Praise for the novels of Michelle Sagara

"Remains rooted in the vivid and relatable contemporary-yet-epic sensibility of the other Elantra books.... Spending more time on the streets of Elantra is always a treat."

—*Tor.com* on *The Emperor's Wolves*

"Exciting… Both new readers and Sagara's long-time fans will be delighted to visit the land and people of Elantra."

—*Publishers Weekly* on *The Emperor's Wolves*

"This world feels so complex and so complete."

—*ReadingReality.net* on *The Emperor's Wolves*

"A satisfying combination of contemporary-feeling secondary world city-based fantasy, and go-big-or-go-home epic."

—*Tor.com* on The Chronicles of Elantra series

"Well-crafted… Readers will appreciate the complex plot and many returning faces in the vast cast of characters. This magical thrill-ride is a treat."

—*Publishers Weekly* on *Cast in Wisdom*

"Full to the brim of magic… Beautiful and intricate…a breathtaking read."

—*Word of the Nerd* on *Cast in Wisdom*

"This is a fast, fun novel, delightfully enjoyable in the best tradition of Sagara's work. While it may be light and entertaining, it's got some serious questions at its core."

—*Locus* magazine on *Cast in Oblivion*

"First-rate fantasy."

—#1 *New York Times* bestselling author Kelley Armstrong

"No one provides an emotional payoff like Michelle Sagara… It doesn't get any better than this!"

—Bestselling author Tanya Huff

Also by *New York Times* bestselling author Michelle Sagara

*Look for the next story in
The Chronicles of Elantra,
coming soon from MIRA.*

SWORD AND SHADOW

MICHELLE SAGARA

mira

Recycling programs
for this product may
not exist in your area.

ISBN-13: 978-0-7783-1177-5

Sword and Shadow

This is a work of fiction. Names, characters, places and incidents are either the product
of the author's imagination or are used fictitiously. Any resemblance to actual persons,
living or dead, businesses, companies, events or locales is entirely coincidental.

This edition published by arrangement with Harlequin Books S.A.

For questions and comments about the quality of this book, please contact us
at CustomerService@Harlequin.com.

Mira
22 Adelaide St. West, 41st Floor
Toronto, Ontario M5H 4E3, Canada
BookClubbish.com

Printed in U.S.A.

This is for John, Kristen, Jamie and Liam,
the other half of our family—
even when we were separated by the pandemic for well over a year.

CHAPTER ONE

"THERE WAS A TIME I HATED HER," AN'TELLARUS said.

Her voice was soft, the words almost affectionate. If Elluvian had ever been able to relax in the presence of An'Tellarus, that softness would have put him on edge. As it was, the edge upon which he found himself was like the peak of a mountain; he couldn't move an inch without falling. Words, in this case, were substitutes for movement. He therefore said nothing.

She had offered him both a chair and refreshments; he had declined, and was now grateful to have done so. He had come at her "invitation," and accepting hospitality implied a length of meeting he wished to avoid. He could pretend ignorance of whom she spoke, as she hadn't mentioned a name. But he knew.

Were the words meant to shock him? To anger him? To invite a similar dislike? All of her words were traps, but they weren't persistent; only if he escaped her quarters—and the High Halls—intact, could he be certain he had evaded them.

Had she been one iota less powerful, he would have declined the invitation.

An'Tellarus was far more at home in her personal quarters than any visitor would be; she both sat and availed herself of the refreshments Elluvian had refused. "Your eyes are a lovely and unfortunate shade of blue," she said, above the rim of her glass. Hers were a blue-green. "Come. If I wanted you dead, you would be dead. No subtlety on my part would be required. Sit, Elluvian."

As if he were a dog. "I am under time constraints, as you well know."

Her smile, as she offered it, was genuine. That was the most difficult thing about An'Tellarus. "You are not nearly under the time constraints you will be. I almost regret the inconvenience it will cause you." Her smile deepened. "I give you my word that I intend no harm to you today. Will you not join me?"

He did not, could not, trust her. The fact that she was kin made it harder, not easier. That, and the fact that she knew of his past. But he understood that she intended to extend this meeting; turning on heel and leaving was tantamount to suicide.

"Elluvian. You have never learned the art of grace. We both know that you will remain in my quarters until I have finished; we both know that I will decide when we are done. Is that not so?"

"An'Tellarus," he replied, emphasizing her rank.

She frowned. "You will give me a headache. You were easily the most stubborn of your kin, most of whom are dead." She watched carefully.

He nodded.

"Do not wish that the rest would join their number." Her smile returned. "Very well. You will stand, and I will speak as if you were the least significant of servants."

He was called the Emperor's Dog, frequently to his face,

and as it was materially true, he shrugged. He had no pride to prick. It was both his signal strength and, in the eyes of his people, his greatest weakness. It had certainly been a point of contention between Elluvian and one of his only surviving relatives over the past few centuries. An'Tellarus's eyes, however, retained their green; if she desired to descend into a lecture over being properly Barrani, she would not give into it today. It was the only mercy he was to be granted, and, in keeping with An'Tellarus, it was small.

"I have called you here to ask a favor."

He could not prevent his jaw from clenching. He did, however, find flexibility in his legs; he sat. This was not the first time he had been asked a *favor*, but the color of her eyes didn't imply the cold rage of imminent death.

"I am to return to the West March in the very near future."

Which would be a relief to everyone in the High Halls who had any reason to either interact with An'Tellarus, or who was too new or foolish to avoid her.

"I expect that I will not be greeted with great hospitality— that has ever been the case."

"You have guards."

"Indeed. I do. I wish you to be among them."

"Just how little hospitality are you expecting?" His tone, unlike hers, was sharper. He didn't trust her, and the trek to the West March would eat months of mortal time. Were it not for his duty to the Emperor, and his duty to the Wolves, those months would be a triviality. The Lord of Wolves, however, had survived what Elluvian considered to be the last assassination attempt for the next several years; the office was, if woefully undermanned, stable. The newest of Elluvian's recruits had settled into the job he had been given, and he was quick, bright, and often otherwise invisible while standing in place.

Helmat both prized and trusted the young Severn Handred.

Rosen approved. Jaren had not yet returned from his last hunt, but Elluvian felt almost certain—or as certain as one could be with ever-changing mortals—that Jaren would approve. Mellianne was…herself. Suspicious, and wavering between protective interest, envy, and resentment.

The office could survive a few months of his absence.

"When do you plan to leave?"

"That will depend on you."

He had an inkling of what was to follow.

"I wish you to bring Severn Handred with you."

The request was both expected and surprising, the latter because of the timing. Severn was only barely of age in mortal parlance. He had—there could be no doubt—experience with Barrani, but until his induction into the Wolves, that experience had likely been singular. He had met a single Barrani man, had been taught to read and write, and had been tested for the magical abilities so prized by Elluvian's kin. That Severn himself did not seem to understand those abilities seemed clear to both of the Barrani currently in this room.

"Severn Handred does not report to me. I am not his superior officer."

"I am aware of that."

"I cannot fulfill your request."

"Oh? You serve the Emperor directly; the boy serves the Emperor. While mortals are difficult and their hierarchical convolutions often mystifying, the Emperor is not mortal. You will have, and carry, more weight with our Eternal Emperor than the boy—or his Wolflord. If you request it of your Emperor, he will grant the request."

"It is clear to me that you have not met the Emperor," Elluvian replied, wry rather than stiff. An'Tellarus was unusual for a Barrani Lord, but she made assumptions. "The first question he will ask—and I consider it perfectly reasonable—is why. If

I cannot answer that question, the request will be denied. The existence of that request will, however, pique his interest."

The green in her eyes dimmed. "Come up with an excuse. You are surely capable of that."

"Perhaps you wish to speak with him in person. It would be highly unusual for a Barrani Lord to visit a second time, but I am certain he would allow an appointment to be made."

"Now you are beginning to annoy me."

"An'Tellarus."

"If you cannot gain permission from the Emperor, I am certain the Lord of Wolves would grant what you ask."

"The Emperor is the better choice if you wish for success," Elluvian told her, his expression and tone bland and neutral. "But if you wish it, you will have to offer an explanation for the request."

The last of the green faded from her eyes. Elluvian wasn't afraid of this woman; there was no point. If she desired his death, he was dead. He waited, impassive now, impatience falling from him just as green from her.

"You are both tedious and unobservant. I thought better of you."

"An'Tellarus. Perhaps you will point out the ways in which I have been unobservant today. Should I trouble you to catalog all of my incompetencies, Severn Handred will have passed of old age by the time the tally is complete."

"Would he?"

His smile was practiced artifice; he adorned it with no words.

Her smile was, he was certain, genuine, there was so much edge in it. "Very well, child. Play your games if you must."

"It is not I who plays games, An'Tellarus. I confound most of our kin because I do not. I am the Emperor's servant. His dog, if you are unkind. I obey his commands when they are given; I do not scheme to escape them. If you ask a question,

I will answer it truthfully where possible; if I cannot, I will not. What do you want with Severn?"

"As I told you before you descended into your particular brand of surliness—and I must assume you are capable of better, as the Emperor has not yet reduced you to ash—I once believed I hated her."

He did not ask *who*. He waited.

She nodded as if in approval, although the color of her eyes didn't shift. "She had everything, you see. Everything I wanted at the time. She was heir. She was respected—feared, perhaps—and in the fashion of our kin, she was powerful. Her magical gifts manifested far earlier than mine. She was considered flawless." She looked down at her hands as they rested in her lap.

"Ah, but that was not why I thought I hated her. Her power was of a particular type—and she was beloved of the green."

Elluvian frowned.

"You have heard that, surely?"

"No."

"What have you heard?"

"She made a foolish decision for reasons no one of our kin could understand; she almost brought ruin upon her line and she did not inherit it. In the end, she died."

"Do you know how?"

"No; it was not relevant to me. And you, who might know for certain what happened to your sister, forbid all discussion of it. I am not certain I would have survived asking irrelevant questions. Many did not."

She nodded. "We do not forget. It is perhaps the only thing I envy mortals: they do. Even if their lives are short, they burn so brightly—and memories are consumed by the swift passage of their time. It is not so, with us." She lifted her chin, exposing the eyes her downcast expression obscured. Her eyes were shaded purple. "No body has ever been found."

He looked away, as most did when confronted with evidence of grief.

"You have perhaps seen the statue I left in the hall. The boy did not recognize her."

"And you expected he would?"

"I had hope, yes."

"An'Tellarus—her fall was centuries past. She has not, to my knowledge, been seen in our world for centuries in *any* calendar. The boy is mortal. Unless you believe she still lives, how could that even be possible?"

"Hope is bitter. It has always been bitter; it is a vulnerability we would do well to discard entirely."

"Perhaps you could start now."

The air crackled. "I see you are without even a smidgen of empathy."

"An'Tellarus."

"Very well. You are undoubtedly *busy*. I will allow you to return to your various labors. But I am leaving within the ten-day, and I expect both you and the boy to be present." She rose, indicating by the shift in posture that Elluvian should do the same. "Your presence, however, is not required. If you are unable to attend me, I will guard the boy personally."

Elluvian's eyes were indigo when he rose. "You will not touch Severn Handred."

"I will not kidnap him, if that is what you are implying or inferring from my words. If I am not to simply pluck a random mortal of my choosing off the streets—and yes, I understand how laws of exemption work—he is, by the reckoning of the mortals, an adult. Should he choose to accept my invitation, yours will be the criminal act should you choose to forcibly prevent him from accompanying me."

Elluvian was silent, considering the woman who stood

before him. Grief, if it had not been illusory, had been vanquished—as it so often was—by anger.

"You surely do not think that you are the only avenue I might take to approach my goals? I wish permission from those to whom he owes service, but I am fully aware that service in the mortal world does not have the weight, legal or otherwise, that it does in ours. Should he choose, for his own reasons, to venture to the West March, you cannot prevent it. I will endeavor to keep him alive; dead, he is of little use to me."

"Ten days?" he asked, the words low and grudging.

Her smile was ice and steel. "Ten days."

A knock on Severn's door was not a normal occurrence. He had neighbors, but they—like he—tended to keep to themselves. The woman to the left did so because she had fled here from family. He knew very little about the tenants to the right; they had two children, both capable of running, shouting, and shrieking as if noise and sound were not a danger.

Here, with doors that locked and walls and ceilings in decent repair, it wasn't. The noises of the city beyond the walls were constant, consistent; theirs were simply competing sounds in an enclosed space. That had not been true of his childhood.

He adapted, as he always had, to different truths, new facts. He did arm himself before he chose to answer the door, but not in a fashion that would be obvious to the visitor. He calculated risk, always, but he was now a member of the Halls of Law, and his address was in the smaller pool of the Wolves' official records. It was likely a missive from one of the Wolves—Elluvian, perhaps.

Severn was not yet in a position where he could afford a household mirror of his own. Had a mirror been a prerequisite for the job he now held, he would have given up all but the scantest of food to purchase one. The Wolflord didn't deem it a necessity; he appeared to dislike mirrors, although much of his time in the office involved their use. The Wolves had no other way to reach him if they needed to pass on information except by foot and door.

He had settled into this small set of rooms; they weren't home, but no rooms would be, no matter how large or grand. And he knew, when he opened the door upon two Barrani men, one carrying a sealed scroll, that he would have to move again.

"An'Tellarus wishes to speak with you."

"When?"

"At your earliest convenience." The messenger's face was smooth and expressionless, as if the young man he addressed was not a mere mortal who lived in the Barrani equivalent of a poorly repaired closet.

"It can't be today," he said, standing in the door.

"She understands your time is both precious and encumbered. If you cannot speak with her personally, there will be no hint of reprisal. But she wishes you to read this before you make your decision." He handed Severn the scroll case. When Severn failed to take it, he said, "The enchantments are entirely privacy-related; the seal itself is enchanted, and it will not break for any but you."

Severn took the case.

"We are not to wait for an answer. If you wish to meet with An'Tellarus, she will venture into the High Market both this evening and tomorrow evening. She can be found at The Rose Café, and she will make reservations for two— or three—under her name." The man bowed. His bow was low enough, exact enough, it made Severn uncomfortable.

I am uncertain that Elluvian will pass my message—and my invitation—on to you. I will not tell you that he is untrust-worthy; I am certain you do not require the warning.

*I wish to extend an invitation—to you, although I will ac-
cept Elluvian's presence if you deem it necessary—to visit my
homeland. I offer you the hospitality of Tellarus for the duration of your stay. I have my own reasons for extending such
an unusual invitation, but I am aware that you must find, in
the end, your own reasons for accepting.*

*I therefore offer answers to a question—if it is a question
you have ever asked yourself.*

*Do you wish to know more about your family? Do you wish
to know—or perhaps locate—the Barrani who took guardian-
ship of you in your early years?*

*I offer you information about both—but I will not give you
that information in the heart of a city governed in its entirety
by either a Dragon or the High Halls.*

*I await your reply; if you do not reply, I shall assume you
have grown past these questions and you have no interest in
the answers to them.*

Yours,
Cediela, An'Tellarus

Severn still had the clothing Elluvian had insisted on pur-
chasing for his first visit to the High Halls. It was appropriate
for his meeting with An'Tellarus, and he wore it. He understood that clothing made a statement without the need for
actual words. He understood as well that shaving was necessary; that he be totally clean and well-groomed. He knew
how to walk as if he owned the street—to walk as if he belonged there. He didn't strut; he didn't call attention to himself; he simply walked as if these streets and the buildings
that they contained were his home.

He looked as if he lived here.

There was a trick to this. It required observation, but he'd
observed the city and its many streets, had spent hours watching how people simply walked—or ran—through them. He

saw the people that were treated politely, the people that were treated with care, and the people that were treated with barely veiled contempt, and he matched patterns in each case: age, gender, race, at first, but within those categories, clothing, hairstyles, chosen colors. Some people were attended by private guards. In some cases he felt the guards a waste, in others, necessary; there were people who seemed desperate to belong, and they made choices that were as ostentatious as possible.

Desperation had never, ever been his friend; it did not—with far fewer immediate consequences—appear to be theirs, either.

He saw no Barrani on these streets, although this was one of the areas of Elantra where Barrani who were willing to mingle with the merely mortal might go and still retain some scrap of social dignity among their own kin. He saw no obvious carriage, saw no empty spaces in the streets in which a carriage, concealed by magic, might be parked.

But he saw The Rose Café, its broad glass windows tinted and constructed in such a way that the café's name was rose-hued, transparent glass behind which customers filled the many seats. It was past dinnertime, and the seats had not yet fully emptied, but even on the wrong side of the glass, Severn saw that An'Tellarus hadn't lied: she sat, alone, at a table meant for two. The tables around this small table had been cleared, and no customers occupied them.

He swallowed, forced his hands to uncurl, and entered.

"Do you know," she said, her voice almost songlike, trapped as it was in the currents of mortal conversation that could not entirely fade into the background, "I was not certain you would arrive." She looked past him, nodded, and then lifted a hand. "I hope you intend to join me."

"I would be honored, An'Tellarus," he replied, in Barrani.

"I hope you continue to hold that sentiment when we

are done speaking." Her smile was gentle but marred by something that implied a grimmer emotion beneath its surface. Then again, she was Barrani—and not young, by the reckoning of her people. Certainly not by the reckoning of Severn's. "I see you have not brought Elluvian with you."

"The invitation was not mine to extend." Severn offered her a low, perfect bow.

"You have such pretty manners," An'Tellarus said. She did not add *for a mortal*, but it was, and would always be, implied. Even so, he smiled.

"My teacher would no doubt disagree—much after the fact. He was never entirely satisfied with my use of etiquette."

"I am sure you have very little reason to practice it; it would be entirely out of place in most of mortal society." There was a question in the words that theoretically contained none.

"My teacher said that manners are a tool, but when they are necessary, it is essential that those tools remain in my grasp." She nodded, as if this had answered the question she hadn't asked. She was, to his eye, everything that he had been warned to avoid.

But she had offered answers to a question that had haunted Severn for much of his childhood—if she had them. He'd considered this with care while he dressed; meeting her was a risk because he didn't understand what she wanted.

People—mortal or no—wanted things. Some of those things would be of use to Severn; Lord Marlin wanted a Wolf, and Severn wanted the employment; their wants overlapped. He couldn't see a way in which what a Barrani Lord of the High Court desired would be in his best interests. He couldn't be entirely certain the information she offered was true.

He couldn't be certain it was entirely false, either. From the moment he had traversed her apartment in the High Halls, he was aware that she knew more about his teacher than Severn himself did, that she knew something about the lessons he had learned before his teacher had departed the fiefs in which he had remained hidden for decades.

His teacher had never answered questions, and Severn had learned—quickly—not to ask them. What he had wanted, in the fiefs, was survival. What his teacher had offered was exactly that. He would teach Severn how to survive. But his lessons hadn't been practical. Severn had learned to read, to write, and to speak Barrani. He had learned something of Barrani history, as seen by his teacher. The teacher who was quick to point out that history itself was confabulation, something that was tainted and weighted by those who wrote the reports of events.

Nor did he consider such reports to be lies. *Severn, we are each concerned with the detritus of our own lives. We each live within a story constructed of events we have chosen—or events that we have had no choice in, but that nonetheless affect us. What I might tell you of the history of my people is colored, always, by the events I have personally seen, or those that have affected my freedom and my own kin.*

Rare are those who come to history with an interest in the events that have no personal meaning. They do, however, exist. You might call them scholars. You might call them Arcanists. I will tell you now that should you be unfortunate enough to encounter an Arcanist, you must avoid speaking with them or interacting with them at all. Power of a particular kind is the focus of their lives; they have devoted the whole of those lives to amassing more power.

It had made some sense to Severn, in the cramped room in which his lessons were taught, the ragged books on shelves surrounding furniture in decent repair. He had considered stealing some of those old books—but in his limited experience, they were without value. Very, very few of the people he could easily reach could read. Those that could would find no value in these books, and if he went farther afield, possible customers might simply take them rather than trade in coin.

You think like a Barrani, but your thoughts are too obvious, his teacher had said, his eyes a green that implied deep amusement and a smidgen of approval. Severn had, of course, said nothing.

Why do you pay attention to me?

Perhaps because I miss the days in which I could purchase and keep humans. The green had shaded to blue. Severn was uncertain if his teacher lied but understood that this discussion was now over. Perhaps in the future he might return to it—but never bluntly.

An'Tellarus was nothing like his former teacher. She was both warmer and colder. It was warmth she offered now; he could see it in the color of her eyes. But surrounding that hint of green was a wall of blue.

Severn was accustomed to walls. In some fashion, they were far more comfortable.

"You are thinking of your former teacher."

He nodded. She didn't ask, and hadn't demanded, that teacher's name. He would have given it to her because he was certain that the name itself had been yet another mask—a lie that was not quite lie but was very far from the truth. His master was not so foolish as to give a mortal child information that could harm him, or harm them both.

Because she had not asked, he said, "I have not seen him since I was roughly ten years of age."

"Roughly?"

"It's common for orphans to have little knowledge of their actual date of birth."

"Ah. Of course. Clumsy of me."

He understood that clumsiness was artifice here, but regardless, as the balance of power was in her hands, this approach was more comfortable for him. It was…unusual to have Barrani care about his comfort at all, even those absent of malice.

Be cautious. When in the presence of Barrani, never lower your guard.

To his teacher, the natural arrogance of the Barrani made the entirety of the mortal world a pale, harmless place. Severn, however, was mortal. He understood the rough edges of power in the fiefs, and he could see the overlap between those and the struggles of the Barrani—only the stages and the props were different. He therefore had learned, early, never to lower his guard, period.

But he had also learned to manage appearances; to be less obvious when his thoughts strayed to considerations of theft, of personal survival. He could be pleasant; he could be threatening—but each of his responses came from a measured consideration of their utility in a given situation.

"Barrani are seldom orphaned in a like fashion—although perhaps you are aware of this. Birth and awakening are highly scripted, highly ceremonial; our young cannot wake without the intervention of the High Lord's Consort. We know the date of our birth, and if for some reason we are uncertain," and her tone implied that this was never the case, "those dates are recorded in the High Halls. It is not so, I am told, of mortal births; there is no ceremony and no interference required for a mortal infant to arrive, whole but small, into our world.

"You do not know where you were born?"

She asked the question casually, softly, but there was an edge hidden beneath the gentle velvet of her chosen words. He didn't need to lie, but had he, he would have. "No. Mortal memory is not Immortal memory; the time of our infancy is long forgotten even when we have lived a simple handful of years." He exhaled. "You said you have possible information about my parents."

She smiled, but the smile was complicated; ice and fire together that might end in the destruction of both. "I did."

"Do you still believe it to be true?"

"I believe it to be true more than yesterday, and more than the day before."

"What do you ask of me in return?"

"I wish you to accompany me on a journey. I will be returning to the lands of my birth in less than two of your weeks, and I am desirous of company. Your company."

"Why?"

"I find you interesting, of course. In my youth, I would have done all in my lesser power to possess you." Her smile sharpened.

He understood her meaning, but the enslavement of his kind was in the distant past now, well beyond the reach of his span of years, or the lives of his parents or grandparents, whoever they had once been.

"Do my parents still live?" It was not the first time Severn had asked this question of a Barrani.

"That, I do not know. The lineage of mortals was never our concern. But what information I have I will give you." She studied his neutral expression, her eyes shifting color, the green giving way to the blue that seemed the sole resident of Elluvian's eyes. "I was told often in my childhood that I should not play games. Games are dangerous and their consequences not so easily separated between the act and either victory or defeat. What do you think?"

He stopped himself from shrugging as she observed him. "I am only a mortal, and I have not lived among the Barrani."

"Indeed. But I would hear your answer."

"I cannot see how that is true, unless the word *game* is defined very differently among your kin. To my eyes, and to my admittedly scant experience with Barrani, games are your entire way of life. It is the stakes over which those games are played, and the board upon which the pieces are set, that differ—not the intent."

"Oh?"

"Victory or defeat."

She exhaled and nodded. "One day I would very much like to meet this teacher of yours. At your age now, we would be close to our infancy, and such knowledge is not easily retained—and yet, you have done so. Very well. The information I wish to impart—about your birth—cannot be imparted here, where the High Halls watch and the High Lord has spies everywhere. It is close to our Leofswuld— perhaps a handful of your years from now—and we will all be commanded to return to the High Halls." At Severn's expression, An'Tellarus smiled. "*Leofswuld* is the word we use when there will be a changing of the guard. It is quite probable that soon, we will have a new High Lord.

"Until then, I do not wish to disturb our kin. I do not wish them to interfere with my life or my own plans. There are places in my homeland which are immune to the machinations of the High Lord and his court, and the information you seek rests at the very heart of the safest of those places. If you agree to accompany me, I will take you to where you might ask your questions and receive your answers."

He was silent, considering the color of her eyes and the position of her hands; she was so still she might have been holding her breath. He had noted, on his first introduction to An'Tellarus, that she was never completely still.

"Where is your homeland?"

"In the West March of our kin."

"When would you need my decision?" His voice was almost flat; he might have been sitting at his desk, considering the information Records contained before attempting to draw conclusions from possible patterns. Nothing in his expression gave An'Tellarus purchase.

He had learned, not from his master, but from other children, other mortals in the streets of the fief of Nightshade, that eagerness must be hidden and contained. The greater the desire, the less it must show.

"I leave within the ten-day, with or without you." She watched him. When he nodded she frowned, but added no further words.

CHAPTER TWO

"IF I WERE YOU," ROSEN SAID AS SEVERN ENTERED the office, "I'd head back out. I have a few things I need picked up."

Mellianne said, from across the room, "I can go. Severn's been tasked with a report that tabulates four years' worth of petty Hawk investigations, but only the relevant bits." Her tone clearly indicated that it was needle-in-haystack work, or something more disgusting than hay.

"I don't think he'll thank you," Rosen replied, with a shrug that said she'd made a good faith attempt to stand between the newest member of the Wolves and his dire fate, whatever that happened to be.

Severn glanced at Mellianne and then turned his attention to Rosen.

Rosen shrugged. "Elluvian graced us with his presence. His eyes were the color of midnight. Barrani skin is pale; his was chalky. I might have called it gray were it not for the red highlights."

"He wasn't red." Mellianne's snort was almost louder than her words.

"His knuckles were. You did notice his hands were fists?"

Mellianne shrugged; Severn instantly interpreted that as *so what*. It was a gesture he knew well enough to use himself on rare occasions. None of those were in this office. But Mellianne was brittle when in Elluvian's presence; she was hostile when his name was mentioned. Severn didn't understand the entirety of their history and had little desire to do so.

"I notice you're not leaving."

Severn nodded. "I need to take a leave of absence. I'm not certain how I would apply for that."

"Or if it would be granted?"

He nodded again.

Rosen exhaled. "Then there's no way for you to avoid this. How long would the leave be?"

"Six to eight weeks."

Mellianne's chair scraped floor as she left it. "You haven't even been here for a year and you think you can take two whole months off?"

Rosen lifted a hand, which Severn considered pointless. He'd learned that Mellianne was very difficult to shut down. Better, though, not to fuel the fire; he failed to answer.

"Would this leave involve a trip out of the bounds of the Empire?" Rosen asked.

Severn nodded.

"What a coincidence," she said, in a voice dry as tinder. "You might as well take a seat—at your own desk—while you wait. Elluvian went to talk to Helmat; they've been closeted together for the past forty-five minutes. Given his expression, they'll probably be at it for at least another hour. My suspicion is that your request and Elluvian's mood are connected."

Severn offered no reply.

"Helmat's not going to like it. You want to go?"

"Yes."

"He's *really* not going to like it. Have you discussed this with Elluvian at all?"

"No. Is there a reason I should?"

"It involves the Barrani. If you haven't spoken to Elluvian, it involves Barrani who reached out to contact you directly. Which is not against the law, of course. Given Elluvian's anger, the Barrani is someone with whom he has personal history."

"This isn't about Elluvian's personal history," Severn finally said, although his belief in the words was fading as they left his mouth. "It's about mine."

Rosen winced. "You're so self-controlled it's easy to forget your actual age." She exhaled. "I won't ask. Helmat undoubtedly will. You are free to remain silent. The Emperor is entitled to information about our personal lives; the Wolves aren't."

"You'd answer?"

"I would—but I wouldn't be giving Helmat anything he didn't already know. In your case, I'm not certain that's true, so I offer it as information: he is not legally entitled to demand knowledge about your personal life."

"Is the Emperor?"

"Yes. But Helmat is not the Emperor. Regardless, in future, do nothing with or for Barrani of any name or stripe until and unless you've passed it by Elluvian. If he's okay with it, you can proceed—with caution. In Barrani eyes you're mortal. You're not one of them. You'll never be one of them. Our handful of years and our comparative frailty make the whole of our lives inconsequential."

"They're not inconsequential to the Emperor."

"No; it's probably why we can coexist with Barrani at all. They're not playing nice because they have any respect for us—they're playing nice because the Dragon can burn them to ash. And will if they interfere. Why are you requesting a leave of absence?"

"It's a personal matter."

Rosen exhaled again, a neat trick since inhalation had been almost inaudible. "Take a seat," she repeated. "And get some work done. You're good at detail work."

Two hours later, the door to the Wolflord's office opened. Mellianne had skipped lunch and had remained at her desk, glancing at the closed door as the time passed. Severn, however, aware that he could do nothing to change the pace of the meeting between the Wolflord and Elluvian, had returned to Records. Having a mirror of his own hadn't changed the nature of the work; it had certainly made doing it more convenient.

He had started with reports about murders and the investigations surrounding them, because those reports were timely. The Hawks interacted with the Imperial Mages, and he had come to appreciate the reports the mages made. Although some were florid and lacking in easily accessible facts, most were precise, concise, laying out facts without comment.

When the cases weren't murders or terrible assaults that didn't tip over into murder charges, the Hawks were far worse at filing reports to Records than the Swords. He could see the holes in the net created by those missing reports, because he was looking for commonalities. All of the missing or late reports he attempted to track down had to be routed through the Wolflord; Helmat Marlin was the public face, the only public face, of the Wolves. Rosen had explained the procedure in such a way that it made sense: the Hawks and the Swords were not as secure with their information as the Wolves, and the Wolves could be at risk if their identities were easily discovered.

He frowned. In the absence of reports—some delayed by up to a year—he looked for patterns. The type of reports delayed were often minor; trespassing, when such trespass didn't involve the domiciles of the wealthy, minor theft, minor assault. He looked at the officers involved in those late reports, looked to see whether specific officers always lagged in report time. He looked for areas of delay across the various city districts. He made no notations as he did, rising above details to see what looked like a very patchwork web.

See the patterns. Understand the flow of power. Understand the places in which you might stand, as a rock does in the rushing currents of a moving river. You will not survive if you cannot do this.

He had never doubted it. He had become adept at standing, not in the current, but by the side of the river, watching, observing. Alone. Always alone, now.

There is safety in numbers, when one is mortal; that has always been offered as truth. Among my kind, it is often true, as well, but for entirely different reasons. When you are alone, when you are isolated, you become a target—and you are an ignorant target. You do not know what others intend, what others might have planned for you. It is a delicate dance, this safety in numbers; you must never appear to be weak.

You must never appear to be desirous of power. Only when you have power, only when you are certain of it, can you declare yourself.

To who? He had asked so long ago it was one of his earliest retained memories.

To anyone, Severn. To me. To any of my kin who might teach or guide you. They will do so, always, for their own purposes.

And your purpose?

To that, there had been no answer. Nor had he pressed for one, for he already understood that he was helpless; parentless in the streets of a fief, safe because his rarely glimpsed guardian was Barrani, and mortals didn't tangle with Barrani unless they wanted their finite lives to be much shorter.

He shook his head.

Are you lonely?

Are you?

The Barrani do not feel lonely, was the eventual reply. *Those who are cursed with such feelings die in their youth.* He had watched

Severn, his eyes an odd color in the dim light; not blue, not exactly, but absent any green. It would be a year before he recognized the purple mixed with the natural blue, and years before he understood that purple was the shade of grief.

Perhaps that is not the entire truth. Am I lonely? I do not know. But even if the answer were to be yes, it is almost irrelevant. Loneliness does not drive or control me. I have said that fear is the worst driver; you must never allow fear to make your decisions for you. But loneliness shades easily into fear.

Elluvian stood over Severn's shoulder. He was certain the young man was aware of his presence, but his awareness did not impede the work he now did. It was, to use an Elantran phrase, scut work; Elluvian considered it petty and almost irrelevant. He generally relegated the Hawks and the Swords to that same category; their concerns involved mortals, and with rare exceptions, mortals were also petty and irrelevant. Even if one rose to power, the power flowered and died, just as hothouse plants did; it left no permanent marks.

No, the only mortals that did or could were those who had gained either the favor or the enmity of the Emperor or the High Court. And Severn Handred appeared on the edge of achieving both.

Helmat was angry. This particular anger was likely to fade with time—if his new private survived. Elluvian waited. Severn worked. It occurred to the Barrani that the work itself had taken hold. If Severn was aware of his presence, he considered it harmless. Had Elluvian any pride to prick, he might have been annoyed.

"Private."

Severn glanced up immediately.

"The Wolflord wishes to speak with you."

"Records pause," the newest of the Wolves' recruits said. He rose instantly and tidily, and left his desk.

★ ★ ★

"Rosie said you've applied for a leave of absence." Helmat gestured and the door behind Severn shut with an authoritative click. The room was now soundproof, among other things.

Severn nodded. He stood, hands behind his back, chin tilted toward the surface of the Wolflord's desk.

"I'm not of a mind to agree to your request. I am, however, considered a reasonable man."

Not, Severn thought, when he was in this obviously foul mood. He nodded again.

"Convince me. You have yet to complete a full year; your tenure here has been, as I am certain you are aware, exemplary. The Emperor himself has been pleased with the work you've done. Rosie even likes you—and that's rare."

Severn frowned.

"Have you not realized that? She's a pragmatist—she'd have to be to continue her work here. Other jobs and other desks have been offered her, but she chose to stay when she could no longer perform the duties for which she was known. Desk work doesn't suit everyone."

Severn nodded again.

"It appears to suit you, which is unexpected. Regardless, you would not be manning a desk while you take your leave. The timing is suspicious."

"Suspicious?"

"Elluvian has also requested a leave of absence. I gather, from your expression, that your request and his request are linked."

"I wasn't aware that he'd made the request when I made mine."

Helmat nodded. "Tell me where you believe you'll be going." It wasn't a question.

"To the West March, the western stronghold of the Barrani."

"On your own?"

"In the company of An'Tellarus of the Barrani High Court."

"What is your purpose in accompanying her?"

"I don't know. She doesn't need me as a guard. If she wished investigative work to be done, I wouldn't be the person she'd choose. The Empire doesn't encompass the West March, and the laws there aren't Imperial laws."

"Meaning you wouldn't be safe."

"I'll be as safe under An'Tellarus's care as I would in the High Halls under Elluvian's."

Helmat snorted, but the purple tinge receded from his face. His jaw, however, remained clenched. "You know what happened to Darrell."

"I know what Mellianne thinks happened."

The Wolflord exhaled. "If I didn't need you here, I'd tell you you're wasted on us. You would have a promising career as a diplomat ahead of you. You're good at telling the truth while implying the opposite and allowing your audience to draw their own conclusions."

Severn said nothing; he waited. He waited without fidgeting, as most of the rest of the Wolves did, consciously or unconsciously.

"Darrell was young. He lived on the edge of the warrens. He was a very, very quick learner when it came to purely practical elements of this job. His knife work was second only to Elluvian's. His ability to move unseen was remarkable. He applied himself to every aspect of this job that involved ground hunts.

"He was your age, inasmuch as records of his birth date could be ascertained. He accompanied Elluvian to the High Halls on three occasions. He did not return to the office after the third visit."

This matched what Mellianne had to say, shorn of the rage and anger.

"Elluvian believes that you are better with weapons than young Darrell was. He is, however, the only person to believe that; the weaponsmaster thinks you will need a few years to reach that level—if ever. Why do you think Elluvian believes you are Darrell's equal?"

Severn shrugged. "You'll have to ask Elluvian."

"He is particularly impressed with the work you can do with two blades; he feels that two daggers, or two swords, might be your specialty."

"The weaponsmaster doesn't agree."

"No. Odd, isn't it? The only circumstances in which Elluvian has seen combat prowess would theoretically be in the training room. While you've aided in investigative search, you have not—*ever*—been sent as an executioner. Nor has Elluvian while you've partnered him. Elluvian and I have had several discussions about this very topic; none of them were satisfactory to me.

"And now, he wishes to take you to the West March. I'm against this."

"It's not Elluvian who wishes me to travel to the West March. It's An'Tellarus."

"Oh?"

"I'm uncertain of his actual relationship with An'Tellarus—I believe she's an aunt, but I'm not certain that 'aunt' means to the Barrani what it means to us. I believe she does have some affection for him."

"Why?"

"She's openly critical and openly dismissive."

"So are many of the Barrani High Lords."

"She doesn't call him the Emperor's Dog. Ah, no, perhaps she does—but there's an openness to the criticism and dismissal that implies disappointment, not betrayal. She expects better of him, and he's failed to live up to that better. But... she expects better. She doesn't appear to expect obedience. It's..." He trailed off.

"Maternal?"

It was the word that Severn had been attempting to avoid. "It seems—to me—to be more like nagging and less like threats. If she truly felt he was a danger to her, he'd be dead."

Helmat's brows rose. "An'Tellarus has a very small file in the Imperial Service Records. She's not considered to be a political player, although she is both old and a Lord of the High Court."

Severn nodded; he knew. He'd attempted basic research about her position among the Barrani. In the High Halls, she was considered Lord, and having seen her rooms, she was senior. There was almost no information about the West March. The implication that information existed was present in the gaps, but he'd run immediately into a wall of complex permissions. He was certain that his attempt to find the information would be—had been—noted.

He had made no further attempts.

"Do you believe Elluvian will be safe if he travels with An'Tellarus?"

He considered the question from several angles. "I believe he'll be as safe with An'Tellarus in the West March as he might be in the High Halls."

Helmat's snort was louder. "Boy, I want you to speak plainly."

"I think she likes him. I think she wants more for him because she doesn't understand what this job means to him."

At that, the Wolflord laughed. "Neither does he. He was born in the West March. It's where he first met the Emperor, who was not, at that time, Emperor. They were on opposite sides of the third Draco-Barrani war. I don't believe it will be safe for Elluvian to venture there."

"You don't think he's safe in the High Halls, either."

"No."

"You think it'll be less safe?"

"Yes." Helmat began to drum the desktop with his fingers. "What do you think you're doing?"

"An'Tellarus believes she has information about my parents."

"Your parents?" Bushy brows rose again.

He nodded.

"Your parents were mortal. Do you know who they were?"

"I know nothing about them at all." Severn's voice was low; it was the only way to keep it steady. "I have no memory of ever seeing them. I've always wondered."

"How on earth does a Lord of the High Court have access to that information?"

"I don't know. I can't assess without seeing the information itself."

"But you believe she has what she's offering."

"...I believe she might."

"What does she want from you, boy?"

At this, Severn cracked a smile. "I don't know. She finds me interesting and amusing. If I had to guess, I'd say she hopes to find the Barrani man who taught me when I was a much younger child."

"You're her bait?"

"It's just a guess—but it's the only thing that makes sense."

"Have you given her his name?"

"No."

"Has she asked?"

"Not directly. I don't expect the name I know to yield results for her."

"Elluvian doesn't trust her."

"Of course not. They're both Barrani."

Helmat's bark of laughter was a short stab of sound. "He trusts me."

Severn nodded. "It's why you're the Lord of Wolves. But...

we're mortal. If you fail his trust, it won't cost him more than a handful of years; it certainly won't cost him his life."

"He trusts the Emperor."

"That's different."

"Oh?"

"Trust is irrelevant. The Emperor is a far greater power. Any oath between them is predicated entirely on the Emperor's generosity. If he failed to trust the Emperor, nothing would change. I think he finds the Emperor...frustrating."

"Noticed that, have you?" The smile the words evoked lingered a little longer. "Elluvian would be grateful if I failed to give permission for your outing."

"Yes. Or if the Emperor did. Either of those would prevent the risk, and neither would be his fault." The Wolflord's expression shuttered as Severn watched, anger and amusement leaving the lines of his face. "You don't want me to go."

Helmat shrugged. "The work you're doing in reconciling the Records information is valuable. You have an eye for detail—"

"Elluvian says I have an eye for petty detail."

"He would. If it were up to Elluvian, all of the mirrors in the Halls of Law would be shattered, never to be replaced."

"He has Barrani memory."

"Yes. Why is that less relevant?"

"He can only remember things he's heard, seen, or experienced himself."

"Exactly. Barrani are solipsists. If it's irrelevant to his life, it's irrelevant. This, however, doesn't appear to be irrelevant. I would like to deny the permission you've requested. I would, in other circumstances."

"But?"

"I believe you'll attempt to tender your resignation if permission isn't granted."

"Attempt?"

"You're a Wolf. You serve the Emperor directly. Permission to resign is required. The Emperor's permission. If you request that permission and it's denied, your journey to the West March will be seen as flight. A rare act of treason. You hadn't considered that?"

"Not seriously."

Thick brows rose, an invitation to continue.

"I considered the odds that you'd reject my request very small."

"You didn't spend two hours closeted with an ill-tempered Elluvian."

"I'm almost certain I will in the very near future."

The Wolflord laughed again. "Lineage is everything to most of the powerful Barrani."

"Of course it is—it's the source of their power."

"And will it be the source of yours, in the end?"

"No. I have no desire to play happy families with strangers. If they even survive."

"Then why?"

"I've always wanted to know."

"Is it worth your life?"

"If my death were guaranteed, I wouldn't go. I don't know what An'Tellarus wants, but if it were something as simple as my death, I'd be dead. If you wanted me dead, I'd be dead. If Elluvian wanted me dead, I'd be dead. If I have to make decisions based only on the possibility of failure, I'd never be able to take a step at all." He swallowed. "I want to know. I've wanted to know for half my life."

"Elluvian doesn't think six weeks is feasible. He considers eight to be the minimum required. Ten is optimal."

Severn couldn't stop himself from wincing.

"By granting permission, I'll be losing access to both my newest recruit and Elluvian. During that time, if the Emperor desires the execution of a Barrani individual, the work will fall on entirely mortal shoulders."

"Elluvian doesn't have to go to the West March."

"If you go and Elluvian remains, I'll have to deal with Rosie."

For the first time today, Severn laughed.

"Were I your age, private, I'd go."

"And at your age now?"

Helmat shrugged. "I'd still go. But I knew who my mother was. I had rumors about the identity of my father—but in the warrens, fathers are irrelevant. My mother never wanted my father to find me. Or her. She was a tough old lady, sharp as a knife, blunt as a cudgel. She had words to say about my father. I won't repeat them.

"But my reason for going at this late date would be different from yours." He smiled, the smile all edge, the cast of his brow etched in lines of pure malice. Severn could see two things in that expression before it once again shuttered: rage and distant youth. "I won't pay you for the time. I expect you to do what you need to do, survive it, and return to me."

When Severn left the office, Helmat didn't close the door. He therefore heard the shuffling gait of the one Wolf whose injury prevented a more even step. Rosie entered his office.

"Your paperwork." She walked to his desk and dropped a small stack of papers on its surface.

"You don't approve."

She shrugged. "I worry, but worry has kept me alive so far. Severn's not a talker, but...he's going, one way or the other."

"And you expect me to bow before the inevitable."

She glanced pointedly at the paperwork. "He asks for nothing. He asks a lot of questions, but they're never personal. This is. It's important enough that he *has* asked. It means he's going. I don't like it. Are you sending Elluvian?"

"That's not up to me."

Rosie whistled. "Elluvian's gone to the Emperor."

"I didn't ask."

★ ★ ★

Elluvian's dislike of throne rooms was well-known to the man who occupied the relevant one. The Emperor therefore arranged the opening of the much smaller audience chambers used when dealing with less publicly political business. Elluvian was not grateful; he was instantly suspicious.

Since suspicion made no difference, he failed to act on it. He arrived at the appointed time. The Imperial Guards were brisk and thorough, or as thorough as it was possible to be; they made no attempt to disarm Elluvian, and no attempt to question his presence. They knew the Emperor's schedule, and they knew Elluvian on sight.

They did not usher him in, which was highly unusual. They simply opened the much less ostentatious door and allowed him to pass through it. Demands that one visit the Emperor unarmed were the palace norm; it was a conceit that allowed the Imperial Guards to work in relative safety. But the presence of weapons meant very little to a Dragon, unless the weapons were one of The Three. Elluvian had never possessed, and had never desired to possess, one of the near-legendary Barrani swords.

To his surprise, the Emperor was not seated upon the throne this room possessed; he was standing by the peaked, narrow window, its stone arch rising almost directly from the floor to the ceiling. It was the width of perhaps two men, and its clear glass reflected the Emperor's face; his back was toward Elluvian.

Their gaze met in reflection.

"Is it time?" the Emperor asked, his voice a draconic rumble at odds with his chosen appearance.

"Time?"

"It is seldom you request an audience, regardless of the difficulties you face. In general, when you are involved in complicated investigations, it is I who summon you. This is the first time I can recall in recent memory in which you have taken the initiative." He turned, slowly, from the window that overlooked the city at the heart of his hoard.

"You intend to return to the West March."

As this was stated as fact, Elluvian simply nodded. "Your permission is required."

"Do not play games with me; I have had a difficult month." At Elluvian's raised brow, the Emperor grimaced. "If I execute all the people who are irritations, I feel that I will regret it in the future. At this moment, that future seems impossibly distant."

"I hope I am not one of those irritations."

"No. Were you, I could kill you without particular concern; the Barrani are unlikely to rally around your death as a political show—that would be too much farce even for the most fractious Lords of the High Court."

"The High Lord would not raise a brow, no."

"But there are others who might."

Elluvian privately doubted this and said nothing.

"Tell me," the Emperor continued, "about An'Tellarus."

For the first time in centuries, Elluvian was frozen in shock. None of this shock was on display; only the gap between question and answer implied it. "She is not much involved in the politics of either the Empire or the High Court," he finally replied, his words measured.

"So I surmise given the scant information her name dislodges. Even during the final war between our peoples, hers was not a name of any renown, and her family is largely rooted in the West March; most are not Lords of the High Court. But she is old; she has survived two wars; she is rumored to be independent to an unusual degree for one who wields so little influence or power."

Very few of the High Court would agree with the assessment the Emperor had offered; they would agree that she was old—but age among the Barrani implied power; it was the young who were weak or foolish who perished, their deaths largely ignominious and irrelevant.

"You are not considered old among your kin, but you are no longer considered a youth. And the West March was subject to its own civil war in a past you experienced."

Elluvian could not deny this, and did not try. It was during the last war between the Dragon Flights and Barrani war bands that Elluvian had first encountered Dariandaros. He had not been Emperor then. And Elluvian had not been what he now was.

"What does An'Tellarus hope to achieve?"

"The reason An'Tellarus is feared," the Barrani Wolf replied, as he leaned against the edge of a long table which was a flat mirror when it was activated, "is because very few can begin to guess at any of her goals. Did she contact you directly?"

The Emperor's smile showed predatory teeth. "She did."

CHAPTER THREE

ELLUVIAN HAD DEVELOPED TACTICS WHEN DEALING with younger mortals. They were so much a part of his routine he found them a stumbling block when dealing with Severn Handred. The rough edges of ego and insecurity that characterized both Mellianne and Darrell were absent; someone else had gone through the effort to grind them smooth in a childhood that felt distant to Severn.

He suspected—had suspected since the first time he had heard Severn's High Barrani—that that teacher had been Barrani, but if he had, he had been monumentally patient and exact. The possibility that Severn was simply himself, Elluvian had rejected outright. He had spent centuries among the mortals, after all.

His attempts to force Severn to pay attention were rendered useless. The moment Elluvian began to speak, the boy listened. His silences were not the silences of a wandering or bored mind; when he broke them, his brow slightly furrowed, it was clear that his questions were relevant to the information Elluvian intended to impart. Helmat had seen this clearly from the beginning, which frustrated Elluvian.

The Wolflord set tasks that leveraged Severn's focus, Severn's ability to see patterns of behavior or neglect, and those tasks had been accomplished well.

"The Barrani do not change as quickly as mortals do. Twenty years in mortal circles can see large upheavals; in Barrani circles, that is far less true. None of the names I have given you are irrelevant; there are two or three who have edged into adulthood in our terms, but they are still considered too young to be meaningful."

Severn nodded. His nod was flexible; it did not imply agreement.

"I expect you to memorize all of the names and all of the lineages before you depart, and you have seven days. You will require clothing suitable for a personal companion to An'Tellarus. She is the head of her line. Some excuses for ignorance will be made due to your race."

"I don't believe people expect An'Tellarus to be predictable."

Elluvian exhaled. "No. Do you believe this will work in your favor?"

Severn was silent for almost a minute. "No," he finally said. "It might work against me. It might not. An'Tellarus's rivals and enemies will no doubt question everything. They won't question her. They'll try to question me."

"Yes. Understand that some of those questioners are almost outsiders; they fled to the West March when the Empire rose, and have remained there in the shadow of wars that are ancient to you."

"But not to the Barrani."

"No."

"Because Barrani never forget."

"Indeed." Elluvian exhaled. "It has been two centuries since ownership of mortals was legally forbidden in the West March. The West March did not immediately follow the custom of the High Court and the High Halls because those customs were dictated in their entirety by the Eternal Emperor. Imperial law states that mortals are sentient, and sentient beings cannot legally be owned."

Severn's shrug was noncommittal.

"You disagree."

"I agree that it's against the Emperor's law."

"And you have come to understand the practical reach of that law."

"I understood long before I crossed the river," the private replied. "The fiefs aren't subject to Imperial law, either." He looked to the corner of the desk; a simple, reflective mirror awaited his command. "An'Tellarus has offered to attend to my attire." There was a slight question in the statement.

Elluvian was certain his eyes were too dark a blue for anything resembling nonchalance. "No. I will see to it. Do not trust her."

"I don't. I trust that she wants me alive, for now. I don't understand what she hopes to achieve. Letting a mortal loose among the Barrani of the West March is like a thrown gauntlet. But—" and here, his smooth brow rippled as his eyebrows tried to meet over the bridge of his nose "—I can't see clearly enough to understand what her game is. I cannot think of a single reason a random mortal would aid her cause—because I don't think she has a cause."

"She does. And before you ask, no, I have no idea what that cause is. But if you think you are bait set in a simple trap, you are likely to be disappointed."

"It's what makes the most sense."

"Yes. An'Tellarus has never been a lord who condescends to make sense." At Severn's expression, he added, "It is clear you feel kindly disposed toward An'Tellarus."

"And clear you don't," Severn countered. He did not do what Mellianne or Darrell would have done; did not do what Jaren or Rosie would have done at his age. Only Helmat in his youth—his angry, violent youth—would have failed to follow the statement with a question, and at that, only because Helmat had considered confession of ignorance a besetting weakness.

"You are far too pragmatic to take such an extraordinary risk with your life in order to obtain information that will change nothing."

Severn was silent, waiting.

"It is not just An'Tellarus that causes confusion in this circumstance," Elluvian finally said. "It is you. Were you Helmat, and he your age, I would understand your drive. Were you Darrell or Rosie, I would see your motivations clearly. Kin, however, does not mean as much to you as it once did to them. You are capable of utter, implacable loyalty to things that do not motivate most. And yet you are willing to abandon your duties to go to the West March for a period that might stretch to three months.

"Why?"

Severn's shrug was the entirety of his answer. He turned once again to the materials Elluvian had commanded he absorb. "The position of Warden doesn't seem to exist in the hierarchy of the High Halls. Can you explain it?"

Elluvian exhaled. "Helmat will die if you die."

"What?"

"He'll try to kill me, and in the history of the Wolves, that has never worked out well for the mortals."

A hint of smile accompanied Severn's shake of the head. "Warden?"

"As you wish. The West March is not simply distant geography; it is the largest gathering of my kin that exists outside of the Empire's boundaries. There is a reason for that. You are aware that the fiefs exist because of the Towers; the Towers exist to keep the heart of the fiefs caged. The Shadows that exist in *Ravellon*, the area encircled by the fiefs, are the largest existential threat the Barrani have ever faced. The fact that it poses the same threat to any sentient being does not change that fact. The Barrani seldom care about the difficulties other races face. The exception, of course, being the Dragons.

"There were small pockets of Shadow at the height of the final war between our kin; they were spread thinly across the vast plains of the Leontines and the forests of the Barrani. They were thickest in concentration near the West March."

"Was the West March as heavily settled then?"

"Yes."

"The Shadow gathered there because of the settlement?"

"That is our supposition, yes. The West March is not, and has never been, the seat of Barrani power. To our race, that is the High Halls, and will remain so. It is in the High Halls that the Test of Name exists, and the Test of Name is an emblem of power."

"Have you faced that test?"

"I have. An'Tellarus has as well—it is the reason she is lord. The Warden's position is not defined by that test. In the West March, it is a position of honor, and it is perhaps the highest position one can achieve if one does not choose to make the pilgrimage to the High Halls. There is a power in the West March which is unique and ancient, and symbols of that power persist."

"The Warden rules?"

"Ah, no. Not currently. The ruler of the West March is the Lord of the West March, and in general that position is granted by the High Court—the High Lord." Something in his tone must have offered warning to the youth; he truncated the dialogue. "Study what I have given you. If you have questions, I will attempt to answer them. If the West March is the land of my birth, I have become something of an outsider there; I am tolerated, but never welcome."

Severn nodded, as if he understood. And given it was Severn, he probably did. To Elluvian's surprise, Severn rose.

"I'll be back soon. I have a request to make. I'm not sure the information here will be enough."

Ybelline Rabon'alani was not within the Tha'alani quarter she theoretically now ruled when she received Severn's message. It was brief, the information it contained simple: he wished to speak with her, if possible, within the week. If her schedule was too busy—and it was—he would not have the opportunity for another two to three months; he would be leaving at the side of a Barrani High Lord for the distant West March.

The message wasn't written; he'd approached one of the Tha'alanari who worked within the Halls of Law. Draalzyn was not called in as an interrogator; his function was different. It was the only reason that he'd been allowed to continue to work at all. He did not find the constant presence of humans comfortable, but that was to be expected. No one was comfortable around people whose fear—implied or explicit—was constantly directed at them.

Draalzyn knew who Severn was; the entirety of the Tha'alanari knew. They didn't know all of Severn's interactions with their castelord, but they knew the castelord viewed him favorably; she didn't consider him an enemy to the Tha'alani, but rather, and far more unsettling, a friend.

Severn interacted with Ybelline from time to time, but always at a respectful distance, one that didn't imply fear of the Tha'alani racial ability to read minds. He had offered her access to the events that had scarred him; he hadn't struggled to hide himself.

But he didn't have to struggle. He was self-contained, his thoughts his own—one of the very few examples of a privacy that did not lead, in isolation and loneliness, to the peculiar madness that gripped so much of humanity. The Imperial Service didn't fear Ybelline in the same way they had feared her predecessor; she understood this. She was

young, she was—by human lights—*pretty*, her beauty marred
only by the racial stalks that protruded from her forehead.
She was not considered intimidating. They understood that
she, like any of her kind, could read their deepest, darkest
secrets—but they were far less afraid of what she might do
with those secrets.

She was Tha'alani. She had no desire to expose herself to
their internal thoughts—but she had been trained. She could,
and remain both herself and sane. And she could keep that
knowledge from the Tha'alaan.

She rose from the desk she occupied; it was tucked into a
corner in the part of the palace that was considered the most
secure. Very few of the people who visited the Imperial Security offices could, or would, catch sight of her; there were
no windows, and the door was warded. The ward itself was
unusual; it was far more like a door knocker than a lock. It
informed the occupant of this airless, windowless room that
a visitor had arrived.

It also showed her an image of who it was. She glanced at
the mirror on her desk and waved it to life. "Saidh Mankev."

Her supervisor's dour, expressionless face filled the mirror's
width. Ah, no—it wasn't expressionless; he looked apprehensive. "Ybelline?"

"I have received word from the Tha'alanari; my presence
is required."

The apprehension receded from his human face.

"I'm fine, Saidh. It isn't an emergency."

"Will you be returning today?"

"I'm uncertain. I think it unlikely."

"I'll call the guards."

She hid a grimace, and understood, in so doing, why so
much was often hidden when dealing with people who had
no access to the Tha'alaan. "I will be visiting the Halls of
Law," she said.

"The Halls of Law has made no request—"

"No. I will be visiting the Wolves."

"No request has been forthcoming," he repeated. "They know the procedures we require."

"It is a caste court matter; the caste court is not beholden to the same procedures." She exhaled. "I wish to speak with Severn Handred. He has not been asked to hunt; his hunt is not being reviewed. If you wish, the guards can remain by my side at all times."

His profile filled the mirror as he turned to speak to someone Ybelline couldn't see. She couldn't hear what he said. "Are they attempting to pressure you in any way?"

"No, Saidh. It is caste court business; Helmat has become particularly reluctant to ask the Service for aid."

"Because you're a young woman," Saidh replied, saying the quiet part out loud. Saidh was unusual in many ways, but Ybelline was almost comfortable with him—or as comfortable as she could be given the nature of the forced service the Tha'alani offered the emperor.

"Helmat is old-fashioned," she replied, smiling. "He considers me too frail."

"He's not usually this foolish."

"He is who he is." Her smile deepened. "I'm grateful that you are who you are."

He nodded gruffly and cut the connection.

Saidh Mankev lacked what most of the Imperial Service thought of as human warmth. Ybelline considered this as she made her way to the Halls of Law. She wore the uniform of the Service, which, for the Tha'alani, included a cape with a hood meant to somehow obscure the racial antennae of her people. She had pointed out that as capes were considered official uniform only for the Tha'alani, it obscured little; Saidh had considered this with his usual frown of thought.

From that point on, capes with hoods became part of the official uniform for everyone. Those directly beneath

Saidh—and far above Ybelline in Imperial rank—were displeased; they felt it made them look like dress-up assassins. The fact that the Tha'alani required them for safety was irrelevant. Was it wrong to feel a glimmer of satisfaction at their resentment and discomfort? Saidh, being Saidh, probably didn't notice. He was concerned with the protection of, the survival of, the Tha'alani under his care. He was not afraid of them.

She hoped that he survived as head of Imperial Security for a very, very long time.

If the hood drawn down over the forehead might fool the casual eye, it did nothing to fool the Hawks who stood guard at the main doors; she felt their instant tension, and yes, the disgust they couldn't quite conceal. They weren't unprofessional; they made no attempt to pepper her with questions she couldn't legally answer. They were even polite, which was not always the case. She passed them as they stood to the side to allow her into the Halls, and if they muttered or whispered behind her back, they waited until her back was far enough away she couldn't hear it.

She understood their fear; she was part of the Tha'alanari. She had touched human minds many, many times; she understood their need for secrecy. But she pitied them because that secrecy was all they had. They didn't have each other; they didn't have the experience of tens of thousands of people from which to draw courage and strength when choices and circumstances became too difficult.

They thought she *wanted* to know their secrets, because knowledge was power. It was power for the Immortals as well. Ybelline had never touched any of the Immortals; it was illegal. The Eternal Emperor had made that quite, quite clear.

But in the past, the Tha'alanari had been drawn, time and again, into the power struggles of the larger Imperial Service; they had been expected to perform extra-legal duties at the behest of their superiors, entirely off Records. The

Tha'alanari didn't trust mortals. How could they? They had seen far, far too much. Saidh had never asked for any information that would not become part of the internal Service Records.

He understood the intricacies of caste law; he understood that Ybelline was castelord. He had considered dropping her entirely from his roster on the day that position was confirmed. She was never certain why he hadn't. He had only asked if she wished to remain and continue with her duties to the Eternal Emperor. She had said yes. Inasmuch as any of her people had choice, it was true.

To her surprise, Saidh had seemed relieved. "The effect the mortals have on you—and the effect you have on the mortals—is less difficult. I will make adjustments to your interrogations as needed." He had been, and continued to be, true to his word. It was odd, but Saidh trusted Ybelline. He was possibly the only person in the Imperial Service who did, Tha'alani excepted.

She had very pragmatic reasons for not wishing to ever betray that trust, but they were not the only reasons.

He is mortal. He's the head of *the Imperial Service.* Scoros was not amused. She couldn't see his expression—he was in the Tha'alani quarter and she was in the Halls of Law—but she could feel the shape of his jaw, the heat of his annoyance, and beneath that, the seed of worry.

He is not beloved of the people he supervises, either. He's cautious, he's thorough, and he is immune to bribes.

You like him. Scoros's tone skirted accusation.

I do. If it were in my hands, I would never see him again; I would withdraw all our people from the Service in a heartbeat. You know this. But you also know why we can't. If we disobey the Emperor, and he chooses to reduce parts of the Tha'alani quarter to ash, I would be where he starts. And we would get no support from any other quarter; no other caste court would extend a hand in aid. We do what we do to protect our people.

Scoros was not mollified.

He serves as we serve. I don't think he loves the job, but he does it. He makes as much truth of the job as he can. He sees clearly. And I'm sorry, she wasn't and he knew it, but I would far rather a human I can respect, and maybe even like, than otherwise. He has done nothing yet to earn my distrust.

He's the head of the Service.

There will always be a head of Service. You know he's better than almost any other person we've dealt with in his position.

Since this was true, Scoros changed tactics. *Why are you going in person to the Halls of Law? Why do you not ask Severn Handred to visit us instead? He would do it.*

This was faster.

Ybelline, a new voice said.

She considered Helmat's ridiculous protectiveness and almost sighed. She considered her own people above such condescension; they *knew* she was powerful. But if they didn't consider her weak because of her gender, they certainly considered her fragile because of her age.

And that was unfair. She listened to the quiet lectures offered by fellow members of the Tha'alanari as she made her way to the smallest suite of offices in the Halls of Law: the Wolves.

Rosen was startled when Ybelline asked permission to enter; the wards glowed and the doors rolled open. She jumped out of her seat, but she didn't move quickly.

"There must be some misunderstanding," Rosen began. "I have no outstanding requests for a member of the Service to come to the Halls of Law." She looked almost flustered, which was unusual. Ybelline drew her hood down around her shoulders.

"There are no outstanding requests," she said, her smile genuine. "I am here as castelord, at the request of Private Handred."

"Records," Rosen said. "Severn, you have a guest."

"Who?"

"If you put aside your work and head to my desk, you'll see." She looked up from the mirror. "He doesn't seem to be expecting you."

"Ah, no. I don't have an appointment. But he asked if he could speak with me, and I had business close by, so I chose to answer his request in person."

"Take a seat," Rosen then said.

"Does Helmat know I'm here?"

"He does by now. It's not necessarily Helmat I'd worry about, though."

"Oh?"

Elluvian's door opened at almost the exact same time Severn's did.

"Oh."

Helmat's door was soundproof—but only in one direction, although the sounds from the outer office could be muted at his command. He was aware of the activation of the door wards, and in general, gave the notifications he received by mirror a cursory check. The wards recognized the visitor.

His personal mirror showed her: Ybelline Rabon'alani.

He hadn't requested the presence of a Service investigator; she was, he could see, wearing Service uniform.

"Saidh Mankev."

The mirror remained flat, and a voice he recognized said, "Saidh Mankev is currently occupied in a meeting. Do you wish to leave a message?"

"No."

The faceless voice coughed and then said, "Saidh wishes me to inform you that he has no idea why your visitor chose to visit; it's caste court business and has nothing to do with the Service. If you wish to know why she has arrived at your office, you might ask her." Another cough. "Sorry, Helmat.

He also wishes me to remind you that you, like he, have no sway over caste court business."

Ah. It was Anderson's faceless voice. "I'll keep that in mind." He rose, walked to his door, and pushed it wide open. "If the two of you," he said, to Elluvian and Ybelline, "are about to argue, do it in here." It wasn't a request, but Helmat wasn't in the business of making requests in his own damn space.

Elluvian and Ybelline acquiesced immediately; they were in his office for five minutes before Severn joined them. The private offered a deep bow to the castelord; she returned a nod. It looked out of place given her uniform.

"I am not here on Imperial Service business," Ybelline said, smiling. She looked, as she most often did, serene; her eyes were the resting gold of the Tha'alani.

Severn glanced at both Elluvian and Helmat. "I didn't expect you to come to the office in person," he said, the words implying surprise—and gratitude. "I tried to make clear to Draalzyn that it wasn't an emergency."

She nodded. "You are not the type of person to make such a request unless you feel it is urgent, and I admit some curiosity."

"Does this…request…have any relevance to your leave of absence?" Helmat demanded.

"It does," Severn replied. He exhaled slowly. "I wish to speak with Adellos."

The name dropped between the Tha'alani and the mortal private like a stone. Her expression, however, didn't change.

"Why?" The question was direct, unadorned, and uttered by each of the three people in the room who weren't Severn.

"I've requested a leave of absence," he replied, "as you just heard. I'm to travel to the West March."

Elluvian's eyes were undiluted midnight. Ybelline's were now flecked with green. "You will travel with Elluvian?"

"With An'Tellarus."

"And Elluvian," Elluvian said.

"I'm not sure your presence will make things any safer." Helmat coughed.

Ybelline, however, held Severn's gaze. "Adellos has never traveled to the West March."

"No. But he is close friends with a man who spent almost the entirety of his life there."

"His *childhood*," Elluvian snapped. "He is only barely considered adult by our kin."

Severn nodded. "There is no one else I can ask."

"You could ask *me*."

"You haven't lived in the West March since the founding of the Empire. I know things change slowly in Barrani society—but not that slowly. And I don't trust An'Tellarus to tell me all of the necessary information."

"You don't even know what necessary information *is*."

Severn nodded again. He then stepped forward, until he stood less than a foot away from Ybelline Rabon'alani. She understood what he was offering but shook her head. "I will ask Adellos. I cannot compel him. And for reasons you must understand, it would be far better for everyone concerned if we spoke with An'Sennarin in person." She hesitated, and then added, "I believe he would be willing to speak with you, but I cannot be certain."

"It's why I wished to speak with Adellos. Adellos can be certain. I considered making the request directly," he added, lowering his chin, "but An'Sennarin is at the heart of the High Court; he can't afford to be seen to be making a mistake. I don't wish to inadvertently cause difficulty for him."

"And you don't believe you will be causing Adellos difficulty?"

"Not political difficulty, no. I don't believe my request will threaten Adellos's survival within the Tha'alani quarter."

"Very well. I will confer with Adellos." She closed her eyes.

★ ★ ★

Adellos had every reason to refuse the request, and Severn had every reason to avoid Adellos. Adellos had attempted to murder him in the heart of the Tha'alani quarter. But the private seemed to understand—even forgive—the attempt; he was not afraid of Adellos.

Ybelline was far more hesitant. If Severn understood and forgave, she still struggled—because what she had seen, what she had learned, could not be shared with the Tha'alanari in any way. Adellos's attempt was an act of madness, something decided in his self-imposed isolation, without the advice or the experience of those who might have faced similar decisions before. Adellos had been forcibly retired; she hoped that, cut off from the pressures of the office of castelord, he might at least return to the peace and serenity of his kin.

She could keep this calculation from Adellos in the Tha'alaan. But he was perceptive enough he might assume it anyway. She wanted to ask Severn why he intended to go to the West March, but the destination made clear that this was about the Barrani, and about Barrani politics—the politics of poison and madness, in the opinion of the Tha'alani. She wanted no further secrets she was forced to bear in isolation; she was certain there would be more than enough of them before she, too, was allowed to put down the burden of rulership.

Ybelline.

She raised her chin; it was Adellos. Had she lost enough control that she had contacted him subconsciously? He was *done* with the work of the castelord; he was allowed to rest in peace. She felt her cheeks redden.

Apologies. I did not intend to bespeak you here.

No. You have taken an interest in the boy I attempted to kill. You took an interest in him the first day—and I have seen all the ways in which that interest has proven correct. He is not, to my mind, dangerously insane, although he is mortal.

He wants to bespeak An'Sennarin. He is, I believe, afraid that any public interest on his part will be to the detriment of An'Sennarin. And he knows that you can bespeak An'Sennarin directly if it is necessary.

All of this is true. What do you wish me to do, castelord?

She felt the sting of the words. *What do you wish to do?*

I am viscerally opposed, he replied. *But while it is visceral, it is instinctive. I have had decades of hiding and protecting the information you now contain, and I understand that I cannot see clearly. I do not believe your private will harm An'Sennarin. I know An'Sennarin will not harm your private. But I do not think the mortal should be going to the West March, and I do not think he should trust An'Tellarus.*

It wasn't a reply.

Adellos continued. *No. What I wish, now, is what I was denied for so long: a chance to confer, to examine the possible benefits and the risks, to make a decision after considering all elements carefully in the presence of someone I can trust. And there is only you. Only you know, and only you will know, going forward.*

"I will have to return to the Tha'alanari before a decision can be reached," Ybelline told Severn. "But I believe Adellos would be willing to speak with you. Understand that I will not and cannot command him, but I will ask."

CHAPTER FOUR

THE THA'ALANI QUARTER HADN'T MARKEDLY changed since Ybelline Rabon'alani had become castelord. This visit, however, was much like Severn's first one: the streets weren't empty and children lined them, some attempting to look uninterested and some openly, vividly curious. The Tha'alaan contained interactions with humans; in a city the size of Elantra, it was impossible to avoid them. But the Tha'alaan wasn't a substitute for actual, lived experience, as cautious and eager curiosity implied.

As usual, older Tha'alani kept a watchful eye on both the children and the human visitor. Caution didn't tip over into fear because Ybelline herself had chosen to meet Severn at the heavily guarded gate. She was castelord, not Emperor; Severn wondered if any other race had a castelord who was greeted with such open affection and warmth.

Not for the first time, he envied the Tha'alani.

One child—gender wasn't obvious—approached Ybelline, tugged on her skirt, and was lifted in the castelord's arms. They then turned to Severn. "Does it hurt?" they asked, eyes hazel, the Tha'alani color that implied worry, not fear.

He blinked.

The child frowned and hesitantly reached up to touch the stalks on their own forehead.

Ah. "No," he told the child, smiling. "I was born this way. I've never had them."

"Never?"

"Never."

"But how do you hear? How do you talk?"

"I can hear what you say now."

The child's stalks wavered in air as they turned to Ybelline. Ybelline's smile was gentle. "I don't think most human children learn to speak to each other until they're older."

The hazel color intensified. Severn's smile deepened as he recognized the expression: pity. He was almost certain she might offer the same expression to a starving stray cat if one crossed her path.

"Can I try to talk to him?"

This did cause an older man to intervene, although he remained silent, holding out his arms to take the child from the castelord. If he admonished the child, the words were silent; they could speak without opening their mouths.

"Perhaps another time," Ybelline told the child. "Our guest has come to speak with Adellos this morning, and we will be late if we linger here."

The man relaxed, although he didn't allow the child to return to Ybelline. "You are welcome here," he said to Severn. "More positive memories of interactions with your people would be welcome in the Tha'alaan." A reminder, possibly unintentional, of the memories that did exist—even if most of the people here couldn't touch or experience the worst of them.

Ybelline nodded. "Apologies," she said to Severn, voice soft. "There might come a time when the presence of someone who is not of our people elicits less obvious curiosity or excitement—but I fear that will not be soon."

"Would it be safe to talk with the child?"

The castelord's eyes were gold. "Almost certainly. But there is a risk, and it is a risk I think you understand. I was once a child, just as she is, and it would not have been safe—for the Tha'alaan—had I made that request at the age she is now, and you were willing to accept it.

"Secrets break so many things," she added—in Barrani. "But once you have begun the keeping of them, revealing them is dangerous for multiple reasons. Your race is a race of secrecy, but at heart many of you desire to set that secrecy aside. It is not so with the Barrani."

He switched to Barrani to reply. "No. And it is of the Barrani that I have come to speak."

"So it is," a familiar voice said. While Ybelline and Severn had been interacting with the child, Adellos had approached them. Severn had been instantly aware of his presence; no doubt Ybelline had noted it as well. He had chosen to take his lead from the castelord, but as Adellos had broken his silence, he turned.

He offered Adellos a Barrani bow—the respectful bow offered to a superior. The only difference between the gesture he offered the Tha'alani and the bow he might have offered An'Tellarus was that he chose how long to hold it, and he rose of his own accord.

"You have been well taught," Adellos said.

"I came to it young."

"You must have. I could not execute a bow half as good."

"You were castelord; among the Barrani it would not be expected of you."

"Come. I have prepared refreshments. Ybelline?"

"I will join you if Severn desires it."

Severn, however, shook his head. Adellos met Ybelline's gaze. He held it; to Severn's surprise, it was the castelord whose eyes moved first.

★ ★ ★

"She is worried for you," Adellos said. "But you are not worried."

"No."

"Why?"

"I understand the reason you tried to kill me."

"And you believe I will not have a reason to make a similar attempt?"

"It would break something in Ybelline."

"She is not that weak. But yes; the trust between us is tentative and fractured. It is not entirely shattered. It would be costly to her—and she is castelord now. Do you not believe your inquiries will cause difficulty for An'Sennarin? Do you believe that he would have no desire or need for your death?"

"I am, I admit, uncertain. But given what I know of his history with the Tha'alani and his rise to power, it's a risk I'm willing to take."

"And as you have chosen to take the risk, so have we." We. Severn noted it. "We have reached our destination. This is my home."

It looked, to Severn's eye, like any other dwelling in the quarter; small, but in good repair. The former castelord had not gained obvious wealth from his previous position. Tha'alani furniture was almost entirely rounded—the edges of the tables, the chairs, even the doors, and rounded, well-worn furniture filled the visible rooms.

"Please, be seated. Let me go to the kitchen."

Adellos had no servants, either. He lived a life, now, that would suit Severn. Severn sat at the table the Tha'alani had indicated, and waited while food, on a large, round tray, was brought to the table. Drinks were brought on a second tray—from the scent, some type of tea.

"I am uncertain of your preferences."

"I grew up in the fiefs. Anything is better than nothing," Severn replied.

"You must tell me of your fiefs sometime," Adellos replied, his eyes gold, his expression serene—as if Severn might randomly visit at any other time. "An'Sennarin is willing to speak with you."

"Through you?"

"For the moment."

Severn nodded.

"It would be difficult for him to meet you directly; he might do so in the presence of An'Tellarus, but that has other complications. She is, to his mind, someone who is old enough and powerful enough to flout convention at her own discretion."

"And he is newly come to his title and his position as the head of his line. I understand. I find An'Tellarus... intimidating. Unpredictable."

Adellos's smile was different, if genuine. "What do you wish to know?"

"An'Tellarus has invited me to attend her when she returns to the West March."

Gold eyes instantly developed flecks of vivid green. "When?"

"Seven days from now."

Green eclipsed gold. Green was the color of rage or fear, in Tha'alani eyes; it was the color of happiness in Barrani. "Has she said why?"

"It's An'Tellarus."

At that, green receded slightly. "What excuse has she given?"

"She wants company."

"What believable excuse has she given?"

"None. As I said, I find her both intimidating and unpredictable. I cannot see what she wants of me, but the West March is not Elantra; I might be the only mortal present. The Tha'alani are curious. Their curiosity is...like a child's curiosity. There are no games in it, no allusions to power or personal gain; they want to know things that are stubbornly unknown.

"The Barrani aren't like that. I can't see what she hopes to gain—or whom she hopes to offer deadly insult. Our information about the West March is scant."

"An'Sennarin says you are dealing with An'Tellarus, who defies rational explanation. But he asks a different question."

"He wants to know why I'm considering accepting the invitation."

"Indeed."

Severn exhaled. "I told you: I grew up in the fiefs. I'm not sure what that means to either you or An'Sennarin. I was an orphan; I would not have survived had I not had a guardian."

Adellos nodded.

"The guardian was Barrani."

Green eyes.

"When I was very young, I accepted his presence as a matter of course. He taught; I learned. But I have no memories of my parents, either father or mother. It didn't bother me when I was young."

"It bothers you now?"

"Not exactly; the knowledge won't change my childhood and it's unlikely to change my life. But I know that other children, other orphaned children, aren't taught and protected by Barrani. In the fiefs, they aren't protected at all much of the time. If you don't have family, you'll die. I was nine years of age before I realized that I, too, had had mortal parents. I know nothing of them. I know nothing about my place of birth; I know nothing about where I was found. I asked my guardian only once."

"What did he say?"

"Nothing. His eyes were midnight. It was the first time I had seen them that color—but I knew what it meant."

"You did not ask again."

Severn nodded. "An'Tellarus said she might have information about who my parents were—and she would give

me that information in return for my company to the West
March."

"Do you know the name of your guardian?"

"I know the name he used. I don't believe it is a name
used by the Barrani."

"And you are curious, now, about why he chose to protect you in your childhood."

Severn nodded again. "It's the only reason I believe
An'Tellarus might have the information she says she has."

"What does she have to gain? Do you believe she wishes
to locate your guardian?"

"If she wished to locate him, she has the resources."

"An'Sennarin points out that you have access to impressive resources within the Imperial Halls of Law."

"So, in theory, do the lowest of servants within his domicile."

At that, Adellos chuckled. "Humans are more Barrani
than Tha'alani are."

In Severn's opinion, any race was more Barrani than the
Tha'alani, part of the reason he envied their children. But
he didn't envy them the fear and the hatred of outsiders, or
the dire consequences that arose from them.

"Very well. What do you wish to know about the West
March?"

Severn withdrew a notebook from the interior pocket
of his jacket. "An'Sennarin lived in the West March until a
few decades ago."

Adellos nodded.

"The West March isn't part of the Empire, but it's part
of the domains ruled—in theory—by the High Lord whose
home is. There's going to be a power structure, which might
be similar to the power structure of the High Halls. We
know far more about the High Halls and its various lords
than we do about the West March.

"The brother of the heir to the High Lord's throne is Lord of the West March."

"Yes." Silence followed the word, and in that silence, Adellos's expression changed several times, as if he were having a conversation without words, and in very compressed time. He finally exhaled. "An'Sennarin says the Lord of the West March is unusual. He is powerful, and it isn't wise to anger him—but he is harder to anger than many Barrani who have held that position in the past.

"He is not entirely trusted in the West March; his closest familial ties are pure High Court. Does that make sense to you?"

Severn nodded; he wondered that it made less sense to Adellos, who had known—and had clearly conversed with—An'Sennarin for half his life.

"He does not believe An'Tellarus intends to cause difficulty for the Lord of the West March. Ah, no, I am being corrected. He does not believe her purpose is to cause difficulty for the Lord of the West March. Although she speaks of him as one born to the West March, she speaks without rancor; were he born there, she would likely approve of him."

"She is part of the High Court."

"She is powerful, yes. She has passed the Test of Name. But she does not dwell within the High Halls; she visits, and those visits generally flaunt her disdain for the High Halls in one way or another. She last visited for an extended period when An'Sennarin was brought to court by his former lord."

"Did she disapprove of the previous An'Sennarin?"

"An'Sennarin says *disapprove* is too flimsy a word."

Severn's smile deepened. He could well imagine that. "Is she tolerated because she's powerful?"

"In An'Sennarin's opinion, it is mostly that—but it is also the fact that she will go away. She has no designs on any of the positions granted lords of note. The Consort does not care for her, but the Consort's daughter—the future Consort—

holds her in esteem. She has always treated An'Tellarus with genuine respect."

"The High Lord?"

"As you imagine, his respect is stiff; were she less powerful, I do not imagine she would claim living quarters within the High Halls itself. An'Sennarin cannot see how her return to the West March would cause complications for the High Lord."

"And for the rest of the West March?"

"He is more troubled. He agrees that An'Tellarus is as you've described her—but I believe, inasmuch as he feels affection for Barrani Lords, she would be one of them. She has always been politically astute in circumstances where the consequences of being less astute would be too high. And her enemies have learned to walk and speak with care in her presence.

"If one is to attack An'Tellarus, the attack must be swift and it must succeed."

"Does An'Sennarin expect she'll be attacked?"

Silence.

"Does my presence give ammunition to those who might seek to unseat her?"

Adellos exhaled. "My apologies, Severn. An'Sennarin has asked—and I am willing to grant the request—that the two of you speak more directly. He finds my interpretation mildly frustrating, as he believes you—and he—share more of the same concerns, from the same context."

Severn met Adellos's gaze. "Are you willing to take that risk?"

"I was castelord, and I spent my adult life in the Tha'alanari. I can contain a conversation that occurs between the two of you, and I can keep it from everyone—save Ybelline. She will know if she desires to do so. She cannot contact An'Sennarin directly." There was a warning in the martial green of Adellos's eyes.

Severn accepted it. His prior investigation of Tha'alani murders had made clear that Ybelline could, should she choose to, speak the True Name of An'Sennarin. But perhaps the nature of True Names did not allow it. Adellos's reaction made clear that he believed she could. None of the people involved in this conversation wanted that.

But An'Sennarin was not like the rest of his kin; he was clearly willing to accept that risk. For now. And it would be a risk that continued into the foreseeable future because every castelord would have access to Adellos's particular memories.

Adellos had already attempted to kill Severn to protect that knowledge, and Severn had not touched the Tha'alaan through anyone but Ybelline. But he agreed with An'Sennarin. Adellos as interpreter added time and confusion to a very necessary discussion.

Adellos drank tea and waited until Severn nodded. "Pull your chair closer. I am an old man, and you are young and healthy. I would prefer greatly if you would clear the table and lie across it on your back."

Are you lonely?

Two voices asked the same question.

Severn opened his eyes. He recognized An'Sennarin; An'Sennarin's eyes were a steady blue, lighter in color than the indigo that indicated visceral emotion. The Barrani man didn't look young; he looked like any other Barrani male. Knowledge of his youth was an exercise in research.

"No," he said, answering the question. It was only when he voiced a response that he understood it was not An'Sennarin who had asked it of him. He recognized the first voice; it was the voice of his guardian. He did not recognize the second, although it was a soft tenor, almost shorn of the curiosity the question implied.

Memory was not a guide, here. He would have side-stepped it entirely had the question not also been asked of

An'Sennarin. When, where, and by who were not instantly revealed—nor did he ask. An'Sennarin was here in the same fashion Severn was: in spirit.

"I owe you a debt." An'Sennarin's voice was soft, cool but not cold.

"I release you from it," Severn replied, well aware that debt between Barrani often ended in bloodshed and death.

"Almost any interaction between Barrani ends in bloodshed and death," An'Sennarin said, although the blue in his eyes lightened, making room for green. "I was not an orphan when I first caught my lord's attention." The green dimmed. "You never knew your parents."

"No. I can't miss what I've never known. But…" He wasn't speaking aloud, but had he been, his voice would have dropped to a whisper. "I want to know even if it won't change anything."

"They might be alive."

"They might. But even if they were, I spent childhood without them. They are family in theory, not practice."

"And the family you did have?"

He shook his head and almost pulled away. He had shared these memories with Ybelline as a prerequisite of accepting the work the Wolflord had offered, but he did not wish to add the burden of those memories to Adellos.

"How did you meet An'Tellarus?" An'Sennarin asked.

"Elluvian introduced us. Ah, no. She demanded Elluvian's presence on the day I accompanied him to the High Halls."

"You did not go to meet her?"

"We went to meet Lord Corvallan and his wife, Cassandre. An'Tellarus…intercepted us. She intended to test either Elluvian or me, possibly both."

"And you survived."

Severn nodded. "She wasn't intent on killing me, but she wouldn't have been upset if she'd succeeded. She wanted to know, I think, that I wasn't flimsy enough to die to an invisible sword strike."

"That was foolish. Were you a Wolf then?"

"I was."

"In the West March, there are no laws of exemption that govern the caste courts. There *are* laws, but the application of consequences is directly proportional to the power of the person accused of a crime. Were she to make that attempt in the West March, it would signify nothing; at worst, she would be required to pay a price for property damage." At Severn's raised brow, he added, "Inasmuch as there are laws on the books, damages come under loss of property. It is a holdover of the days in which—"

"Humans were slaves."

"Not just humans, although they were more common."

"And now?"

"Slavery is illegal, by the will of the High Court. It is not the Eternal Emperor that the West March fears—but if the High Lord and his closest confederates are not allowed to own slaves, with the implied advantages of that ownership, the courtiers of the West March are to be likewise deprived. It has been long, even in the time of my kin, since slaves were so owned. But slavery is a legal term."

It was a warning.

"Are there mortals in the West March?"

"You might find a few—but only embedded in the homes of the powerful. It is not unlike owning a precious kitten; it is difficult to keep them from being either injured or stolen." An'Sennarin's skin reddened. "I apologize for the implication."

"No apologies are necessary. I have some experience with the general attitude of the Barrani, and I take no offense at it. Offense would have served me ill as a child, given my guardian. And seeing the world through Barrani eyes prepared me for later life in the fiefs."

"And in the human court?"

Severn shook his head. "The human caste court isn't the power the High Court is. I don't imagine a single Barrani anywhere is unaware of who the High Lord is. Most of us have no idea who the lord of the human caste court is."

"Do they exert so little influence, then? They might kill you and call for a caste court exemption."

"It's unlikely to be invoked, and even if it were, it wouldn't be accepted. The laws of exemption require both parties—criminal and victim—to invoke. If the victim wants Imperial justice, they simply refuse, and the investigations proceed as they normally do."

"Truly?"

Severn nodded. "Most of the crimes referred to the Halls of Law fall under the possible exemption rules."

"There is no such law in the West March."

"No. Who is the law in the West March?"

"In theory, the Lord of the West March."

Severn nodded. He reached for his notebook and remembered where he was. He understood that theory was relevant to Barrani, because customs and etiquette followed theory with a vengeance. "In matters pertaining entirely to the West March?"

An'Sennarin grimaced. "It's complicated. In the past, the Warden."

"But not now? Is there no Warden?"

"Oh, there is. But the man who currently occupies that position is new to the role—and he has never made the pilgrimage to take the Test of Name." At the mention of the test, his eyes darkened to a familiar indigo. "Had he, his authority would surpass the Lord of the West March's authority."

"Could he take it?"

"Any Barrani can take the Test of Name; some are sponsored to do so if their family circumstances do not allow easy travel. But few survive the test; they enter the Tower and they fail to emerge. There are no families of any note in the West March who have not lost kin to that test. The beloved son of Lord Avonelle was lost to it; the current Warden was close to his brother and his resentment of the High Halls is therefore deeper.

"Lord Barian is the current Warden of the Green—the full title. He is addressed, however, as Warden." As An'Sennarin spoke, an image of a Barrani man formed to Severn's right. "You will not see the scars in public."

"Scars?"

"The green tests, and it leaves its mark. It is not as deadly as the Test of Name; less than a quarter of those who enter the green perish, and if they do, their bodies are returned to their kin."

"How many pass the Test of Name?"

"Perhaps a fifth."

"So sending your children to take the Test of Name is highly likely to be a death sentence."

"Better death than failure," An'Sennarin replied, his voice the epitome of bitterness.

Severn understood. "I don't agree."

"No—but you are not Barrani. I have taken the test. I have become both a Lord of the High Court and the ruler of my familial line. There are constant challenges to my authority, and there will be constant challenges for at least a century, possibly two. If I survive, however, I will have power. Lord Barian would not make the pilgrimage."

"You did."

"I had no choice. My parents were dead and my extended family leaped at the chance of power. If I failed, it was of little concern. If I passed, they expected to be bathed in my reflected glory. I tried to run away," he added, the bitterness twisting his mouth and the lines of his brow. "And one of the three people I considered a friend suffered a terrible accident; she did not die. She could have. It was made very clear to me that she could have."

"Are you certain she survived?"

"I have not seen her since. An invitation to the High Halls has been issued in my name."

"She hasn't accepted."

An'Sennarin shook his head.

"Have you asked An'Tellarus to at least ascertain that she lives?"

"I cannot." He swallowed words, and silence descended upon them both for minutes. "If she still lives, if I ask some-one of An'Tellarus's stature to check on her, it will be clear to all of my enemies that she is still a grave weakness to me. If it were not for me—" The words broke. An'Sennarin lifted a hand as if to ward off further questions, but those questions did not come from Severn. He understood. He waited.

"My apologies. I seldom speak of this; I am not yet capable of viewing it objectively."

Severn's voice was soft. "There are things of which I cannot speak, even now."

"Then perhaps you are no longer a child. I was told," again, bitterness seeped into his words, "that it was regret and the ability to keep secrets that defined adulthood—and apparently, as I am speaking with you now, I have only the first and none of the second. Again, I apologize." He blinked. "No, Adellos." It was obviously a reply. "Severn Handred asked a question I could easily answer—but it led to unexpected emotional cliffs. He is not to blame in any way.

"It is not expected that discussing the bare facts of Barrani hierarchy, known to any child of any background, should cause…difficulty. The fault lies entirely with me." Words that no Barrani of any age should easily utter. Severn knew it; in theory, An'Sennarin, Barrani by birth and upbringing, must know it better. But the words were offered with concern and without guile—and again, that was unusual.

Ah, Severn thought. An'Sennarin is worried about *me*. Adellos had already tried to kill Severn once; the worry made sense. He said nothing, waiting.

After another long pause, An'Sennarin continued. "Lord Barian's younger brother died in the third war, his older failed the Test of Name in the High Halls. But his younger brother did not undertake the Test of Name, either.

"His mother, Lord Avonelle, was forbidden that test by her lord, well before our time. By the time her father died, she could not easily risk her life in a pilgrimage to the High Halls. In her view, death is better than failure. It is a bitter view for Barian; he would have far preferred his brother's life. I do not believe his brother wished to leave the West March, but his mother demanded it—Lord Avonelle is powerful in the West March. Her husband is head of his line, but it is acknowledged that she is the ruler. Anger her and you will not survive long."

"What is her relationship with An'Tellarus?"

An'Sennarin winced in a way he wouldn't had they met in person. It was answer enough. "Let An'Tellarus lead. Let An'Tellarus speak."

"If she allows it. She might well demand I speak or perform instead."

Another wince. "Yes. But if she wishes you there, she will not allow harm to come to you, and if she is incapable of protecting you, Lord Avonelle is the one who will pay the price. An'Tellarus has, in the past, destroyed entire families, root and branch, in her august displeasure; the eldest among us still remember, and fear of reprisal stays many a hand."

"As she no doubt intended."

"Yes. I don't believe she enjoyed the slaughter, but she felt it necessary: do it once, do it without mercy, and it will echo down the ages as the warning it must become."

"Are there any other lords of whom I should be wary?"

"You should be wary of every breathing person you meet,

but yes. Avonelle has allies, and some are more likely to act against you for concessions to their own lines, as they would not expect to survive An'Tellarus.

"Kin is not everything to Barrani—in mortal terms, in yours, I would say it counts for nothing. But the pride of kin is ferocious. That pride is where the ties of family are seated." He began to list names, to list alliances, to speak of the histories between the various families, and the enmities and rivalries that still echoed.

He did not mention Elluvian at all, until the end. "Will Elluvian travel with you?"

"That's his intent. He's not happy that I've been invited."

"Elluvian's story is known in the West March. He is not well-respected there."

"He's not well-respected here, either, but I don't think he cares."

"No. Usually, lack of such care implies power; the powerful do not need to be concerned over small details and niceties."

"In Elluvian's case?"

"Elluvian is family to An'Tellarus. None of us are certain what the exact connection is; some believe she is mother, some aunt, some believe there is no blood relation at all. Elluvian is not well-liked in the High Halls; he is similarly disliked in the West March. I would almost tell you that your journey would be safer were he to be left behind."

"But?"

"It is clear to me that An'Tellarus wishes his presence; she is no fool. She understood, before she issued the invitation to you, that he would come." He exhaled, although breath was, in theory, unnecessary in this space, which consisted only of two people against a gray, featureless background. "It is possible that Elluvian is her goal. If she invites you, and she has reason to believe you will accept that invitation, Elluvian will join her. He would not join her, otherwise. Even should she command it; she is matriarch, yes—but he is the Emperor's Wolf. He is not beholden to her. If she wanted Elluvian to accompany her, you present an actual lever that has not been available to her in the past.

"I will send a letter with An'Tellarus; it is a letter of introduction. My parents are dead, but I have cousins. It is possible that they might be of aid to you. I owe you a debt."

Severn shook his head. "It is the other way around. I owe you a great debt."

"You do not."

"The Tha'alani—"

"No. I acted to protect them—too late. You were barely born, if you were born at all."

"You did what I would have done and survived it. What the Tha'alani have now, you gave them."

An'Sennarin shook his head. "It is I who owe you a debt. I will make that clear. If they can discharge that debt, I will owe them; I will not say any will act out of the goodness of their hearts. But...it is not unknown, in the West March. It was not unknown in my childhood." He closed his eyes, and Severn felt a wave of homesickness so strong it left a lingering envy in its wake. He had never felt that about any place he had ever lived.

No, his home had been people. Two people. And then one. And then none.

"But Severn, I must give you one warning: stay away from the heart of the green."

CHAPTER FIVE

"YOUR LACK OF FEAR," THE FORMER THA'ALANI castelord said, as he accompanied Severn to the gates, "is astonishing. I am surprised that you considered making your request of Ybelline. Perhaps more surprised than you were when I consented." Adellos spoke Barrani in the streets of the Tha'alani quarter. Very little Barrani existed in the Tha'alaan, and while some Tha'alani could speak it, the memories required to access the little-known language were less easily reached without focus and effort.

Severn followed suit. "I understood, in the end, all of the different motivations in this case. I would have done what An'Sennarin did—and perhaps what you did—were I in your position." He had done worse.

"Would you?"

"Yes—if it were possible. I prefer Ybelline's approach, but yours makes sense to me; it wasn't personal."

"Ah." Adellos shook his head. "I am grateful for Ybelline. I am grateful you survived my momentary madness. You understand because you have more experience with Barrani. But at a distance, I understand it less and less well. You are young; you will go to the battlefield while those of us who are too old or too feeble will remain behind."

"You like An'Sennarin."

"Yes. Affection is dangerous for those of us who have such broad responsibilities. But he is worried for you. He does not trust An'Tellarus."

"No, of course not."

Adellos chuckled. "And yet he, as you, desires the ability to trust. He is, and has been, homesick—but he will summon no one to the High Halls. What he has endured he would never demand of anyone he cares about. He will write your letter."

Severn hadn't doubted it. But he understood that it was difficult to lie in the Tha'alaan. The Tha'alaan was not just a collection of disparate words and thoughts; it was a form of true communication.

"You must survive your outing," Adellos said, as the guards that manned the gate came into view. "He had to struggle not to tell you not to go, because he understood that it would be pointless. I believe he will feel some guilt if you perish in the West March. And yes, the guilt is not his—but perhaps his association with the Tha'alani has broken some essential Barrani trait in him; he will feel responsible for not trying hard enough to dissuade you."

"Tell him that I work for the Emperor and have been asked several times to accompany Elluvian to the High Halls. The West March can't be worse than that."

"You have amused him; he agrees. Thank you for that. Take care, Severn. You are a Wolf, but you have made connections with people you did not know before you became one, and those connections, living and breathing, will grow in ways that none can easily foresee."

You should not simply ask questions to receive answers; answers, even if the speaker believes them, are one small thread in a tapestry. Truth is, and has always been, subjective when speaking of or to other living beings. It is best, when you begin, to know the truth before you ask; you can gauge much about the speaker and the speaker's intent from the response you are offered. As they so often did, his master's words returned to Severn; the echoes of that voice were strongest in the presence of Barrani.

Severn glanced briefly at Elluvian. Elluvian was dressed for the High Halls, not the office—as was Severn himself. Some of the clothing Elluvian had purchased for Severn's first visit to the High Halls saw unintended use now. It wasn't particularly ostentatious, but it spoke of the money Severn didn't actually have; it offered the patina of confidence, the implication of the wealth from which humans derived power.

None of which would impress Barrani, near or far. Here, all eyes would be on An'Tellarus first, Elluvian second; any attention paid her human attendant would be the attention offered a novelty, a curiosity. Her own servants—there were half a dozen visible—treated both Elluvian and Severn as valued guests; if they felt otherwise, none of it showed.

The carriage itself was Barrani style, the exterior slender, the wheels flimsy to the eye. It was pulled by two horses, not the four that usually accompanied the more traditional carriages used by mortals, or the six that were often required when the Dragon Court went traveling on official business.

An'Tellarus entered the carriage first; she was followed by Elluvian. Severn waited until he was summoned, noting An'Tellarus's eyes. They were green. Flecks of blue could be seen but they were scant. Elluvian's, of course, were blue, the shade too dark to denote caution, but pale enough otherwise to imply safety.

"Sit across from me," An'Tellarus said. "Elluvian can sit beside me; I would far rather see your face than his, his expression is so unpleasant."

Elluvian took the seat beside An'Tellarus in silence; there was nothing at all unpleasant about his expression that Severn could see.

"I am so delighted that you are actually here. Until you entered the carriage, I felt almost certain some malign fate would prevent it." She gestured; an envelope appeared in the palm of her hand. "I have been asked to deliver this to you. You are bidden to offer the letter of introduction to one of three people; it is highly likely that you will have the opportunity to meet two of them. The opportunity to speak with the third is far, far harder to create."

Something in the way she spoke caused Severn to straighten in his seat. This minor shift in posture delighted An'Tellarus; she laughed—a full-throated sound that Severn could not recall ever hearing from a Barrani before.

"What has the young An'Sennarin asked of you?"

"Nothing. Nothing at all."

"And how did he know to offer this letter?"

Elluvian cleared his throat. "I spoke with him, of course."

An'Tellarus rolled her eyes. "Of course. Given your usual social grace, I highly suggest young Severn read the letter before its intended recipients; he might be in for a very unpleasant surprise, otherwise."

"I highly doubt An'Sennarin would visit his displeasure with me upon Severn."

"That is true. He is young; he has yet to understand the true value of selective treachery. I am certain he will do so in time." Her smile deepened. "I did."

"You cannot possibly compare An'Sennarin to yourself; the circumstances in which you came of age were markedly different."

"And you feel he is innately more decent?"

"He is young," Elluvian replied, with a graceful shrug.

Severn, however, said, "Yes."

Both sets of Barrani brows rose at the bald, simple answer. Severn met their gazes—An'Tellarus's more blue, Elluvian's less so—and then turned his attention to the letter in his hand. It was sealed; if he was allowed to read it before he passed it off, the seal was unlikely to be magical. "There are three possible people to whom I might offer this letter, according to An'Sennarin. Will you tell me what you know about the third—the one I might have trouble meeting?"

An'Tellarus's eyes shaded back to green. "I would be delighted."

"Do not get involved in the affairs of the Barrani," Elluvian said—at the same time. The older woman and the younger man glared, without bothering to turn their heads to make sure the cause of those glares received them. The amount of green and blue in their eyes seemed to combine to be a constant.

Elluvian's advice was good advice; it was the advice Severn would have offered anyone who found themselves in his position. It's what Severn's absent guardian would have said.

Do not be greedy. It is greed that ruins men. Act when you have the information and the ability to succeed. Plan, Severn.

I can't plan in ignorance.

No. But the gaining of information is very, very risky. If you have learned nothing else from me, learn caution.

For the first time in years, Severn wondered what advice his guardian might have given him if he knew of An'Tellarus's offer, and Severn's decision to accept it. He had, only once, made a choice of which his guardian had not approved—and it was the last time he had seen him.

See what is in front of you. Hear how others describe it; hear the stories they make of it—but see it clearly, or you will not survive.

An'Tellarus, Severn thought, understood the early lessons he'd been taught, even if she couldn't be certain what they were. She knew how to be seen, how to confound expectations. She knew how to behave in a way that made observation irrelevant. What did she want of him? What did she want of his presence?

Some clue was to be found in the color of her eyes. He had asked a question that had pleased her enough she was willing to answer it. And she clearly knew the three people An'Sennarin thought might accept his letter of introduction without resultant ill will. It was likely she'd already read the letter, and likely that An'Sennarin wrote it with that expectation.

But it was because she had seemed fond of An'Sennarin that Severn was willing to trust her intent when it came to the new, young lord. He couldn't imagine that most Barrani would approve, not yet—perhaps not for centuries. Possibly never if they truly understood the motivations that had led to his unseating of the previous ruler.

To Severn, however, the reasons defined the lord. He understood that he could not, could never, count An'Sennarin as a friend. A mortal friend, a human friend, would be a weakness An'Sennarin couldn't afford, and Severn was not Adellos, to offer friendship in utter secrecy. In different circumstances, he would have been willing to serve An'Sennarin, especially now. It was now that his grasp on the seat he'd taken to protect the Tha'alani was the most tenuous.

Are you lonely?

The echoes of a question they had both heard. Perhaps they'd both asked it themselves. Severn had barely understood the question the first time he'd heard it. He shook his head to clear it; An'Tellarus's eyes were a steady green, but he had been silent for too long.

"If I am correct," she said, when she saw she once again had his undivided attention, "the third friend of whom you speak is Yvonne of the Darrowelm clan. She is still young— younger in all ways than An'Sennarin, although to our kin the difference is negligible. They were childhood friends, at a time when it was thought An'Sennarin would remain an insignificant, minor Barrani beneath the notice of the High Court.

"She has never undertaken the pilgrimage to the east."

"Is she still considered a child by her family?"

"That, of course, is the excuse given by Darrowelm. If you are unlucky, you will meet some of them." Her lip curled in distaste; Severn noted it. "I do not know the extent of the injuries she received."

"Injuries?"

"I do not know how much An'Sennarin has told you of his past in the West March."

"He has said very little."

She did not ask him when. "He was, as I said, considered insignificant; a young child of a branch family of little value or note. I am certain that those in the Sennarin hierarchy will regret this estimation—if they survive it."

"An'Sennarin did not strike me as punitive."

Her smile was all edge. "I did not say that he would be the source of their regret. But he is, as you must understand, in a very tentative position. Where I can, I have offered him support—but my support, as all support, is a double-edged blade. Those who would see him fall would see my support as proof of his inherent lack of fitness to rule. You have something you wish to add?"

"He wears the crown."

"Indeed. He has proven himself capable of at least that—but succession wars often leave many dead who briefly lifted that same crown. Darrowelm is not a family well-known or well-connected to the High Court. But they are one of the subtle powers in the West March. I have visited Yvonne once. The visit was heavily supervised. She moved slowly, and I believe her appearance was slightly altered. More would have been insulting to me, and if we are not allies, they do not wish my enmity in the West March."

"Are her injuries relevant?"

"Yes. And they were inflicted at the command of the former head of Sennarin, with the possible help of some of the Darrowelm servants."

"Why?"

"You have the impatience of a mortal."

"We lack time," Severn replied, expression grave.

She laughed. "You do, indeed. Very well. We are tested for magical aptitude when we are approaching our majority. Some are tested far, far earlier than that—that aptitude is key to power. The Barrani do not have children at the ferocious rate of mortals, but attempts have been made to breed for magical abilities.

"The current An'Sennarin was not the result of such attempts. But when he was finally tested, he showed a depth of ability—and a range of ability—granted to few. He is not yet the power he will grow to become if he survives, but the seeds of that power were noted. You know that he is an orphan?"

Severn nodded. "It's something we have in common."

"He was not an orphan when he was tested."

After a silence that extended as Severn considered the implication of the words, the young Wolf said, "Their deaths were a result of the test? They didn't want their son to be sent to the east?"

Her smile was far warmer. "Indeed. But the An'Sennarin of the time desired his presence in the High Halls. There are few Arcanists of note allied with Sennarin. The boy would have been of incalculable value to him. The loss of his parents was a tragic accident," she added. "There are rudimentary laws that govern the West March, but there are some cases that are never investigated. I have a base appreciation for the Eternal Emperor's laws—when they do not, of course, apply to me. The West March is not ruled by those laws.

"Because of the tragic accident, the boy was then taken in by elder cousins—those more amenable to the previous head of the line. When An'Sennarin came of age, he was sent to the High Halls to take the Test of Name. He was considered of value—but the Arcanum is extremely political, and the course of his studies would be heavily impeded had he not proved the strength of his name. You don't approve."

"It seems to be a death sentence for most Barrani."

"It is. Or worse. It can break a person for many decades."

"Enough," Elluvian snapped.

"…and we are, of course, forbidden to speak of what we suffered. For people of power, breaking such rules is almost expected; I will not personally suffer from my indiscretions."

"You are not High Lord," Elluvian said, blue darkening in his eyes.

"No, of course not. But Severn does understand what I implied."

"They'd kill those to whom you spoke. If they could not determine who, they'd kill all of the people in their reach, to be safe."

"Indeed. But to do that, one must assume that I would stand by while my people were murdered for my indiscretion. This is in all ways a faulty assumption. It is far better, however, for no word of indiscretion to reach the wrong ears."

"Nothing you've said would be considered such an indiscretion," Severn replied, in perfect High Barrani.

"No. But even the mention of such discussion could cause difficulties."

Elluvian's expression was the definition of icy. He offered no further interruption.

"The current ruler was not of a mind to obey the commands of his family's head. He was at home in the West March, and it was the only place he knew. He made this clear—foolishly, in my opinion. He could not be punished or broken if he was to be of future use, but other children with far less value could be.

"Yvonne had an accident. It was not considered accidental enough by those of the western court; if she was insignificant, there was some sense that the young man might not be, in the future. Yvonne survived—but at some cost, and I do not believe she ever fully recovered. After her injury, he understood that similar accidents would continue to plague those for whom he cared, and he surrendered and went to the High Halls.

"I believe you know more of what happened afterward than either Elluvian or I."

Severn's gaze fell to the letter of recommendation. "Does An'Sennarin think that now is the time to take such a risk?"

"I cannot answer that question. You will have to ask him in person when you return. But Severn, caution is necessary. There is a reason rulers never display open or obvious affection: such affection becomes a weapon in the hands of one's enemies."

"It was known that Yvonne had been used as such a weapon?"

"A fair question. Yes, I believe it was known—but not widely. As I said, An'Sennarin came from an insignificant branch family, about which there was nothing to know."

"Do you believe Yvonne is heavily guarded because of this?"

"I would be interested to hear what you, an Imperial Wolf, think."

"I don't have enough information."

"And you make no assumptions?"

"Faulty assumptions can be fatal."

She nodded with approval. "You were well taught, for a mortal."

He said nothing else.

An'Tellarus and her party made use of inns along the merchant roads until they reached the border of the Empire. They made use of inns along those same roads to the west of that border. Accommodations for three guests, two servants, and four guards were in no way difficult to find—not when the leader of the group was possessed of a large amount of fairly obvious wealth.

Severn professed an ignorance of geography beyond the boundaries of the city of Elantra. It was a partial truth. He had not often traveled outside of Elantra itself, but his teacher, being Barrani, considered Barrani strongholds of interest— as if he suspected Severn would one day have to navigate within them.

There was a large gap of merchant road between the last inn and the boundaries that defined the West March on a map. Severn knew that the inns used by the Barrani from this point on were entirely ancient constructions—similar to the Towers that ruled the fiefs.

"Do you know where we're going?"

"The West March," he replied, noting the color of An'Tellarus's eyes. Elluvian's had remained the steady blue many mortals assumed were the Barrani's only eye color. An'Tellarus's eyes, however, showed a much more accessible range of emotion.

"Do you imagine that we will travel there without pause?"

"No."

"Well?"

"I am uncertain if we will set camp and remain there, or if we will enter the Hallionne."

She glanced at Elluvian.

"I will camp," Elluvian said. "I will not enter the Hallionne." Severn looked to An'Tellarus.

"It has been a long time since I have entered the Hallionne," she said. "But I believe it will be safest for you to do so."

"Not safe for you?"

She smiled. "It will be safe for me, but in general, it is not my preference. This is not the first time I have traveled with mortals, although the last time was centuries ago. The forests here are not entirely safe for one of your kind, as we learned to our detriment the first time we made the attempt. If you ever travel to the West March again, you will discover that many of my people prefer the risk of the night forest to the possible danger the Hallionne poses. But the Hallionne have long slept since the last war.

"How much were you told about the Hallionne?"

"Very little."

"Ah. Well. We are approaching the gateway for the first one now."

Severn looked out the window; he could see nothing but forest. The path to the forest, like most Barrani roads, was clear, but it ended in a large, circular clearing. No sign that this clearing had been used by any traveler in the near past was evident, but the carriages stopped, spreading out along its edges.

An'Tellarus glanced once at Elluvian, shook her head, and stepped out. The sun was setting, but night hadn't yet darkened the forest; Severn could see the trees that encircled the clearing. Only one stood out to him; it was easily the largest of the trees, and the only one with roots that rose above the ground. He turned toward it.

"Yes," An'Tellarus said, coming to stand beside him. "That is the door." She turned to one of the two armored men who had accompanied her. "Has Elluvian already departed?"

They nodded in unison.

Elluvian clearly didn't consider the Hallionne a threat to Severn. He had vanished without a word of warning.

"Why do you think this is safer for me?" he asked, voice soft; Barrani hearing would carry the words to anyone who chose to listen anyway.

"Is this not the first time you have been in this forest?"

He shook his head.

"Ah. I did not lie. The forest presents danger for mortals. It can, in the wrong circumstances, present danger for any of my kind as well." She walked past Severn to the trunk of the tree; there she lifted her hand, placing her palm against tree bark. That bark melted, exposing the wood that lay beneath its protective covering.

Severn exhaled and drew a dagger. An'Tellarus raised a dark brow, her eyes narrowed. "What are you doing?" she asked, voice soft as threat.

"I can't enter the Hallionne if I don't offer it blood," he replied.

"Did I tell you that?"

She knew she hadn't; Severn didn't bother to answer—not with words. He made a small cut in the mound of his left palm, and placed that hand against the surface of the wood. The wood itself began to fade, as if blood was a solvent. Nonetheless, he waited until An'Tellarus passed beyond what had become an arch before he sought to follow her.

"You do not need to offer the Hallionne your blood a second time," she told him, her voice trailing over her shoulder.

"I've never entered a Hallionne before."

"And you waited until I had entered first."

"You are An'Tellarus. I am your guest." When she failed to move, he added, "The Hallionne consider the precedence of entry an important part of etiquette."

"They do. It is almost hard to believe that this is your first experience. I do believe it," she added. "Come. Mortal inns are small, cramped, and inconvenient."

They were better than sleeping on the ground, in Severn's opinion, but his opinion wasn't the relevant one here.

"We shall eat, and we shall sleep in safety." She hesitated. "The Hallionne can function in a state of sleep—try not to wake them."

The warning she offered was one he had heard before. He wasn't given to daydreams, even in his childhood, but he had wondered about buildings that seemed to respond to their occupants in a hospitable way. The only experience he had with such buildings were the distant Towers of the fief, buildings of dread and death, ruled by their necessary lords.

The halls that they entered—and apparently An'Tellarus's servants and guards had chosen to remain outside—were airy and light, the ceilings clear enough that were it not for the color of the sky, he would have thought them nonexistent. An'Tellarus's eyes were blue—but a blue that possessed flecks of green. She was not afraid to enter, and even felt at home here.

Severn, naturally cautious, almost felt the same—and that was a warning. Obvious threats could be observed and countered. This was far more subtle; it induced him to drop his guard; it invited him to feel that that guard was unnecessary. Perhaps it was. He followed An'Tellarus into a dining room that felt entirely Barrani, but resembled no room in the High Halls that Severn had seen; there was far more wood and far less stone, for one. But the style of chairs was different, as well, far more curved and of slightly varying heights; one side of the table appeared to be a small bench.

An'Tellarus took the seat that defined the head of the table; Severn, at her slight nod, took a seat on the bench closest to her. He was surprised when food appeared on the empty plates. If the Hallionne wished to offer hospitality, it wasn't entirely individual; the food on Severn's plate matched the food that appeared on An'Tellarus's.

But his glass was filled with water; hers with a dark crimson wine.

"You don't drink," she observed.

"I've seen what drink does to people who are too careless."

"You would never be too careless."

"That's what those people thought as well."

"You don't trust yourself?"

He shrugged. "I'm aware that there are possible consequences

I can't foresee. If it were necessary to drink wine, I would drink it."

"The Hallionne doesn't consider it necessary."

"Because you don't."

She nodded, frowning. "You are an enigma."

"So, according to both An'Sennarin and Elluvian, are you."

She smiled then. "It is protective coloration. It is far better to appear to be unpredictable. The expectations the Barrani have of each other make that far more simple; we are a rigid people. Mortals are far more variable. What do you think An'Sennarin wishes for?"

Severn frowned.

"You do not expect that he has offered you his tacit support—and the letter of introduction—with no possible benefit to himself, surely?" Her frown was tighter as she observed him. "I see you do. I had assumed that your teaching would be better than this."

"Why?"

"Pardon?"

"Why do you believe that about the lessons I was given?"

"I wonder. You have never spoken the name of your teacher aloud—perhaps because I have not demanded the information."

"I'm not certain the name would be relevant. I think it highly likely he used a name that wouldn't be traced should I encounter Barrani in the future. So do you."

"Indeed. But nonetheless, I am curious—and in this place, the only person who might hear your answer is me. Tell me, what was the name he gave you?"

"I called him master or teacher, depending on his mood," Severn replied, voice more carefully neutral than An'Tellarus's. "But he was known as Regellius on the rare occasions we had visitors."

Her frown deepened. She had no reaction to the name;

her eye color didn't change. As Severn expected, it wasn't a name she knew. "Visitors? Mortal?"

"Not always."

She smiled. "I see. And if I were to ask you the names of the visitors?"

"I was four years old," he replied, his voice far graver than hers. "Our memory isn't Barrani memory, much to the annoyance of my teacher."

"He did not have visitors when you were older?"

"When I was old enough to understand the significance of visitors, I was no longer with my master."

"Your expression says I should not ask why your master left."

He nodded.

Her laughter filled the hall, echoing there long after it had otherwise vanished. "You are impudent, child."

He nodded again.

"Do not share that impudence with any of the people you will meet from this point on. Dignity and honor are almost everything to most Barrani—especially those who are, or would like to be, powers. I believe you feel rudimentary trust for An'Sennarin—and very little trust for me. Would that be correct?"

"I would not insult you by openly trusting you," he replied, in perfect High Barrani.

She laughed again. "Did your master say that?"

"No. He trusted me because the consequences of misplaced trust were nonexistent."

"Is that what he told you?"

"Not directly. It's what I inferred."

"He taught you what was most important to learn. Power is its own hierarchy, and the powerful are seldom threatened by the powerless. Do you know what I wonder, Severn?"

He waited. When she added no further words, he understood the question was a test. "You wonder why a Barrani man involved himself with a mortal orphan at all." When she nodded but offered no words, he continued. "You wonder why the lessons he taught were Barrani lessons—Barrani language, reading, history—when those would appear to be irrelevant to a mortal life."

"I do," she said, surrendering words when she was satisfied with his answer. He felt a pang of nostalgia, none of which he allowed to show. "Let us speak about An'Sennarin's friend."

CHAPTER SIX

AN'TELLARUS WAS SIMILAR TO SEVERN'S MASTER in one way: any discussion started with a preamble. "Power is hierarchy among my kin. Power implies freedom. Your expression has become extremely guarded. You don't believe it."

"Power brings attention, and attention brings enemies."

"Yes. In order to remain a power, you must deflect or, better, destroy those enemies. Your life becomes a game of cat and mouse, and your role—cat or mouse—can feel extremely uncertain. Your master didn't consider himself a power. You understand that our own view of these things is oft muddied and subjective. Tell me, with your imperfect childhood memories, do you consider your former guardian to be powerful?"

"He lived in the fiefs, in hiding, with mortals." Severn shrugged, as if he were still in the fiefs, and looked down at the tabletop, at his mostly empty plate.

"Very clever, young man." Cleverness clearly didn't always amuse An'Tellarus. "It is not, however, an answer."

He took a risk. "Most Barrani would believe it was an answer."

"I am not most Barrani, I am An'Tellarus."

"I have no answer to offer."

"I want your opinion; I will not judge you for it."

He exhaled and set his utensils down across the plate. "He didn't fear his guests. They weren't impressed with his living conditions—they were blue-eyed to a man. Or woman. But they treated him with respect and concern. I believe they wanted him to return home."

"I see. I will not ask you where that home theoretically is; I am certain you do not know. And yet you did not seem surprised by the Hallionne. Perhaps he chose to give you the upbringing of our saner kin."

"Saner?"

"If he did not speak of the less sane, I will not. Perhaps, one day, Elluvian will enlighten you. If he speaks, listen. I will now tour the Hallionne—I like to inspect small changes. Will you join me? You are mortal and require sleep, or so I have oft been informed."

Severn rose and offered An'Tellarus an arm, which was the entirety of his answer. Her eyes were once again green. "Do you wonder that I don't fear the Hallionne?"

He shook his head. "I understand that most of your kin aren't comfortable within the confines of the Hallionne, but don't believe they have reason to fear them."

"It depends on their intent. The Hallionne prevent assassinations and the less savory of our political games. To do so, they must be aware of their guests in a way other guests might not. They can read the thoughts of those who choose to accept the hospitality they provide."

Severn nodded.

"This doesn't surprise you."

"It wasn't explicitly presented that way, but no."

"You have no fear of your thoughts or secrets being known."

"To the Barrani—or most of the Barrani—I have no secrets that could be a threat."

"But that is not the case for me," she said.

"You don't believe that your enemies could pressure the Hallionne for those thoughts and secrets, if the Hallionne even retained them."

"No. There was once a small lake here; come. Let us find it."

There was a lake that would not, by Elantran standards, be considered small. It was girded by the tallest trees Severn had ever seen, but they looked and felt almost familiar. If the Hallionne was awake, it offered An'Tellarus the illusion of privacy; no one came to disturb her. Severn stood by her side. There was only one chair, and she took it as if it were a throne.

An hour of silence later, she dismissed him; he bowed and retreated, stepping back until she was out of view. He then exhaled, turned, and found himself in front of a door; the door opened as he approached it. No words were said; he simply stepped through the door, and found himself in a hall. Although the floors were wooden, a faint light shone from the heart of some of the planks, and he followed the light as if it were a solid path.

In this way, he found a room—a set of rooms—very similar in architecture to the rooms he had occupied throughout his life in Elantra, or the fiefs that preceded it. He entered, found a bed, and removed his clothing, leaving only his weapons in easy reach. He could sleep while leaning against walls or doors—and, in fact, had—but here, he felt no need to practice that level of caution.

And An'Tellarus was, of course, correct; mortals required sleep.

★ ★ ★

I want you to consider two things today.

Severn nodded. He glanced, briefly, at the familiar confines of the rooms in which he had spent much of his life to that point: faded furniture, threadbare carpets, and shelves in excellent repair. Books lined those shelves, and those books, having passed through his hands—his child-sized hands—were not in as fine a condition.

I'm dreaming, he thought, curiously displaced from himself; he wasn't entirely comfortable in the body of a child he hadn't been for over half his life.

But the voice of his master was strong, an anchor against even the experience of reality.

Yes. I did not expect you to visit the Hallionne so soon—but mortal years pass so quickly the experience and lessons amassed in them give rise to inaccuracies. If you wish, you may choose different rooms in which to have this discussion. It is not a lesson, Severn. I cannot teach you what you must now know. Either you have learned it, or you have not.

And if I have not?

You will perish. The Hallionne will not allow you to come to harm; it is not the Hallionne that will kill you. But if you are here, you walk death's road, and there is a very, very narrow edge you must navigate to successfully escape that road's ending.

Has this happened before?

Of course. And, at the same time, never.

Severn closed his eyes. He didn't regret his childhood; he didn't miss it. In childhood he had had no power and no skill of his own, and the gaining of what power or skill he now possessed had been fraught. This wasn't the first time he had faced death. It wouldn't, in future, be the last. But to hesitate was worse because there were worse things than death. A clean death, a relatively painless death, was the best ending he could hope for.

Or it had been, when he had been a child.

He chose rooms that were familiar to the man he was now: the indoor training rooms used by the Wolves. Although the Swords and the Hawks trained in the open yards under the supervision of weaponsmasters who had apparently trained all their lives to deliver a bellow of sound that wasn't an actual shout, the Wolves never joined them. The composition of the Imperial Wolves was never exposed to the other two branches of the Halls of Law; only Helmat and Rosie, now that she did not accept missions, were visible.

There were far fewer Wolves than either Hawks or Swords, and the space requirements were not as pressing. The lessons—the fraught lessons in which Wolves were expected to both recognize and react to magical attacks before those attacks killed them—were conducted in a large, windowless room that contained no furniture beyond a practice weapon rack; there were suits of armor of various types which could be donned to focus the lessons or refine them, but beyond that, nothing but wooden floors.

Even the walls were absent the paintings and insignias of the Emperor which otherwise graced the open and public halls beyond the Wolves' closed doors.

I see. I do not consider this a suitable practice chamber.

You said this was not an actual lesson.

All of life is a lesson, both the quiet and almost invisible parts and the...more colorful events. As his master's disembodied voice spoke, the light in the room changed, the magical illumination giving way to a far more natural light, although the walls and floors remained as they had been remembered.

Severn looked up; he saw sky. Sky, and breaking its clear open lines, high branches and leaves. A compromise?

Yes, in a fashion. Life is compromise. But there are some things that should never be compromised. The young cannot often discern the difference; they make choices that hew to their parents' or guardians', and often do not question those choices. There would be little to gain from it. Children—even ours—are without power.

As Severn listened, the voice gained direction and solidity. Beneath the boughs of the high trees, shadowed by them, a man emerged from the wall farthest from Severn. He wore a cloak of an indistinct color—gray, or gray-brown, or perhaps gray-blue; the color shifted and moved although the man who wore it didn't. That had not been his master's way. He had been still, and could remain still, for hours on end; he had taught Severn this skill, although of all the lessons Severn had learned, it had been the most difficult to master.

His master's eyes were blue, of course; they had never been any other color in Severn's memory—a memory that was clouded by the distance of childhood.

"You are not here."

"No. But I have been here; I requested a boon from the Hallionne and it has been granted. Do not underestimate the power and flexibility of the Hallionne. My kin—some of my kin—fear the Hallionne, but that is also to your benefit. If you can reach the Hallionne, you will find shelter and safety.

"Ah, no. If you can reach any Hallionne with the exception of Alsanis. I will not warn you not to enter; entry is strictly prohibited and you will not—even with your skills—be allowed to so much as approach Alsanis. But you might see him, or what remains of him, if you are here. You are traveling to the West March."

Severn nodded.

"Do you travel alone?"

"No."

"Do you travel in the company of Barrani?"

"Yes."

His master's eyes shaded instantly to the blue that had always signaled displeasure. Severn hadn't seen that expression for almost half his life now, but felt it viscerally. He showed no signs of that reaction; obvious reactions had long since been trained out of him.

"Who?"

"An'Tellarus."

The silence that followed caused some of the darkest blue to ebb from his master's eyes. Severn wasn't ignorant enough to relax. "How did you come across An'Tellarus? You have not been foolish enough to dare to enter the High Halls, have you? She is known to be...almost chaotic among our kin; she is in all ways unusual. This does not mean," he added, glaring balefully, as was his wont when he meant to drive an important point home, "she is harmless or safe."

She was certainly neither. Severn nodded.

"Well?"

"One of my companions is Elluvian of Danarre."

To his surprise—a surprise he almost certainly failed to completely veil—his master uttered a short bark of laughter.

"You serve the Emperor's Dog?"

Severn said nothing.

"Come, child." The laughter had not lightened his master's eyes. It had darkened them, shifting their color into something that resembled a deep, deep purple. "If you serve Elluvian, you serve the Emperor."

"You disapprove?" The question was controlled, almost indifferent; the impetus behind the question less so.

"We each have our own circumstances; I cannot approve—or disapprove—without further information. I will tell you, however, as you are in the Hallionne, that Elluvian is not the safest of companions for your journey."

"He has not chosen to enter the Hallionne."

"Ah, no. That is not what I meant, and I perceive you understood that. He is dangerous, Severn; he is broken."

"An'Tellarus?"

"She is dangerous because she has never broken. But she has always been indulgent in unusual ways, and her alliances have not always been alliances of power; our kin have long failed to understand her."

"That implies that you do."

"No one can fully understand the measure of another person. But I do not find her as unpredictable as most of our kin would. Dangerous, yes—the powerful are always dangerous. I hope you have not forgotten that."

"It was the earliest of your lessons. No, master. I have not."

"Tell me, why do you journey to the West March?" There was something in the question that reminded Severn so strongly of his lost childhood he had to bow his head. He was no longer a child, to seek the open approval of anyone to whom he did not owe a duty. And yet, some part of the child remained.

"I seek answers," he said, his tone bland. "I seek information that has always been beyond my reach."

"And it is An'Tellarus who has offered you those answers."

"She sought my service as a guard. It is not an entirely credible request."

"And you accepted."

"In payment for that service, she offers information about my parents."

Silence.

The walls of the room flickered in place, as if they were made of pure light and something had passed between his eyes and the source of illumination. Above, the skies shimmered in the same way; the only two things to remain solid were Severn and his master.

"Were you still under my care, I would tell you to turn back."

"You would advise it?"

"I would command it."

Severn nodded. "You are no longer my guardian, and the debt of duty I owe is not to you."

"It is to the Dragon Emperor."

"It is to the Eternal Emperor."

"Who would not send you to the West March; it is beyond his reach. The flights that damaged it in the three wars never broke it; they could not. You are not here because of the duties you have undertaken for the Emperor."

"The duties I have undertaken on occasion take us beyond the borders of the Empire, but no."

"I did not raise you to die so pointlessly."

Severn said, "I cannot assess the truth of that. I was a child when last I saw you. I am not a child, now, by the reckoning of my kind." He paused, and then smiled. "I have no intention of dying."

"It is not your intent that matters, or that will matter. An'Tellarus might keep you safe, but there are many secrets contained in the West March, and some of them are living, breathing things that desire to feed—and will. Do not continue this."

"You have said—you have always said—that history is important. Our making and our breaking have roots in the loam of history; it is from those that we become." He spoke High Barrani, Court Barrani. "My history began before you—but you are the history I know. You know what An'Tellarus knows." He didn't attempt to hide behind the carefully chosen words; he met his master's gaze and held it.

"It is not mine to tell."

"Were you not the one who said that knowledge is not the domain of any single individual?"

"I was. If I told you what I believe she knows, would you turn back?"

Severn didn't answer.

His master, grave now, said, "That, too, is an answer. If it is simply information you seek, and I offer it—"

"It is not yours to tell." Severn looked down. "And I have offered her my services; I cannot now simply recant and flee."

"Why not?" The question was sharper, the eyes narrower as Severn lifted his face to meet them once again.

Severn shrugged. "If, in the end, I accomplish what she wants and she doesn't give me the information, I won't accept such an offer again. But what she chooses to do is not what I choose to do. I've agreed, and I will abide by that agreement."

"Do not tangle with An'Tellarus's many enemies. In your

city, it might be safer, but the West March is no part of your Empire, and the customs of the West March are not entirely the customs of the High Court. Do not trust her. Do not trust Elluvian."

Severn nodded.

"Do not—"

"Trust you," he finished. "I know. I've never forgotten."

"You are too young."

Severn nodded again. "I'll always be too young in your eyes. It's not, therefore, your vision I must rely on." He turned, seeking a door, an exit from this place.

"No. Sadly, it has never been my vision. If I could, I would join you. But any place in which we might meet is not safe for you."

An'Tellarus had said that the Hallionne was not awake. Severn wondered just how much a sleeping Hallionne could accomplish. He had no doubt that the illusion he had faced was his master; the man hadn't changed at all in eight years of absence.

He'd known, as a child, that the day would come when his master would simply close his doors; that the safety of knowledge, and the lessons that conferred it, would vanish. It had been the cause of anxiety in his childhood; he had understood then that surviving on his own was a very unlikely outcome.

He'd discovered that mortals were nothing like his master. They could be far more indulgent, far more patient, or far more deadly; they were also far louder, as if the sound of their lifted voices contained their desire to be heard in the brief span of years they were given. Severn had never been comfortable in the streets of Nightshade; the retreat to his childhood home had been a blessing of silence and stillness.

But as he grew, his master had insisted that he walk those streets; that he learn something new to him, that he bring that knowledge back, where the two of them could dissect it, interrogate it, absorb some parts of it. Severn didn't assume that he brought relevant or useful knowledge to his master; he didn't assume that those lessons taught his master anything.

Not then.

But his master had said that if knowledge was general, it was the specificity that made it interesting. His master didn't know the people who lived in the buildings that surrounded them; did not know the children that played in the streets under the watchful eye of their grandparents. He understood their language, but didn't understand their choices, which is why he found mortality oddly fascinating, both repellent and vulgar, yet vibrant and dynamic. Only the ugliness seemed commonplace to him; it was the ugliness of the powerless. Many of the Barrani suffered that powerlessness.

The least powerful of the Barrani were far stronger and faster than the average mortal. The most powerful of the Barrani were so far above the ground on which Severn stood he might never be noted at all.

Severn had asked him, perhaps a year before his master had left, why his Barrani master was involved with a mortal.

"It is a good question, an intelligent question. What should my answer be?"

Severn had frowned. "I don't know—that's why I'm asking."

"What have I told you about asking questions of the Barrani?"

"I must know the possible answers before I ask."

"Yes. Why?"

Severn sighed. "...Because that's the only way I can assess the relative truth of what I'm told."

"Indeed. Were you perhaps under the unfortunate illusion that I am not Barrani?"

"...No."

"Then tell me: What should my answer be? I am living in your fiefs." They weren't Severn's fiefs, but he knew better than to offer correction during a lesson. "I am living anonymously; there are very, very few of my kin who dwell in this place, beneath those Towers, in the lee of the great Shadow. What might impel me to serve as your guardian and your teacher?"

I don't know was the wrong answer in any circumstance, even if it happened to be the truth. Severn was silent for a moment, considering the question with care. "You would do it if your lord ordered you to do it."

"And?"

"You might do it in exchange for something you desire. You might do it if someone to whom you feel indebted asked it of you."

"All of these are possibilities."

Severn exhaled. He'd been young; he'd almost forgotten the reason for his question. That had no doubt been his master's intent. "I asked the wrong question."

His master had nodded.

"Why would any Barrani have interest in me? In the past, I might be considered a promising slave—but I'm not a slave."

"No? Perhaps not. But you live in conditions the least of our slaves would never have been forced to endure."

"We don't—"

"Not *we*, but *you*. You personally."

"You never owned slaves."

His master's brows had risen; if human memory wasn't Immortal and perfect, Severn could still recall his master's expression. "Why are you so certain of that?"

But Severn shook his head, retreating. He'd known he would get no answers that day.

In the darkness of his room, he considered the Barrani he knew. Elluvian, An'Tellarus, and An'Sennarin. He had spoken with Cassandre and Corvallan, both of the Mellarionne faction. He knew better than to trust Barrani, but there were layers of distrust, and there were certainties within those layers; neither Cassandre nor Corvallan would hesitate to cause him harm if it served their purposes. An'Tellarus would at least pause to consider. Elluvian would not betray Severn unless at the Emperor's orders—or Helmat's.

But An'Sennarin?

An'Sennarin, who had risen to political power at, for Barrani, meteoric speed? He had advised Severn not to go; he had, however, written a letter of introduction for those he considered friends—men and women of little power or significance, a remnant of his old life.

Severn could trust An'Sennarin. Perhaps, with age and time, that would become less true; the games Barrani played, they played for survival, and that was bound to have an effect. Yet he'd taken power not for himself or his Barrani friends, but for the Tha'alani. And now, the only way to lay down that power was to die.

Severn wondered what his master would have thought of An'Sennarin, and more important, what he might have made of him, had An'Sennarin grown up in a run-down, small apartment in the heart of the fief of Nightshade.

Understand what others want, not only of you, but in its entirety. The moment you understand what they want, you can begin to navigate the currents of their plots. Not all those who have such wants will be inimical to you—but if you are to survive, you must clearly see the difference before you set foot in the currents they cause.

He was frustrated. Frustrated and apprehensive.

His master had intended that Severn come to the West March. If the unexpected interview, similar to a mirror's view, had been planned, it had been planned for a reason. In none of his most childish fever dreams, in that distant set of rooms, had Severn believed he would be where he now was: under the protection of one of the Hallionne, on the road to the Barrani stronghold of the West March.

But his master had.

His master recognized An'Tellarus at least well enough to know of her reputation; he recognized Elluvian of Danarre in a similar fashion. His master, however, had not known that

Severn would travel with either of them. He was certain his master would have little knowledge of the new An'Sennarin.

So: he either intended or expected that Severn would—somehow—make a journey to the West March. Why? Had he intended to one day bring Severn here himself? And if so, why had he abandoned his student?

Abandoned was perhaps the wrong word, at least in Barrani. As if his master felt there was room in his ward's life for only one person, he had vanished when Severn had found Elianne and her mother.

Are you lonely?

It had been almost the last thing his master had said to Severn. Severn had had difficulty understanding the question, it seemed so out of context.

Lonely?

That is answer enough, child. I have kept you long from others of your kind; I have kept you safe—but safety, in the end, is a state only the dead achieve permanently.

They're dead, not safe.

Dead, there is nothing that can alter their circumstances or their state. You are unusual for a mortal, but you are mortal, and mortals require things I cannot give. Perhaps you have found friends because you understand this.

I found friends because you told me I had to find friends. I found friends because you wanted me to investigate mortal lives and mortal stories you haven't heard yet.

You will find things you did not seek when you seek at all, his master had replied. His eyes had been blue, but it was an odd shade of blue. *I have done what I can, for now. How you handle yourself, how you handle the mortals around you, will be proof of either my success or my failure. I will be waiting.*

He had never expected that his master would remain by his side. He didn't confuse the role of "father" with the role of teacher. He didn't believe that anything that had existed in that distant apartment, where hunger hadn't been an issue, and the cold couldn't kill him, would remain in his hands. Had he trusted his master?

Yes. But he had trusted him to be Barrani. That, at least, he had learned.

Why had his master taken him in? And...from where?

Why were the answers to questions he had asked for the entirety of his life to be found, somehow, in the West March?

He couldn't sleep, and in the end, he rose, missing the mirrors and Records of the Halls of Law, even if those Records didn't extend to the West March. He began to review the names of the Barrani An'Sennarin had noted as powers within the hierarchy of the West March, and he looked at the names of Barrani for whom An'Sennarin had offered official introductions.

Two, An'Tellarus thought, would be simple to meet; she considered the letter of introduction trivial given that she herself was all the introduction required. But the third?

Yvonne of Darrowelm. It was Yvonne of Darrowelm that An'Sennarin had been most concerned about. He hadn't asked Severn to investigate; she was Barrani. Darrowelm, further, was one of the houses that could be considered a threat. Instinct guided him, here.

On some level, he felt a debt to An'Sennarin—one that the Barrani Lord would never claim he owed, because An'Sennarin would never publicly claim a mortal as a friend.

No, he had seen where that had led, and the cost, in the end, had been paid by the innocent. An'Sennarin wouldn't take that risk again. But the powerful among the Barrani had no friends. They couldn't afford friends.

Severn Handred, orphan resident of the fief of Nightshade, couldn't afford not to have friends. And so, he had made friends, had found a second home—a very different one—with mortals. One was now dead. One would kill him if she ever got the chance—and he accepted that. He deserved it.

He didn't intend to repeat that mistake; did not intend, as surely An'Sennarin did not intend, to repeat it with different names and different causes of death.

Elianne.

It would be a long night.

CHAPTER SEVEN

CHIMES WOKE SEVERN IN THE MORNING—OR WHAT he assumed was morning, given the ambient light. It had been many years since he'd heard those chimes, but they were familiar. He was surprised to feel a tinge of nostalgia and rose quickly to dispel it. The room in which he had slept contained windows, but those windows boasted no glass and no shutters; birds could pass freely through them, although none had, as of yet.

He rose, dressed, and walked to the open windows, pausing there.

The forest beyond his window was not the forest through which An'Tellarus's party had traveled. The difference wasn't subtle; the trees were younger, beyond his wall, their bark a silver-white. His master had once said the Hallionne were similar to the Towers of the fiefs, but with very different imperatives.

He listened, but the chimes had stilled, and after a moment he turned toward the doors of the room that led to the hall. The halls were filled with the same light that illuminated his room: sunlight, from the gaps in the ceiling above.

That ceiling was now a canopy provided by the thick, sturdy branches of trees; they wouldn't stop rain or snow, but Severn suspected they wouldn't face either here.

An'Tellarus was waiting for him. He'd expected that she would wait in the dining room they had used the previous evening; he simply followed the floor, which glowed a few yards ahead of his feet. He had no sense that this hall was the hall he had traversed to reach his room, which was disorienting.

Severn felt the dislocation of constantly changing geography. The resultant inability to get any sense of the lay of the land was difficult, and he wondered if some who refused to enter refused for that reason. In the future, he'd certainly consider it. But maybe not; the Hallionne had been built for a reason, and given Severn's lack of familiarity with the forests and their native wildlife, refusing certain safety might not be the soundest of decisions.

He chose to trust the Hallionne; the Hallionne was not, after all, Barrani, and even his master considered the Hallionne to be painfully—and occasionally inconveniently—neutral. But they attended to the needs of their guests. Wherever the Hallionne led him now, it was what An'Tellarus desired.

The hall didn't end with a door; it ended with a wide arch, the top of which, like the ceilings above, were entwined branches. But these branches didn't appear to be attached to anything as solid as a trunk; he thought they were a type of clinging ivy, with smaller leaves and thicker vines. Beneath their grasp, pale stone pillars were almost entirely obscured by leaves.

Beyond the open arch stood a small table. On one side of it sat An'Tellarus. The table was long, but low. It wasn't meant as a dining table of any kind. Food, however, had been laid across it; odd, brightly colored fruits Severn had never eaten, and oddly shaped breads. As he watched, small dishes with very thinly sliced meats and cheeses appeared.

An'Tellarus chuckled. "Good morning, Severn. Did you sleep well?"

"I slept," he replied. "Honestly, I would have preferred to skip sleep."

"Oh?"

"I've never been inside a Hallionne before, and might never visit one again. I would have liked to see more of the interior."

"Even had you explored to your heart's content, it would not necessarily signify useful knowledge; the Hallionne is a living place, and as living places, it grows and changes with the passage of time."

"A mortal lifetime?"

"Even so. Come, eat. Keep an old woman company." Severn's brows rose, and she chuckled. "Yes, of course I am attempting to solicit sympathy. It amuses me to see how much you know of our kin, and I receive answers to questions I am not forced to ask." She inclined her head to the second chair; there were only two.

Given the blue of her eyes, Severn nodded politely and took the chair.

"You will see many things on the way to the West March; we will visit another—and different—Hallionne. But once we reach the water, you must fall silent, and you must behave in a way that implies you are an impeccable servant. Small errors of grace will be forgiven, as you are mortal—but large errors will not. They will be seen as my personal failing.

"You understand that there are no Imperial laws that might protect you here."

"Yes."

"There are, however, laws; they generally involve property. If you are killed by anyone who does not first seek my permission, they will have wronged me, and they will be expected to pay in one way or another. In the worst case, they will die."

Silence.

"Do you not believe me?"

"I believe you. I also believe it has nothing to do with me as Severn Handred; I might be a beloved dog or cat; I might be a precious family heirloom. The punishment you devise is a simple warning—"

"Not simple at all."

"A complicated warning, then. It's meant to remind people that you are a power and you are not to be trifled with. You are certainly not to be attacked by anyone who is not prepared to show a like power in response. If you make clear your intentions with regards to your companions, only those who feel certain of victory in any encounter with you will deign to play the game."

Her eyes were blue, but the blue had tinted; they seemed almost violet in the sun's light. "That is not the first time I have heard those words—but I was much younger and far less inclined to consider them good advice. It almost cost me my life. You will come to understand, if you do not already, that anger is a useful tool. Your anger. My anger. But it cannot ever become the master; it cannot be the driver.

"I will play at anger, should that become necessary; I may even genuinely feel it. But I *am* old, Severn. We remember, as you cannot, all of the events of our lives. And anger can become embers if one handles it with care. You will see the water. You might also, depending on the speed of our overland travel, see the great birds we call the Dreams of Alsanis."

"The Dreams of Alsanis?" He frowned. "Alsanis is Hallionne."

"Yes, but lost to us for centuries now; he touches our world from time to time only through his dreams. Be wary of them. You do not consider yourself responsible for the nature of the dreams that take you in your sleep; we do not hold him responsible for them, either. But the dreams of a Hallionne can be deadly."

"You said the Hallionne sleep."

"Yes. But Alsanis's sleep is not the sleep of the Hallionne we now occupy. It might have been, but the Hallionne in the heart of the West March had ties to, roots in, the green." She waited, but Severn continued silent. "You have heard of the green."

He nodded.

"I wish to meet your master."

"I have no way of contacting him."

"No. No, I am certain you do not." She exhaled. "Very well. I am An'Tellarus. I was not born An'Tellarus, and I became An'Tellarus almost—but not entirely—by accident. We are an old family, but we were not always considered a significant one."

That had clearly changed.

"I was not considered the heir. I was not considered suitable to be the head of the family."

He waited.

"My sister was. And you may not believe this, given my current position, but I, too, thought no one was more suited to rule than she. I have met only one Barrani, ever, who reminded me of my sister. But that woman survived."

The silence shifted, and Severn understood that he must carry part of the burden of this odd conversation. "Your sister did not?"

"No. She left one day for the heart of the green. She did not return."

"You are certain she died?"

"The green told the Warden that she had passed beyond all help. Yes, we were certain. But we could not recover her body, and we could get no information about the nature of her passing. I am not proud to say the anger and loss maddened all of Tellarus; small wars were started, and accusations were the only conversation available between two families, of which ours was one."

"The other?"

"You will meet descendants of the other in the West March because I will meet them. An'Avonelle is the current head of that family; she is not a Lord of the High Court. She desired to travel to the east and enter the Tower to prove the strength and value of her name; her father would not allow it. He, too, had not deigned to be judged by outsiders; he was of power and relevance in the West March, but the West March was considered of secondary import. The High Lord was a cold, autocratic man, and An'Avonelle's parents considered him pretentious and largely useless.

"I see I have surprised you. I told you: the West March is not the High Halls. An'Avonelle's father, while he lived, made it clear that the High Lord had bent knee to a Dragon—as all Lords of the High Court must. He would not seek approval or the company of fallen, cowardly lords."

Severn was accustomed to maintaining a neutral expression; this time it took effort.

An'Tellarus smiled. "Yes. There has been historical tension between the High Court and the West March for some centuries." The smile dimmed. "You understand why we—as Lords of the High Court—must bow to the Emperor."

"The fiefs."

"Yes. The six Towers and the danger they were created to protect us from. *Ravellon*. There can be no substantive war anywhere near the borders of those fiefs. To bow to a Dragon is the heart of pragmatism when the possible consequences of continued hostilities play into the lord at the heart of *Ravellon*. What do you know of those Shadows?"

"If it weren't for those Shadows, the fiefs wouldn't exist," Severn replied.

"Have you encountered them?"

He shook his head. "Only Ferals. They live in *Ravellon*,

but come to the fiefs to hunt when the sun sets. They're not considered a danger by the fieflords."

"And you have seen nothing else?"

"No."

"You understand the Barrani; we bow where bowing is necessary. But we bide our time, Severn. We wait for the moment when such bows will be rendered irrelevant. I have sworn my oath to the Dragon Emperor; I am a Lord of the High Court."

"This makes Avonelle your enemy."

"*Enemy* is a harsh word, but yes. To those with ambition, I am powerful; to those whose ambitions encompass only the West March, I am almost a traitor. But things are further complicated; the Lord of the West March is also a Lord of the High Court and son to the current High Lord. The current High Lord is not considered a friend of the West March, and his son—his indisputably powerful son—is therefore a man upon whom the figurative crown sits uneasily.

"Were it not for the dire consequences his death would cause, the Lord of the West March would not have survived. But he is not a simple Lord of the High Court; he is second son to the High Lord, and one of the two contenders for the High Seat. He has made some concessions; his main abode is in the West March. He proved himself long ago—to many factions in the West March. Not all, but we are Barrani."

"How?"

She smiled again, as if he were a clever child. "He bespoke the Dreams of Alsanis—and they replied. The water hears him—and that is the first and most critical test of suitability. But the water hears many people, and the Dreams of Alsanis, few. When he has chosen to temporarily withdraw from the political arena of the West March, he has not retreated to the High Halls."

"They would hardly be much of a retreat."

"Indeed. But if he wishes to become High Lord, he must

make stronger alliances within the High Court itself. The alliances he has managed to build in the West March will be of ancillary support only."

The way she said this was odd. Severn dissected the wording, lifting his head to meet her gaze when he had finished. "You don't believe he wants the High Seat."

She clapped. It was both condescending and embarrassing; he felt a slight warmth at the clear and obvious sign of approval—an approval he shouldn't want. "He has claimed—as have many before him—to have no desire at all to contest the eldest's right to rule. But in his case, I believe he speaks truth. He is dangerous, Severn. Do not forget that."

"If he doesn't desire the ultimate power, how is he more dangerous than you?"

She laughed then. He wondered what she had been like when she had been his age—a child, in Barrani terms.

"I *really* desire to speak with your master. But I will answer your question. Understand that the answer is personal; it is not authoritative."

Severn nodded.

"It is believed that the Lord of the West March truly reveres his brother, the official heir."

He waited, but she offered no further words—as if this simple statement were the entirety of her answer.

"You are young, even for a mortal. Perhaps you do not understand the lengths to which those with strong attachments will go when they feel the objects of those attachments are threatened." She frowned; her eyes never left his face. "Perhaps I am wrong."

He said nothing. Had she asked, he would have continued to offer nothing. But he knew. "Do you think he is intemperate? Does he suffer from lack of self-control?"

"No."

Severn nodded. "Do you base your concerns on actual events?"

"No. I am old; it is a supposition, given what I know. He has removed himself from the pressures of the High Court; he has removed himself from the race. But not all are content to allow him to absent himself; their true colors, and the pressure they will apply, will only come into effect in the event of the High Lord's passing."

"And if he does not consent to take the High Seat?"

"He will die. It is likely that he will die, regardless."

"His older brother does not share his affection?"

"Ah. No, I did not say that. But those who support the elder wish to see their support rewarded. It is a mistake," she added. "But the Barrani sacrifice those of lesser power when it is necessary. We have many, many pawns and few pieces of considerable power. The Lord of the West March is not a pawn."

"Do you support either?"

"No. It matters little to me whether one or the other takes the throne. If I had to profess a preference, it would be for the heir."

"Why?"

"The Lord of the West March is, outsider or no, a better lord than those who seek to replace him here. But I would say that his enemies in the west are those who support the line Avonelle, and I am of the line Tellarus. Avonelle would perhaps produce an acceptable ruler—but they would solidify their ancient power by their reign. I will not tell you how you should, or must, behave; I will not insult you. But there are tensions that have survived centuries between us. I will let you know, in one way or another, when we meet families who are loosely connected to Avonelle.

"Your presence will ruffle feathers."

Severn frowned. He studied An'Tellarus, her eyes almost green. He didn't believe that her purpose here was trivial, although he couldn't be certain. What he could be certain of was that she would find discomfited rivals highly amusing.

"I will not ask what An'Sennarin asked of you; I doubt you would tell me if I did. But I caution you to move with care. An'Sennarin is a power in the West March, but he is now in Elantra; his reach is not as long as it might be were he to come home.

"An'Sennarin would be my candidate of choice for the position of Lord of the West March should the current lord fall."

Severn stilled. What had she said? The most important affinity was for the water. And An'Sennarin definitely had that. "Have you made that clear?"

She smiled again. "No, child."

"Then why are you telling me this?"

"An'Sennarin is struggling to maintain the power he took. He was not an ambitious child; had you asked, I would have said his only desire was to come home. That, however, was never going to be allowed—the water hears him. He is, should he survive, a considerable power, and that power is only likely to grow. Perhaps one day, in the future, the water will hear him no matter how far away he is forced to dwell."

"You like him."

"In truth, I like the Lord of the West March as well. I do not understand what caused An'Sennarin to murder his lord and take his lord's place—I was quite surprised. But I have seen him several times since that insurrection, and he is markedly unchanged; the weight of power bows him, but it has not yet broken him.

"I also feel a certain fondness for you. I think there are reasons the two of you met—although I cannot clearly see them. You did not contact An'Sennarin by mirror; you did not contact him by letter. He did not contact you in either of the accepted fashions, either. You are not sensitive to the water; he could not bespeak you through fountains or wells." Her eyes had shaded to an uncomfortable blue.

She knew.

She knew that An'Sennarin's True Name was known by at

least one of the Tha'alani—the former castelord. Not a man easily assassinated, and given the nature of the Tha'alaan, that death would not necessarily destroy the knowledge of the name itself.

Ah, Severn thought. *This is a test.* "I asked the Imperial Service to arrange a suitably private meeting."

"And he obeyed?"

"He condescended to grant it."

He thought she might press him for more precise information, she held his gaze for so long. But in the end, Severn did not fail the test. There were things of which he could not safely speak. Given the cost the Tha'alani had already paid, it was a lesson he did not need to learn, and a test he would never fail. "If he offered to write this letter, I feel there must be something he hopes to gain."

"He did not ask anything of me."

"No. Do you believe that he wanted nothing of you?"

Severn almost nodded. Would have, had Elluvian asked the question. But An'Tellarus had asked, and he now evaluated An'Sennarin again.

"...No."

"What do you feel he desired?"

Severn had no answer he wanted to share.

If Severn had no desire to share his thoughts, An'Tellarus's questions weren't trivial. He'd assumed, in part, that she wanted his company in the West March because it would annoy Avonelle and Avonelle's satellites. He still believed that to be true. But he now believed that lacking that annoyance, she would still have asked for his company.

He had been taught to distrust Barrani. Every Barrani with whom he had shared actual conversation offered the same advice. He had trusted his master, regardless; his master had not approved. But absent approval, his master made clear that trust was not a single thing; it was not all-encompassing. Severn could, as an example, trust his master to offer him food that was not poisoned; he could trust his master to teach him the bare necessities. He could even trust his master to protect him, for as long as that master felt protection was required.

At the age of five, the elements Severn could trust were almost the entirety of their sheltered world.

But now? At the age of eighteen? His master had intended that he come to the West March; that much was clear. For what purpose? He was not Barrani, not part of the Barrani power structure. What could he do here that would be advantageous to Barrani? He understood only part of what An'Tellarus wanted—indulgence in petty malice. Petty malice was, and could be, a way of life, but had that been her only way of life, she wouldn't be An'Tellarus.

An'Sennarin could hear the voice of the water. He could hear it more strongly than Ybelline. An'Tellarus didn't consider An'Sennarin's seat to be secure. Was Severn here to somehow secure that seat? To strengthen the child An'Tellarus considered the best choice for Lord of the West March in the future?

Severn believed—strongly—that An'Sennarin hadn't desired power. Those who didn't desire power seldom kept it. Was there an advantage to An'Tellarus to fortify An'Sennarin? He was young, his power unstable; she was old, and her power solid. But surely, if that were the case, she was better suited to stabilizing that power than a lone mortal Wolf?

Three people he personally knew were involved in some fashion in the West March: An'Sennarin, An'Tellarus, and his absent master. The only person he had a hope of understanding was An'Sennarin.

"You are thinking," An'Tellarus said. "As I wish to give you some time to do so, we will walk to the next Hallionne."

Carriages would make no headway in the forest, and Severn hadn't learned how to ride; it was one of his master's frustrations. While there were, of course, horses and wagons in the fiefs, they were scarce, and those that rode them purely as transport were bound to attract notice. He had begun to learn, with the Wolves, and in a part of the city where riding a horse wouldn't attract the same attention, but he had not mastered it yet.

Elluvian met them when they exited the Hallionne. His eyes were blue, but it was the resting shade. An'Tellarus told Elluvian to scout ahead. He reminded her that he didn't serve Tellarus. This amused her; given Elluvian's stiffness, Severn gathered that amusement wasn't a dependable reaction.

Only two of An'Tellarus's guards remained; they took the rear.

"Sennarin is a family with roots in the West March?" Severn asked.

An'Tellarus nodded. "But it was an ambitious family at its heart."

"You've said Avonelle is ambitious."

"Yes. Avonelle, however, consolidates power only in the West March, as its prior ruler had a deep grudge against the High Court. It is considered a family of note only in the West March—the backwater of a once proud and glorious stronghold. Power is in the eye of the beholder, but the High Court is considered *the* power, even here. Sennarin is similar to Tellarus, although Tellarus is more certain in its reign. The previous lord of Sennarin was of the heir's faction."

"You said—"

"Yes. The heir does not dabble in factions in any serious fashion. But the support of the Lords of the High Court is both useful and necessary, regardless. Both of the possible heirs hold their factions because they are not the only possible rulers. But you must know this."

"Might makes right."

"Indeed. If the Lord of the West March does not politic against his brother, the lack doesn't mean the brothers have no enemies. The High Lord is old, which signifies only power; he is tired, which is different. I think it is possible that you will see the change of rulership in your lifetime."

"Does the West March support a third contender?"

She chuckled. "Yes, of course. But that contender is of the High Court. I believe that if An'Sennarin wished it, he could present a notable threat; Sennarin has long held power in the High Court. It is not as significant as Mellarionne."

"Cassandre's faction?"

"And Corvallan's, at the moment." She frowned, her eyes shading to a darker blue at the thought of the couple. "Avonelle could not aspire to rule the High Court. The current ruler did not make the trek to the High Halls. She did, however, send one of her sons; he failed to survive the Test of Name.

"She could not send the only surviving son."

"Why?"

"He is the Warden of the green. He could have retired from that position—but his retirement would weaken Avonelle's power here. She then sent nieces and nephews."

"Did any succeed?"

"No. There is a reason the less ambitious denizens of the West March fail to send their offspring to the east. The Test of Name has killed far more of our kind than even the wars. Success is a certain way to proclaim personal power, but the risk is high. An'Sennarin was not sent by his parents; he was called by the previous ruler. He did not answer that call until his parents were dead, and his friends in danger. I would have considered him far too soft, far too empathic, to survive the test. He had no desire to take it. I was therefore pleasantly surprised."

"Did you know him well before he went to the east?"

"I believe that's the first time you've asked that question." Her tone was a mixture of frustration and approval. "Yes. I knew him. I knew his parents. They were all children to me, but they were pleasant, if loud. There is a charm in the openness of the young; their ready joy or despair. Their passions and dreams have not yet been muddied or broken; they see the trees and not the ash those trees will inevitably become.

"It is a conundrum; we are drawn to the young, we are delighted in them, and we understand that if we cannot break what attracts us, those children will not survive. Far better to be aunt than to be parent, but even then..." She shook her head. "It is not safe to love, Severn. Love causes a pain from which we cannot protect ourselves. It is therefore unwise in the extreme to show favoritism or affection to those for whom we feel it.

"Understand, however, that such shows can be used to great effect when they are not genuine. It is our nature to seek weakness. Our nature to exploit it where we see it. But we, too, were once young and hopeful—it is why we understand the weakness so well. Those that seek weakness in too broad a fashion might mistake our pretend affection for actual love; they might act against those they deem 'loved.' It is a slow way to rid oneself of enemies, but it can be effective."

"An'Sennarin isn't old enough to see love as certain ruin."

"No. But he is old enough—barely—to understand love as weapon; to understand that it is the most effective of weapons because it is one that we hand to our enemies. They cannot hurt us if we do not feel. It is advice I give all of the children: do not love. Love is weakness and pain."

He nodded. "My master made that clear, many times."

"Yes." She, too, fell silent.

It was companionable, this silence; he knew, without asking, that she was thinking about the ways in which she had learned that lesson.

"Is it better," he finally asked, "to love nothing? Does the pain render all joy meaningless?"

"What do you think, child?"

"I think if you love nothing, you have nothing to protect. What is the point of power, then?"

She smiled, but the expression was one of pain. "You are young."

He shook his head. "The Eternal Emperor isn't young, but...he protects the empire. He protects his people."

"Does he? You are a young Wolf, or so I am told. Does your very existence as a Wolf not refute this? You are his executioner. You kill. People die all the time in the Emperor's Empire. His power does not protect them."

Severn exhaled. "It doesn't protect all of them, no. But no one can protect everyone. No one can be in all places at all times."

"And so you believe in him, regardless?"

"Not him, exactly. But I'd rather devote my life to protection than destruction."

"And yet you kill."

Severn shook his head. "Not yet. Not for the Emperor. Sometimes there is no other way."

"Do you believe that?"

"Yes."

CHAPTER EIGHT

THE JOURNEY TO THE NEXT HALLIONNE TOOK several days. Lessons that had at one point been theoretical were put into practice here, and Severn was surprised at how difficult the transition from city to forest was in practice. The city, in his early years, hadn't been safe; the forest, absent the roving packs of Ferals and gangs, should have been safer. But everything about his surroundings was unfamiliar. Elluvian had no difficulties, and An'Tellarus, a rich and powerful woman, seemed to be at home in the wilderness. He took his cues from them.

"The forests here are likely to be safe," Elluvian told him, as they returned to the campsite with dead wood.

"Which means we're not close to the next Hallionne."

Elluvian nodded. "The Hallionne are not Towers. Understand that. They were created with a different purpose in mind. They are fortresses, regardless—but they are meant to be sanctuaries."

"Sanctuaries you won't enter."

Elluvian exhaled. "No. But that is not entirely because of the Hallionne itself; if I am cozened within a Hallionne, I will be at the beck and call of An'Tellarus. I prefer to avoid that." There was the hint of a question in those words.

"I dine with her," Severn said, answering that hint. "She's made no move to harm me."

"What does she discuss?"

"Her childhood home. The tensions that arose in her youth. The tensions she perceives—politically—now. I don't understand what she wants or expects of me."

"That was always her way. So few do; she is hard to predict." The words were sour, but Severn sensed no enmity on the part of Elluvian—just a weariness that seemed to deepen as they continued their overland trek.

He was surprised when they came to a cliffside, because An'Tellarus called a halt there. "I am in need of a bath and decent food," she told her companions. To Severn she added, "The Hallionne is here."

Severn was the only person present who could be said to be in need of a bath. He had clothing suitable for a servant of the High Halls, and clothing suitable for street work—but the latter was in dire need of cleaning. He allowed An'Tellarus to lead. Elluvian once again declined the hospitality of the Hallionne. He indicated Severn should follow An'Tellarus.

"Elluvian," she said, before he could vanish, "we will take the portal paths from here."

"I will join you in the West March," was his stiff reply.

"Stop being such a stubborn child. The Hallionne is not awake, and neither circumstances nor my own abilities will change that. You are not required to remain within the Hallionne, but in the morning, you will join us."

The interior of the Hallionne Severn entered resembled the High Halls, in that it was stone; the floors were marble, not wood. An'Tellarus glanced at them, frowning, and as they followed the long hall, the marble was replaced by a more familiar interior wood; the wood was dark, the planks wide. The pillars and arches didn't change, nor did the height of the ceiling.

An'Tellarus's steps were crisp and slightly faster than normal; she was annoyed with Elluvian and didn't bother to hide it. But the hall was long, and if the sound of her steps echoed in the curved stone of the ceilings they passed beneath, that echo slowed.

"I will need a reminder in the near future," she said, without looking back at Severn. Before he could ask, she added, "I know there was a reason I never killed that boy for his obvious lack of respect, but at the moment, I cannot recall what it was."

"Many Barrani choose to avoid the Hallionne," Severn said.

"Yes. And the Barrani are, as any race is, composed largely of fools."

Severn coughed; it was not what he'd expected. "I don't believe my master chose to remain in the Hallionne."

"Your master—whoever he was—was a Barrani of some note who chose to live in a mortal hovel while raising a mortal child. I hardly consider him to be the wisest of men. I wish we had left Elluvian behind."

"Why didn't you?"

"As you have no doubt seen, I am not his lord." She slowed, exhaled, and turned back. "Yes, I have the standing to exclude him from my personal party. I cannot, however, deny him the West March."

Severn was certain that wasn't the reason she hadn't tried. He said nothing, waiting.

"And yes, he will be a distraction. I am aware that no protection is perfect; there are those who will find you a quaint oddity, those who will find you a genuine curiosity, and those who will consider your death or injury a personal slight or insult to Tellarus. But you will not be considered anything but a pawn. People will wonder why I brought you. It is a way of passing time in the long twilight of our kind.

"They will, however, be more concerned about Elluvian, and much of their calculations will therefore involve him. If you are a curiosity, you are harmless. He is not. He is the Emperor's Dog, and he has been known to hunt Barrani at the Emperor's command; that command has taken him beyond the borders of the empire. There are those who will worry, and those who will mount solid defenses against his presence. While they are doing so, they won't have time to spare for you."

"Will he survive?"

She smiled. "He has survived so far. Head to your room; I will head to mine. This close, I can see that your need of a bath is far greater than my own." She glanced back and added, "He is in more danger in Elantra than he is in the West March, but his enemies have far greater freedom of movement here."

The bath was set into the ground; had the water not been so warm, Severn would have called it a pool, instead. This Hallionne didn't have ceilings open to sky; all was stone. He wondered if Barrani preferred the sky. His master had made clear that the Hallionne responded to the needs of its guests, and as he had seen the floor shift from marble to wood as An'Tellarus traversed it, he had no reason to doubt the words. But this bath, those high ceilings, the pillars that supported them, none of these were Severn's experience or preference.

He rose quickly, returned to his room, and found his clothing—the correct clothing for attending An'Tellarus in the High Halls—laid out across the bed; they were spotless. He imagined that his traveling clothing would be spotless as well.

Here, for the first time in years, he felt the loss of his master keenly. There was very little to remind him of the

choices he'd made on the last day he had seen that master—
choices he had not realized, at that time, would lead to his
abandonment.

He wasn't a person who wasted time on regret; beyond
an examination of the circumstances, there was little benefit
to it. He could take the bitter lessons, learn from them, and
make better choices, or at least make different mistakes; he
couldn't change the past.

But to understand the lessons, he had to understand the
context. Why had his master abandoned him without warning? Without explanation? What had he hoped a ten-year-old
human boy could learn that would be of value to a Barrani
teacher?

Are you lonely?

This was the question that kept coming back to him in
the privacy of thought and the safety of isolation. That, and
his answer.

No.

During dinner, An'Tellarus continued her somewhat ad
hoc lessons. "Tanniase, heir to the line Kosmarre, has served
Avonelle for some time; he is pragmatically loyal. I would
consider him her most significant supporter. He is an ambitious man—ambitious enough to have made the trek to the
east, and to have survived it. He takes care not to mention
the tower of test or the High Halls when he is in Avonelle's
domain."

He was therefore a Lord of the High Court. "He doesn't
reside in the High Halls."

"No. For the moment, the High Halls are not his goal.
I doubt he will stay in the West March forever, but there
is something in the West March he must achieve before he
leaves, as so many ambitious people do. He would not be
content with a mere guest room in those halls—he wants
what Tellarus has."

"Exactly what Tellarus has?"

She chuckled. "Perhaps. He does not aim at Tellarus directly, but would not weep were I to lose my life or my significance in the High Halls. Yes, if he could be given the quarters I occupy there, he would be satisfied for some time. Rumors indicate that he is fond of his parents, inasmuch as he can be. He will not become the head of his family by the murder of his parents. He is not An'Kosmarre, and is therefore forced to treat me with the respect due the head of Tellarus." Her smile deepened.

"Was Lord Tanniase involved with the difficulties Ollarin faced before he became An'Sennarin?"

"That, I cannot answer. Nor can I answer—before you ask—if Avonelle was involved. Understand that power is concentrated in the hands of a few, but that power is not a sword—it is a web. If the previous An'Sennarin requested an insignificant favor of the lord of Avonelle, it is highly likely she would have granted it without much concern. Asking her to intervene, asking her to see that Ollarin was uprooted and sent to the east, would be considered almost trivial."

"Almost?"

She smiled again. "Almost. Ollarin could hear the water more clearly, more strongly, than any of his generation, or the generations that preceded it."

Severn frowned. "You said Avonelle wants to be Lord of the West March."

"I did."

"She can hear the water."

"Yes, but to a lesser degree; I would say that the current Lord of the West March is more adept—but not so much more that her ability pales in comparison. It would have been a trivial request, but one that suited her ambition. If she fulfilled the request—and again, I am uncertain that it was her hand alone that achieved it—she would be rid of a possible rival without staining her own hands with his blood.

There is a danger in destroying those things beloved of either the water or the Dreams of Alsanis. If she were to see to his death personally—or even his absence—it might endanger her. One cannot be Lord of the West March when the water itself is hostile.

"I am not entirely certain it is relevant at this point. An'Sennarin is where he is, and distant from his kin; he will not be able to leave the High Halls for some time if he wishes to solidify his power there. No one in the West March will now take an open stand against him—and there is incentive to bury the circumstances, or their part in the circumstances; they are not foolish enough to believe that he does not resent them.

"Ah, perhaps I am wrong. Avonelle is not foolish enough; Tanniase might be. Had Ollarin not been forced to the east, he would not have become An'Sennarin. Tanniase might feel that he did the boy a favor, that, in fact, An'Sennarin should be grateful. He would have remained insignificant and powerless had he remained in the West March.

"If things go well, you are likely to meet neither. If things go poorly, you are likely to meet both. I have seen your reflexes; they are good. I expect you to survive. You have questions?"

"I'd like to know more about Darrowelm."

"An'Darrowelm?"

"When do you use 'Lord' instead of 'An'?"

"Your master did not make this clear?"

"I was told that An was necessary to denote the ruler of family, but you don't seem to use it consistently."

"Oh?"

"Darrowelm is a family in the West March. You refer to Lord Darrowelm. Is it meant to be an insult?"

"It is a safe insult. 'An'Darrowelm' denotes respect. 'Lord Darrowelm' is technically correct; anyone in the West March would know to whom I refer. You can safely refer to him as

Lord Darrowelm while you are in my presence. He will not expect you to understand our forms of address. If he makes an issue of it, he does so with an intent to insult me, and I quite honestly do not care. It is not enough of a mistake that your life would be the price for assuaging his annoyance."

"You've said little about Darrowelm. He is not considered a power?"

"No. He was not."

"I believe one of An'Sennarin's friends was of Darrowelm."

"Indeed."

"The one you've implied it would be most difficult to see."

"That is not where you should start, no. Darrowelm is an old family, which has been its sustaining grace; it has never been a power in the West March, although it has been elevated of late."

Severn nodded. "In the past three decades?"

"Yes. Perhaps the past four." She exhaled. "I will not be helpful should you set your sights on Darrowelm."

Severn nodded again.

"...But Elluvian might. He will not be happy—but that child was ever dour." She smiled. "Why Darrowelm, Severn?"

"I want to know if Yvonne of Darrowelm is still alive."

"And if she is not?"

He frowned. "If she is not, An'Sennarin has two friends in the West March."

For the first time this meal, An'Tellarus frowned. "That is cold."

"It is a possible fact. Facts are neither cold nor warm; they are facts."

"I believe I have some small inkling of who your master is." She exhaled. "Yes, if she is dead, it is a simple fact. But I believe such a fact will, exposed, cause more harm than good."

"Do you think she's dead?"

"I think it possible."

He nodded. "Why?"

She lifted a hand, palm out. "I am not a suspect in Imperial custody. You are not in the Empire. You have no right to question me, except the social right I deign to give you. I am under no obligation to answer. Is that clear? Hood your fangs, wolf cub. Hood them carefully; bare them only when there is no other choice that remains. I believe we are finished here." She rose.

Severn rose with her, and tendered her a very correct bow, acknowledging the gravity of her power and her age.

"No. You have not offended me. If Yvonne is dead, Darrowelm will do all it can to conceal that fact; Lord Darrowelm is not a fool. Yvonne, alive, gives him leverage over An'Sennarin; dead, it might instill enmity. Only if he has the support of Avonelle, with whom he is loosely associated, will he survive that enmity."

Given what Severn knew of An'Sennarin, he disagreed. But he did so in silence. He understood the value of her information, but it felt oddly incomplete, as if there were facts that she had concealed. Such concealment would be simple; he knew nothing of the West March. He knew nothing of the secrets that the West March contained for those, like him, who were not born and bred to it.

None of what she had told him so far made his presence here a necessity to An'Tellarus.

Did she want him here to investigate on behalf of An'Sennarin? Did she want him to deliver this letter of introduction to Darrowelm?

Morning came with chimes. Severn woke, packed, and shouldered his gear; he paused, made the bed, and left the suite of rooms. An'Tellarus, who professed to be a late riser, had decided to forgo breakfast. Severn, however, found a small satchel which was clearly meant to be taken on the road.

To Severn's surprise, Elluvian was waiting for him at the end of the hall; An'Tellarus was nowhere in sight. As they often were, the Barrani Wolf's eyes were a blue.

"I see you've survived An'Tellarus's company."

"The Hallionne wouldn't allow her to kill me," Severn replied. "But I have the advantage of being mortal. She might see me as useful; she can't see me as a threat."

"You serve the Emperor."

"The Emperor's law is irrelevant here."

"No doubt she's taken pains to point that out."

Severn nodded. "You don't fear her."

"Anyone sane would."

"You work for the Emperor's Wolves."

Elluvian laughed; it was a brief bark of sound. "I'm concerned that she's decided to take the portal paths. Your leave is long enough that we could travel overland and still have time to return."

"Are the portal paths dangerous?"

"They're risky."

Severn waited.

"The paths are created by the Hallionne; they travel between points long established by the Hallionne—but those points are impossible to map. The will of the traveler defines how quickly the paths reach their destinations—but the will of the traveler often defines which directions the paths will take."

Severn considered the words as they began to walk down halls that looked remarkably similar. "Is there a risk that the travelers end up in different locations?"

"Yes." Elluvian exhaled. "I think the risk small, but real. It is not often that the Barrani choose the portal paths."

"Why do you think she chose them?"

"She's An'Tellarus. I'd prefer the overland route, but there are different risks overland. You lived in the fiefs. There are—on occasion—creatures similar to the Ferals in the forests. But they are not considered a genuine threat." Before Severn could ask what would be, Elluvian continued. "There are areas outside of the West March which were once devastated in ancient wars—before the Dragons—that are far less safe to traverse, even for An'Tellarus. No overland route crosses them, but in the desert, dangers that are far deadlier can arise."

"You don't think her decision is based on the possibility of that danger."

"No." He exhaled. His eyes remained a dark blue. "I have already discussed this with An'Tellarus. We take the portal paths." He hesitated, and then added, "If she expected the journey to be without danger, she would not insist I accompany you. I would normally meet you outside of the West March. I have my own reasons for traveling separately; they are not good enough for An'Tellarus."

After a pause, Severn asked, "Why do you obey her?"

"A good question," was the bitter reply.

It was a question Elluvian had asked himself for centuries. An'Tellarus was not his lord, although, ironically, in his youth she would have been the lord he chose had the choice been his. His lord, now, was the Eternal Emperor; he had no other. Elluvian considered himself among the most pragmatic of men; he had had to be, to survive childhood.

In the early years, An'Tellarus had been the practical choice; she had power. But her exercise of that power had been, and remained, unpredictable. Perhaps two-thirds of the time she followed the lines laid out for Barrani rules. It was the other third that made her both interesting—which he would not admit aloud while he lived—and frustrating.

Her anger was legendary, and with reason. Whole families had been destroyed, root and branch, in the lee of her rage. But he knew the difference between that rage and her constant irritation and disappointment. He had once asked, in frustration, what she expected of him.

"Are you a child, Elluvian, that my expectations define your choices?" The chilly contempt in her voice prevented any further questions.

But she hadn't abandoned her association with him when he had chosen to *serve* the Dragon. He thought she understood why, and that was discomfiting. But to the extent that Elluvian of Danarre was a free man, it was entirely due to the Emperor. And that freedom had come to him during the final Draco-Barrani war. Nor had it been the happy accident of the casualties that war had inflicted upon his kin.

No; it had been deliberate.

The Dragon, his enemy, had led the flight under his command to the lord Elluvian had thought never to escape: his father. And that father, An'Danarre, had died. So, too, had most of Elluvian's immediate kin.

Before the death of An'Danarre, Danarre had been considered a power; it eclipsed all others in the West March. Tellarus was an ancient line, but it was no rival to Danarre; in comparison it had been quaint, an echo of ancient history. So, too, Avonelle. The families that had once formed the base of support for Danarre still existed in the West March, but they had never managed to regroup, to reconsolidate, their former strength: there was a large void that had once been filled by An'Danarre. He could not be replaced.

Elluvian had been grateful for that. No doubt Tellarus had been grateful as well. None of the Barrani could be accused of assassination. The death of An'Danarre had been laid squarely at the feet of the Dragons. An'Danarre could be mourned, feted, respected as a victim of the war: he unified, in his death, who had once divided to conquer.

Elluvian had never mourned.

An'Tellarus had never expected mourning. She had never

demanded that he follow those social forms of grief, aping an emotion that was the exact opposite of what he felt. Others, of course, had.

He was your father.

Yes. Yes, he was. And he had birthed all of his children into a nightmare of slavery from which they could never hope to escape: he knew their names. He had forced them to surrender either the names or their lives. Elluvian had seen both fates: the death or the slavery. He had been far more cowardly than his dead older siblings, killed slowly and terribly to set an example: he had given his True Name into his father's keeping.

And he had yearned for the death that had terrified him.

What had family meant to Elluvian? His sisters and brothers—for his father had had many wives and they had birthed and wakened children at his command—had been kin, but enslaved, as he was enslaved. There was very little they could do for each other, and even had they the desire, familial closeness was forbidden. It was a threat to An'Danarre. All such affection was.

An'Tellarus was not family to An'Danarre, and not family to most of those siblings—those dead, buried siblings. But she was kin to Elluvian's mother, and she had grieved his mother's death. Perhaps because she had, Elluvian felt drawn to her. Drawn to family even if family itself was the nightmare of his life. After the fall of Danarre, that had persisted. She was kin, and for no good reason, that connection still mattered.

If it brought joy, it might have made sense. It brought frustration and a certain sense of inferiority instead. He disliked feeling that he was a constant disappointment to a person who should, in theory, have been irrelevant: he had chosen his oaths.

But he remembered, as he walked beside the newest of his recruits, the first day of the long and unceasing funereal rites for the dead. If he had hated—and *hate* was too pale, too insignificant a word—his father, he likewise felt no grief for his dead siblings; instead, he felt relief and gratitude. Having made the choice to survive by surrendering their True Names to their father, they discovered that there was no more escape: they could not choose to die when they realized that death was the better option.

Their names had been taken—as Elluvian's had—when they were children, and the control that formed around the holding of the name had been far more absolute than it might otherwise have been with an adult: between adults, there was a struggle for, a fight for, dominance.

To those who had been raised with no concept of freedom, such a struggle was inconceivable.

An'Tellarus understood. She had never demanded grief, and her own emotions, complicated and revealed only by the color of her eyes, had been almost akin to his own. She didn't understand his choice to serve the Emperor—possibly because Elluvian had never chosen to explain it. He was already despised by the majority of his kin; he sought no further animosity. The truth would demand that animosity.

"Why do I obey?" Elluvian repeated, as they turned a corner that led to steps that sloped down. "She is the only person who was willing to claim me as kin. She is the only family left me."

Severn nodded then, as if those words had weight and meaning. And of course they did: the boy was here to learn about kin he had never met and could not therefore remember.

The portal path was not a path in any sense of the word. Severn understood this when he reached the end of the stairs, Elluvian by his side, and was confronted with forest. The sky above that forest was bright and clear; there was no stone ceiling in what Severn had expected to be basement. An'Tellarus had clearly been waiting for some time.

The trees were tall, the bases of their trunks thicker by far than Severn, but unlike the forests above, there were no fallen branches, no fallen logs or toppled trees, no insects. Light passed through branches as if branches were oddly colored windows.

An'Tellarus looked exhausted, which was highly unusual; her eyes were a darker shade of blue than their usual neutral state. "I see you found Elluvian."

"He was waiting for me," Severn replied. He didn't ask An'Tellarus if she was feeling poorly. She was not the kind of person for whom one could safely demonstrate concern.

"Has he discussed the portal paths?"

Severn nodded.

"Good. It will save me some trouble." She gestured, and rope appeared in her hands. "I do not believe there will be trouble, but it is always best to come prepared. Loop this around your waist." She lifted her head and looked to Elluvian. "You will do the same."

"And you?" Elluvian said.

"I am not against caution when caution is mandated by circumstance."

Elluvian allowed Severn to wrap—and loosely knot—the rope around his own waist before attempting to do the same. "Why are you moving in such haste? What event do you fear to miss?"

"I fear to miss nothing of grave import," she replied, her voice decidedly cool. "But young Severn is here for a limited time, and I wish to waste none of it."

"If he is either lost or dead, you will have wasted all of it."

"There is a reason I tolerate your attitude." She glanced past Elluvian. "I am not concerned about the unknown dangers presented by the portal paths; it is the unknown dangers that might await our arrival that is of the greater concern."

"And you are rushing to meet them."

"Enough." She finished knotting the rope around her own waist. "If you must continue to natter, do so while we are on the move. We will still require some time in the passage between Hallionne Orbaranne and the West March proper."

"You intend to travel only as far as Orbaranne?"

"Orbaranne has agreed to anchor the path from her end. Inasmuch as such travel can be safe, this will be safe."

If Severn had ever imagined walking into a painting, he thought it would be much like this forest. Absent weeds, insects, and birdsong, the light that permeated the trees was ominous as shadow, it seemed so sculpted and hard.

An'Tellarus had taken the lead; Severn followed. Elluvian was left to pull up the rear. Had the rope that now bound them together been longer, Severn was almost certain the Barrani Wolf would have remained out of sight. As it was, the rope between them was almost without slack. They walked in silence.

The silence itself was wrong; he couldn't hear the sounds of either their footsteps or his own. This was not a forest. The ground beneath his feet was firm. He wondered if the path and its appearance conformed to An'Tellarus's request—or demand. The unnatural silence remained unbroken; if discussion was possible here, An'Tellarus or Elluvian could start it.

The light remained as it had first appeared, and in the silence it was difficult to gauge the passage of time; the shadows cast by trees didn't budge. He was certain they made progress, but couldn't say how much. Had he been told they'd been walking in place, he would have believed it. This forest was nothing like the overland forest through which they'd previously walked; he was certain it was nothing like the forests that surrounded the West March. This was not a place for the living.

Child.

He frowned. "An'Tellarus?"

"Now is not the time for conversation," she said, without turning back.

Severn knew, but he wanted to hear her voice; to know whether or not the space in which they now walked might distort it. It did not. He then repeated this test. He called Elluvian by name. He half expected silence as Elluvian's response.

It wasn't. "What are you looking for?"

"I wanted to know whether voice or speech is affected by portal passage." The rope between Elluvian and Severn tautened.

"What do you hear?" The Barrani Wolf's voice was both softer and sharper.

Severn shook his head. "Nothing, now."

"An'Tellarus."

Her answer: she began to move more swiftly.

CHAPTER NINE

CHILD.

The voice was stronger. What had been almost attenuated no longer seemed distant.

An'Tellarus continued to walk. If he slowed at all, she'd notice immediately. But there was no sign that she'd heard what Severn heard.

Elluvian, however, moved quickly enough to stand almost by Severn's side. Voice low, he said, "What do you hear?"

Severn shook his head, raising a hand to forestall further questions. Although he did hear the word, repeated once, he couldn't pinpoint the direction from which the voice came. Two single-syllable words made it harder.

Child, why are you silent? It has been so long.

Severn glanced at Elluvian, who now walked by his side. "Did you hear that?"

Elluvian's eyes darkened. "Do not listen. Do not answer."

Do you not remember?

The voice drew closer, and closer again, as syllables faded. The speaker was nowhere in sight. Elluvian and An'Tellarus were, but beyond them, behind them, and to both sides, the perfect, sterile forest remained empty.

I have been waiting. You are late. Come.

The words were Barrani. They were High Barrani. But the tone and texture of the voice were oddly familiar: there was emotion in it. Regret. Fear. Desire. Severn stumbled, as if the words were solid enough to be felt.

Elluvian grabbed his right arm, his knuckles instantly whitening at the strength of his grip. "An'Tellarus!" The word was a bark of sound, better suited to the training rooms than this forest.

An'Tellarus turned then to look over her shoulder. As she did, the trees that had girded the portal path lost color. They became gray, as if they'd surrendered solidity to become the ghost of a forest. The branches above faded first, and Severn saw sky without impediment: it, too, was gray—but it wasn't still.

An'Tellarus said a single word that Severn didn't understand. Elluvian's grip tightened enough that Severn's hand began to numb. "Don't look up," the Barrani Wolf said, voice low.

Up, however, seemed to descend as the last of the tree line vanished in all directions. In its place sky covered everything, and in that sky, in the distant horizon, he could see what appeared to be a flock of birds. At this distance, they were black in color. He didn't know enough about birds to even try to assign them a species; they were wings and motion, a shade against the gray of sky. He couldn't even guess at their size; there was nothing to compare them to.

"Elluvian," An'Tellarus said, in an august, almost imperial voice. "Do not let go of the boy. We will need to run, now." She picked up her pace. Barrani clothing, unlike mortal clothing, never seemed to be an impediment to movement. Severn could run, and had, but he couldn't keep the pace An'Tellarus set for any length of time; she seemed to simply lengthen her stride, but he had to sprint to keep up. It was that or be dragged. The rope's knot was tight, and the rope itself—supplied by the Barrani Lord of both High Halls and West March—seemed unlikely to break.

He wanted to ask her why she seemed to be running toward the birds; he was almost certain the appearance of those birds was the reason she chose to run. He didn't ask. He found it hard to run with Elluvian attached to his arm, but had no hope of shaking Elluvian off if the Barrani Wolf didn't voluntarily release him.

He remembered, as Elluvian paced him, a similar flight in a totally different situation. He'd been running through the streets of Nightshade, Elianne in tow, her stride shorter because she was five years younger. They had both been children, both orphans. He wondered if this was how she had felt then: stumbling, in flight from a danger she didn't completely understand, Severn dragging her by the wrist because he was afraid she would fall too far behind.

But she had run doggedly; she had done nothing deliberate to break the silence. She had trusted that he would explain when there was time and safety to do so. Severn had no such faith, but he believed that both An'Tellarus and Elluvian were genuinely concerned with his safety.

He, too, was concerned. The birds became larger as they ran; their wings seemed to exude black smoke in a dark swirl, an afterimage left by their motions. The birds weren't crows, as he thought they must be at a distance; they were far larger than that. Nor were they the gulls that dotted the harbor like winged, noisy rats.

If storm had been given form, he thought it might look like them: they didn't caw or screech, as birds did, but when their beaks opened the birds spoke with the voice of thunder.

He remembered something An'Tellarus had said: the great birds were the Dreams of Alsanis. Dreams weren't daydreams, and some, as Severn was well aware, could turn the corner into nightmare without warning or pause.

Nightmare, however, one could wake from. He knew he wasn't asleep, no matter how strange and formless the landscape had become. He focused on An'Tellarus's back, not the flight of birds. It was hard; the birds filled the sky, became the sky. He knew time had passed, but he wasn't yet incapable of maintaining his sprint.

"Do not speak to the Dreams," Elluvian said with no obvious exertion; the run hadn't come close to winding him. "If you hear them, if you understand them, don't let them know. They shouldn't be here—but they're more dangerous here."

Severn stumbled, righted himself—or was righted by Elluvian. The dangers he'd expected of the West March, the dangers of which he'd been warned, hadn't included the dreams—or nightmares—of Alsanis.

An'Tellarus raised an arm, pointing ahead. Given the lack of trees or identifiable structures in the gray space, he could immediately see what she'd indicated. She said nothing, but continued to run toward what appeared to be a lone person, standing on ground as gray as the sky, facing them. That person made no move to intercept or to run toward An'Tellarus; she simply stood and watched.

The decreasing distance between them allowed Severn to see her more clearly. She appeared to be his age, perhaps slightly older, and everything about her implied that she was as human as he. Everything except her eyes. The eye color of a person standing at the distance she was shouldn't have been immediately clear. But distance or no, it was: they were all of black. Her hair was plaited behind her back; it was as gray as sky or land, but it had a very clear texture.

Only when they had halved the distance did the figure move; she brought both of her arms up, to the sides, and held them overhead as she lifted her face, exposing her chin. Her skin was the color of the sky. The hair that had been bound escaped as if bindings could no longer contain it. She brought her hands together in a clap of sound and light—as if the birds were thunder and she, lightning.

Around her, from the ground to either side, pillars rose, and rose again; above those pillars stone began to form. He recognized the style of architecture; he'd last seen it in the High Halls. The stone was ceiling, shelter from this particular storm—or so An'Tellarus seemed to believe, for it was to that forming hall that she ran, dragging Severn and Elluvian in her wake, the rope between them taut enough it would have cut off Severn's breath had he not knotted it with care to avoid that outcome.

The birds were thunder, and beneath Severn's feet, the ground shook in time to their voices, as if it might break on command. His hand was now numb, Elluvian's grip was so tight. The hall that grew up around the stranger grew closer and larger—as did the birds that flew almost directly above it.

The stranger opened her mouth; she spoke, and light illuminated the sky. Severn couldn't understand her words, but knew they *were* words. An'Tellarus slowed; Severn's sides were now trembling, and his legs would feel the effect of the forced sprint for some time.

But it was odd: were it not for both An'Tellarus's and Elluvian's near panic, he might have been lost in the gray landscape, but he wouldn't have been terrified. He knew, given their reactions, that he could die in this place—but he didn't viscerally believe that that would have been his fate.

The birds inspired awe, in the way the distant southern cliffs could at the right time of day: there was a majesty to their presence, a natural beauty that could never be achieved by the people who lived beneath them, it was so vast, so much larger than their individual lives. So, too, the Dreams of Alsanis.

If he were to fear something, he might have feared the woman who waited, arms raised, as they approached. But

An'Tellarus wasn't afraid. The moment her foot touched the floor that had risen beneath that woman's feet, she slowed her punishing pace, slipping from a fast jog to a stately walk as Severn stumbled in the transition.

Elluvian released Severn's arm as his feet touched stone, raising his face to look at the contours of the arch above their heads.

Severn could no longer hear the rumbling voice of the flying storm above.

"Hallionne Orbaranne," An'Tellarus said, bowing as if the rope around her waist was a tasteful, common adornment. Elluvian didn't bow; he set about loosening the knot that tied him to Severn. Severn waited until he was done, and then did the same; the rope dropped to the floor, anchored only by An'Tellarus.

"Cediela," the Avatar of the Hallionne replied. "You are welcome here. My apologies for the last stretch of your journey. Alsanis is...restless; I believe his dreams have turned dark. We had not expected that level of unrest to disturb you so far from the green."

An'Tellarus rose. "We?"

The Hallionne nodded. "There is one guest staying within my domain at the moment. If you do not wish to see him, I will make certain your paths do not cross." The words tailed up at the end, as if she were asking a question.

An'Tellarus's expression was complicated. To Severn's surprise, she reached out almost gently and placed a hand on the Avatar's left shoulder. "I cannot call you child," she said, her voice as soft as he had ever heard it, "as you are not young, even by our reckoning. But forgive me if I make that mistake; to me you will never be old."

The Hallionne Orbaranne said nothing but made no attempt to evade An'Tellarus's grip. In the end, it was An'Tellarus who moved. "Forgive my manners," she told the Hallionne. "And allow me to introduce my companions."

"I know Elluvian of Danarre," Orbaranne said. "He has visited me before. But the mortal, I have never seen."

"No. I beg you to allow me to claim full responsibility for him while he dwells here."

Severn shook his head. He withdrew a dagger and made a shallow cut in the mound of his left palm. "I am not a child in the reckoning of my kind," he said, in Barrani, to Orbaranne. "And I am not a pet or a dependent."

She nodded and held out a hand, palm up. After a brief hesitation, he placed his cut palm across hers; her skin was cool. She felt, and looked, like a young human woman.

"You don't sleep."

"I do," she replied, the hint of a smile bracketing her lips. "But…I am more often awake than the others."

An'Tellarus was majestic in age; she walked as if she could own the world if she desired to do so. Severn knew that the Hallionne were buildings constructed by gods in the distant past; they were therefore ancient. But he couldn't see the Avatar of this place as ancient or terrifying. He wondered if she'd been mortal when the Hallionne had been created around her.

"Yes," she replied.

Ah. He hadn't asked the question aloud, knew that no hint of it was implied by facial expression alone. This was why many Barrani chose to avoid the Hallionne.

"Yes," she said again. "Please follow me; we will move someplace more welcoming to guests." She turned and led the way, but even walking she said, "I seldom have Barrani visitors."

"Your current guest is Barrani," An'Tellarus said. "As are we."

"Elluvian will not stay," Orbaranne replied. "But I would be grieved to lose him in the outlands; let him leave the normal way."

"Do you often have other visitors?" Severn asked.

SWORD AND SHADOW 151

"Not often, no. I haven't had mortals visit for many, many years. Even before their slavery was outlawed entirely, they were seldom allowed to enter."

"You forbid them entry?"

She turned, her brows raised. "I? No, of course not. Their masters, however, did, on those occasions when the masters were willing to accept my hospitality."

Ah. Of course. "Some of those slaves chose to remain within the confines of the Hallionne?"

"Yes. They preferred to pass their days here. The Ancients didn't differentiate between the sentient races when it came to the imperatives they carved into us. And if I'm honest, I appreciated their company. They didn't suffer here." She paused, and then added, "And some are buried here, even now." She then turned to An'Tellarus. "Do you wish to go to your rooms, or do you wish to visit the great hall?"

"Is that where he is?"

"Yes."

"And he is aware of our arrival?"

"Yes. He has not commanded your attendance."

"I imagine he would not," An'Tellarus replied. "Yes; allow me to visit my rooms but tell him I will attend him in an hour. We do not intend to remain here overnight."

"Very well."

An hour was only barely enough time for Severn to wash. He chose to dress in the clothing of a servant of significance, not for the sake of his companions, but for the sake of the unnamed guest.

Although he'd been taught about the Hallionne, he hadn't heard that at least one of these majestic buildings had a mortal at their heart. That she had been one wasn't in question, and he'd heard something in her voice as she spoke of the succoring of slaves that reminded him of his master's final question.

Are you lonely?

He did not and would not ask, of course—but he imagined that the companionship of those who found a greater freedom in a confined space had been welcome to her. He was also certain that had they asked to leave, she would have let them; he was almost certain she would have had no choice.

The Hallionne's Avatar met him in the hall, as if she'd been waiting without motion for Severn to emerge. She then said, "Follow," and began to walk. He wondered if, had the previous Hallionne been awake, a physical representation would have replaced the glowing lights embedded in the floor that otherwise showed him the way.

"Yes," she said, once again answering the question he hadn't spoken aloud.

"Does that require effort on your part?"

"Effort?"

"Hearing the thoughts I do not put into words."

"No. You don't need to speak Barrani if you're not comfortable with it; I can understand any language you choose to speak. The Hallionne were designed to respond to the needs of their guests; they were also designed to keep each individual safe from the machinations of any other guests. I don't hear your thoughts as thoughts; I hear them as if you never stop speaking."

"Is that true for any other guest?"

"No. Elluvian's thoughts, while he remains within my borders, are clear, but they are far quieter than yours. An'Tellarus, I cannot hear unless she wills it. And yes, you could learn to do what An'Tellarus does, should you believe it necessary."

"Will it take longer than my natural span of years?"

To his surprise, Orbaranne laughed. "No. If you stayed for a few days, I could teach you. Or I could let you experiment and tell you what the results of the experiment are."

He shook his head. "Can you speak to me without speaking out loud?"

"With difficulty, yes, assuming that you're asking if I could do so while you were in the company of others. As we are now, there would be little point."

"Can you tell me what the black birds were?"

"You already know: they are the Dreams of Alsanis."

"You could hear them."

She nodded.

"What did you say to them? I couldn't understand the words, but it seemed to me that they did."

"I told them that they were lost."

"Were they?"

"They should not be here. I am not certain how they arrived, but..." And here she stopped, as if choosing her words with care. Or as if choosing none. "The latter," she finally said. "I believe you should speak with my other guest. An'Tellarus is waiting."

"Who is your other guest?"

"Lirienne," she replied. "But he is commonly called the Lord of the West March." As she spoke the name, she smiled, and the eyes that had seemed like the darkest of blacks became a warm brown, almost a hazel.

"Does his arrival have anything to do with the Dreams of Alsanis?"

"You will have to ask him." She turned a corner that Severn had not seen until the moment she moved; he suspected, until she did, that the corner hadn't existed. They entered another hall, at the end of which were double doors; both doors were open. Beyond them he could see An'Tellarus; she was seated, her gaze upon the man who stood opposite her, near the windows that allowed light to flood into the room.

These windows were heavily glassed, although the sky outside was clear for as far as the eye could see. Elluvian was not in the room.

"No. He offered his regrets and retreated," Orbaranne

said. She entered the room slightly ahead of Severn and came to a stop less than a yard away from her other guest. "My lord," she said, offering him an odd bow.

"Will you join us?" he asked, smiling. It wasn't his smile that surprised Severn; it was the color of his eyes. They were almost entirely green.

As Severn followed Orbaranne into the room, he glanced at An'Tellarus; her eyes were an almost martial blue. He wondered, briefly, if any two Barrani could have green eyes at the same time and in the same place; he doubted it.

Severn offered the Lord of the West March a perfect obeisance; he dropped one knee to the ground and bowed his head.

"Rise."

He rose just as perfectly, aware in the moment that this was the reason that his master had been so particular about his etiquette. He stood before the Lord of the West March as someone almost beneath significance, and he had no other way to show that he acknowledged the difference in their respective power.

"You are the young man who's keeping An'Tellarus company on her dreary voyage." To Severn's surprise, the Lord spoke Elantran.

Severn glanced at An'Tellarus. "I wouldn't say it's been dreary." He chose his mother tongue as well. "Unless everything becomes dreary when you've lived for centuries."

"Well, Cediela? Is all of life dreary?"

"Questions such as these are endlessly wearying," An'Tellarus replied. "As you requested, we waited for young Severn. Will you now tell us why you traveled here? Beyond the obvious," she added.

Sparks of blue added themselves to green eyes.

The Hallionne's Avatar bowed low. "I will leave you to your discussion," she said, her voice soft.

"Remain," the Lord of the West March said. "Cediela teases; she means no harm."

"She is annoyed, my lord."

"Yes, she is. But her annoyance is entirely at me, and I've dealt with it before. I wasn't with you when you went to greet your guests, and your input may be of value to them." There was a slight emphasis on the final word.

"I wish to be on the road soon," An'Tellarus told him.

"Indeed."

"It would be best if you did not immediately follow."

"I'm uncertain that that is true." Blue finally overwhelmed green; the softer lines around mouth and eyes stiffened. The Lord of the West March was now willing to converse. He walked away from the window and sat in the chair opposite An'Tellarus's. He didn't command Severn sit.

Neither did An'Tellarus. Severn moved to stand behind her chair, to the left, as was the proper place for a valued— or trusted—servant.

"I did travel solely to keep Orbaranne company; it has been long since I went on retreat, and I was desirous of rest and the clarity of thought that comes with it. But I arrived very recently, and the Dreams of Alsanis have been very, very active of late."

"That is not entirely unusual." Although her eyes were no longer visible from Severn's position, her tone was distinctly chilly.

"Indeed. It has happened three times in the past century. Ah, no. It has happened three times in an obvious fashion. But the Dreams have grown restless in the past few decades."

Silence. It was eventually broken by An'Tellarus. "You fear Alsanis's prisoners are somehow taking action."

"That was my supposition, yes." The Lord of the West March then turned to Orbaranne. "The Hallionne Orbaranne does not believe that this particular manifestation is due to Alsanis's prisoners."

"Why?"

"She can, on occasion, hear Alsanis—as we must—through those dreams. Often, they speak in the voices of those imprisoned, but not this time."

An'Tellarus's silence, if brief, felt weighty. "...The green."

"That is our fear, yes." The Lord of the West March folded his arms; his eyes were now a dark shade of blue. "And it is at this time that you have chosen to return to your homelands—in the company of Elluvian, the last scion of the once great house of Danarre, and a random mortal youth.

"Cediela, what game are you playing? The Warden is even now marshaling his forces in the event of unforeseen emergency. I would be displeased and disappointed were that emergency to be you. The webs you spin in your games have long been so convoluted, so complicated, a spider might grow motion sick while attempting to traverse them—but it has been many centuries since those games were played in earnest. I do not wish to see the return of those games; many of our kin were lost to them."

"It was not I who began that particular game." Her voice had gone from chilly to something darker. Severn had always understood that An'Tellarus was a power, but he hadn't truly felt it. He did now. She reminded him, in that moment, of Nightshade. "And were it not for the finish, I might still be entangled in it."

"I was not Lord of the West March then. It was not therefore my people you were killing."

"And you believe I have come to somehow reinstate that past slaughter? With someone who is *almost* outcaste and a young mortal as my only soldiers?"

The silence was meditative; the Lord of the West March shifted position until his hands were steepled beneath his chin. "...No. But I, as you, dislike coincidences." He lifted his chin then. "Boy, your name?"

Severn didn't answer; he waited for An'Tellarus's signal.

"His name is Severn Handred." It was Orbaranne who replied.

Severn considered his options, aware that Orbaranne was listening—and aware that the Hallionne would reveal all thoughts she considered relevant to this man, this ruler of the West March. He was uncertain that other Hallionne would do the same, but perhaps they would; the information did not immediately kill him, and their only imperative was to keep their guests safe within their own borders.

"Yes," she said.

What occurred beyond their borders was not their concern. No, he thought, it wasn't their responsibility. The information given to the Lord of the West March would not be acted on within the Hallionne itself, if that action would lead to Severn's immediate death. He considered this a cheat but was well aware of how little his opinion counted.

"It is not relevant," Orbaranne replied. "And you are not wrong. Will you answer my lord's question?"

Why did she call him her lord?

"I do not choose to answer that question," Orbaranne said.

"No, of course not. But I'm not Barrani, and I'm not a citizen of the West March. I don't have to answer yours, either. The Lord of the West March is a guest. I'm a guest. If my teacher wasn't wrong, we have—we should have—equal weight."

"Your teacher?" It was the Lord of the West March who now asked.

The Hallionne Orbaranne couldn't answer the question because Severn had no useful answer to give the man she called her lord.

"My teacher," Severn replied. "But he also said the Hallionne slept. Orbaranne doesn't."

"You make a statement, mortal from afar."

Severn nodded as An'Tellarus stiffened; he added no further words. Orbaranne must understand—as her lord did—

that he was here in service to An'Tellarus, and it was therefore An'Tellarus's decisions that were paramount.

"She is of the West March," Orbaranne said.

"Yes. But you must know by now that the Barrani of power seldom give commands to other Barrani of power; everything is oblique, a request that doesn't risk the consequences of disobedience for either party." But as he watched her, he wondered if his words were correct. He had no idea what happened to those chosen as the heart of a building such as this. Clearly they didn't age in the natural way, for Orbaranne's Avatar was human. He bowed to An'Tellarus, although she couldn't see it given her position. The Lord of the West March could.

"He is an interesting mortal," the Lord of the West March said to An'Tellarus.

"I find him so. And I imagine I will not be the only one."

"Cediela, why have you returned? I did not expect to see you for a handful of years."

"Was the peace boring?" she asked, in the same indulgent tone she often reserved for private discussions with Severn.

"You are well aware that a ruler does not consider peace boring."

"And aware as well that the ruler is still Barrani. Come. Do you honestly believe that the Dreams of Alsanis reacted to a mortal stranger, one barely out of childhood?"

"I do. I would not have had I not witnessed it myself." This answered a question Severn hadn't asked: the Lord of the West March hadn't been at Orbaranne's side at the end of the portal path but appeared to have seen the events that unfolded. "And I would have ignored it had the mortal not traveled here beneath the shadow of Tellarus's mighty wings. You have told the boy nothing."

"He is not here as adviser, Lirienne. He is here as companion and guard. Or do you perhaps regale your servants with the minutiae of your plans?" The answer was obvious;

he therefore returned silence. She changed the subject. "How long have the Dreams been so restless?"

There was a long pause as the Lord of the West March, blue-eyed and unblinking, gazed at An'Tellarus, his expression almost frozen in polite neutrality.

"Come. You know that the Dreams of Alsanis have never spoken to me in any voice I could hear or understand."

Severn once again bowed to the Lord of the West March. "If you feel the discussion is difficult and you wish privacy, I will leave."

The Lord of the West March nodded. An'Tellarus, however, lifted a hand, well aware that it was her permission Severn required. She waited. Severn almost wished he could see her face, but only to see the color of her eyes; he knew her expression would give nothing away.

"Very well." The Lord of the West March rose. "It has been just under a week since the Dreams have become almost unstable. Where there were one or two Dreams, there are now a dozen or more; they cast great shadows across the West March when they fly, appearing and disappearing without notice or warning." He lowered his chin. "I can understand perhaps a quarter of what they are saying."

An'Tellarus's hands tightened on the arms of her chair; her back straightened.

"They do not speak with one voice; they speak with many. And they seldom speak our tongue. Of the languages I have heard, there are three: our tongue, the language of the Ancients, and a language long lost to the mortals who once spoke it."

"Mortals?" The word was sharp.

"Orbaranne."

The Avatar nodded. "It is a tongue I understand, but they do not respond to the speaking of it. And Lirienne is correct; it is a lost language. The tribe who once spoke it freely are long gone from this world."

Was that the language Severn had heard when she had shouted at the flying shadows above them?

Orbaranne turned toward him. "Yes," she said softly. "It was. You heard it." She glanced at the two Barrani. "They did not."

CHAPTER TEN

AN'TELLARUS ROSE FROM HER CHAIR AT ORBA-
ranne's words, turning toward Severn, just as the Lord of
the West March had done. Her eyes were as dark a blue
as her conversational opponent's. "We thank you for your
warning, Lord of the West March," she said, lowering her
chin in recognition of the difference in their rank. "And
we will take care to avoid the Dreams should we encounter
them overland.

"As always, Hallionne Orbaranne, I remain grateful for
your hospitality."

"The Dreams are not the only change," the Lord of the
West March said.

An'Tellarus exhaled. "While I understand this conversation is necessary, I hope, Hallionne, that you can accommo-
date my busy schedule."

"Understood, An'Tellarus."

Severn felt an odd chill in the air; he saw a flicker of light
from the corners of his eyes. Nothing else changed. What
exactly had Orbaranne understood?

"Time," the Hallionne replied. "Time will no longer pass while you are conversing."

"Orbaranne." The Lord of the West March's voice was soft; it carried a hint of concern.

"I am fine, my lord. It is not too taxing."

"It is also unnecessary."

"I mean no harm to you or your kin; nor would I condone such machinations at this time," An'Tellarus said. "But I would like to keep my companion off the board, and it is clear that your desire to have this conversation works against him."

"The timing of your visit is not coincidental."

"No. No, it is not. You know it and I know it. But the boy did not until you first spoke; he knows it now. What else will he learn, when he does not have the ability to affect any of these difficulties? I wish him to see our circumstances through as unfiltered a viewpoint as he can; he may note things we do not."

"You claim he is so naive that he does not view your invitation with suspicion?"

"He is mortal."

"That is not an answer."

"It is the answer I choose to offer. I do not expect mortals to understand all of the complexities involved in Barrani games; those games start long before their birth and often end long after they pass of old age. If it amuses me to have his company at this time, and his company will cause no harm to your rule and those you value here, I see no harm in it. If you see harm, it is you who must now come to me to explain it."

"I do not recall that has ever made a difference."

"Then your recall is deliberately poor." There was heat in those words.

"I was not Lord of the West March the last time we differed so greatly in viewpoint."

"No. Nor was I An'Tellarus. But we have both risen to the positions we now occupy, and our roots are planted in the times we did not. No game I play endangers you. Orbaranne knows this to be true."

"No game you play *deliberately* endangers me. But we have both seen the ways in which even the best of intentions led to disaster and loss. If you must visit at this time, you might allay my suspicions by leaving your companion within Orbaranne."

She chuckled. "You barely believe that yourself. Do not burden the poor Hallionne with the attempt; if she hears what we think, she is not built to be as expressionless as we are when we converse. I understand what you have offered; I feel it is unnecessary. It is not entirely on my behalf that the boy has traveled this far."

"On whose behalf would you claim he acts?"

"An'Sennarin," Severn replied. He had answered the question silently, but Orbaranne had withdrawn, bowing head to hide the face and expression that An'Tellarus had said was so easy to read.

The Lord of the West March frowned, his perfect brow collapsing for a moment in the center. "An'Sennarin? Truly?"

"You would know if I lied." Severn reached into his interior pocket and withdrew the letter of introduction An'Tellarus had conveyed to him. He handed it to the Lord of the West March, closing the distance between them to do so.

The Lord of the West March took the envelope, glanced at the name written on it, and returned it. "Why are you running errands for An'Sennarin? How did you meet?"

Severn thought then of An'Sennarin. He didn't know what An'Sennarin wanted of him, but perhaps that was because An'Sennarin did not—or could not—risk putting it into words. He had his own beliefs, and he felt a debt to that

Barrani he was certain he would never feel for another Barrani again, saving perhaps Elluvian.

Yvonne of Darrowelm was, in his opinion, the heart of the unspoken matter. Perhaps he had come to ascertain fully whether or not she'd survived; that news would be of import to An'Sennarin either way. But he hoped that he could find her alive and carry word of her survival to the High Halls.

An'Sennarin was young. It was likely that the Lord of the West March viewed his reign as temporary and precarious; An'Tellarus certainly did. There was very little a mortal could do to make it less precarious—but inasmuch as it was possible, Severn would try.

"I am not at liberty to answer that question," Severn said. He considered what Elluvian's reaction would be to the conversation, the question that the Lord of the West March asked, and the possibility that Severn would actually dare to answer it; in spite of himself, he grimaced. Helmat would be furious—probably at Elluvian, but there would be temper enough to go around.

Orbaranne's gaze, which had been drawn, time and again, to the Lord of the West March, now narrowed as she studied Severn's expression. He could see the black of her eyes clearly, could see the tightening of her lips, and could see, as he watched and studied, the slow, rueful rise of the left corner of her mouth. "You have not practiced," she said, voice soft, "but I believe you understand now how a certain opacity of thought is achieved. I will tell you that you need not fear my lord. He holds no ill will for your master—if indeed An'Tellarus can be called such.

"The advice he would give, should he break the impasse An'Tellarus has constructed, is simple: be very wary of Avonelle and Darrowelm. It is above Avonelle's abode that the Dreams of Alsanis are drawn, and they are almost angry. You will not understand, but An'Tellarus does: do not visit the green during your stay."

"The green?" An'Tellarus said, speaking to the Avatar.

"We believe it is the heart of the green that is driving the Dreams of Alsanis; we cannot bespeak Alsanis himself, and we cannot therefore confirm this suspicion. I do not need to tell you to avoid Alsanis."

"We have no choice."

"You cannot enter Alsanis as you have entered me, no—but do not attempt to cross the borders that define his outer reach. If you can aid the young An'Sennarin, my lord will be pleased—but he would caution you against making the attempt. You will draw attention as you are now, but the attention will be far worse if the Barrani understand that you are an Imperial Wolf."

Silence followed the last two words Orbaranne had spoken.

"Cediela, you didn't." The Lord of the West March's eyes now tinted purple, although the shift was hard to ascertain given the darkness of the blue.

"I did not make him a Wolf, no." She frowned at Orbaranne. "And he is not exactly wearing a large tabard that proclaims that service. I will trust you to keep this entirely to yourself."

It was to Severn the Lord of the West March turned. "Boy, you are young. Do not be foolish. The Wolves are feared, yes—but this far from the seat of their power, they will be hunted if their identities are known."

"I would not be here were it possible to trust the Barrani to do what must be done," Severn countered.

The Lord's brows rose, and then, for the first time, he laughed. "I see now why Cediela found you interesting. You husband your boldness, but it is there. I have met the young An'Sennarin. I knew him when he was considered too young a child to leave the perimeters of my domain. I do not know how his inexplicable struggles have changed him, but I will see for myself sometime soon. In the meantime, I judge your intent worthy, if highly dangerous. Very well. You have received what warning I can offer.

"But I will offer another. The Dreams of Alsanis cannot be heard by most of our kin. You heard them."

"It is possible he could hear them because they flew in the outlands, near the portal paths," An'Tellarus offered.

The Lord of the West March continued as if she hadn't spoken. "And you heard, as well, the voice of Orbaranne when she attempted to bespeak them. Do not speak of that to anyone in the West March."

"Why?"

"Because, boy, mortals *cannot* hear the Dreams. Not without an interference I am sure you have not experienced. You do not wish to be known. Absent reasons to pay attention to you, most of my kin will consider you beneath notice or relevance. But remember: there are rat hunters for a reason; there will always be those who attempt to eradicate what they consider vermin."

Severn offered the Lord of the West March an almost perfect bow.

The great room vanished around Lirienne once An'Tellarus and her mortal had departed. The passage of time—or its lack—followed An'Tellarus; Lirienne was content to wait. Only when the room reasserted itself into something smaller did he look up.

Orbaranne could, as she chose, sprout Avatars wherever such Avatars were required; there might be a hundred, and there might be two. She was, after all, the heart of the Hallionne that bore her name. But she never chose to do so when Lirienne visited.

He understood why, but had never asked. If the Ancients should ever return to the lands they had all but abandoned, he had very pointed questions for them. The first, the foremost, would be Orbaranne. He did not, could not, understand why she had been chosen to helm a Hallionne.

She had been mortal. In spite of the brevity of mortals' existence, there were those who Lirienne considered distinct—and responsible—choices. Orbaranne would not have been among them. From the first time he had entered her Hallionne centuries ago, he had known, immediately, that she suffered; she was god within her realm, but the realm itself was a cage. She could not leave it. Could not venture out when her loneliness became all but unbearable.

"I am not lonely," she said, as the door opened. "I haven't been lonely for a long time, now."

He smiled at her Avatar; reaching out, he brushed her left cheek gently. "No, not now."

"An'Tellarus is worried."

"I know. Is she as worried as I am?"

"I think maybe...more." She leaned into his hand, closing her eyes. It was affection, no more; eyes closed, she could still see everything that occurred anywhere in her domain. "She was as surprised as you were when I told you both that Severn could hear me speak. She means you no harm," she added quickly.

"I know. But unintended harm is still harm. Did Severn come as agent for An'Sennarin?"

"I think so. By the end of your discussion he focused his conscious thought much more deliberately. He likes An'Sennarin. He's far more wary of An'Tellarus. And I cannot read her well. It is not my place, but..."

"You want to trust her."

She nodded. "...Will you go?"

He drew the Avatar into his arms, wondering—as he oft did—how she perceived the gesture. Did she feel warmth? Did she feel heat?

As if to answer, she slid her arms around him and leaned into his chest.

"I will not go unless and until there is clear danger. I am curious about Severn Handred, but I cannot yet perceive his use; I believe he will seek Darrowelm. He can make mistakes, if few, that might be excused by his ignorance. He is both mortal and young. He might accomplish what we—An'Tellarus and I—could not easily accomplish without bloodshed and death. She is already enemy to Avonelle, but that enmity is civil, for the moment.

"Come. There is nothing more that you can tell me, and nothing at all that you can do to control or bind Cediela."

"You wouldn't want that, even if I could."

He smiled. "No. She is not a friend, but she is not an enemy, and with the exception of Avonelle, she remains outside of all struggles for the succession."

"But you don't want the throne."

"Yes. But Barrani see truth at such a slant that our truths oft sound like lies to those who listen." This was not the first time he had told her this; it would not be the last. Orbaranne often liked the familiarity of repetition. He could do very little else for her and was content to offer her that.

"You are certain the boy is not here as a hunter."

She nodded.

"Then you must tell me what you think he will do while here."

She shook her head.

"I did not ask what he thinks he will do. What do you think?"

"I think there is no way he can avoid Darrowelm or Avonelle. But there is another problem."

Lirienne stilled.

"The Dreams of Alsanis are tangled and dark. I told him he should not touch them should they land; he should not allow them to touch him."

"You believe they might try."

"It was—I think—the mortal they sought. They cannot

bespeak him, not yet, but…Alsanis dreams of the green, and the dreams are twisted."

"It is too early for the ceremonies."

She nodded again. "I believe An'Tellarus intends to approach the Warden." She bowed her head again; he could feel the contours of her face through the clothing he wore.

"Orbaranne, look at me." When she failed to obey, he pulled back, sliding a finger under her chin. "I have said I will not leave; I promised you the time, and I will give it unless an emergency arises. Come, let us talk about other things."

She was tense in his arms.

"What do you fear?"

"I could not give you the name of his master; he did not know it. I don't think he ever used it; he called him master or teacher."

Lirienne stilled.

"But…I saw him. I saw the image of him in Severn's thoughts. He has been a guest here many times; like An'Tellarus, he is more than willing to remain within my domain when he travels."

"Who is he?"

She was silent for a beat, her expression dark; she closed her eyes tightly. But in the end, she did not answer—could not answer, he thought, although she strained against that imperative. He did not understand the range of imperatives that governed Orbaranne; did not understand why she could introduce Severn herself when he failed to surrender his name at Lirienne's request but could not yet speak the name of this unknown visitor.

"Hush," he said, once again lifting both of his hands to cup her cheeks. "It is not necessary for me to know."

She shook, but eventually nodded. "In the green," she said, "I think something is waiting."

"For Severn's master?"

"For Severn."

He asked no further questions.

An'Tellarus's eyes were a martial blue for the duration of their short walk to the exit. She said nothing, her lips slightly white around the edges. The gear with which Severn had made the first part of the trek was waiting for them just to the side of doors that had rolled open at their approach. He grimaced. He still wore the clothing best suited to an important servant, but An'Tellarus had made clear that the time to return to his room to change had long passed. She was not happy.

Elluvian was equally grim. He met them outside of the exit. Severn paused to look over his shoulder: Orbaranne was a castle, not a tree, not a cliff face. He wondered if that was a side effect of being awake, but didn't ask. Nor did he ask if he might take the time to change into traveling clothes; the answer was clearly written in the color of An'Tellarus's eyes.

"Have you seen the Dreams of Alsanis?" she asked of Elluvian.

"No. But the Dreams do not speak to me. If they fly, I am irrelevant."

Her eyes narrowed. "I am certain that some part of that is your choice."

This surprised Severn; it clearly didn't surprise Elluvian. From his weary, almost long-suffering expression, it was what he expected.

"Is it yours, An'Tellarus? If you choose to do so, can you bespeak the Dreams?"

She snorted inelegantly. "I have had a difficult day; do not make it more wearying by your pointless questions. You already know the answer. And as you do, I must believe you are attempting to annoy me."

There was a particular type of unfairness that seemed to spring up, from time to time, between family members.

Their interaction reminded Severn that they were, in some fashion, family.

"Perhaps you might explain my words to young Severn," An'Tellarus continued. "If you fail to do so, I might."

"Oh please, An'Tellarus. Do. I am very curious to see what explanation you might offer a mortal Wolf."

Severn wasn't. He had no desire to be caught between An'Tellarus and Elluvian. "How long will we travel by foot?" he asked instead.

"Orbaranne was gracious enough to allow us to exit at the farthest western edge of her boundaries. We should not be more than three days from the borders of the West March," An'Tellarus replied. She glared at Elluvian.

Elluvian failed to note it. It was going to be a long three days.

Three days of travel involved eighteen hours of walking per waking day. An'Tellarus called a halt to allow Severn to sleep; she called extremely brief halts to allow him to eat. From the moment she left Hallionne Orbaranne, she had not otherwise stopped moving.

Although she had threatened to regale Severn with tales of Elluvian's past, even she considered it unwise, for she said nothing. She did, however, wear disappointment very loudly on her sleeve; she reminded Severn of an old woman he knew whose children worked at one of the market stalls. He understood that anyone annoying those very adult children would get the sharp side of the old woman's tongue— but her children might have preferred that, given how often she nagged and criticized them.

He couldn't be certain. His childhood had encompassed only a Barrani master as "family"; the family he'd built later had been severed by death. And more death. In neither of those cases was An'Tellarus's behavior the norm. Had he not been sent out, time and again, into the streets of the fiefs to simply observe others who lived there, he would have had nothing against which to compare it. He might have believed that the older woman hated and despised the younger man.

He didn't believe that now, but was nonetheless grateful to be Severn Handred and mortal, with no chance whatsoever of familial connections to the head of Tellarus. He was certain Elluvian wished he could say the same.

But if Elluvian was uncomfortable in An'Tellarus's presence, it was a kind of expectant, weary discomfort; he knew what to expect, and knew he couldn't avoid it—but he had no plans to end the misery by ending An'Tellarus's life. Elluvian had made clear that he stood no chance against her, but Severn was far less certain.

An'Sennarin, however, felt only genuine affection for An'Tellarus; his emotions in the Tha'alaan made clear to Severn that she was, to An'Sennarin, a much-loved aunt. A terrifying aunt, to be certain—but one who would never turn the force of her fury and power upon Sennarin.

In family squabbles, it is best to understand the full context before you make any attempt to intervene. At a remove, should the conflict be minor, any choice you make will be seen less as support and more as interference. Love among our kin is not expressed easily; there is far too much risk in it. You will understand this when you are older.

His master's words oft returned to Severn; they returned now. But in the past, had his master sounded almost sorrowful when he had begun this particular, inexplicable lesson? Or was that simply the detritus of poor mortal memory and the experiences that lay between those words and this moment?

When An'Tellarus slowed her walk, Severn understood that they had almost reached the border. He couldn't see or sense it, it was so artfully hidden; this forest resembled the forest through which they had trekked for days. But he reached for his pack.

"Yes," she said. "I would prefer that you change. Your

clothing is respectable, but the stains of travel mar it." And by association, An'Tellarus. "Elluvian."

"I am not here as either your servant or your guard," Elluvian replied. "If issue is to be taken with my clothing, so much the better." The words sounded almost dire; he was not in a good mood. Had not, Severn thought, been in as bad a mood at any time they had crossed paths in the Halls of Law.

An'Tellarus exhaled; it wasn't a sigh, but rather a sign that her own temper was fraying.

Severn changed. He had a small mirror, meant for shaving in a pinch, and a rough strap against which to sharpen his razor, and he used both, the normalcy of the actions steadying. There were no clouds in the sky that he could see, but he could hear, faintly, the sounds of thunder. He chose to keep this to himself when a brief glance at Elluvian made clear that Elluvian had not.

Severn couldn't see the Dreams in the air.

But he became aware of the people in the forest, many high in the treetops, but some in the long shadows cast by the trees themselves. Elluvian was no doubt aware of them, but when Severn caught his eye, the Barrani Wolf shook his head. Guards, then. Guards that both An'Tellarus and Elluvian expected.

None of those guards confronted An'Tellarus and her party; she had the right to be here. If they noted a mortal in the midst of the small number of Barrani, it made no difference. An'Tellarus proceeded with august grace, until she reached the banks of a circular river. Ah. The water she had spoken of.

An'Tellarus moved her right hand briefly, as if flicking her skirts; Severn understood. He was a servant here, and he was meant to wait on his master.

But the river, if it could be called that, didn't wind its way through trees. The air above it was open to sky—and at that, a sky so crystal clear and so pristine it looked artificial. Above the water flew a single black bird, its wingspan large in comparison to the slender width of its body. It spoke, its voice elemental, shorn of actual syllables.

Severn had neither need nor ability to answer. Here, he must be as unremarkable as possible.

"Elluvian."

Elluvian nodded to An'Tellarus. He stepped forward to the edge of that water, and knelt before it; he lifted a hand, and laid his palm against the water's moving surface.

The water rose, river becoming a rising wall. Beyond that wall was a pillar of water that now rose into the sky; only when it had stilled did the river wall once again fall back into its banks. A bridge formed, lifting itself from the ground, the pale stone almost gleaming in the sunlight. An'Tellarus nodded as Elluvian stood.

"Apparently you are still considered of the West March to the water," she said, her voice pinched.

"A pity," Elluvian replied, under his breath.

"Come. Unless you wish to return to your home, you will be forced to endure mine."

Elluvian didn't reply, but he did follow when she began to walk across the bridge.

To Severn's surprise, there were no guards awaiting them when they left the bridge. But there was a gate: a large, intimidating gate that might, at a distance, be mistaken for crystal. It wasn't; it was a thing entirely of water.

Here, An'Tellarus stopped; she tendered this gate a perfect obeisance. Elluvian did the same. When she rose, she walked into the water, and passed beyond Severn's sight. Elluvian moved to follow but glanced at Severn. "What do you see?"

"I see gates of water."

"They haven't opened?"

"Not for me."

The Barrani Wolf exhaled. "It appears you will have to approach the water as an individual, not a servant."

"Is that normal?"

"No. I will wait."

"She's going to be angry."

"She's always angry."

"What does she want from you?"

"Something I am not of a mind to give." The answer was a wall. Severn asked no further questions. "Be quick. Our actions—or inactions—will be observed."

Severn immediately tendered these unmanned gates a perfect Barrani bow—one that made clear he was insignificant in comparison to the water itself. He started to rise but stopped as the shadows across the ground shifted beneath his feet.

Elluvian cursed. At any other time, that would have been enough to cause Severn to rise instantly to his feet—and to reach for possible weapons. But instinct told him to remain as he was. Not even when he heard thunder did he override that instinct. His hands remained by his sides.

Rise. Rise, Severn of Handred.

Only then did he straighten.

What Elluvian saw as an open gate was not, in Severn's vision, a gate at all. It was a sculpture made of ice without the dusting of frost that usually accompanied ice. Taller than Severn by shoulders and head, the sculpture was that of a woman, her long hair trailing past her shoulders and becoming absorbed in the swirl of water that resembled a robe. Her face was colorless, but not featureless.

Only when she held out a hand did he realize she was not sculpted in ice.

He hesitated then, aware of the warnings given him by An'Tellarus on their journey to reach the West March. There were two things he should not do: the first, hear the Dreams of Alsanis, and the second, the voice of the water.

But...the sculpture itself hardened into familiar lines, dwindling almost in place until he faced a much more familiar woman: Ybelline Rabon'alani. He could not enter the West March's hidden city if he didn't reach out to touch the hand offered him, and he therefore couldn't follow An'Tellarus's advice.

Reaching out, he placed his palm across the palm that lay, translucent but solid, awaiting him.

CHAPTER ELEVEN

HE ALMOST EXPECTED TO HEAR YBELLINE; HE HAD taken the water's hand for that reason. When the water spoke, it wasn't in a familiar voice.

You are welcome here, the water said, speaking as the Tha'alani might have done. *I have come to meet you, Severn Handred, at the request of one who has always been close to me.*

Who?

Ollarin. You call him An'Sennarin now, but he was not always thus—and perhaps, in a more gentle time, he might set down the mantle and return to us; it is all of his desire.

Can he speak to me?

Not in this way. It was difficult for him to convey a message to me, although we are ever connected in our own ways.

Can you contact him if I...have a message to pass on?

Not easily, no. He must concentrate or he must go to where the water is—and that has not always proven safe or wise. I do not know if he will risk it. He is concerned.

So was Severn. He didn't choose to pass that on.

If I find that his friend is alive, what does he want me to do?

He will be relieved. I believe it better if his friend is not alive.

Better for who?

For Ollarin. Even now he is trapped in the webs woven around her existence; he must trust that she is in truth alive.

Do you know?

No. If I could lie, I believe this is the time I would choose to do so—to Ollarin, for both his safety and his peace.

If she's alive, could he protect her in the High Halls? Would it be better if she were there, not here?

There was no answer. The water fell away from his hand, and as it did he looked up; she was gone. Beyond where she had stood was the gate: it was a gate of metal, but finely crafted, a work of art in which metallic leaves caught sunlight, suggesting unnatural vines. Those gates now rolled open.

Elluvian was, of course, dark-eyed. His glare fell on Severn, and then away. His lips moved, but Severn couldn't hear his words because thunder smothered all other sounds. It was closer than it had been. He wondered how long he had been standing in one place and looked up as a shadow crossed over him. Dream, he thought. Nightmare. Were they substantially different?

He meant to ask Elluvian if the Dreams were substantial or ghostly; if their claws and beaks could rend and tear flesh, or only cause the chill attributed to ghosts. But he had no need. As the shadow grew larger and larger, it screeched. Elluvian froze but didn't bend or leap out of the way. Neither did Severn, as if somehow standing still could prove anything to those who might be watching.

Maybe it would have. But as the bird passed overhead, its claws brushed the top of Severn's hair. Something teetered there for a moment before falling from its nest; Severn opened his hands to grab it. A small branch, similar to the detritus left by a passing storm, rested in his hand. It was as white as ivory, its leaves a sparkling emerald.

"Don't stand there," Elluvian snapped—in Elantran. "We need to move. Now. Do not fall behind."

Severn didn't ask the obvious question. Sliding the small branch into the inner pocket of his very fine jacket, he nodded. Elluvian passed through the gate, Severn on his heel.

Given Elluvian's tone and the color of his eyes, Severn wasn't surprised to see guards materialize on the other side of the gate. He hadn't seen them through the gate's open bars, but understood these gates probably functioned as a portal.

Elluvian came to a halt in front of An'Tellarus, who was standing in the center of the road. Her eyes, like Elluvian's, were indigo; from a distance they looked black. The guards arrayed around her were three sword lengths' distance, but those swords had been unsheathed and pointed inward. She was highly unamused.

The guards weren't amused, either; to Severn's eye they looked nervous, although their expressions were Barrani. Their eyes matched An'Tellarus's in color, and they were just a bit too stiff, too perfectly still.

The circle of swords broke and re-formed far more loosely as Elluvian and Severn came into view. Severn thought Elluvian would stop there. He was wrong. Elluvian uttered two words and leaped *above* the grounded Barrani. Severn simply veered as all eyes were captured by Elluvian's leap. It was beyond impressive; Severn had no hope of matching it, no matter how hard he trained.

He didn't hesitate. He left An'Tellarus behind, sprinting to catch up with Elluvian as the Barrani Wolf's feet once again touched ground. Elluvian didn't look back. He'd given Severn an order, and Severn knew better than to disobey it. He was also certain that none of the guards would dare to injure An'Tellarus.

★ ★ ★

The West March wasn't small. Severn couldn't be certain of pursuit; he heard no clanging armor, no sounds of armored feet, at his back. Barrani could be silent, and Barrani armor was lighter in weight than the more ceremonial armor required of the Swords—but not so light that it remained soundless.

No one raised voice at Severn's back.

Still, Elluvian didn't slow. Severn watched the Barrani Wolf's back; it became his goal as he ran, as if Elluvian were a criminal at the end of a long pursuit, and only Severn could catch him. But he noted the streets and the roads; noted when they narrowed and thinned in number; noted when the trees that surrounded those streets became forest. Even then, Elluvian continued to run.

He considered what might have happened had they both been mortal. Entering the gates at a run, avoiding any interaction with those who manned them, racing through those standing in the streets as if they were simply part of the landscape. Nothing good, at least not for Severn. Flight would almost certainly engender pursuit and suspicion.

He had been taught about Barrani life. His interaction with the Barrani in Elantra had made his master's stories feel quaint, distant. Now, however, he saw things that he had never seen and could nonetheless recognize.

When Elluvian came to a sudden, graceful stop, Severn's tread disturbed both dirt and undergrowth.

"You're out of practice," Elluvian said. "If An'Tellarus doesn't keep you busy while you're here, we should train."

Severn shrugged, taking a moment to catch the breath Elluvian didn't apparently need. Elluvian's eyes were predominantly blue, but the blue had lightened into a normal, resting shade. The parts that didn't contain blue were purple, a purple that blended into blue rather than overwhelming it.

Severn looked away, as he had often done when confronted with grief.

"The tree behind me, to your right—the large one—is a door," Elluvian told the private. "Doors of this kind exist almost nowhere else."

The first Hallionne's entrance had been a tree as well. "Are they common in the West March?"

"No. But you must know that. The buildings we ran past are far more common, and house perhaps half of the occupants of the West March. Perhaps less."

"An'Tellarus will live in a building like this one?"

Elluvian nodded. "An'Tellarus, An'Avonelle, An'Darrowelm." At the mention of the last lord, purple vanished from Elluvian's eyes. "If ascertaining the fate of Yvonne of Darrowelm were as simple as entering—and exiting—a small complex of buildings, do you think we wouldn't know? There is only one entrance, and that entrance very like this. In order to visit Darrowelm at all one must have two things: trust in the safety of the interior, and permission."

"Only those three families?"

"Ah, no. There are other families, lesser than Avonelle and Tellarus, who nonetheless have ownership claims to homes such as these." Elluvian touched the bark of the tree.

This, Severn thought, was Danarre's—or what had been left of it. Clearly these dwellings were unlike Elantran dwellings; if left empty for too long in Elantra, new occupants would arrive.

Elluvian exhaled. "Come," he said. "You will be the first guest these halls have seen since the last war."

The strange dislocation Severn felt when entering portals was so faint he might have been imagining it, given they seemed to have entered a vestibule. The space was too small to be called a foyer. It possessed walls and a door at the far end.

"You are remarkably quiet," Elluvian said, as he opened that door.

"There are no good questions to ask," Severn replied. "And none I think you'd care to answer. Ah, no. There is one."

"And that?"

"Will our...departure anger An'Tellarus?"

"Yes."

"And will our destination mollify her at all?"

"You really are more perceptive than most of the young Wolves have been. *Mollify* is perhaps too strong a word." The door opened into light; Severn could see pale planks on the other side of the door, and in the distance, curved walls that were composed of varying shades of brown. "I've retreated to this residence perhaps a handful of times since the end of the war, but I have done so furtively, and I have never brought a guest.

"I do not consider this my home. An'Tellarus does." He exhaled again. He stepped through the open door and into the room itself, indicating that Severn should follow. He approached the middle of this room of wood and light; in the center was a pillar—a tree trunk by look and feel, around which a narrow set of steps twined. "In older days, the hall might be used to entertain visitors—or to greet them properly. But we did not live on the ground." He began to climb the steps, his feet silent, his movements careful. "We did, however, bathe there." The implication was clear.

There was no guardrail near the stairs to prevent the careless from falling, just the trunk to one side and the flat steps themselves. Those steps weren't nailed into the tree, nor were they separate from it; were it not for the uniformity of shape, Severn might have thought them perfectly placed branches.

Elluvian climbed for some time; Severn half suspected that the stairs were irrelevant to the Barrani Wolf, but perhaps not. Although the stairs rose up, and up again, Severn had no sense of open sky, although the light that filtered in implied it.

"Here." Elluvian leaped from the stairs to rough, wooden flooring; Severn did the same. "You can see much of the West March from this perch. If you are careful, you can see the abode of Tellarus. Beyond, you might see a glimpse of Avonelle."

"Darrowelm?"

"Not from here, although if we moved, it's a possibility. I haven't been overly concerned with the politics of the West March since the end of the war. I'm indirectly involved with them because An'Tellarus will not let go." He exhaled. "I'm being unfair. Danarre was utterly destroyed by the Dragon Flights—one of the few clans that was. An'Danarre held nothing back when he rode to war; none of his kin, none of his servants.

"I was the only survivor. To An'Tellarus, I am therefore An'Danarre. Or could be, if I chose to resurrect my fallen line." He glanced at Severn, as if expecting questions, but nodded in approval when none followed.

"You serve the Emperor."

"Indeed. She's entirely too optimistic. Unless and until I disavow that service, Danarre cannot stand." His smile was odd, crooked. "She believes I owe it, not to my father, but to my fallen kin. But my fallen kin would have reveled in the destruction—they would have willingly given their lives to see An'Danarre fall."

"Enough, Elluvian."

To Severn's surprise, they were not alone.

Elluvian turned in the direction of the voice—possibly because the man who had spoken carried a wide wooden tray upon which sat a pitcher, two glasses, and an offering of different fruits. "Apologies, Eldanis. I did not expect to wake you."

One brow rose over an eye that was almost entirely green. "I have slept for long enough that I even feel the weight of this tray. But the others are undisturbed." When Elluvian took a glass, he continued. "I dreamed, Elluvian."

"Of what?" The Barrani Wolf indicated that Severn should likewise avail himself of refreshments, but his eyes had narrowed as he studied Eldanis's face.

"Of mortals," the man replied.

"You must have heard his voice. This young man is Severn Handred; he is one of my Wolves, in the distant heart of the Dragon's Empire."

Eldanis's eyes lost their green.

"I am not here at the behest of the Emperor," Severn told him, voice measured and quiet. "I am here at the invitation of An'Tellarus."

This didn't change the color of the servant's eyes, although a grimace crossed his face and passed, as if a cloud's shadow had briefly blotted out the sun. "I would ask to what end, but An'Tellarus's answers engender more confusion than they resolve. I did not hear her voice, when I woke."

"Oh, she isn't here," Elluvian said. "I thought it best to leave her to deal with the ceremonial guard."

They hadn't looked all that ceremonial to Severn.

"At her command?"

"Ah, no."

Eldanis smiled then. "You have grown more bold or less cautious in the years you've been away. You left her at the gates?"

"We did."

"They did not stop you?"

"No. I thought it best things remain that way. I had not intended to visit my old home, but it seemed the most expedient. Now I am less certain. Severn has traveled to the West March as An'Tellarus's servant and companion; his race will draw enough attention. The fact that he followed me will not help him maintain invisibility. She is, however, perfectly capable of venting her outrage at a handful of guards near the gates.

"But now that you are here, Eldanis, I have a question for you."

The man bowed.

"What did the Dream of Alsanis drop into the mortal's hands?"

Eldanis stiffened and rose, his eyes rimmed in gold. It was the Barrani color that indicated surprise, a color that Severn had seen seldom in his life.

Severn turned to Eldanis. Elluvian clearly trusted him, inasmuch as Barrani trusted at all, and any information was welcome. He slid his hand into his interior pocket and pulled out the small branch that had landed on his head. In the light that filtered through much larger branches here, the branch seemed a twig, but it retained its ivory color, the leaves emerald. They were hard to the touch, as if emeralds had indeed been somehow sliced thin and worked into the shape of leaves. The branch felt more like jewelry than tree against his fingers.

Gold eclipsed the blue and green that had been Eldanis's eye color.

Elluvian's eyes remained a steady, darker than normal blue.

"You took the boy to the green?" Eldanis demanded, voice losing the neutrality of respect from servant to master.

"We ran from the gates to...here. No, we did not pause in the green. We would need the Warden's permission to even touch its periphery." His tone made clear that he thought that permission wouldn't be forthcoming.

"Then where...where did this come from?"

"As I said: it was dropped by a Dream of Alsanis—into the boy's hands. It was, I believe, meant for him to carry. What do you see in it? I see leaves."

Eldanis didn't turn back to Elluvian; he focused on Severn.

"If you desire entry to the green, you must show this to the Warden. Do not reveal it where other eyes can see it. Even the Warden's servants are tied tightly to Lord Avonelle, and she will be *most* displeased. Her displeasure in the West March is something you must avoid."

Severn nodded as Eldanis returned the branch to his hands, although his gaze remained fastened to it. "Master, I would speak with you privately."

"The boy is sharp and observant; I do not believe we need to hide things from him if he is somehow meant to deal with the consequences."

"I do not understand how he can," Eldanis replied. "The last time I saw a branch such as this, it was not offered by the Dreams of Alsanis; it was offered by the green. The Warden of the time carried it, and he planted it in the grove that straddles the green and the city here. It is only in such a place, we were told, that it might take root and grow—and its growth is unstable."

Elluvian frowned. He glanced at Severn; Severn shook his head. Beyond the spoken words, Eldanis's meaning was opaque.

Severn frowned. "You said the Warden controls access to the green."

Eldanis nodded.

"Was it the Warden who delivered a similar branch in the past?"

"Yes."

"And the Warden who planted it?"

"No."

"You saw it planted?"

"Yes."

"Could I plant this?"

"No. Not yet. And as you are mortal, I would have said not ever. But Elluvian's eyes are sharp; if he saw the Dream of Alsanis drop this into your hands, you are meant to carry it. And if you succeed, you are meant to plant it."

"Succeed? At what?"

Eldanis glanced at Elluvian.

Elluvian once again exhaled. "Are the shards of Tyron stirring? Rumors of such did not reach the east."

Eldanis said, "An'Tellarus is here, now. In her wake, a mortal whom the Dreams of Alsanis have gifted such a sign. Do not show that gift to anyone, not even An'Tellarus, unless she mentions it." He understood that An'Tellarus was Severn's master here, and knew, as well, that the option of refusal didn't belong to mere servants. "It is yours, but you must be well aware that it is customary among our kin to kill those who possess the things we cannot otherwise have, in the hopes of possessing them ourselves."

"And you don't desire it."

"No. But the Dreams do not speak to me in any language I understand; they do not speak to my lord. I do not believe they bespeak An'Tellarus or any of her living kin—and that might be a cause of bitterness for her."

"But what are the shards of Tyron?"

Eldanis hesitated.

Elluvian grimaced. "We do not want him entangled in any of the business of the West March. Some fool no doubt has sought to disturb the green to take one of the ancient treasures it has long harbored—but that has nothing to do with us. It appears I must leave to gather rumors. Take the boy to the baths and have him cleaned up; I am certain An'Tellarus will be here before I return."

"Severn is to go with her?"

"...Yes. He is still safer by her side than by mine. I will find what information I can." To Severn he added, "You are not to leave this place until and unless An'Tellarus arrives. If she arrives before I do, you may follow her. Do not mention this discussion, and do not mention the Dreams."

Severn said, quietly, "She saw."

"No doubt. She has long seen things which others would have missed, and those who were entangled in it paid the price. Helmat will try to kill me if I lose you here, and I will be forced to defend myself. In case I have not made this clear, Helmat is a decent Lord of Wolves, and I have no replacement for him. If I am forced to undertake that role..."

Severn shrugged. "I'll be dead. Is there anything worse you could do to me?"

"I promise to be suitably inventive."

Eldanis obeyed Elluvian's command. He led Severn back down the narrow stairs toward what Severn assumed was a bath. He was half-right. It was a large fountain, in a room not much smaller than the room the stairs occupied. Eldanis stopped to one side of the fountain.

Severn stared at him with growing discomfort. This wasn't a bath. It was a large, intricately wrought fountain, stone and iron used in its construction, when nothing else he had seen was anything but wood.

"It is Danarre's bath." At Severn's expression, Eldanis nodded. "This is Danarre. It is what remains of a once great fortress. We do not call our master An'Danarre, as is his right, unless we are foolish enough to wish to anger him. Not even An'Tellarus uses that name. But some of us have served Danarre for all of our lives. I will not answer your questions—should you have any—about his past; it is his past, and his to share, reject, or embrace.

"But this is where we bathed, should it prove necessary or desirable."

"It's a fountain."

"Indeed. It is a fountain; it was crafted with care and magic and much thought, for the water must flow into Danarre, and it must flow out; water cannot be trapped or caged. Not

water such as this. It is delicate, yes—but I assume you have
no intention to cause harm here."

"No. I wouldn't survive it." He glanced around. "Do you
have towels I might use?"

"Yes, but they are unnecessary, as you will no doubt see.
No one will interrupt you while you bathe, but if perchance
you require assistance, I will come." He bowed, as if Severn
were Elluvian's peer, and not An'Tellarus's servant. When
he rose, however, he hesitated. It was the first sign of uncertainty Severn had seen in him.

"I have been forbidden to speak to you of things that are
common knowledge among my kin."

He nodded.

"Ask An'Tellarus, but only when you have reached the
relative safety of her domicile." He hesitated again, and then
added, "Ask her about Lord Tanniase, if the opportunity
arises. I will leave you now."

Severn disrobed, feeling oddly exposed. He'd disrobed
in similar fashion by the banks of streams and rivers on the
march, but he felt far less comfortable here. He knew why:
the water. He understood what Eldanis didn't say. This water
was the water of the West March, and the water of the West
March was the ultimate defense for those who dwelled within
its boundaries.

He had been given no brush, no soap; he couldn't imagine dumping dirty water into the circular river that girded
these lands. Tentative, he held a hand out, and the water that
fell from the height of the fountain's crown splashed across
his palm. No voice accompanied the droplets that formed.

He exhaled, climbed up to the fountain's rim, and gently
lowered himself into the large basin beneath its height. The
water in the basin wasn't still. There were currents beneath
its shallow surface, like muscle beneath skin. The water didn't
speak to him here; no hand rose from its surface.

He closed his eyes.

Any attempt to speak to the water was met with a stubborn silence. If this fountain was somehow connected to the water which flowed through the channels around the West March, it didn't retain its sentience. Perhaps, had Severn been An'Sennarin, it might have. An'Tellarus had said that An'Sennarin was gifted in that regard.

Severn wondered if An'Sennarin would have been the choice of the Dreams of Alsanis had An'Sennarin been An'Tellarus's companion. It was an idle thought. He wouldn't get an answer. If it were safe for An'Sennarin to come to the West March, Severn had no doubt he would be here. Perhaps there were reasons he remained in the High Halls—reasons that had little to do with the power he'd gained when he'd killed the previous lord.

An'Sennarin had never wanted that power. He had taken it to save the Tha'alani. Perhaps he had not yet come to realize that the power itself was a tool that might be used to save others.

And perhaps Severn didn't understand the weight and use of Barrani power. If it was a tool, it was living, breathing; it grew or it withered, the strength inherent in the authority dependent upon the person who attempted to wield it.

It wasn't a responsibility Severn had ever desired. He could barely be responsible for one person; he couldn't imagine the weight of being responsible for hundreds. He could not imagine what the Emperor faced, daily, in his attempt to rule.

He exhaled. Becoming a Wolf had been expedient; it gave him access to the one person he had sworn—and failed—to protect. It had given him access to legal money, and that money had given him a stable roof over his head. If he hadn't dreamed of being Emperor as a child, he had dreamed of having a home of his own.

Restless, he rose; the water curled around his feet in permeable chains. "Am I not clean enough yet?"

No answer. Of course not. He did sit again, sliding farther into the water; it was warm, now.

If he'd chosen to apply for the job as an act of convenience, of expedience, both had shattered upon his first meeting with Ybelline. What was left in the wake of that shattering was an entirely different determination. No, he didn't want the power—and the responsibility—of a ruler. But seeing the Tha'alani, seeing what they had suffered, he was absolutely willing to serve the man who made the attempt to protect them. He was willing to face the literal Dragon. He was willing to take the power the Dragon had granted the Wolves and use it in an attempt to make certain that the serial killing of the Tha'alani never happened again.

His experience in the fiefs hadn't taught him to value life. Even his master, being Barrani, hadn't thought to teach him that life, in and of itself, had value—not when it belonged to other people, most of whom would no doubt be enemies, petty or not. Living with Elianne and her mother had taught him the value of specific lives, but he understood that was personal. If Elianne had become the sole focus of his struggle toward adulthood, he'd never expected she would be as important to anyone else.

No, only when he had crossed the bridge in search of her had he come to understand that to the Emperor, life had value. The lives of those he would never meet deserved his protection, inasmuch as one Dragon could offer protection to those he would never see, never meet, and never interact with.

You cannot rule others if you cannot rule yourself. Do you understand, Severn? It is self-governance that is the first hurdle you must cross.

Even here, old lessons returned. He smiled almost bitterly. "I don't want to rule others."

And will you then be ruled? You rule or you are ruled. He could see his master's expression, when he closed his eyes. It was a familiar expression: he'd seen it cross Elluvian's features when Elluvian was frustrated with the Wolflord. *You dream of living "together." You dream of an equality, a harmony, that does not and cannot exist.*

But it did. It existed in the Tha'alani, if nowhere else. His master had never interacted with the Tha'alani. If he ever did, Severn wondered what he would see, or how he would interpret it.

Severn knew humans couldn't, overnight, transform themselves into Tha'alani. Greed, envy, fear, and jealously would prevent it. What the Tha'alani taught their children effortlessly couldn't be taught so easily to people who couldn't hear each other or understand each other so completely.

Humans had to look inward. They had to take control of their own impulses; they had to know when to act on them and when to retreat from them. That, he'd been taught. He had learned. He had never rebelled against those early lessons.

Was he still a child, then? Was he still someone who required a master, a lord, a cause—something larger than he was, something more powerful, more innately worthy? He shook his head, thinking of his master; remembering the rare, pinched expression transform his otherwise serene face.

The Emperor was a Dragon. Severn was a mortal. Given the absolute difference between their power, Severn's service to the Dragon was natural and expected. His survival would depend on it. Not even his master would have argued against it. Elluvian accepted it as the natural order.

But that wasn't why Severn chose, in the end, to serve. It wasn't why Helmat chose to serve. It wasn't why Rosie continued to man a desk when the injuries she'd taken were too severe to allow her to hunt. If Severn decided to walk away from the Wolves, he could disappear into the crowd, as he'd done for so much of his life. He had a choice. Elluvian's hunt to catch him notwithstanding, from the moment he walked into Helmat's office, he'd always had a choice.

Then why was he here? Why had he left Elantra?

He wanted to know about parents he had never met, never seen, parents who had left no trace of themselves in his life other than his mortal existence. He wanted to know about his family—a family that was a fairy tale, a story, a daydream. What would finding the truth mean? What would it change?

He was frustrated and rose again. He knew, pragmatically speaking, that it would change nothing. It wouldn't change Severn Handred. It wouldn't change his choices. It wouldn't justify his existence—no, that was something he himself was meant to do, for better or worse.

Yes. But even for those in the Tha'alaan, that is the truth. In small ways—or large—they find their purpose, their goals, their paths forward. Do you understand yours?

He looked up as the fountain water stopped its constant fall. It had gathered above him in an almost familiar pillar.

An'Sennarin will speak to you, if you permit it.

"I do."

CHAPTER TWELVE

I OFFER APOLOGIES FOR THE METHOD OF COMMUNICATION. *I have taken a walk, and I sit on a rocky outcropping; the ocean is fierce today; the clouds gather above. Adellos is almost beside himself with worry.* This last was said with amusement.

If he's worried for me, he wastes his time. I would have come to the West March even had you argued against it.

Ah, no. He is worried for me. The ocean water is wild and untamed, and it is difficult to find the parts of the water that listen. In the West March, the water does listen—but it cannot speak to most of my kin.

Why can it speak to me?

I do not know. The water believes it is because I can speak to you and have spoken to you; you have touched the Tha'alaan.

You don't believe that.

It makes sense to me, but I am not a scholar; I have not tested or confirmed. I...do not know, but Adellos feels you are different.

Different?

Yes. Mortal, as we are not, but...closer to our kin than your own in some fashion. You surprised him.

I don't think I surprised Ybelline.

I do not know. She has never spoken to me the way Adellos does—I don't believe she can.

She knows your name.

Yes. And I believe Adellos's fear was that you would also know it. But you have not made the attempt to bespeak me, either.

Hearing it isn't the same as speaking it.

No. It is not something I understood when I was young. There was a question in the statement.

It's what I was taught when I was young. I might hear a name spoken—but speaking it requires will and intent, and it poses a risk to me. Less of a risk than it would pose to one actually born Barrani; I have no True Name.

Your lessons were more complete than ours. Ours were simple: never, ever do this or Bad Things will happen. But...Adellos has been the truest friend I have, and he knew my name. He used it. Barrani, he added bitterly, *cannot truly be friends.*

You have Barrani friends here.

I have childhood friends there, yes—but children are not adults. I am the head of my line. I have allies, not friends.

Severn wondered if he believed that. Or if he believed that yet. His master had made that sentiment clear many, many times: people of power didn't have friends. They couldn't afford them. Severn had listened and had absorbed that truth— but it had been distant from him in his childhood, and distant in his youth as well: he was mortal, and he would never have the power of which his master spoke.

But he understood why Adellos had never abandoned An'Sennarin—and he knew that Adellos, being mortal, would become a thing of the past when old age ended its descent. Adellos would become a memory. In the Tha'alaan, what Adellos had done would be a poison; to An'Sennarin it was salvation. Yet it was the same set of actions.

Are you lonely? The same question haunted them both: Severn Handred. Ollarin. For both, the answer had once been No.

I have questions for you, Severn said, shying away from both the question and the changing nature of its answer.

I thought you might. I will answer whatever I can.

First: Do you have reason to believe Yvonne of Darrowelm is still alive?

Silence. Severn thought he would get no answer, but an answer did come. *Yes. But I am not certain that I can trust that reason; I am too entangled in the answer. I hope too much. When I proved difficult for the previous ruler, they allowed a letter to pass from Yvonne to me. In it, she spoke of things men of power would have no interest in; the handwriting was definitely hers.*

How long ago?

Twenty-three of your years.

You have not heard from her since?

No. No attempt to meet with her has been allowed. Perhaps, should I travel to the West March in person, Darrowelm would have no choice—but I am not so secure in my position that I can afford to take that risk.

I will take that risk for you.

You are not An'Sennarin.

Severn nodded, understanding the intent in the words. *What does she look like?*

An image formed behind Severn's eyes: an image of a young Barrani woman. To his surprise, her hair was a tangled mess. She had no distinguishing characteristics—she had the long, black hair of her kind, and the smooth, almost flawless skin. But her cheeks were smudged with dirt, and her eyes were a brilliant green. It was the first time Severn had wondered if the almost preternatural cleanliness and tidiness of the Barrani was a learned trait and not a natural consequence of age.

An'Sennarin laughed. *It's learned. It's learned the way mortal grooming is learned.* The laughter faded quickly. *Where are you?*

I'm in Danarre now.

…Danarre?

I don't know if you'd call it a fortress, but I came here with Elluvian.

If you meant to pass with as little notice as possible, that isn't the place you wanted to be.

Yes. It's apparently difficult to enter.

Without permission? Yes.

Is it possible?

There's no way for you to test that now—unless your companion chooses to revoke his permission.

He won't. Apparently Darrowelm has a similar stronghold.

Yes.

And Yvonne would be in that stronghold?

Yes.

Is it impossible to escape?

…I am uncertain. She could sneak out, and often did—but she wasn't considered essential to Darrowelm; she had very little power. Her parents were proud that she worked as a servant in Darrowelm, but she wasn't considered of import otherwise.

Until An'Sennarin. Severn didn't say this, but it wasn't necessary.

I'll have to test it.

No! The word was more felt than heard, and after a pause, An'Sennarin spoke again. *No. It's far too much of a risk. If you're caught, you won't survive. You must be skilled; Adellos feels you are. But no one is flawless, and first attempts often end in failure.*

Yes. Severn exhaled. He had an idea, but it wasn't one which An'Sennarin could affect. *You have two other friends in the West March; they weren't as difficult to see as Yvonne, according to An'Tellarus.*

No—to her, they wouldn't be.

Will they, or can they, help?

…I don't want them dragged into this if it can be avoided. They're more or less safe where they are, and they haven't been used against me.

Severn was an Imperial Wolf, an expendable mortal.

They will not think to tie you to me, An'Sennarin said, almost awkwardly. *You are in the greater danger—but if you are tied to any Barrani, it will be An'Tellarus or Elluvian of Danarre.*

Severn nodded. *What can you tell me about the Dreams of Alsanis?*

An'Sennarin was silent for a long moment, but it was a silence of confusion, as if the conversation had taken a turn into an almost entirely foreign language. *Alsanis is Hallionne, and his sole attempts at communication are...not entirely voluntary. The Dreams of Alsanis are great birds, and they fly and speak with his many voices. It's considered significant if you can hear them.* This last held a depth of bitterness Severn hadn't expected.

You could hear them.

I could. And I was proud that I could. The bitterness was now blended with humiliation.

I heard them.

Silence.

I heard them, Severn repeated, *and when I entered the West March, one of the great birds dropped something.* He then showed An'Sennarin the small branch with its glittering leaves.

An'Sennarin was once again silent.

You don't think it was accidental.

Not if you could hear them, no. Severn— Words trailed off. *You must not show that to any who did not see it.*

Elluvian knows.

He is an Imperial Wolf, as are you. He is the only person in the West March with whom you might safely share the information—but even then, it is not safe.

What are the shards of Tyron?

Once again, An'Sennarin fell silent; Severn could feel the hesitance that marked his words when he finally chose to speak. *They are the blades of the green, and those blades are given to the chosen champion of the green—or so the legends say. To us, even as children, they were a daydream: perhaps, one day, if we were good enough, we might be called to the green, and we might be tested there.*

Tested?

Yes. The green—as any Barrani—tests.

To what end?

To determine—or so stories say—the worthiness of the one who wishes to wield them. I have never seen those blades. Almost none of my kin have; they have remained hidden within the heart of the green for the entirety of my life. Perhaps you could ask An'Tellarus. He spoke doubtfully. *But the shards are coveted; in the West March they are more significant than The Three—those ancient weapons crafted to kill Dragons.*

Why?

Again, I do not know. We knew The Three existed; there were those, among my kin, who had even seen their use on the fields of battle, and in the skies. But the shards, we have not seen.

They weren't meant to kill Dragons.

No; they are older than that. Why do you ask?

Because the branch seems to be some part of the story of the shards of Tyron—a story, I was informed, that any child of the West March knows.

Children's stories are short on detail—but yes. In theory, such a branch means the green has invited you into its heart. In practice, there's no way to reach the green through that branch; if you have it, and you approach the Warden, it is likely that he will allow it. But he is of Avonelle, and it is also likely that An'Avonelle will accuse you of theft. If she takes the branch, or if the Warden does, it will be passed into other hands.

Severn nodded. *Could An'Tellarus be trusted with this information?*

If, as you say, the Dreams left it to you upon entry into the West March, it's highly likely she already knows. Severn...do not trust her overmuch. I trust her with the matters in which she's proven reliable, but...she is old, and the old play games to while away their endless time. It's highly likely that she had some knowledge, some sense, that the time was coming when the green might seek a wielder for the shards.

If the shards have remained hidden all this time, how could she possibly know that they might come to me?

Exactly. But I think it can't be a coincidence. If the Dreams and the green are acting in concert, they meant for you to have this…as if they were waiting. An'Tellarus is not a child of Elantra, but of the West March. She was young when Alsanis wasn't a prison. She has seen the shards in use before, one of the few who will remember it. The shards were meant to be an honor conveyed by the green, and the green is the heart of the West March.

Then why would she think I would have anything to do with them?

It made no sense, but the facts aligned in such a way it was almost impossible to believe it was coincidence. Severn's master had taught him much about the Barrani and their ways—but much of what he'd also taught was relevant to the West March, not the High Halls. Having taught, he then abandoned his student in the heart of the fiefs.

Severn had always wondered why but had assumed that it was because Severn had chosen Elianne and her mother, had chosen a mortal life, not the Barrani life for which he'd theoretically been prepared. Now? He felt he understood far less than he had on the day An'Tellarus had made her offer.

Who was the last person to wield the shards of Tyron?

I…do not know. I know of the first, but he is story and legend; there are none now who were alive when he was alive. But I do know that many have made the attempt to retrieve those weapons, as if those weapons would be their truest crown. There are, no doubt, ambitious people who are, even now, making that attempt. Do you want them?

Why would I? They're Barrani weapons.

An'Sennarin's smile was complicated. *Mortals fear us*, he said, *because we have power. And mortals ally with us because we*

*have power. Power, in the end, is a tool—but it is also a mantle. I
have power, now.*

Power, Severn replied, *hasn't freed Yvonne, if she still lives.*

*That is because my enemies also have power. If I had power
greater than theirs, she would be free. I did not want this power. I
took it because it was the only way to stop the Tha'alani murders
from destroying the Tha'alaan. But now that I have it, I find I cannot simply walk away; it has become something that I must both husband and protect. I do not want it to fall into the wrong hands again.*

No.

*But…were it not for your interference, in the end, the cost to the
Tha'alani—and Adellos—would have been much higher. You faced
the Dragon in his den. Because you are what you are, the Dragon
listened. Adellos and I have talked for hours about the nature of power
and responsibility; Adellos believes it is impossible to retain power for
a long time without being changed by that power. He gives himself
as an example. Sometimes, it's our inability, our natural weakness,
that prevents us from making the wrong choices, choices we would
not make if not for fury or fear.*

I understand his choices, Severn replied. *I do not fault him for
them.*

He almost killed you.

*Yes—but I understand why. I'm happy that he failed, of course.
If he feels guilt, he shouldn't.*

*His guilt is his to bear, as mine is mine. But the point I was
trying to make is this: he could do what he did because he has the
power to do it. That same power ended the life of my former master.
Neither he nor I regret that.*

Severn didn't, either.

*The shards of Tyron are powerful weapons. They are also sym-
bolic weapons. I do not know if they are simple blades that respond
to the power of their wielder, because no one knows. But Adellos
suggested that perhaps it's not the* power *of the wielder to which
they respond, but the wielder themself.*

Adellos may be many things, but an expert in Barrani artifacts isn't one of them.

An'Sennarin laughed. *No. He says an external view is sometimes useful when all known information is questionable. And he adds that the Barrani almost consider power a sacrament, suggesting that the lack of any wielders in the last several centuries might support his view. But beyond sounding pinched and annoyed, I believe he is now truly worried.*

You said he was worried before.

Yes, that's what I thought. But...this is deeper, and darker. Dark enough that he has withdrawn entirely from me while I have this conversation.

He's afraid you'll hear the darker thoughts. Severn thought this ridiculous, given An'Sennarin's life to date and in the foreseeable future.

An'Sennarin thought it ridiculous, as well, but it reminded him that Adellos was Tha'alani, and he treasured that. Severn understood why.

Yes. I cannot give you more information about the shards. Adellos suggested that the early and far more martial memories contained in the Tha'alaan have no information to offer, either. What I can tell you is this: if, for some reason, An'Tellarus intended for you to enter the green, it means she is willing to accept your death. She can't possibly believe that you would somehow retrieve the weapon and return it to her; she therefore means for you to take it.

That's not why I followed her here.

No, but that will be irrelevant to An'Tellarus. If she means for you to somehow take the shards, she no doubt wishes to prevent someone else from taking it. Perhaps she chose the timing of her visit for that reason and no other. I don't know if she will give you information if she hasn't mentioned anything so far, but in order to navigate the West March as safely as you can it's information you should attempt to obtain.

I need to know who wants the weapon.

Everyone who could possibly wield it would want the weapon; you

*need to find out who is going to make a serious attempt. And that…
will involve the green, the Warden, and—I am sorry—An'Avonelle.*

Darrowelm?

Darrowelm supports An'Avonelle, but the support is subtle; Darrowelm has long chosen to remain in the background. If An'Tellarus is willing to play her games more publicly, information will come from that—but that is when you will be in the most danger from my kin. I must go; I will be missed soon. If it is possible, I will reach out to you again. I believe Adellos is now attempting to gain more information from other sources. Those sources will not be Barrani in nature, he added, almost wryly.

Severn, the water said, when An'Sennarin's voice had fallen silent. *There are things you must do for Ollarin while you are here. Where I can, I will help.*

He nodded.

Severn was dressed and ready when Elluvian came to find him. The Barrani Wolf's eyes were blue, and his hands, balled in fists, were white-knuckled. Severn waited for Elluvian to speak. Elluvian, however, was grimly silent. For the first time, Severn wished Helmat were with them.

"Was our absence noted?"

"It was."

"An'Tellarus?"

"They wouldn't dare to raise sword against An'Tellarus. She was most displeased, and they cannot afford to anger her further. They might not survive angering her to the extent they already have."

"Who were they?"

"They serve the Warden of the green, in theory; they're the rough equivalent of the Elantran Swords. But they're not Swords, and they're not beholden in the same way to the law, such as it is."

"Who do they serve in practice, not theory?"

Elluvian forced his hands to relax; it took time and obvious effort. "That is less clear. I believe fully half serve An'Avonelle, mother of the Warden."

"Then they aren't normally present when the gates open?"

"Not in those numbers, no. Clearly An'Tellarus hasn't been particularly secretive in her travel plans." He exhaled. "And to be fair, which takes effort at the moment, the Dreams of Alsanis have been very active, and such activity has often presaged...difficulty in the West March."

"Difficulty?"

"Yes. There's a reason the West March was built to stand in this place. It's home to the green, and it's the green it must protect. During the last great war, the Barrani and Dragons fought; that is common knowledge. What is less commonly spoken of is the role played by Shadow."

Severn stilled.

"*Ravellon* is not the only place where Shadow rose to threaten the living; there were other dells and glens in which Shadow, escaping from *Ravellon*, made its home. The effects of that Shadow are still felt in the West March; with luck you won't see them." He waited for questions; when Severn asked none, he continued. "There are times in the past when Alsanis wasn't a prison, and in those times, when Shadow sought to infiltrate the West March, he carried warning to the Warden and families of note.

"He can't do that now. But his dreams have served as warning since he sealed his doors. Even if we can't hear the Dreams themselves, we can see their numbers grow. They're dark, now—things of storm and shadow that fill the sky periodically, as if struggling to find freedom."

"Can they fight?"

"Pardon?"

"Can they attack?"

It was clearly not the question Elluvian had been expecting. His eye color couldn't get darker, but his eyes changed shape as he considered the question. "They can," he finally replied, with uncharacteristic hesitance. "And have been known to do so from time to time—but very rarely. They are birds in form, only."

"They can clearly affect physical things. They dropped the branch." He left the branch in his interior pocket.

"That wouldn't be considered complete proof of your claim."

"It's a physical object."

"It's tied to the green, and the green has some roots in the Hallionne. When Alsanis was forced to close his doors permanently, he attempted to sever those roots—but the green is older than the Hallionne, and not even Alsanis could extricate the green from himself. The green and Alsanis remain connected. The branch that you carry is from the green, and it was likely given to the Dreams because the Dreams are not trapped in the same way Alsanis is, and they have full freedom of skies the green cannot reach.

"I don't hear the Dreams of Alsanis; almost none of us can. But you did, and that will be noted unless An'Tellarus makes certain those who understood what occurred are dead."

Severn exhaled. "I'd prefer she didn't."

"I'm sure they'd prefer she didn't as well. But they were there for a reason, and that reason wasn't service to An'Tellarus. If I had known, I would have done all in my power to forbid this pilgrimage. The Emperor will forgive your death as a natural consequence of the choice you made in ignorance. Helmat, however, will not."

"I have reasons for making the choice I did—and I imagine An'Tellarus's purpose won't be served if I spend all of my time in your home."

"I have reasons for journeying with you, and I assure you that *my* purpose will be best served if you remain here."

"Will your purpose have more weight than my own?" Severn's voice was soft.

"What do you think?"

"You'll be loyal to the Emperor's will, even if we're not in the Empire."

Elluvian's brows rose. Severn had startled a laugh out of him, even if it was short and tinged with outrage. "You will, of course, avoid uttering such sentiments where any other ears can hear them. You're not what I expected when I first found you in the streets, tailing An'Teela. You are not what I expected, having found young men and women for the Imperial Wolves before. No, I will not imprison you here; I'm almost certain I would be forced to kill you or injure you badly enough you couldn't move.

"If I were to detain you, I would have to face An'Tellarus myself. She is…irritable and annoyed when she's in my presence, but she's never been enraged; I would be unlikely to survive it."

"Is she waiting for me to join her?"

"What do you think?"

"She's waiting."

"Impatiently. At the moment, her ire at the guards must be seen to, but that won't cost her more than a day or two."

"Is the Tellarus home as secure as this one?"

"I note you fail to mention my family name."

"You don't seem to appreciate the name."

"No, I do not. But this building is both more and less secure than Tellarus. Although it's active, there are very few servants and guards. If we were breached, we couldn't mount a proper defense. But if we had more people, there would be gaps in security as they both left and arrived. She has more people."

"If her method of entry is like yours, the gaps won't be significant."

"No. And if you could exploit those gaps to enter, you wouldn't remain undetected."

"Could you?"

"I have permission to enter; she has withdrawn it only

twice in utter disgust but reinstated that permission when she commanded my presence. I could exploit those gaps. I am recognized by Tellarus. You, however, are not."

"Have you ever tried?"

Elluvian stilled. "What are you actually asking?"

"I want to try sneaking into Tellarus."

"Instead of using the door as her guest?"

"It's...a possible proof of concept. I want to attempt to enter, undetected; if I'm detected, she won't kill me. Probably. It's the only way I can experiment."

"I could throw you out, and you could attempt to reenter."

"There are very few people here; Tellarus is a better test case."

Elluvian's eyes narrowed, but the blue had lightened enough they no longer looked black at a distance. "If you fail?"

Severn shrugged. "I fail. I can assess the reasons for failure and make a more informed decision at that time."

"This isn't about Tellarus. You want to enter Darrowelm."

Severn nodded. "If this building were like a Hallionne, it would be impossible; I'd have to resort to different tactics to gain entry."

"Such as?"

"Offering information about Tellarus to Darrowelm."

"That, An'Tellarus would kill you for."

"Yes, if the information were true."

Elluvian exhaled. "Don't let your brief acquaintance with An'Sennarin become your burden or your doom. His current course is prudent: he gathers and solidifies his power. If he cannot demand entry to Darrowelm yet, the time is coming when he can't be so easily ignored."

Severn shook his head. "Yvonne can still be used against him. I'm almost certain it's already happening."

"It's the reason the young are seldom rulers: they haven't shed the sentiment and hope that defines childhood. The young take risks. If they survive those risks, they develop scars, they harden themselves, and they emerge as contenders. Or," he added softly, "they die. An'Sennarin was far too young to take his family's throne; he is still too weak to endure the cost of power.

"But if he survives, he will become what he's expected to become. And when he does, he won't care about Yvonne, except perhaps on darker days when nostalgia is overwhelming. Do not involve yourself in purely Barrani affairs."

Severn nodded. "I wish to attempt to enter Tellarus in secret," he said, as if Elluvian hadn't spoken at all.

"Very well."

CHAPTER THIRTEEN

ELLUVIAN'S RESERVATIONS WEREN'T SUBTLE. THEY weren't silent. He made one attempt to pull rank, but Severn shut it down; he was unfailingly polite and reasonable but wouldn't budge.

In the Halls of Law, Wolves were the only branch that often operated without backup. Severn had no partner with which to patrol the city. Elluvian came closest because Elluvian continued to supervise many elements of Severn's training, just as he had done for every Wolf. When the Wolves graduated from Elluvian's training, they were left to navigate the duties assigned them on their own.

Severn had not, in Elluvian's estimation, progressed far enough to be called a graduate. He made this clear.

Severn nodded. "I value your lessons and your opinion," he said. "But Mellianne has graduated, and we're evenly matched." He waited for objections; none were forthcoming. Elluvian was Barrani; he could no doubt lie with ease. But he took his duties to the Wolves seriously. He wouldn't argue a point that was demonstrably false. "Were we in Elantra, you would, of course, accompany me.

"Here, your movements are heavily watched and scrutinized; if you accompany me, the possibility that I'm actually an Imperial Wolf will arise." Severn spoke crisp High Barrani.

"You will require a guide. You have no knowledge of the geography of the West March. It is unlike Elantra in almost all particulars. The best option would be to have An'Tellarus accompany you. It will not prevent suspicion, but she is so random in her actions, it will cause less of it."

"I do not require a guide; I do require a map. Are Records used in your halls?"

"Not as such, no." Elluvian exhaled. "Maps do exist, but geography changes, given the season of the year and the passage of time. You will not be in danger in the streets of the West March if you have An'Tellarus as company."

"I intend to meet her."

"You will have to reach Tellarus to, as you put it, meet her. There is some separation between our homes, and the road from here to there might be patrolled."

"New patrols?"

"Of course. It is possible that the whole of the West March is now being patrolled by the guards of the Warden."

"The ones you think report to Avonelle."

"Directly or indirectly, yes."

"How common is magic in the West March?"

"If you mean its practice, it is more common here than it is in Elantra; in Elantra, the streets are largely occupied by mortals, most of whom evince no magical ability. Here, low-level magic is often used, but this will cause you no difficulty. You might not even be aware of the spells."

"Offensive magic?"

"Also rare. Here, the Barrani of the West March prefer to use the more practical and readily accessible swords."

Severn could disguise himself more than competently— but none of those disguises would allow him to pass as Bar-

rani. Barrani armor was light and flexible in comparison to
the varying levels of armor used in the Halls of Law. As full
armor—with helm—was Severn's only hope of walking the
streets as if he belonged there, he discarded the idea.

"I want to check something," he finally said, when Elluvian had failed to move out of the only exit. He turned on
heel and headed to the stairs, taking them two at a time. He
followed them all the way up to their natural ending, which
was a wooden platform. There was no safety rail, but the
outer edges of the platform curved up; it reminded Severn
of a flat bowl.

He felt wind, here; it moved through his hair and across
his cheeks, surprisingly chill in its touch. He then looked out.

Elluvian had followed, frowning. He joined Severn on
the platform.

"That's Tellarus, right?" Severn asked, in Elantran.

"Yes."

"That's Avonelle."

"Indeed."

"And that one is Darrowelm?"

"Yes. I fail to see why you ask. You are not going to leap
from here to a similar lookout in Darrowelm."

"No."

Elluvian grimaced. "That was intemperate. Why did you
ask?"

"I want to compare the geography on the ground to the
geography I see here."

"To what end?"

The question made almost no sense to Severn. This must
have shown, because Elluvian exhaled, audibly and deliberately.

"The tree to which you dragged me when we gained entrance to this city was one of many. It's not nearly physically
large enough to *be* what it looks like once you enter the door
it contains. None of the trees that we passed were."

"You never fail to surprise me," was the dry response. "Do continue."

"But upon entry, I was informed that this building was not a Hallionne; that its dimensions were not fully extensible at whim. It's…a giant tree-home." Severn's turn to grimace. "I had the sense—and this could be entirely wrong—that this particular tree has grown into this particular home; they're almost one thing."

"That's an extremely simple way of describing something more complicated, but yes."

"What I see from here are similar trees."

"Yes."

"They occupy the same space."

Elluvian frowned.

"What I don't see—from here—is the West March itself."

"Ah. I believe I see your difficulty. You've been taught much about our kin and our customs, but clearly not all. These homes exist in a forest of their own; the roots overlap what you would consider reality. If you look to the north, you will see trees of similar height and shape to the one you now occupy. Those are fallow; they are, and have remained, unclaimed."

"Were they always empty?"

"Who can say, now? But the way into them has been lost by the descendants of those who once occupied them."

"Fair enough."

"What do you want to know?"

"I want to know how to get into the forest I can see from here. I don't understand how that forest works."

"It is said—and this is hearsay, not the word of a heavily invested scholar—that these trees, as you correctly call them, have roots in the green. The soil they touch is the earth of the green itself. The green *is* a space similar to a Hallionne, although there's no central intelligence that we can perceive. The dimensions of the green, from the interior, don't match the dimensions of the West March. The green itself—when it's open to us— is expansive in a way the towns of the West March are not."

"You've never tried."

"I? No. But it has been tried before, admittedly never to my knowledge from this height. Those who seek the forest and find it can often claim such a home for themselves. But they did not approach from a claimed home. I believe they explored the green. Some never returned."

"They were lost in the green?"

"Or to it, yes. The green gives, but as any power, it is to be treated with respect and care. My kin can, from time to time, forget that."

"And the others—the ones who did return?"

"They didn't find what they sought." He paused and then added, "they felt they had been away for weeks—but years had passed in the interim. The green," he said, repeating the words in a different tone, "is as close to the Ancient as you will find in this world. That is my belief.

"And we were taught, frequently, not to—"

"Anger the Ancients." Severn finished the commandment with a wry smile.

"One who can control the green would be a power impossible to reckon with."

Severn nodded. "My master didn't speak of any attempt to control the green."

"No; he sounds wise, and the very concept would be considered profane by the wise. It is perhaps something I should not have said aloud while standing here."

"Do you think the green cares?" It was an honest question.

"No. I would be surprised were I to be told that the green listens to most of us."

"The green hears the Warden."

"The green hears the Warden—but I'm uncertain that what it hears is speech. There are rituals and sacraments that the Warden offers the green, but those are private, not public. They might not seem practical to you or I, but they are the way in which a Warden proclaims his presence. He is, in some fashion, heard.

"But he doesn't command the green. He beseeches. Were it not for the fact that the Warden is the gatekeeper, it would not be an enviable position; men of power do not plead or beg. It is his permission you will require should you have cause to enter the green. The Warden is Barrani, and persuasion of the more natural kind will work. Threats might, but no wise man threatens the Warden while the Warden is within the West March."

Severn assumed that those lacking wisdom had tried it before, but it was irrelevant; he would never be in a position to threaten the Warden for entry into the green.

"Perhaps you might allow An'Tellarus to speak with An'Darrowelm before you attempt what you mean to attempt."

Severn shook his head. "If I can avoid that, I will—I don't want to give them any chance to prepare. But...I want to see the interior of Tellarus before I make an attempt to breach Darrowelm."

"Your grasp exceeds your reach, private."

Severn's smile was sharp and brief. "So I've been told."

Elluvian spent the next day by Severn's side. Severn chose to visit each of the platforms that grew out from the trunk of the tree—one of them his designated room. The lower platforms had less of a view. Beyond the edges, he could see the trunks of regular trees; a glimpse of Tellarus came into view only through the gaps between those trunks. The distance was far too great to cover by jumping, but Severn had already given up on that as an option.

Instead, he measured the distance to the forest floor.

"Have you ever pushed someone off a platform?"

"No. Not that the possibility wasn't tempting, but the only person to visit who might enrage me enough was An'Tellarus."

"It seems like an ideal place for a murder, though—invite your victim in, push them off a platform, and lose their body in a forest that no one can search."

"A sound theory," Elluvian replied, in a tone that implied he was about to correct it. "But the dead do not remain within. Dead, the bodies are returned to the West March. It is true that the damage done would be the falling damage, if the person pushed was not powerful enough to prevent that death."

"If they were, they wouldn't find themselves in the forest. I assume that's also been tested."

Elluvian's smile held more amusement and lasted longer. "Yes."

"I find it hard to believe that Barrani children don't make the attempt."

"Falling from the greatest heights would be their deaths. Falling from the lower heights would cause injury. Yes, I am certain some of us were foolish enough to try in our scattered youths—who among us didn't daydream of finding homes of our own from which we could found new familial lines?

"If your plan involves entry into this forest, you will need to develop a new one. But please do it quickly. An'Tellarus has sent two angry messages via her servants; I believe she'll be patient enough to vent her spleen in a third. Instead of a fourth, she will arrive in person, and if Barrani do not breathe fire as our ancient enemies do, she will certainly make the attempt."

Elluvian was wrong.

An'Tellarus didn't have the patience to send another message. She arrived in Danarre in person. She had clearly been given permission to enter Danarre at one point or another, and Elluvian hadn't considered it smart to revoke it. She therefore found Severn while he was lying across the ground, his face over the edge of a platform, his eyes narrowed.

The forest was quiet, and in the end, that quiet caught and held his attention. He could hear wind through branches but couldn't hear birdsong or the drone of insects. Both had been prevalent in the overland leg of their journey. He was accustomed to the noise of a city and had found the forest's silence the most intimidating thing about it—but that silence was full of quiet sounds. This forest was not.

"What are you doing?"

Severn glanced up, saw An'Tellarus's pinched expression, and abandoned his prone position in one swift, graceful motion. He then tendered her a perfect bow. As a gesture, it provided a brief escape from her glare.

Elluvian wasn't by An'Tellarus's side, although she wasn't alone; she was accompanied by two guards who stood at a respectful distance. Her clothing wasn't travel clothing. It was also far more ornate than the clothing she'd worn when she resided in the High Halls. In particular the collar, which rose stiffly around her neck and toward her head as if it aspired to become a crown.

"I asked you a question."

"I was looking at the distance between this platform and the nearest tree."

"Why?"

"Not all of the trees in this forest are homes. Many are not. I've been told botanists won't be able to answer questions about why—but at this height, the normal trees are closer. Elluvian expected you tomorrow."

"That boy doesn't have the sense he was born with." She spoke in very clipped Elantran.

"I would have attempted to find you, but Elluvian considered it unwise," Severn replied, in High Barrani.

"Then he's not entirely brainless. He could, however, have sent word."

"He thought you might be attending to the problem with the guards that greeted us; he didn't wish to intrude."

She snorted. "I hope you don't actually believe a word of that drivel."

"I do, actually. It might not have been the entirety of his reasoning, but from my view, it's reasonable."

"Nothing that child does is reasonable."

"Am I to attend you, today?"

"Not dressed like that, you aren't."

Severn bowed again. "If you will give me a moment, I will change."

A moment drifted into ten, twenty, thirty; at that point, Severn ceased to keep count. He could hear the raised voices of two Barrani, and he recognized both of them: An'Tellarus and Elluvian.

It was Eldanis who came to retrieve Severn from his room.

"How long will their discussion last?"

"To call it a discussion is charitable," Eldanis replied. "They might argue until the sun begins to set, but the argument won't end; they'll simply retreat and wait for the right timing to begin it again. Why do you ask?"

"If I have a couple of hours, I'd like to try something. Do you have rope?"

"Pardon?"

"Rope. Not twine, but actual rope."

"Yes, although it is not a supply in heavy demand."

"Would it be all right for me to use it?"

"To what end?"

"To test a theory."

"I would advise you to be very careful of such tests at the moment." It wasn't a no. Eldanis's eyes were blue, but given the argument in progress, Severn was surprised they weren't darker. "Considering An'Tellarus's current mood, I would also advise that you wait, if that is possible. When she has reached the limit of her patience, she will leave—and she will expect all of her entourage to be ready to leave in that same instant.

"If you are anything like the children this house once held, the estimation of time for the results of your experiment may be wildly optimistic; if you are not ready when An'Tellarus wishes to leave, your absence will be noted. I will, however, bring a large coil of rope and leave it in the guest room for your later use."

Over an hour later, An'Tellarus stormed down the stairs. Severn was waiting by the door; he offered her a silent bow, and followed immediately behind her when she failed to acknowledge it. Her two guards deliberately left room for Severn; if they disapproved of the presence of a mortal, no sign of it showed on their faces.

"I loathe that place," An'Tellarus said, when their feet touched the footpaths that encircled the entrance of Danarre. To Severn's eye, it was a tree; when he looked up, it had branches, not platforms.

Severn failed to ask why. He failed to ask anything, although he did sweep dust off the small train of her dress. She accepted this as if it was to be expected. Severn would have to thank Eldanis later.

His intent to attempt to sneak into Tellarus didn't survive An'Tellarus's august displeasure; she left no room for any questions, let alone possible favors. As he'd so often done in the past, Severn went with the flow of the figurative river, especially when the currents were raging. He had no time to admire An'Tellarus, and no other chance to personally attend her; he served as an unusual adornment.

She made no attempt to proceed as if she owned the streets and merely condescended to walk them, which was what he'd expected. Then again, she had no need. The streets were very sparsely populated. None of the people brave enough to remain in them made any attempt to interact with An'Tellarus. Severn wouldn't have, either, had he the choice.

"We have a meeting to attend," she finally said, when the storm of her rage began to pass. "It will be held, for the moment, in Tellarus. We have an invitation to visit Avonelle, and I wish to accept it. I have words for its master."

Yes, the opportunity had been lost for the moment, but when the river met a standing rock, the water flowed around it. If he couldn't use Tellarus as practice, he could use the information he would receive from his visit.

Tellarus was very similar to Danarre on the interior. The entrance vestibule was elegant, the walls were more intricately carved with leaves and vines. The leaves were adorned with emeralds and sapphires. Those gems shed light; the interior of the entry wasn't nearly as dark as Danarre's had been. But Danarre wasn't open to guests or visitors; there was no one Elluvian felt the need to impress.

Leaving the entryway, Severn entered a room that was as round as the room which contained Danarre's slender stairs; similar stairs wound around the trunk of a tree from which platforms grew.

"What are you studying?"

"Architecture," Severn replied. "Eldanis said these homes grow, and I'd wondered how similar—or different—the two homes might be."

"And?"

"They're similar—at least so far. Do you also have the fountain?"

"No, sadly. The fountain, as you call it, is one of Danarre's features."

"Do you have no water, then?"

"We have no fountain. Water is captured through rainfall and redirected to where it is needed."

"Does Darrowelm have a fountain?"

"Yes. Darrowelm is old. Avonelle does not, but you will find a fountain of similar construction in the home of the Warden. The home of the Warden," she added, "is always occupied by the current Warden; it is not a property that is passed down through a specific family." She exhaled. "We have some time before we are to meet our guest. I would have you explain what happened when the gates to the West March flowed open before the guest arrives."

Severn considered his options, and he considered the woman who stood before him. Elluvian and Eldanis had been insistent that he remain silent about the Dreams and their odd gift, and in other circumstances, Severn would have agreed. But An'Tellarus was her own circumstance; he would have bet any amount he owned that she had seen what the Dreams had done.

And that she had seen the water.

"Are we to meet the guest here?"

"No. Follow me. When the guest arrives, they will be led to where we will meet." She turned and headed toward the stairs, and he followed her like a living shadow until she reached her destination.

There were chairs on this platform, and a long, low table that seemed to have grown out of the same wood upon which it stood. But here, too, there were carvings around the edge of the platform, and vines that grew—or fell—from above. Here, there were birds as well. Birds, not the dreams of an isolated demi-god.

To his surprise, An'Tellarus indicated a chair with the brief nod of chin. "I am here as your servant," he began.

Her eyes narrowed instantly. He sat.

"You were seen with Elluvian. I understand why he felt the need to leave, but it would have been better had you

remained; you are now tied to the most troublesome denizen of the West March. I will therefore have you attend me
closely for the next several days to attempt to quell rumors
that have already begun to circulate." Her eyes were indigo.
"You should, however, feel honored; it is the first time Elluvian has condescended to bring guests to his ancestral home
in centuries."

"The Dragon Flights destroyed most of his family?"
Severn asked.

"The *Emperor* destroyed them." And Elluvian served the
Emperor. "I see by your expression you now understand why
his service and loyalty are viewed so harshly. It is why your
association will fall under immediate suspicion; it is well-
known that the Emperor employs mortals for any roles of
note. And it is known that Wolves do not curtail their hunts
when their quarry flee the Empire."

Severn nodded.

"I could *strangle* him."

"He was afraid that my interactions with the water had
been noted."

"The water?"

"And the Dreams."

"It is a fair concern; I am certain both were noted. The
timing was impeccable—if one wanted to make certain you
leave the West March as a corpse."

"Elluvian was not responsible for either the water or the
Dreams."

"No—but he reacted in panic instead of actually using
his brain." Severn had begun to understand that An'Tellarus
used Elantran when she was in a foul mood. Insults existed
in High Barrani, of course—but the insults were subtle and
took time to properly construct. "I noted the opening of the
gates was...unusual. And I noted the Dream of Alsanis; at
the time I was grateful that there was only one such bird."

Severn nodded; there had been several on the portal path.

"You could hear the Dream."

Severn nodded again.

"You could hear the water."

"I am not Barrani."

"I'm not certain that doesn't make it worse." She lifted a hand. "You will show me what the Dream dropped. Now."

She had, as suspected, noticed that as well. He reached into his shirt pocket and removed the branch.

Her eyes were an odd blend of colors: green, purple, blue, and a brilliant gold. In the chaos of emotion so unusual in the Barrani, she failed to immediately find words. But wordless, she held out a hand, and he placed the branch across her palm. He was almost mortified when the edge of one of the leaves cut her.

"Are you surprised?" When Severn failed to answer—there was so much to find surprising—she added, "That our blood is the same color as yours." The cut was, to her, insignificant. "It was my fault. The cut is a simple warning: I am not to grasp and hold what was not offered directly to me."

The leaves had not reacted that way to either Eldanis or Elluvian, and An'Tellarus had not, to Severn's eye, held the small branch any differently than either of them.

"It has been long since I have seen such a branch." Her voice was soft. "A long time, and in the end it came to heartbreak and loss." She had reverted to High Barrani, and now stared at the leaves that lay flat against her palm; there was something almost musical in the tone of the words she spoke. "But the branch did not become a tree, in the end. Greed, ambition, and power destroyed even the hope of a sapling.

"Have I spoken to you of my sister?"

She had. But he thought she needed to speak, and said, "A little—but I am mortal, An'Tellarus; our memory is not your memory."

"No. I understand that intellectually; it is hard to understand it viscerally."

"Did you last see such a branch when your sister still lived?"

"You are perceptive. Yes. Yes, I saw it then. I resented her less by that point than I had for much of our childhood—and I bitterly regret the entirety of that resentment now. So many years wasted in pointless feelings of inadequacy, I failed to make memories that might have otherwise sustained me."

He frowned as she spoke. "Tell me about her."

Her black brows rose, gold ringing blue irises. When she smiled, the smile didn't suit her face or her clothing; there was nothing martial about it. "I told you there is only one Barrani I have ever met who reminds me of my sister; you are unlikely to ever meet her. She is the only daughter born to the High Lord and his Consort, and her hair is white. She is considered too soft, too...young."

"Not by you."

Her smile deepened. "No, not by me. But I made that mistake to great cost in the past, and I will never make it again. Strength, to our kin, is defined martially, as you must know. It is our ability to kill—when necessary—that makes us powerful, because to the High Lord and his supporters, fear is power. No one feared my sister. Ah, no, that is an exaggeration.

"Almost no one feared her. She was that rare heir who might have ruled through foundations of love and loyalty. She was not without power, mind; she was not without magic. I am considered personally powerful, but even were I not, I would be powerful regardless, for I rule Tellarus.

"I was not the heir while she lived. I would never have been made heir. And in my bitter, distant youth, I did not understand the why. Why was she *loved*? Why was she honored? She was not significantly better at anything than I was, and poorer at wielding a sword. I could not ask, of course, and perhaps that is why the feelings grew so deep: they had to be hidden. To feel at all was a sign of weakness.

"And yet…she felt, openly; she displayed joy and delight, as if she were still a child and destined to remain so. I wish I had spoken of the things I feared long ago. I couldn't." She shook her head as if to clear it, and her eyes returned to a purple shade. Severn thought she might cry and hoped she wouldn't. If she were sentimental, that would be embarrassing enough. But tears? He wasn't sure he'd survive the witnessing of them.

"What I wanted—what I thought I wanted—she had. She had everything. It is our way: all things are given to the heir, the person who will lead and husband Tellarus into the future. She did not fight for the things she received, not as I, lesser in all ways, was forced to fight; nor did she struggle as I struggled to achieve what I achieved." She smiled, purple still the predominant color in her eyes. "I hated her.

"I hated her, and I loved her; I wanted her to disappear, and I wanted to be able to see her. I could not help but admire her, and I resented her for it. Do you understand?"

"I've never felt that way about anyone."

"I felt it consistently about many people in my youth; fewer as I aged. I found no freedom within myself until I did not, and could not, feel it at all. I did not understand, in the midst of my sorrow and longing, that she, too, might have been lonely; that what she was given was a burden she had no desire to carry. She could not easily put it down—which of us could, who were meant to be the future of our entire line?"

"You miss her."

"Every day, Severn. Every day since—"

"Enough. Enough, Cediela."

Severn turned instantly at the sound of the voice, the conversation shattered by simple words. He rose; An'Tellarus did not. The man who had spoken was not the Lord of the West March, the only other person who had called An'Tellarus by name; he lacked the odd gravitas of one who ruled such a domain.

His hair was the black of the Barrani, his eyes the natural blue, although they, too, seemed to shade into the purple of Barrani grief. He wore robes the color of his eyes; his hair was bound in a single braid, his boots dusty, as if from long travel, although the robes themselves showed no sign of it. The hilt of a sword could be seen beneath the cloak he wore.

"Master," Severn said, the word barely louder than a whisper.

CHAPTER FOURTEEN

"WELL MET," THE MAN SAID. TO SEVERN'S SURPRISE, he bent fully, offering Severn—not An'Tellarus—a bow. It was not the bow of inferior to superior; it was a gesture of acknowledgment.

"I see you have already met Verranian," An'Tellarus said. Grief had receded from her tone; her eyes, as they rested briefly on Severn's expression, were once again blue. She didn't seem to be surprised.

"You have grown much since we last met." Verranian's voice was soft. "But you are still considered young among your own kin." He gestured, as if he were the lord here, and not An'Tellarus; Severn once again sat. He folded his hands carefully across the arms of his chair, allowing his expression to settle into Barrani neutrality.

"I am considered young among my own kin, yes."

"And you do not care."

"I understand how to navigate it. It is otherwise irrelevant."

Verranian's eyes shaded now to green, although blue remained the dominant color. "Did you follow Cediela to the West March?"

Severn nodded.

"How did she find you?"

An'Tellarus lifted a hand before Severn could reply. "It is not necessary that you know."

"Ah. But I did not ask you."

"You are in Tellarus, Verranian. Some respect is due— although you have never been known to abide by the rules that govern most of us."

"I would say I have done so better than you."

"That," she replied, almost echoing Severn, "is irrelevant. Here, while your opinion—when sought—is of value, I am Tellarus."

"What do you think of her?" Verranian asked. He asked it of Severn, as if An'Tellarus wasn't actually present.

"She is An'Tellarus."

His master smiled then. "She is. She is what she was not meant to be—but had she been chosen centuries past, we would not now be where we are. I counseled against the previous choice made."

His comment clearly surprised An'Tellarus. It also annoyed her. "Who were you to offer counsel to An'Tellarus? Who were you to interfere in the inheritance matters of a clan of which you have never been part?"

"Verranian," he replied, his voice and expression almost serene. "But Leveanne agreed with me, even then."

"Enough." An'Tellarus rose. "You petitioned me for this appointment."

"And you granted it for a reason."

"Perhaps, but not this reason."

"You spoke of her yourself; I could hear the song of your words before I placed foot upon the stairs. Can you not hear it, in the leaves and the branches? Even the wind now whispers her name."

"I cannot hear any such thing, as you are well aware; I have no way of ascertaining the truth—or the lie—in your statement. I feel that anyone who believes I am chaos incarnate has never had the misfortune of dealing with you. You are in the West March from which you are often absent, and you have arrived at this time. What do you intend?"

Severn could hear the wind; it wasn't a voice. But in Tellarus he could hear what he hadn't heard in Danarre: birdsong. He listened in the brittle silence that followed what was only barely a question, there was so much suspicion in it. Birdsong? No.

No, he thought; it was unlike the sounds of the overland forests; unlike the cries of the gulls that littered Elantra's harbor or the crows that perched on buildings in the city streets. He heard a name, yes.

It was not Leveanne.

"An'Tellarus, perhaps I should—" he began.

"No. The conversation I have with your *former* master I will have because you are here; it would defeat the purpose to allow you to absent yourself. And surely you wish to hear the explanation he is willing to offer, however meager it will be."

But he found it hard to hear her words as the voices of birds grew in volume—and in proximity. He couldn't rise, couldn't leave his seat, without An'Tellarus's permission; he understood that. But he understood, as well, that there were no windows or walls here. The vines that trailed down in the outline of walls were decorative, not functional.

He turned his face toward them, regardless, because he could now see the moving span of great wings; one bird. Ah, no. There was a second. And neither were birds in any true sense, but here their outlines were solid; he could see the sheen of feathers as they approached the platform; could see the glint of claws as they tore through the vines.

It was absurd to think that An'Tellarus wouldn't be pleased

by the destruction, but sometimes thoughts were absurd, and that was the first one that occurred as he sat almost immobile.

The Dreams of Alsanis pierced what little nod to privacy existed. Severn lifted both of his arms, as if these were somehow trained birds of prey. The Wolves used such birds as messengers when they needed to send urgent messages.

And as if they were those birds, not the dreams of something that was almost god in its own domain, they came to his raised arms, landing, one each, on left and right. Unlike the birds used by the Wolves, they were weightless, and didn't appear to require either praise or feeding at this end of their journey.

No, it was not the name his master had spoken that these birds spoke; what his master heard was not what Severn heard. He had no need now to listen to anything but the Dreams, because neither his master nor An'Tellarus spoke.

Handred.

Not his name, but his family name—a family he didn't know, had never met, and would likely never meet. It would be a lie to say he'd never been curious—but curiosity about his family had started with Elianne and her mother, a tiny bud, a question for which he had never been given answers. Elianne had a mother, if not a father. She had a family, if small. Severn had been welcomed into that family, and he had—

Are you lonely?

No. No, in the end, loneliness was not what he felt in the run-down home of the two. He had been welcomed. He had been given a place—a patch of floor with blankets—which was his own. He had been given food and water, and she had told him, Tara had told him, that if he wanted to contribute in some fashion, the most important thing he could do—more important than providing food or finding better shelter—was to protect Elianne. Tara's love for her daughter was not without frustration and fear, but it was the most important thing in her life.

He had wondered, briefly, if he had ever had that, in an infancy he would never remember. But he hadn't resented Tara's child. Couldn't. He found her instant trust confusing, but in its entirety different from the trust Severn had had in his master. There was a warmth, an immediacy, an *awareness* that he had lacked. What had she called it?

Love.

I love Severn! Singsong words, a child's words. Tara had never said them, not to Severn. But she had to her daughter. Ah. He'd wondered what it would be like to be someone's son. To be someone's child. To have grown hearing words that his master would never—probably could never—utter.

But Tara's utterances had not excluded Severn. And even if they had, Elianne could never exclude him. From the second day of his stay in their home, he had somehow become hers. She'd never irritated him, perhaps because she'd become the answer to the question—the final question—his master had asked.

He closed his eyes.

Handred.

And opened them again. One of the Dreams was perilously close to those eyes; he knew the damage those beaks could do. Trembling, he slowly lowered his arms until they rested against the chair. The Dreams didn't seem to notice the difference in elevation.

The hush deepened.

"I am Severn," he finally said, because the Dreams seemed to be waiting for an answer. "Severn Handred."

Handred's son. Why are you here? Why? Why are you here? The claws on his arms tightened but didn't destroy the fabric that now protected them. *The green is waiting, waiting; the green is crying. Come to the green. Go to the green.*

"I cannot enter the green, not yet."

The green is **waiting**.

The words, the sense of words, were lost to thunder, to lightning. Only pouring rain was absent—but rain fell, regardless; he could see it in sheets of water beyond the edge of the platform.

"I will come to the green as soon as I can," he told the Dreams. They were angry now; he could feel the tremble of their sudden rage. What had he called Alsanis? Almost a god. He wasn't surprised when the bird on his left arm lifted a claw and pierced jacket, shirt, and skin.

It is a promise, a promise, a promise.

Singing thus, their voices a squawk of sound, they rose; as they spread wings, the rain stopped, as if all weather here was just an indicator of mood. Severn was afraid, for one sharp moment, that they would carry him off, but they released his arms and headed into the forest that couldn't be reached except through the green.

Silence fell in the wake of rain and the passage of dreams.

Severn didn't break the silence; it therefore continued until one of Tellarus's many servants ventured up the stairs and onto the platform, bearing a long, oval tray. He was followed by a second servant, who carried another tray, and a third, cloth. They brought these to the table and laid them out, as if they had seen neither the Dreams nor the brief, bright storm.

The attendance of servants and the expected signs of hospitality slowly brought a sense of normalcy to Severn's surroundings—Barrani normalcy, that barbed field of thorns and mistakes waiting to bite the unwary.

In such a situation, Severn relied on An'Tellarus's sense of hospitality; it was her duty to break the silence.

"Would you care to offer an explanation for what just occurred?" This was not the way he'd hoped the silence would be broken. Her gaze, dark blue, would have pinned him in place had it been physical.

"Cediela, the boy is bleeding. Perhaps questions might wait until he assesses the injury done."

She frowned. She hadn't noticed the small rent in the expensive fabric, nor had she noticed the slow spread of blood. Severn wasn't surprised that his master had noted both. An'Tellarus was annoyed.

"He did not injure himself." Severn's master rose. "Come. Let us examine the arm."

"I do not wish to disrobe in front of our host," was Severn's grave reply. His arm stung, but he'd had far worse injuries in the fiefs. "It wasn't deep."

"It was deep enough to seep through layers of impractical clothing."

Severn shrugged, which caused an immediate flash of blue to darken his master's eyes. His former master, as An'Tellarus had called him. "The Hallionne required a token of blood. This is probably similar."

An'Tellarus, never one to depend on delicacy or grace, snorted loudly. "The Dreams of Alsanis are not the whole of Alsanis."

"Permission to enter the Hallionne is granted by the Hallionne," Severn replied. "Or so I was taught."

"In this case, your lessons were inadequate. Even if Alsanis was willing to allow you to enter, you would not be allowed to approach. The Warden's guards would forbid it. Had you somehow stumbled into the West March without an obvious benefactor or master, those with a taste for blood and suffering might have allowed you to pass—but you are now linked to Tellarus, and Tellarus has, on occasion, shown an appetite for the blood and suffering of those who have defied it. None of the guards would dare the consequences they might be forced to bear should they seek to dispose of you that way." An'Tellarus glared at the obvious wound as if its presence offended her.

Given that it had occurred within the heart of Tellarus, it probably did.

"You spoke with the Dreams of Alsanis."

Severn nodded.

"You *spoke with* the Dreams of Alsanis."

"Yes, An'Tellarus."

"And they wish you to seek the green."

"Yes." He hesitated, and then added, "They weren't best pleased with my first answer." He held up the injured arm, as if to emphasize the point.

"No, they wouldn't be."

"Were I Barrani, how should I have answered to avoid their displeasure?"

"Do not ask me." She turned a steely glare upon Verranian. "You may answer the boy, if you are so inclined."

His master's lips were turned up in an odd, fey smile. "What have I taught you of the Ancients? Mortal memory is poor, but not so poor that you cannot recall, surely?"

"The Ancients are not Barrani; they are not mortal; they are not, in any sense of the word the living use, alive at all. No more alive than the sky, the ocean, the earth beneath our feet."

"And?"

Severn exhaled a sigh, an echo of the sounds he made when frustrated as a child—as if repetition of the words offered him by this inscrutable man meant anything to anyone but the man himself. "They do not understand the limits of the living that are not their personal creation. They have will, they have intent, and they create—and destroy—based on the dictates of their nature. But they make no allowances for the will of lesser beings."

"Indeed. What do you understand of the green?"

The temptation to say *nothing* in a short snap of sound proved that in some space of his heart, that child was still alive. But he was not that child, to answer so carelessly, now.

"The green is an Ancient force. It might be an Ancient, bound somehow to this place. We cannot understand the will of the Ancients. We cannot divine their purpose. But…" He glanced at his arm. "They have purpose."

"Will you stand against it?"

Severn shook his head. "The Ancients are eternal. The passage of time—a day, a month—probably means little to them."

"Then the correct answer would have been?"

"I will go to the green."

"Good. Remember it. The details will have to be worked out, of course. But the details are not relevant to the green—they are your problem, or our problem, to solve."

"I see you are not surprised, Verranian." An'Tellarus spoke his name as a dire warning. She lifted a hand in Severn's direction. It was as close to *shut up* as she would allow herself in the presence of strangers.

"You are wrong, Cediela." He spoke hers as a gesture of affection. "It happens so seldom I had forgotten what it felt like." His smile deepened, as did the flecks of green in his eyes. "I believe you must misunderstand deliberately; you are not mortal and your memory is sharp, as was proven by the conversation I interrupted earlier."

"What game do you play? What do you desire in its completion?"

"Why do you ask? Have you not, yourself, been searching for one of your own who might prove worthy? Have you not, as Avonelle, as Darrowelm, sought those who have the spark of promise, and beseeched the green in your own way?"

"No candidate I chose was mortal."

"No, but if you are unpredictable to most of our kin, you are nonetheless Barrani, and your view has always been narrow. Ah, no. No, Cediela, I misspeak. It was not always so narrow."

The air chilled instantly; it crackled, as if it had become, in that moment, a thin sheet of ice even breath could damage. Severn had never seen An'Tellarus's eyes as dark as they had become, and without thought, he rose, narrowing the distance between them in two long, hurried strides.

Her rage was directed in its entirety at Severn's master, her gaze anchored to his, her hands white-knuckled as the crackling in the air grew louder and more certain. Severn spared no glance to his former guardian. Instead he took the risk of laying his hands across An'Tellarus's. They were cold, as the air was cold; they might have been oddly shaped blades, they were so smooth and hard.

"An'Tellarus," he said, his voice soft. Without turning, he said, "You should leave, master."

"There is much we have yet to discuss."

"I will not discuss any of it now."

"Severn."

"Leave, if your intent is to speak with me. I will speak with you later—if you retreat now. I will not speak with you at all while I remain in the West March, otherwise."

"You make a mistake."

Severn did not reply. He didn't hear the movement of cloth or feet at his back, but knew, as he had often known, the moment his master departed. He knelt before An'Tellarus, although he didn't remove his hands. He lifted his face to meet the gaze that, even now, spoke of rage and death, waiting for it to waver.

His master wasn't wrong. He'd made several mistakes in the last few minutes. He shouldn't have moved; shouldn't have interfered; shouldn't have threatened the man to whom he owed his early survival. But last, and most important, he should never, ever have dared to touch An'Tellarus.

He had assumed that An'Tellarus, as so many elder Barrani, had a competent grasp of magic and its use. He'd never seen an obvious display of raw power from her. This was prelude, beginning, the first notes of a song he didn't want her to complete. He waited.

He waited until her gaze moved, her eyes at last meeting his. Her hands twitched beneath his palms. Had he been wiser, he would have removed those palms instantly, reducing the clearly unwanted contact. He couldn't, yet. He couldn't until her eyes, eclipsed by rage, once again returned to the calm midnight of natural night sky.

Midnight was not a color he would ever have associated with calm in the Barrani.

"I could kill you now," she said, but the crackling of power was diminishing by the syllable.

"You did not bring me here to kill me," he replied, speaking softly, softly, as her hands gained warmth from his.

"I cannot now recall why I did. In no universe in which Barrani dwell would it be considered wise; it is the passing fancy of an almost forgotten dream. I had forgotten. I, An'Tellarus, Barrani."

"Forgotten?"

"We do not require sleep when we finally climb out of childhood, as you know. We do not sleep, and we therefore do not dream. And yet, Severn, as children we did. Dreams are not artful; they are not willfully controlled. They can become nightmare when we turn a corner, lift a glass, look over our shoulder.

"Nightmare at its worst, its most intense, will wake us from all dreaming."

Severn, who needed sleep and often dreamed, nodded.

"But perhaps, nightmares can also shift. I have once again moved away from darkness and terror; I cannot tell if I am still dreaming."

Severn removed his hands and once again rose. He returned to his chair. "Verranian isn't of Tellarus."

"No. But he is unusual: he is not *of* a line."

Severn frowned. "He was cast out?"

"No. His family was scattered and destroyed in the wars, the intensity of which reached their peak with the destruction of the Aeries. The Dragon Flights were enraged, and much of the southern settlement was lost; there was no Hallionne to which they might retreat in safety. His kin were in the south." She opened her mouth and then closed it again. "The Dragons had their reasons; it was known that rage would be the result of the Aerie attacks. It was, however, considered a reasonable risk. One day, if you wish to know why, you must ask your Emperor.

"Regardless, Verranian was content to remain without acknowledged kin."

"He is not in Elluvian's position?"

"He is not. Honestly, Verranian has annoyed me enough I need no reminder of other annoyances."

Severn nodded.

An'Tellarus, however, grimaced. "You do not understand— and without guidance, will not—what Danarre once was in the West March. Verranian's line was a side branch of a destroyed family, and of his kin, he was perhaps the only child of note. Danarre's authority was absolute in the West March. If An'Danarre of old had survived, it would be, without question, the family of the first rank; Danarre's children would aspire to be Warden, Danarre's children would aspire to be Lords of the West March. Even in the distant High Halls, An'Danarre was respected and feared. He reigned for centuries. From the moment he took the throne to the moment he died he was unseated and unchallenged.

"Even if your master did not teach you about Danarre, he taught you enough that you will know how very rare that is."

What Severn noted most clearly was An'Tellarus hadn't liked An'Danarre. "A legacy of power is not power itself," he said quietly. "The power of Barrani families can rise— or fall—over time."

"Yes. Do you think Elluvian incompetent?"

"My opinion is irrelevant."

She sighed. "You are, as always, politic. It is almost astonishing. Very well. Elluvian is not incompetent. He is not without power, as his general arrogance must make clear. No one possessed of insignificant power could be the Emperor's Wolf and survive it for so long. Even here, where the hatred of the Emperor is far more personal, he expects to survive.

"He is not a fool, and he is not careless. Even if we are not in the Empire, politics will always be a concern, as the seat of Barrani power is in the High Halls, which shares a city with the Imperial Palace. Elluvian understands that his death cannot be the result of a concerted, open attack—but a concerted subtle attack?"

Severn nodded.

"I will not say more."

"And my master is not the power that Elluvian is?"

"Ah, I did not say that. What has he said of power?"

Severn considered the question from many angles before he offered an answer; there had been too many things said to easily choose one.

"Power was, in many ways, an absolute, but it was also contextual. I might be considered powerful in the streets of the warrens; I would be considered insignificant in the High Halls. Those who had power had choices. Those without still had choices, but few good ones.

"He wished me to survive," he added, almost apologetically. "To survive as a mortal was to be unseen, unheard; to be overlooked. He taught me the skills he felt would be necessary for that survival in mortal streets. Mortal streets were, to my master, annoying, loud, and smelly. But I would not die there if I were careful.

"Power? Power was what belonged in Barrani hands. To me, as a child, power was...Barrani. As I was never to have power, the subtle gradients of the scale of power weren't relevant. I was to watch for and understand the signs of it, but from the banks of the figurative river, not the middle of the raging water."

The answer didn't please her, perhaps because she wasn't certain Severn was telling the truth. He wondered how much she might tell him of his master if he asked. Although his master had been the entirety of Severn's world when he was young and impressionable, he had known him for, at best, ten years—far less than a lifetime, and far less than a childhood even among his own people.

Still, he waited.

"You serve the Wolves," she said. He wasn't surprised; An'Tellarus often took conversational leaps that others wouldn't have even considered.

He nodded.

"Tell me, does Elluvian rule the Wolves?"

It was clear she already knew the answer. "No."

"I will not ask you who does; I don't believe you would answer."

He knew she knew; she had met Helmat; she had been in the office. "It is not something to be discussed with those who are not Wolves, no."

"I will not insult you by pretending to believe I might bribe you for information."

"Thank you."

Her brows rose, the blue of her eyes brightening. "Are any of your Wolves Elluvian's equal?"

"No."

"Why, then, does Elluvian not rule?"

It was a question Severn had asked at the beginning of his tenure as an almost-private, a probationary trainee. It was a question Elluvian asked, as well, often when at his most frustrated.

"Elluvian is not mortal," he finally said.

"I understand that, of course."

Severn shook his head. "The reason he does not rule is

because he is not mortal. The things that concern us do not concern him in the same way." He hesitated, understanding the overlap between Elluvian as a relative of An'Tellarus, and Elluvian as Wolf. "I would suggest that you ask him, but you are both already angry, and his answer—if he bothered to answer at all—would not enlighten you. He does not know."

"That is like him," was the pinched answer. "But my complaints about Elluvian are not the central point I wish to make." She fell silent, watching him, as if her gaze were a prod. "I am curious, though. Do you feel you understand?"

"I'm…not certain."

"Oh?"

"In all pragmatic ways it would make sense that Elluvian lead or rule."

"Interesting. Why do you say that?"

"If I were to rule the Wolves, it would take time for me to rule them well. I believe that in time, I could achieve that—but I would require age to properly wield the authority, regardless. When I achieved that proper rule, it would be limited by the fact of my mortality. In the end, I would have to retire—if nothing killed me first.

"Elluvian is Immortal, as all of his kin are. While it might take longer to become the leader the Emperor desires, once he achieved that goal, he could hold the Wolves' leash for as long as the Wolves were considered a necessity. The early lessons, the early struggle, would carry the Wolves into any foreseeable future. As it is, were I to be lord, someone very like me would have to experience all of the things I had to learn in order to govern. They, too, would retire, and a new leader would take their place—without the same experience. The cycle is never-ending.

"With Elluvian, it would end. It would be done. And we would have continuity; he would be the bridge."

"Very well. But that was not why I asked."

"You wish to know if the Wolflord is more powerful than

Elluvian—but you already know the answer. In any objective measure, he is not."

"But he rules, regardless."

Severn nodded.

"Is he competent?"

This skirted the edge of allowable discussions, from the wrong side. "I believe so, but I have not had enough experience to fully evaluate—and even had I, my evaluation is irrelevant. I will serve, or I will not."

"What are your reasons for service? Why would you, raised Barrani, choose to serve the weaker master?"

Severn's smile was slender. "I serve the Emperor, An'Tellarus."

She snorted. "Very well, that was clumsily asked."

"I understand your point."

"Do you?"

"You are asking why I serve; you are asking me to extrapolate. You are implying that my master is more like the Wolflord in his role and function—in terms of raw power, if nothing else." Severn could assure her that his master was nothing like the Wolflord but refrained.

"I am, in a fashion. You are a perceptive child."

"Understand, then, that inasmuch as he could be, he was guardian and parent for my early childhood; I cannot untangle that from the person he is in your eyes. I do not serve him, but I owe him a great debt. His power—his level of power—is irrelevant to that debt. Were you to tell me he was the least of your servants—"

"Oh, I would never say that. If he were servant, it was not to me; regardless, he would never have been considered minor. But he was always considered dangerously odd." She exhaled then, sinking into the arms and back of her chair. "And so, in a roundabout fashion, we return once again to the conversation that he so rudely interrupted: my sister."

She glanced at Severn's arm; her pinched frown was familiar, an indication of rudimentary trust—or her estimation of Severn's actual power. "Stop bleeding."

He rose. "Allow me to tend the wound and return."

She glanced at the servant who remained at the edge of the platform closest to the stairs. "Stay where you are; if you require supplies, they will be fetched. So," she added, "will clothing. You absolutely cannot be seen in bloodstained clothing while you are in Tellarus; it implies that I cannot even protect my own guests."

"The injury was caused by the Dreams of Alsanis. It is unlikely blame for that will be laid at your feet."

"You would not possibly be thinking that it would be acceptable to allow that information to leave this room?"

"Forgive me," Severn replied. He bowed head to An'Tellarus, in part to hide his embarrassment. She was right, of course.

The servants left and returned, bearing bandages, clothing, and unguent. One would have attended him but stopped at a respectful distance. Severn took what the man held, turned his back—which was difficult—and removed the shirt and jacket, both of which were now ruined. He folded them carefully and set them down on the seat of his vacated chair.

He then accepted the unguent without comment. He wasn't certain what it contained; he was certain that it was beneficial in some fashion. Even were he to be suspicious, he would have used it—sparingly—regardless. In spite of An'Tellarus's brief discussion about the nature of power, the immutable fact was that hers was the power in this room. The Barrani power.

"Tell me about your sister."

CHAPTER FIFTEEN

AN'TELLARUS LIFTED HER HEAD. "LEAVE US," SHE said. Her servants bowed and retreated at her command. She waited until their steps could no longer be heard before she once again resumed the conversation Severn's master had interrupted.

"Her name was Leveanne. Leveanne of Tellarus. As I said, from my perspective, she was loved; I was not. I regret the ignorance of my childhood and my youth; I regret that I spent so much time yearning for the chimerical. Did you know she was beloved of the green? Even the green. I wanted the attention because with it came respect—a respect that did not rely on power. And of course, it was not given to me."

He now expected the purple cast to her eyes, and nodded, unwilling to break the flow of the words she offered.

"What I did not understand as a child, what I did not understand as a youth, and even as a young adult, was the pressure and the isolation that came with all of the things I desired, things I reached for but could not grasp. I did not understand that, being loved in the fashion she was, she was not loved; she stood atop a pedestal, and the pedestal was very narrow at both base and height; one wrong step, one careless movement, and it would tumble.

"What she was known for, she must uphold. She did not plan to be known for those things; she did not build her reputation in a fashion that was comfortable; it was not—like the robes I now wear—a layer that could be donned at need and as appropriate. She, too, was young. To her, they were a cage.

"I felt that all eyes were upon her, and only her, and I wanted those eyes upon me. But she, who had them, felt that what they were looking at was...not her. That she could not move or breathe as herself for fear of disappointing the expectations that grew, and grew, and grew." An'Tellarus exhaled.

"I wish—always—that I could bespeak her once again. I wish that I could apologize, that I could ask forgiveness, that I could listen to her, listen to what she wanted to say, help her with what she wanted to do. It is bitter; death, when it comes, is the final door. The closed door. Beat it and scream at it as one might, it will not open. And now, I am shameful; I am speaking of myself, and not of my sister. It is seldom that I grieve so openly."

Of course.

Severn understood that grief was weakness, if it was witnessed. But if she wished to speak, it was safest to speak to someone like him; he wouldn't speak of it elsewhere, and he would die in decades, taking the secret of that weakness with him. But she waited, and when he realized she both desired to continue and wouldn't unless he carried part of the conversation, he said, "How was she lost?"

"How diplomatic of you. I had expected you to ask the question in an entirely different way. But perhaps not; I can answer the question you did ask. If you ask how she died, however, I cannot. Perhaps your master knows, and perhaps he might answer if you ask; he has never answered either my questions or my father's questions—at some personal cost.

"But if you do dare to ask, be wary. As you have witnessed, there are things about which he does not speak; nor does he allow others to speak of them in his presence." She looked past him, as if seeing only the sky. "In the end, he intended that you come to the West March, as I did. And perhaps for the same reason. Understand, however, that Verranian has never been good at sharing; even his duty was almost a sacrament, a responsibility gifted to him and him alone."

"He served Tellarus?"

"In theory. But you already know the answer."

"He served the heir."

She nodded. "I do not understand why Leveanne accepted his service so readily, so completely; he was—like all servants—almost worshipful in her presence. Only Leveanne was possessed of that gravity in his eyes, and it was that worship that she found most scarring from any other. Do you understand why?"

"How could I? I mean no rudeness but…the master with whom I'm familiar was not a man who was capable of worship or adoration."

"Was he a man capable of raising a mortal child with enough care that the child survived him?"

"Demonstrably." But as the word left his mouth, Severn considered the question more carefully. It wasn't the first time it had been asked, but it was the first time it had been asked by someone other than himself. He tilted his head, gazing at An'Tellarus, who met his eyes without blinking. "…No. If I were told that you had raised such a child, I would believe it. In my master's case I only believe it because I was that child."

"I will not take the observation as an insult, but you must know most of my kin would. Pretend," she added, voice soft, "to care about their opinions if you are subject to them.

"And to answer your question, we lost her in the green."

★ ★ ★

"When?"

"Centuries ago. She walked into the green with two attendants; only one returned."

"My master?"

"Yes. He was the one." She fell silent again. "He did not murder her; he did not lose her deliberately; not even the most suspicious and cautious of my kin could suspect him of that. But he lost her in the green. We beseeched the Warden of the green for both permission to search and information, and we were granted neither."

This surprised Severn. He frowned. "You've spoken of the past before. When you spoke of the enslavement of my kind..." He hesitated, attempting to reformulate words. "Did she vanish when human slaves were common here?"

"Why do you ask?"

"Handred."

She was still, purple once again giving way to blue in her unblinking gaze.

"The Dreams of Alsanis called that name."

"And it is your name, your family name."

"It is the name I was told was mine. I believe it to be my family name, but I have no way of ascertaining the truth."

"No. You are cautious; that is good. The source of that information was a man you both trusted and needed; the existence of kin would be almost irrelevant. Regardless, you are here, now, and that name is centuries old. No matter how long-lived a human, no human could persist for four or five centuries." She paused, exhaling the last of her grief for the moment. "I recognized the name when I heard it. It is why I suspected Verranian's involvement—although I could not, and cannot, see his aim. I cannot yet guess at the game he plays."

Severn shook his head. "You have suspicions."

"Of course I do. We are Barrani. But I was uncertain that

I was not the opponent in this long game. He gave you the name; he did not give you anything else. You did not recognize the statue I left in the hall."

Severn frowned, remembering the lone figure of a mortal man in her hall of curiosities—a hall through which he and Elluvian had had to pass were they to attend her as she commanded. "I think Elluvian did."

"It is not Elluvian's game, in the end. I am certain it annoyed him, which is an added benefit, but it was not my intent. I wished to see if anything about the man was familiar to you; it was not. You were surprised to see a mortal elevated as a statue in my hall, but that was all."

"Was he a slave?"

"Yes."

"Was he Tellarus's slave?"

"Yes." She studied his expression in the silence that followed. "You are not offended."

"I'm not offended, no. I'm not a slave and you no longer keep mortal slaves. What happened in the past can't be changed. According to my master, the Barrani also kept Barrani slaves, and their lives were, in his opinion, far worse."

"And in your opinion?"

"I will never experience Barrani slavery. I have nothing against which to compare. I don't have a True Name. Those who were careless with their names, or those who surrendered them on pain of death or torture, were owned so completely they had no control of their actions should their master act."

Her eyes darkened again, but she nodded. "I found that slave when he was twice your age. I did not purchase him; the finding was entirely informal. But I chose to keep him. He was not delighted by the choice. You are neither surprised nor upset."

"No. His name was Handred?"

"Yes. It was not his family name. It was his name."

"You named him?"

"I would have named him something far more suitable, although I was told the name would age poorly."

"Your sister said that."

"I understand why Elluvian kept you," was her soft reply. "Yes. My sister said that. My sister, who could approach the wildest of creatures unharmed, could approach an almost feral mortal in the same way. She did ask my permission; she never attempted to take from me anything that was mine. Maybe if she had, we would have fought, and my rage would have been shared—and diminished."

"That's not the fate of such fights in the Barrani history I learned."

An'Tellarus laughed. "No. Never waste time with regrets if you can help it; it is idle and dark as a pastime, and it brings no peace."

"Did Elluvian know?"

"I believe so, yes. We were not, at the time, close. An'Danarre ruled and no family interacted with An'Danarre if they had a choice. Tellarus had a choice. We were not a small and powerless clan, to be subsumed by Danarre. But perhaps the powerless called in some fashion to the powerless. You would have to ask him." Her tone implied Severn would get no answers.

"It was your sister who named him?"

"It was. She offered to call him by the name of his birth. Mortal names have no power, but my sister understood that power is...contextual. When he refused, she did not press him, as we had done. Instead, she told him that even the beasts had names and she did not want to treat him as if he were lower or of less value than beasts.

"His name was Handred. I do not know what it means. It is not a word from our tongue, but from his."

Severn frowned.

"She learned it. She taught him Barrani and he taught her

his tongue. I believe she understood the word, but she said it was a name, and mortal names are all alike to us; ephemeral and without true meaning."

Severn considered what she had said. "May I ask a question?"

"You may."

"Do you think my master named me in order to one day catch your attention? To possibly stay your hand if you did encounter me? I believe he always intended that I travel to the West March; I don't believe he intended that I travel with you."

"Why do you think that?"

"From what you've said, your sister was lost at least four hundred years ago. Whole mortal families of renown and power rise—and fall—in a century; there is no chance that I, Severn Handred, have connections to that man."

"In truth, I do not know. Had he simply named you Handred, I would concur with your suspicion; he did not. And yes—at heart, the name was probably meant to move me, but to what end I cannot say. There was never a guarantee we would meet. I would say the exact opposite is true except we did meet, and you are now here."

"Will you tell me why you wished me to accompany you?"

"Not yet. It is not an act of malice to keep you in a state of ignorance, but an act of protection, and perhaps I should know better. I have never been capable of protecting the right things; I have only been capable of inflicting a very high cost when I failed. It stays some hands that might otherwise be raised against me."

He assessed this information and then filed it for further consideration; he needed to see more of the West March before he could begin to draw any conclusions. But he was certain that An'Tellarus and his master were looking at similar things.

Do not let others set the agenda for you.

What choice do I have?

Severn, you always have a choice. Even if the choice is poor, and you otherwise feel helpless, there are choices. They are not banners; announcing them is both unnecessary and unwise. But...when you are in a difficult situation, be aware of your own goals. Do not stand in one spot without a goal of your own; without a goal, you will not look for a path you might follow, no matter how narrow it is. Do you understand?

Yes. Yes, master. I understand.

He exhaled and slid into Elantran for the first time. "I don't know what either you or my master—my former master— planned. I don't know how either of you intend to move forward, or to move me forward. There's something you want me to see on my own—and I don't see it, yet. I won't see it if I remain in Tellarus or in Danarre."

She nodded, choosing to respond in High Barrani. "You are not entirely correct, but yes. Our intentions are masked or hidden, and they involve a history that you are far too young to have experienced. Tellarus and Danarre would be safe for you, but the ultimate safety for any of us is the grave: it is only when we are dead that no further harm can befall us. If death frightens you, think of it that way; it is the way I have approached it for almost all of my life."

"I don't intend to walk quietly to my death."

"No, of course not; I have never approached it willingly. But I believe, if I have struggled with everything I have and death is the final result, there will be a kind of peace in it." She then smiled; it was her indulgent smile. "What do you have in mind?"

"I want to visit Darrowelm."

"That will prove difficult."

"Will it prove impossible?"

"Of course not."

He studied her in silence, thinking. "I don't want Darrow-elm to understand that Darrowelm is my goal; if we go there and nowhere else, it's going to be obvious that Darrowelm is our focus."

"It is highly unlikely that they will assume you have some connection with Darrowelm or An'Sennarin." An'Tellarus looked down at her hands as if they displeased her.

"No, but you do. You're the one who will make the request; you're the one who will command an appointment. And your interaction with An'Sennarin is known."

"It is not well-known."

"You've tried to visit Yvonne before, and the Barrani don't forget much."

"Memory is only useful when one has the intellect to use it wisely; you would be disappointed with most of my kin."

"Good."

She smiled, but it was slender. "You understand that in a straight, physical fight, you will have to work—hard—to survive when you are facing the least of us."

He nodded. "I need to speak with Elluvian."

"That will not be difficult, in theory. I very much do not wish to speak with him again at the moment."

"Your sense of what is dangerous—to me—is based on your experience. I can't tell if you consider me a puppy, a kitten, or a young child. You believe that all things will present a danger, that danger is the base state."

"And you disagree?"

"Yes. Elluvian, if he has done nothing else that satisfies you, has trained mortals for a long time; he has a clearer idea of what presents a danger to someone like me. I understand what you want from him; I don't think he'll give it. Not yet. But...what I need, he might be willing to do."

"And what is it you need?"

"I need to understand how best to spread a web among the families in the West March in a way that doesn't weight Darrowelm." He hesitated, and then added, "But I might need to go to the green, in the end, to achieve what must be achieved."

"Child, you are ambitious beyond wisdom."

He nodded. "Elluvian has the axis of wisdom I need. You understand the Barrani, the Barrani hierarchy, and Barrani power and history far better than I. Probably better than Elluvian. I want the overlap of your viewpoints."

"Without blood?"

Severn winced, a half smile tugging at his lips. "Without my blood, at least."

"And Verranian?"

"He saw what he felt he needed to see. I'm certain I'll see him again—but I'm also certain that he'll disapprove of my goal, should he hear of it."

"He was always odd; he might surprise you."

Severn shook his head. "Not in this."

An'Tellarus chose to move to one of the lower platforms before she summoned Elluvian. "He is likely to be tardy," she said, her expression pinched. "If it is not obvious, he has seldom adhered to a regular hierarchy of power when he has any choice."

Severn had only seen him in his context as a Wolf and disagreed. It was the choice of service that defined his willingness to serve at all. Elluvian considered An'Tellarus family, but Severn labored under no illusions; Barrani didn't often play happy families, given how frequently siblings killed each other in their quest for dominance and power.

A different table adorned the center of this room, and chairs were entirely absent; An'Tellarus called for maps, and maps were brought. Severn studied maps that pertained to the West March proper, not the buildings in which prominent families made their homes. He was surprised to see that some of the significant buildings were not part of this odd forest; the Lord of the West March's was the prime example.

The Hallionne whose dreams flew occupied a large physical space in the southern center of the small city; the Lord of the West March occupied a larger space in the northern center, and the Warden occupied a smaller space to the west of both.

"Have you absorbed the layout of the streets here?" An'Tellarus asked.

Severn frowned. "Are there no other residences?"

"There are, but the West March is not Elantra. The warrens—and the fiefs—do not exist here. Here, and here, these buildings are like your guardhouses, but the guards are from the families; it is our responsibility to keep them and render their services as necessary. You will find some small section of that force within Tellarus; only Danarre is exempt because it almost fails to exist. As such, the guards are resident within the domiciles of those under whose name they tender service.

"It is similar with our craftsmen, our cooks, and our artists. Some few will own their own homes—but those homes, for the most part, would be occupied with the unaffiliated; Verranian, for example."

"How did he become unaffiliated if he served Tellarus?"

"He is powerful enough to have a choice. As I said, he served my sister, and when she vanished, his dedication to Tellarus withered."

"Does he live in such a building now?"

"He has not been seen in the West March for long enough the answer most would give to that question would be no."

Severn nodded again. "You don't think we'll find him at home."

"No. Nor would I try; it is lowering. Should I desire to speak with someone, I summon them. Should they be a peer, we meet in a neutral territory."

"Neutral?"

"Lirienne's abode, for the most part. All Barrani of the

West March are, in theory, beholden to his commands. Should such a meeting occur, we would arrange with the chamberlain and he would open a space—a well-guarded space—for our use."

"Servants?"

"We would, of course, take our own, and if we wished to insult the Lord of the West March, we would also bring our own guards." From her tone he inferred that it happened more often than Severn would have otherwise assumed.

"Would he acknowledge the insult?"

"No, child. Not unless he wished a civil war to erupt within his domain. Such a war within the confines of the West March would cause serious damage to this ancient stronghold. Accidents, such as they are framed, do happen. But such incidents are handled in such a way that a war is not sparked."

"If you arranged a meeting with An'Darrowelm, where would it occur?"

"An'Darrowelm would come here."

"Are there any circumstances in which you might visit Darrowelm instead?"

"Very few." Not a no, but close.

"Besides Avonelle, which families would meet in neutral territory?"

"Avonelle and the Warden, when meeting with Tellarus. Kosmarre, possibly."

Kosmarre was not one of the families who occupied a living, growing tree. "Kosmarre?"

"An'Kosmarre is ambitious. She is not of the High Court, and she is not from as old a family as Tellarus, but her line achieved renown during the final war. She is aligned with Avonelle in most issues that concern the West March, but she prizes appearance and power in a particular way. She might insist on a neutral meeting because of that desire for the appearance of power."

Severn considered this. He looked up at the sound of steps; Elluvian had arrived.

An'Tellarus glared in his direction. "You know I dislike the scent of blood. How dare you visit before you are properly clean?"

Severn turned immediately. He noted no obvious wounds on Elluvian as Elluvian stepped onto the platform. Elluvian tendered An'Tellarus an exaggerated bow; there were no visible wounds on his briefly exposed back, either.

"I assumed your summons was urgent," he replied. "And I did change. I do not consider now the appropriate time to ask the water to cleanse blood." He paused, his eyes darkening. "I note that I am not the only person to shed blood in your august presence."

"If you wish to claim your wounds are the fault of the Dreams of Alsanis, I will accept your paltry excuse."

Elluvian glanced at Severn; Severn nodded.

"I will keep Severn in Tellarus. Danarre is a danger for reasons you well understand."

"Tellarus is not safe," Elluvian said, but quietly. "What happened?" He asked An'Tellarus, not Severn.

"The Dreams of Alsanis came through the forest; I believe they sought Severn. They certainly found him." She exhaled. "And Verranian came."

"Verranian?" Elluvian frowned.

"Do not play games with me; I am far too tired for it."

"It is not a game, An'Tellarus. The name is only vaguely familiar to me. If a game is being played here, it is not my game; it is not on a board with which I am familiar. Did the Dreams come in his presence?"

"Yes." An'Tellarus lifted a sharp hand. "Do not attempt anything foolish."

Elluvian nodded; he had barely moved.

"I mean it."

"I know. I interrupted your discussion."

"It was not at my request; Severn desired your presence, perhaps trusting your input over mine. I chose not to be offended."

Elluvian nodded again and turned toward Severn. In Elantran he said, "What trouble have you stumbled into now?"

"You mean besides the Dreams of Alsanis and the water?"

"Those are bad enough."

"My thinking was any further trouble would be so mundane it might not be noticed."

"A definition of thinking that suits mortals who have no desire to survive." The darkness ebbed slowly from Elluvian's eyes as he glanced at the map Severn had been studying. "How much has An'Tellarus explained?"

"Of her purpose in bringing me here? Nothing. While I'm here, I have something I'd like to do, if it's at all possible."

"Survive."

"Beyond that."

"And if I refuse?"

Severn was silent.

"If I command you to refrain?"

"We're not here as Wolves."

"You remind me of someone in his angry youth. It's a small wonder he survived. I fear that it will be a large wonder if you do. Tell me what your objective is." He slid his hands behind his back, his head tilted toward the map as if it mildly offended him.

"I want to enter Darrowelm."

"And when you do?"

When, not if. "I want to ascertain whether Yvonne of Darrowelm is alive, and if she is, if she's imprisoned there."

"And if she is?"

Severn said nothing.

"Tell me what you're planning."

Severn turned once again to the map that seemed to hold

Elluvian's attention. "If we speak to An'Darrowelm, we do it from Tellarus."

"Yes. That's not ideal."

"No, not for my purpose."

"You can't storm Darrowelm in the absence of its lord; could you, the West March would have been obliterated during the wars."

Severn nodded, unsurprised. "Darrowelm has no reason to think I'm connected to An'Sennarin."

"An'Tellarus will be considered An'Sennarin's ally."

Severn nodded again.

"I don't want to meet with anyone of note; I want to observe them. I'm here as An'Tellarus's pet, her mortal servant. I'll be noticed, but I won't be considered too relevant."

"You don't understand the nature of the Dreams," Elluvian said, after a pause in which he considered Severn's words. "The Dreams that came to Tellarus, you can hide. The Dream that approached you as the gates to the West March opened will be far more difficult; you were seen."

"You were seen as well. How many Barrani are likely to believe that you weren't the target? Most can't hear the Dreams—or so you've both said."

Elluvian's smile was sharp, unpleasant. "You are far too perceptive. So: I'm to be thrown to the figurative wolves, then?"

"Wasn't that your intention? You are, to the knowledge of those who had a brief glimpse of what occurred, the intended target of the Dreams."

"Yes. It will satisfy many of the people of power in the West March—but not all. If the Lord of the West March had concern, he would not be fooled by such naive assumptions. He is not, but inasmuch as there is a Barrani in power I would consider safe, it is he. There is one man, however, who will not be fooled."

"Who?"

"The Warden of the green. Lord Barian."

"The man I need to meet to enter the green at all."

"Indeed. I am willing—barely—to draw the ire and attention of those with significance in the West March, but I offer this one warning: Kosmarre has petitioned the Warden."

An'Tellarus stiffened. The words had a meaning to her they didn't have to Severn. "Petitioned for what? Entrance?"

"For entrance into the heart of the green, there to ask for the green's permission to take the test of Tyron."

CHAPTER SIXTEEN

THE REASON AN'TELLARUS HAD MENTIONED Kosmarre was evident then. She stiffened at Elluvian's information, her hands curving slightly as if they would become fists.

"Very well. I forgive your impudence for the moment. Severn, you will have to change."

Again. "My clothing is at Elluvian's home."

"Ah. Elluvian will bring your clothing, but in the meantime, we clearly have clothing we can spare." Some of which he was now wearing. "My servants in the West March maintain a certain style; perhaps it is best that I dress you." She lifted her chin; she had never once raised her voice to call for any of those servants. Gestures, like magic, summoned one.

"You will take Severn and see that he is properly attired as a Tellarus servant of note."

The woman nodded, her hair falling over her shoulders as she bowed to her lord. She then turned in silence, pausing once to look over her shoulder when Severn failed to instantly follow. He carefully gathered the ruined clothing and crossed the platform. Although he now knew where some of the significant buildings were, he hadn't yet pin-pointed Darrowelm, Avonelle, Tellarus, or Danarre. Then again, they were probably trees, and took up as much space as large trees did. He couldn't test the entry point to Tellarus as he'd intended, which meant the consequences of failure would be much higher.

He followed the servant down the steps.

The servants attempted to take the ruined clothing from him; he allowed this only after he'd retrieved the few necessary things from the interior pockets of his jacket. One of these was the branch itself. He took care to remove it as unobtrusively as possible.

He couldn't ignore An'Tellarus's game, even if he understood neither the rules nor the objective, but he couldn't be immobilized by it, either; he had made a deliberate decision, set his own goals, and now began to look at where, and how, those goals might align.

The reason he'd chosen to take a leave of absence seemed a dead end. What she'd spoken of so far involved people so long dead they were lost to all but personal history. If, somehow, a human slave in the West March had shared a name with Severn, it seemed likely that the name had been given by Verranian as a commemoration of those ancient events. He couldn't see how those events could be connected to his actual life.

Was he disappointed?

He turned the question over as a comb was run through his hair; scissors and a razor appeared as if by magic, and given the Barrani, it could well have been. He turned his thoughts inward as he was groomed; he allowed a dusting of powder, a spray of something that left a subtle scent in its wake. None of these had been necessary for his visit to the High Halls, but the Barrani who occupied those halls were accustomed to humans, to mortals; they could hardly live within Elantra and not be.

The colors he now wore were lighter and less somber. The jacket itself was without collar, and longer than the jacket considered acceptable for the High Halls. To his surprise, the servant gestured at his boots—as if expecting Severn couldn't speak or understand Barrani—frowning. Severn understood that he was meant to discard those boots. He wasn't of a mind to do so. But the boots were black—or, to be more accurate, gray with dust and dried mud—and they didn't suit the clothing he was given.

Since he had no intention of remaining in the West March, he wanted his boots. They were only a few months old. He couldn't continue mute and obedient, as if he were a living doll meant to be dressed up. "I'm willing to wear different footwear if it will uphold the dignity of Tellarus—but I am not of Tellarus, and I require the return of these boots."

The servant nodded. Eldanis, servant to Elluvian, or at least the remnant of Danarre, had not worked in utter silence. Perhaps there was a hierarchy of servants that Severn didn't understand. She took the boots without grimace, as if their condition was irrelevant, and returned with boots that were softer, the sides taller, the color a pale beige. The heels and soles of these boots were thin, to his eye; they lacked the laces of his normal boots as well.

He pulled them on.

When the servant then offered him a small box, he opened it and stared at its contents, before closing the lid firmly. "No."

This time she frowned.

"I do not require jewelry."

"You represent Tellarus," the servant said, finally breaking her silence. Her voice was unexpectedly deep and resonant.

Severn shook his head. "Normal servants do not require it."

"You are not a normal servant," a more familiar voice

said. Severn turned to see Elluvian, leaning against one wall. "Take the jewelry."

"It's gold."

"Yes. And heavy. It's meant to be noticed. You are not a normal servant; there is nothing that can be done to make you one. We therefore chose a different approach."

"And that?"

"You are a 'servant' in name only; you are to be gilded and clothed in a way that suggests your absolute value to An'Tellarus. If it will make you less uncomfortable, consider yourself a new lover."

Severn's expression became utterly neutral, which caused Elluvian to laugh. The laughter seemed to startle the servant.

"You cannot be invisible; let us grant you a visibility that will draw a very specific kind of attention."

"Lover?"

"She is known to be highly unusual and self-indulgent. Most will assume that her interest is proprietary in a very specific way. We merely intend to underscore that assumption. No one will openly address it."

"If we are to meet with other lords of the West March, I fail to see how this will be an advantage to Tellarus."

"That is not your concern. It is hers, and she has chosen." The echo of amusement drained from the Barrani Wolf's face. Shifting his gaze, Elluvian said, "He will wear the adornments."

Severn handed the box in his hands to Elluvian, crossing the room to do so.

"Don't glare at me, private," Elluvian said, in Elantran. "This is one of the consequences of your decision. Had your entry into the West March been less remarkable, we could risk a more dignified approach. It wasn't, and we can't. I must say you clean up nicely." He exhaled. "The Barrani aren't cloying in their affection, which is seldom publicly displayed.

You won't be required to hold her hand or treat her as if you love her. But precious gems are set in gold for a reason."

"I'd rather have a sword," Severn muttered.

"Ah." He glanced at the servant, frowned, and then said, "Permission will have to be granted for that."

"I was joking."

"Yes, but I believe it a decent point. If we are to play at these games, let us go all in. I'll be right back."

Severn had done many things to survive life in the fiefs. This wasn't one of them. He was surprised at how uncomfortable he now felt. Being a nameless servant hadn't bothered him at all, although the etiquette observed by those at the very bottom of the hierarchy had not been nearly as simple as he'd hoped. Those without power were expected to conform perfectly to the unwritten rules that governed them.

An'Tellarus could do as she pleased because she was lord and ruler.

Elluvian could do as he pleased because he was competent enough to survive it.

Severn was neither, but supplemental lessons had given him the ability to endure with grace. Elluvian was a harsher teacher when it came to etiquette than he had been in almost any other lesson of relevance. Lessons for this particular role hadn't been forthcoming. Severn regretted it; he was certain part of his discomfort with his current situation was the lack of hard rules, the uncertainty about what constituted correct behavior.

When the servant stepped away and bowed, Severn turned to where Elluvian was waiting. In his hands he held a sword. Severn had expected something gaudy and heavily jeweled that would serve as a visible statement; he was surprised at how unadorned the scabbard was. The pommel's height contained one gem; it was large, clear, faceted. It couldn't be a diamond at this size, and it was oddly warm to the touch.

He wasn't as good with swords as with daggers; swords, until he joined the Wolves, were prohibitively expensive, and even if they hadn't been, were harder to learn to use. He'd been making up for that lack ever since.

"It's not a gift," Elluvian warned him, as he equipped it. "This single item would, in my opinion, be enough to declare your current value to An'Tellarus."

"Does that mean I can dispense with the necklaces?"

"No. Don't rid yourself of the rings, either."

Severn was grateful there were no mirrors in the immediate vicinity. "Where are we going?"

"To the east courtyard of the home of the Lord of the West March," Elluvian replied. "Oh, we're not ready to leave yet. We won't be ready for another hour."

"You don't seem to have changed your clothing."

"I haven't—but our paths fork. I won't be attending An'Tellarus in the eastern courtyard."

"Where are you going?"

"I have friends in the West March," was Elluvian's cheerful reply.

"Friends?"

"People who won't immediately attempt to kill me should our paths cross. Then again, they're far more subtle; I'm more likely to face poison."

"Can we trade places?"

Elluvian chuckled; his eyes implied his amusement was genuine. "You are so difficult to discomfit in Elantra—had I known this would work, I might well have tried it."

"You would have had to get it past the Wolflord—and the department budget."

"True, and Helmat would find it far less amusing than I currently do. Be wary," he added, in a far more serious voice. "If you feel unsafe, return instantly to An'Tellarus's side. Do not touch her in public unless she lifts a hand or indicates that she desires it—but you may safely stay within her im-mediate orbit without causing offense.

"This is not unlike offering an arm or hand to someone emerging from a carriage; it is not unlike holding doors or walking on the carriage side of the sidewalk. I am far more confident in your survival now than I was two hours ago, presuming, of course, that embarrassment won't actually kill you."

An'Tellarus was ready in two hours. Stephen saw what he presumed were couriers enter and leave Tellarus at least half a dozen times; he assumed this was in preparation for An'Tellarus's impromptu meeting. It wasn't his place to ask questions, but he did listen for names. He recognized one: Kosmarre. But the other names scattered about as audible de-tritus might well have been personal names, not line names.

There were no carriages, no horses. An'Tellarus considered them wasteful and unnecessary. Severn preferred them, as it narrowed the window of opportunity afforded to possible attackers. It also protected him from the Dreams of Alsanis. He accepted the walk, offering his arm instantly; she placed hers on top of it, and they proceeded down the road. The street itself was stone, a pale stone that seemed, to his eye, to be too soft to serve as an actual road. On the other hand, there were no carriages, no steady stream of wagons and people pressed together tightly enough to become a crowd.

He glanced once, skyward, and her hand tightened.

"Look ahead, or look at me," she said, her voice so soft he almost missed the words. "And be careful. I had not intended to unravel things so quickly, but we do what we must when circumstances shift. It is our ability to do so that defines us."

Elluvian was far more careful than Severn had to be, but his worries were different. If anyone could keep Severn safe here, it was An'Tellarus. Severn didn't understand the game she now played, and because he didn't, he didn't understand the stakes.

Elluvian, given as much information as Severn, understood parts of it better. He didn't understand the whole, but he was now far more worried than he had been when he'd attempted to talk Helmat—and Severn—out of accepting her invitation.

To his eyes, the gift left to Severn by the winged nightmares of Alsanis was a fever dream. There was no possible way Alsanis could believe Severn was the correct recipient of that small branch; no way he could believe that Severn would understand what the branch itself entailed. No more did Elluvian.

But there must be a reason it had been left in his hands.

There must be a reason why Severn Handred—mortal servant of the Dragon Emperor—had been summoned by the green. That branch, and what would flower from it, was tied tightly to the nascent shards of Tyron, a weapon that had not been claimed since the last wielder had passed away, his name returned to the Lake of Life, and to the stories that arose from the loam of death and grief.

It wasn't safe to approach the Warden with his many questions, not now. The Warden was Avonelle's son. But there were others who might be willing to indulge in the intellectual exercises so beloved of scholars and the tinkerers of the mind. Of those, there was perhaps one who would condescend to do so for Elluvian.

Grimacing, he once again entered Danarre. Eldanis was waiting for him.

"Did we receive an answer?" Elluvian asked.

"Yes."

"And?"

"He is willing to meet with you here. I have prepared for his visit, but…Onuri was always odd. I am uncertain what you desire from him."

"Information."

"I suggest, in trade, you offer to open up the archives of Danarre."

"You did prevent me from burning them, didn't you?"

"Yes."

"I do not like it."

"Perhaps it will not be necessary. Neither you nor Onuri are what you once were, but what you once were in this house is perhaps the only thing you have in common."

"If that were the case, he would have refused to visit."

"He was ever and always interested in the archives; on occasion the previous lord would allow him access. He did not care for Onuri but found the results of his studies useful on occasion, which was why he allowed it at all. You are well aware that Onuri is not of Danarre now."

"Enough, Eldanis."

"My lord." Eldanis bowed.

Elluvian intended to make certain Severn suffered for the discomfort he had indirectly caused for many, many years to come. In order to achieve that suffering, the boy would have to survive. Elluvian, like Severn, was looking for information, for strands of seemingly disparate knowledge that would, when viewed in the correct light, reveal the whole of the web.

But he didn't know the green. The sons and daughters of Danarre had never been allowed to enter it. Two had defied that order when their father was absent; they had not survived his return. Onuri, meek and without power, had never dared. Neither had Elluvian. Old habits died slow deaths.

This way.

He heard the echoes of Eldanis's voice and sat in one of the two chairs Eldanis had arranged. He heard Onuri's broken gait, and inhaled deeply, as if bracing himself. Onuri was not the only one, besides Elluvian, to survive—but neither he nor Elluvian had chosen to seek each other's company.

Onuri's eyes, when they could finally be seen, were a resting blue. They darkened when he met Elluvian's gaze.

"Please sit, cousin. Eldanis will return with refreshments, or a meal if you require it."

"I do not. I seldom trust the food offered at meetings such as this—it is usually too rich for my taste. Why have you summoned me, and why *here*?"

"Here is the only place I thought you would agree to meet with me."

"I loathe this place," Onuri replied, voice low, eyes far darker.

"I'm not fond of it, either. An'Tellarus, however, is."

"Why did you return? You are possibly the most hated man in the West March."

Elluvian shrugged. "I can survive it."

"And why did you draw attention to me?"

"You've drawn attention to yourself in the past; this is not new."

Onuri sat; he had only one good leg, the other a gift from his uncle. A punishment that had allowed Onuri to survive in Danarre, in a fashion.

"You spend time in the green," Elluvian said.

Onuri nodded.

"Do you understand why we were forbidden the green?"

"Yes. But you are not your father; you cannot forbid it to me now. I am not of Danarre." He looked down at the hands that rested in his lap before lifting his chin. "But Elluvian, neither are you."

Elluvian grimaced. "If you would meet with An'Tellarus and explain that in a way she can accept, I would owe you a debt of gratitude the like of which has never been seen among our kin."

For the first time since his arrival, Onuri laughed. "Our

current meeting place would severely weaken any argument I might make."

"It's unfortunate, yes. At the moment I appear to be even less welcome in my homeland than I have been at any other time since the end of the war."

"Do you regret it?" Onuri asked softly.

"I regret nothing. Ah, no. That is untrue; where there is life, there is often regret. Do you?"

"No. Sometimes I feel an emptiness that is not regret but..." Onuri shook his head. "Why did you summon me? Do you intend to finally take the mantle of Danarre?"

"And if I said I do?"

"You are not your father."

"That is always the hope."

Onuri looked down at his hands. "Perhaps you have gone too far in your attempt to prove that to yourself."

"Anyone who had the misfortune to live in Danarre under my father must also live under the shadow of that fear. *If I return to Danarre, will it still be what it was?*"

Onuri nodded. He then offered Elluvian a rare, if awkward, smile. "It's why I came."

"I know."

"No—I came because it's the shadow of *your* fear. I am not afraid of that in you." His smile grew lopsided. "But serving the Dragon that destroyed Danarre seems a step too far, even for me. Why did you call for me?"

"You've been staying with the Warden."

Onuri nodded.

"Are there any odd rumors from the Warden's people?"

"Odd rumors? There are always rumors, but would any of those have relevance for one who refuses to make his home in the West March?"

"Not usually, no." He studied Onuri. Onuri who had been scarred and broken but had nonetheless been allowed to survive. He, and a handful of others, now lived and served other families in the West March, but most of Danarre's forces had perished to the flames of the Dragon Flights; even An'Danarre, in the end, could not fight a war from the safety of his home.

Annoying as it was, Eldanis was probably right; he would have to bribe Onuri if he wished answers. "How long have you studied the green?" he asked instead.

"Since the end of the last war. I petitioned the Warden for entry, and when I returned, I was offered a place among the Warden's forces. I cannot fight, and the magic I can use is paltry and insignificant, but...not to the green."

"You spend time in the green?"

"As much time as I safely can."

"Safely?"

"Even as a servant to the Warden, my time is not entirely my own. The will of the green is strongest during the *regalia*, but it is not yet time for that."

"What is the connection between the green and Alsanis?"

Onuri considered the question with some care. "Let me ask a different question first. Among the rumors you are no doubt attempting to track, one has, perhaps, come to my attention." Elluvian waited. "The Dreams of Alsanis have been restless, of late. They gather and fly more frequently, as if they have a message that must be passed on, and no one to pass it to. The Warden has been concerned."

"Is it true that Kosmarre has petitioned the Warden for entry to the heart of the green?"

"Yes."

"Has the petition been granted?"

"It will be, if it has not. The decision to allow entry rests in the Warden's hands, but the Warden is of the West March, not the green." Onuri's eyes narrowed. "Do you intend to petition the Warden?"

"I might."

"Why? You have never expressed ambition of that particular kind."

"You speak of the shards?"

"No, you speak of the shards. It is the entirety of the reason you mentioned Kosmarre."

"I am not feeling kindly disposed toward Kosmarre at the moment; I had a small encounter with two of their servants."

"Did the servants survive?"

"One may have. An'Kosmarre seems to feel I have an interest in things that do not interest me, and their wish to prevent any such possibility is unfortunate."

"Why would they believe this?"

So. Onuri hadn't heard. "The Dreams of Alsanis came to meet my party when we arrived in the West March."

"An'Tellarus's party?"

"I had very little choice in my traveling companions. An'Tellarus was…exceptionally forceful."

Onuri studied Elluvian's face; Elluvian returned the inspection. Eldanis interrupted them, or they might have built silence into a wall that would not be traversed.

"I apologize, Lord Onuri; I failed to fully consider the stairs when I selected this as the most appropriate meeting place. I have laid out refreshments below, in a more suitable environment."

Onuri glanced at Eldanis, and then at Elluvian. Elluvian surrendered. If he was, in theory, the man who owned Danarre, it was not his home; it was Eldanis's. Had Eldanis the blood of Danarre in his veins, Elluvian was almost certain that the West March would once again bow to An'Danarre. He did not. But Eldanis led Onuri down the stairs, and Elluvian took the rear.

He was not surprised to see that the more suitable meeting place was in the Danarre archives, part of which was a library. Surrounded by shelves of books, a long, lone table filled the room's center. It had never been meant for dining of any sort, but that was the use to which it was now put.

The library was not the entirety of the archives, but Danarre had been among the most powerful of the families. This particular library was not easily reached or raided. Without Elluvian's permission—which he had not yet given to any denizen of the West March—it could not be reached at all. But Onuri had been given permission to enter Danarre.

Eldanis did not entirely trust Elluvian to maneuver in a competent political fashion. While he had advised that Elluvian offer this access if he wished Onuri's cooperation, Elluvian had not agreed. And yet, this was where refreshments were laid out.

Eldanis's overstep would have resulted in his death—given his years of faithful service, perhaps even a clean death—in the time Elluvian's father had ruled the line. Elluvian had wanted Onuri to interact without the obvious incentive. To his surprise, Onuri had, but cautiously, the information incomplete.

They had never been allies; when An'Danarre had lived, they had both been tools, slaves. The commonality of experience defined them in some ways, but free from the cage of Danarre, they were substantially different people. Onuri had fallen inward into the realms of his studies, his scholarly pursuit; Elluvian had gone, with alacrity, to the east.

They had not been friends in the past; they couldn't be. No friendship, no alliance, was allowed them, and where it might have grown, the roots were torn out and trampled.

Onuri took a seat, but his gaze now strayed past Elluvian to the shelves in the distance. "This is the only part of Danarre I have missed," he finally said. "I remember some of the volumes, but I was never given permission to read them all."

"That would be a project of many decades."

"Yes, it would. I have transcribed those books I did read, but An'Danarre did not consider the books to be the heart of the archive. I do not believe any but An'Danarre himself was aware of the entirety of the knowledge contained herein; he made deliberate choices about what was, and was not, to be studied by individuals, and the study very seldom overlapped.

"Were I to ask your permission to return to both the library and the archives, what would you ask of me in compensation?"

"I want to know everything you know about the shards of Tyron and the relationship between the Dreams of Alsanis and the green."

"Everything?"

"Only about the intersection of those three; I don't have a decade to sit and listen. There is no way to keep your visit secret. I would prefer that you not try. If you are questioned about the topic of conversation, reveal as little as is feasible. If you require time to reach your decision, you have time—but not very much of it if rumor is to be believed. If you take too long, the information will become irrelevant."

Onuri's gaze was unwavering—but none of it fell on Elluvian; only the library seemed to hold his attention. Had he not been seated, Elluvian was certain he would be standing in front of the shelves, a book in hand.

"How long will your permission last?"

"It depends entirely on the value of the information I receive from you. As I do not know what that information is, I cannot fully assess it beforehand."

Onuri turned toward Eldanis. "Might we have a lighter blend of tea?"

Eldanis nodded and retreated. Only when he had left the room did Onuri bow head to Elluvian. "Agreed. But regardless of the value of the information, I wish a guaranteed two weeks at minimum."

"Done."

"There are rumors—of course—that the Dreams meant to approach An'Tellarus; those rumors are treated with moderate seriousness. There are rumors, and these are stronger, that the Dreams intended to approach you. You have long been absent from the West March, and remain a figure of interest to many of its denizens. The two rumors cannot be quelled; the guardians of the Warden were out in force when An'Tellarus and her companions crossed the border."

"An'Tellarus retreated to Tellarus, but not before she... reprimanded those guards. She was not happy."

Onuri nodded. "She did not remain there for a full day before she demanded to see you, and she entered Danarre—and left it."

"I am not so foolish as to attempt to imprison An'Tellarus. It is highly likely that such an attempt would fail utterly were I not both resident and in full control. Having made the attempt, I would be unlikely to survive it. Do you know why the guards were out in such number?"

Onuri hesitated. "No. Not with any certainty. But everything I have told you so far is absent certainty; some believe one thing, some another. Everyone who pays attention knows that the guards have increased in number, but our beliefs vary."

"What are yours?"

"I believe the additional guards are Avonelle's forces."

"The Warden has allowed this?"

"The guards of the West March are comprised of men and women from all of the primary families. It is possible that Avonelle sent her own guards in an abundance of caution—they will not be allowed the uniform of the Warden in future."

"Because An'Tellarus was angry."

"Furious. Enraged." Onuri's lips twitched. "I always admired her—from the safest possible distance, of course."

"Believe me when I say there is far less to admire when one can't preserve that distance. The timing for such an abundance of caution is…coincidental. Do you think they guard the entrance in number because of Kosmarre's petition?"

Onuri nodded. "Avonelle supports Kosmarre." He hesitated again, and then said, "Lord Tanniase of Kosmarre offered the token of invitation to the Warden."

"Would that token be the emerald leaves?"

"Yes. Someone in the folds of Avonelle seemed to expect An'Tellarus's arrival. They were not so well-informed that they expected yours."

"Tell me the rest, then."

Onuri was silent; it wasn't a silence of hesitation. His brow still furrowed in a particular way when he was trying to sort out useful information from information that would prove irrelevant. "It seemed to one of the Warden's guards—the actual guards, not Avonelle's people—that the Dream of Alsanis had little interest in An'Tellarus."

Elluvian nodded.

"But he also thought the Dream had no interest in you. An'Tellarus brought a mortal in her entourage, and to his eye, the Dream was interested in that mortal."

CHAPTER SEVENTEEN

"I SEE FROM YOUR EXPRESSION THAT HE IS NOT THE only one to believe that," Onuri said, when Elluvian failed to speak.

"Since when have the Dreams of Alsanis concerned themselves with mortals?"

"Did you hear the Dreams?"

Elluvian failed to answer.

"You said Kosmarre sent assassins?"

"I would hardly dignify them with the term; it might imply that they could have success elsewhere in any such endeavor. But it is clear Kosmarre considers me the threat."

"You want that." Onuri exhaled. "What is your goal?"

Elluvian's shrug was broad and almost graceless. It was, in its entirety, a gesture adopted from his newest recruit, his latest student. "I am content to be considered a threat. It is a step up from the general regard in which I am held among my kin."

Onuri retreated. "For better or worse, you are connected with An'Tellarus."

"Believe that I have attempted—frequently—to sever that connection."

A brief flash of sympathy reached, and retreated from, Onuri's face; he had never fully learned to adopt the mask of neutrality. "An'Tellarus has searched for one who might take up the shards of Tyron. It is not a secret. Nor is it a secret that Avonelle has done the same. But Lord Tanniase is definitely in league with Avonelle and her kin."

Avonelle must have been informed of An'Tellarus's travel plans in advance. Elluvian frowned. "Do you consider the token of invitation genuine?"

"That is not for me to decide." As Elluvian opened his mouth to speak, Onuri held up a hand. "But as you have asked, no. No, I do not."

"Does the Warden?"

"He has not made his opinion clear either way."

"You are not concerned."

"No. Those who have spent time within the green, those who have made the green their study, their life's work, are not concerned. The Warden's permission is necessary to enter the green—but that permission is almost ritual. It does not grant power, and it does not control anything that might happen in the green. There are reasons the shards have remained ensconced in the heart of the green—reasons we do not fully understand.

"Even if the token itself is false, as we believe it is, and the Warden chooses to allow entry into the green, there is no guarantee that the petitioner will find the heart of the green. That is up to the green itself. Many are the men and women who have made the attempt; two, in particular, who received what are commonly held to be genuine tokens.

"Both left the green empty-handed. One returned alive. One did not. Lord Barian can bespeak the green, and it hears his voice—but he cannot command. Would not, I believe, make the attempt. We beseech," he added, his voice softer.

"And the green listens. Sometimes the green answers, but not in words. Last year, I desired to see a plant that we have found only in the green; searching did not yield it, and I was many months in the attempt.

"When I was ready to surrender the attempt, I offered my plea to the green, and when I rose, the plant I sought was in front of my feet." His eyes were a pure green, flecked with the gold of surprise, as if even now he could only barely believe it had happened.

"Onuri."

"My apologies for straying from the topic. The reason there is little fear is the nature of the green itself. Even if Kosmarre has somehow been delivered a genuine token of invitation, it is no guarantee."

"But surely Lord Tanniase must be aware of that. Is there some reason this is considered the optimal time to make an attempt? I do not ask for the thoughts of Tanniase—if he has any—but the thoughts of one who lives by the green."

"The Dreams of Alsanis have been restless, and the water, troubled. This has happened before, and has presaged nothing—but those who are desperate will often see signs where there are none. It is a serious question only because of the interference of Avonelle; it is clear that Avonelle expects interference or conflict."

"Why?"

Now Onuri's hesitance was stronger. "The Warden can hear the Dreams," he finally said. As this was common knowledge, Elluvian waited. "They do not always speak in a language he understands, and often when the words are clear the meanings are not, they are so garbled.

"The Dreams are not reliable portents; nor are they reliable warnings. But the restlessness of the Dreams are often...the clouds before the storm. We believe, this time, that it is the green that is influencing the Dreams of Alsanis."

"What does that have to do with Lord Tanniase and the shards?"

Onuri shook his head. "It is not that we have not searched for that answer. We simply do not know. Does Tanniase know something? Does he have some key to the green that even the Warden is unaware of?"

"Perhaps the Warden is aware," Elluvian said.

"It is possible, of course."

"Spoken with so much doubt, I must believe he does not."

"There is concern," he said, his eyes bluer. "Elluvian— you owe me nothing, but in the end, I feel a debt to you."

"I was not the one who killed him."

"Not alone, no. You are the Emperor's Dog; you are the great traitor to all those who observed Danarre from the outside. To those few of us who have survived, that is not what you are."

Elluvian said nothing for a long, long moment. He exhaled more than simple breath. "Kosmarre's paltry attempt must mean that some in Avonelle consider me to be An'Tellarus's entrant into this benighted contest."

Onuri nodded at the statement of the obvious.

"How many believe—as you do—that it is the mortal who is that contestant?"

"I do not know. But Elluvian, one of those people is the Warden."

"Is entry into the green allowed without the Warden's permission?"

Onuri stiffened; it was clear from his posture that this was what he had been afraid of; this was what he had expected. "No."

"Once permission is granted, is it revoked when one leaves? If I have been given permission to enter the green, and the green accepts me, must I then petition for that permission again?"

"Yes. The green is not a Hallionne."

Elluvian watched this distant cousin. "Must you ask permission every time you enter the green for your research?"

"Yes."

"Could you enter without it?"

"...Yes. The green will revoke that permission for reasons we cannot fully understand. There are things one must not do in the green—but none who serve the Warden would be foolish enough to attempt them even were we not taught to avoid them. Do not damage the foliage; do not attempt to cut down the trees; light no fires."

"Torchlight?"

"No fires."

"One more question, then."

Onuri clearly believed that Elluvian's definition of *one* was elastic and bore little relation to actual numbers.

"Does the water in the green speak?"

"I do not hear it."

"That is not an answer."

"If the Warden hears it, he does not share that information."

"In your opinion?"

"What do you think?" Onuri seemed genuinely frustrated. "If you want facts, I cannot give you facts. But opinions? Your opinion—in the ancient home of Danarre—is just as solid as mine."

"I know mine. It is yours I wish to hear."

"If you intend to lie, you must come up with better lies; obvious lies are an insult to the intelligence of the listener."

Elluvian laughed then. "Very well. I apologize for the insult."

"I am aware of how I was once viewed in Danarre."

"Ah, there is Eldanis with tea. I may have cause to contact you again in the very near future."

"I would prefer you did not."

"You have much in common with almost every denizen

of the West March, in that regard. But you will see me, regardless."

Onuri's gaze narrowed. He held his silence while Eldanis brought tea to a table not meant for entertainment. Only when the servant had once again retreated did he speak. "You intend to petition the Warden for entrance into the green."

"If there is anything you might do to encourage him to grant it, it will save you much trouble in the future."

Onuri didn't look alarmed; he looked resigned. "Will you tell me about the mortal?"

"Not yet. But I will be truthful; I do not yet understand enough. He is, among mortals, of interest to me—but that interest would mean little to the Barrani. I did not expect that the Dreams of Alsanis would attempt to interact with him at all. I do not understand An'Tellarus's interest. I had arrogantly, and incorrectly, assumed that her interest was merely a way to annoy me. But all answers lead, in the end, to the green, to the heart of the green."

"And you accompanied him?"

"Barrani have oft failed to survive An'Tellarus's games, and he is merely mortal. An'Tellarus tells me nothing of value. She gives me no information that I cannot glean for myself. Perhaps this is also her way of testing me; I would fail to take that test were the consequences not to be borne by Severn. It was my hope that he would be a curiosity, no more; that he would maintain the invisibility of a servant while he attended her."

"Had he arrived at a different time, that might have been possible. If, however, she intends this mortal to enter the heart of the green at her behest..."

Elluvian knew. "Tell me, does Verranian enter the green?"

"Why do you ask?"

"He is involved, somehow, in this endeavor."

"I wish you had not summoned me; I wish I had refused.

Yes, Verranian enters the green. Until An'Tellarus arrived, the question was often asked in the inverse."

"Oh?"

"Does he ever leave it?"

Severn had been taught to fill a chosen role in the streets of Elantra. He had been taught to fill a different role in its parlors and had recently begun to accompany Helmat as his adjutant when Helmat was forced, by his public position, to join the moneyed and the powerful. He'd observed power in its many contexts, its many guises; had seen how beauty and wealth were used in both flagrant and subtle ways.

As preparation for the Barrani, it was helpful but incomplete.

His first teacher, his first master, had made one thing clear: he must learn to be invisible. To be part of a crowd, if the numbers warranted, but never to stand out while there; to be on its periphery, never at its center.

Elluvian had expanded on those lessons, while accepting their necessity as a foundation. He understood the need to be unseen—but had made clear to Severn that there were two ways to achieve it. This first—the ability that had drawn Elluvian's attention in the first place—was literal: Severn understood how to move through a crowd avoiding notice. He could do so while fleeing; he never panicked. But Elluvian had offered him a very counterintuitive avenue to invisibility. Draw attention. Interact. Be seen. Be heard.

Reveal nothing of yourself while doing so.

People wear masks to hide their faces; let everything about you in those situations be a mask. The clothing you wear. Your language, your posture, even the weapons you carry. Be seen as something you are not, and no one will notice what you actually are.

This had been harder to learn, although Severn had reluctantly acknowledged the sense in it. Elluvian had offered few occasions in which Severn might test the efficacy of the

Barrani Wolf's lessons, and the first two times he had attempted to put them into practice had not gone exceptionally well. They hadn't ended in utter failure, but that was in part because Elluvian had then put those lessons to practice far more competently, far more engagingly, than Severn, stiff with worry, could.

Elluvian's performance made clear what the verbal lessons hadn't; Severn could see the way the Barrani Wolf caught strands of attention, drawing them in toward himself. He could see the way Elluvian—the only Barrani at that meeting of human caste court lords—had almost strutted with the confidence of his immortality and the beauty that naturally graced anyone of Barrani birth. His hair had somehow become adornment, possibly because of the way it draped both down his back and over his shoulders. His eyes had been blue, but hints of green touched his irises, as if he was—for Barrani—actually enjoying mortal company and mortal attention.

He had seemed younger to Severn that evening than he ever had, and Severn had immediately surrendered the floor to his teacher. He had never been good at fighting for attention, because attention was the one thing he had never wanted. Elluvian wasn't fighting for attention, not exactly, but everything about his posture, his voice, his expressions, implied that attention was naturally his.

Some of that attention was bitterly envious, some resentful, some proprietary—all things that Severn had been taught to avoid. But in this second set of lessons, he learned. He saw the ways in which all of those negative responses dimmed actual awareness of who, of what, Elluvian was. In Elantra, that would have been safe.

In the West March, it was not.

Severn considered the risks as he accompanied An'Tellarus; he considered the options available to him. Elluvian at the heart of a mortal crowd could walk, speak, breathe with confidence. Severn at the heart of a Barrani crowd couldn't. But he would soon be at the heart of a Barrani crowd. On one hand, the definition of *crowd* when it involved the Barrani was much smaller. On the other hand, one Barrani could do as much damage as a mortal mob.

An'Tellarus had clearly given up on hiding Severn—inasmuch as he could be hidden, given his race—as a servant. He was aware that Barrani did take mortal lovers from time to time, although *lover* was too strong a description.

"You are worried?" An'Tellarus asked, leaning in to speak. Severn turned his head to smile at her.

Her brows rose before she returned the smile, her eyes blue. "Yes," she said, voice soft. "That's perfect. I will warn you not to smile at others that way."

"Jealousy?"

Her laugh was low and genuine; it set up a tickle down Severn's spine. "I believe you would find it far more trouble than it would be worth. So far, nothing has gone as I imagined it would."

"You don't find that frustrating?" he asked, in Elantran.

"I find it both infuriating and amusing and have chosen to emphasize the latter. It is certainly not boring. Do not wander far from my side."

As he had chosen his role, he smiled again. "Unless you command it, why would I ever want to leave?"

Her hand tightened, as if in warning. Severn's smile deepened. Given his clothing and his position here, there was only one role he could choose.

The east courtyard was perhaps fifteen minutes' walk, given the stately pace of the Tellarus procession. Tellarus guards numbered four, servants two. The guards wore loose chain mail beneath tabards that identified their affiliation. Having worn tabards that were, in their entirety, a lie, Severn nonetheless noticed the Tellarus colors: a dark forest green embroidered in silver, with a gold leaf and vine at its heart.

He realized the colors weren't the distinguishing feature as the east courtyard came into view; no one of note had come here without guards, and the tabards of each were the same forest green. The embroidery differed in color, but it was the symbol at the center of the tabard that appeared to declare family affiliation.

Unfortunately for Severn, that affiliation was hard to differentiate; almost all of the tabards were adorned with a leaf; the leaves were different shapes, but in some cases seemed very similar to his eye. He noticed, made a mental note, counted the number of guards; four seemed to be the standard. If individual Barrani didn't constitute a crowd by Imperial standards, the presence of both servants and guards swelled the numbers.

"Were the presence of guards not a theoretical insult to the Lord of the West March?" he asked, voice soft and warm.

"Yes—but only when he is present. He is absent; the guards are therefore expected and acceptable. I see we are not late," An'Tellarus added, leaning in to speak, her lips turned in a lazy half smile. "Those are Avonelle guards. Those are Darrowelm. Ah, and I see Kosmarre has chosen to make an appearance."

"May I ask if you have any allies in the West March?"

Her smile deepened. "Sennarin, of course, although that is recent. But if you mean will any of those allied families make an appearance today, you must already know the answer." She frowned suddenly.

Severn reached up to touch the corners of lips drawn downward.

Her brows rose, and to his surprise, she laughed—loudly, fluidly, musically. "We were oft told that boldness makes the powerful. You are far too bold."

"I am."

"You might not see it clearly, but the flag of this strong-hold has been raised. It appears the Lord of the West March *is* in attendance."

It had been three days, perhaps four—time was hard to accurately gauge when the method of transportation was so unusual—since they had departed the Hallionne Orbaranne. He didn't ask An'Tellarus if the presence of the Lord of the West March was a good or bad sign. She was probably attempting to assess this as they walked.

"It is likely to come as a surprise to the rest of the attendees," she said.

A servant met them at the entrance to the east courtyard. The guards peeled off, joining guards from other families. An'Tellarus's servants, however, remained at their master's side, as did Severn. The servant led them toward a pavilion, where chairs—indoor chairs, to Severn's eye—and tables had been placed. The sun was not at its full height, but close, and the shadows cast by both furniture and people were short, almost squat.

It wasn't a surprise to any of the Tellarus party that the first person to approach An'Tellarus was familiar to Severn: the Lord of the West March. Severn surrendered An'Tellarus's arm as they came to a stop.

The Lord of the West March offered An'Tellarus a correct nod, one of equals acknowledging a like power. "I see you arrived safely."

"And you as well. We had hoped you might receive a well-deserved rest."

"Not nearly so much as I." The Lord's eyes were blue, not indigo, but darker than the resting blue that defined most Barrani eyes. He turned to Severn. "I hope you find grace and repose in the West March. You are the first mortal visitor I have entertained in my stronghold. May this be a sign of peace between our peoples going forward." He then turned again to An'Tellarus. To Severn's surprise, he addressed her in Elantran.

"I hope Severn's presence here won't lead to the mistakes made in the distant past."

An'Tellarus's eyes darkened instantly, but her lips curved in a beautiful smile. "How daring of you to make such a comment here, when your own difficulties are very much in the present."

"Perhaps," the Lord of the West March replied. "I've heard rumors, Cediela."

"Rumors travel farther than truth," she replied. They had drawn some attention, but no other Barrani approached. Severn wondered how many of them could speak, or at least understand, Elantran.

"Sometimes they are one and the same. I ask you—I will not command—not to play deadly games in my territory."

"Swimming in a river can be a deadly game, Lirienne. Death is not my intent, here. Why did you come?"

"The rumors traveled on dark wings." Severn remembered then: the Lord of the West March could hear the Dreams of Alsanis. Severn might hear them, but he couldn't understand them. Perhaps they had given him the branch in frustration. "And the water is now restless. What have you brought to the West March?"

"Myself, as you must suspect, and a mortal you've already met."

"I will speak to you more privately soon. Both of you." He turned then and offered a nod to a Barrani woman who now approached. Severn glanced at her face, and away, his gaze anchored by necessity to An'Tellarus. "An'Avonelle, it is a delight to see you," the Lord of the West March said, falling back into his native tongue.

An'Avonelle offered the Lord of the West March the perfect bow An'Tellarus had neglected. "The pleasure is ours. It has been some time since I have been called to the east courtyard. I did not imagine that the master of the West March would be here to greet us personally." If her expression was subtle in its joy, her eyes were darker than An'Tellarus's. "We had been told—perhaps erroneously—that you would be absent for some time."

"And such was my intent. But it is seldom that An'Tellarus chooses to grace us with her presence, and I have heard rumors that Danarre has wakened."

An'Avonelle's eyes darkened instantly, although nothing about her posture or expression changed at all.

"It has been long since Danarre was open to visitors—long enough that I have never been its guest. I admit a certain curiosity, although I do not see An'Danarre. Was he not informed?" The Lord of the West March gazed at the visitors as if in warning.

Both An'Tellarus and An'Avonelle stiffened visibly.

Severn listened, and then chose to slide an arm around An'Tellarus's shoulders. "Can it not wait until I leave?"

She glanced at him. "Do not be impertinent in front of other guests."

He smiled. "My lord, I haven't begun to be impertinent yet."

An'Avonelle was not amused. The Lord of the West March was neutral.

An'Tellarus, however, smiled indulgently, her eyes almost green. "Indeed. I look forward to actual impertinence, but later." Her fingertips were cool as she brushed them across his cheek. "But I forget myself, which is intolerable. Danarre has not changed; it is, however, far more silent than it once was."

An'Avonelle's eyes were now indigo, as close to black as Barrani eyes could get. She said nothing for a long beat, gathering her emotions and redirecting them.

"Mortal, what are you called in your own lands?"

"I am called Severn." He released An'Tellarus with obvious reluctance.

"And what brings you here?"

"I begged leave to attend An'Tellarus when informed that she might be absent for *months*. She is eternal; I am not. The months would have been far too long."

"You have known her for a while?"

"In the reckoning of her kin, no." He exhaled.

"And in your own?"

He said, far more seriously, "Not long—but the past is not the future. Until she dismisses me, I will not let her go."

"How...bold."

"Bold," An'Tellarus said, "is compelling."

"And if poorly handled, death."

"I am mortal, An'Avonelle. Death is what waits us from the moment we are born." He then asked An'Tellarus if he might fetch her something to drink. An'Avonelle's fingers tightened around the bowl of a long-stemmed glass; Severn wondered if it would break.

"Please," An'Tellarus replied. "But do not tarry with others."

The Lord of the West March chose to accompany Severn in his search for refreshments.

"It is unwise," he said, in Elantran, "to annoy An'Avonelle."

"I'm sure it wasn't me who annoyed her, and I can't give unasked-for advice to An'Tellarus."

A brief chuckle left the Barrani Lord. "No. None of us can, although those with power have often made the attempt. Did Elluvian travel with you?"

"He traveled with An'Tellarus."

"But did not choose to remain in Tellarus."

Severn chuckled as well. "Would you?"

"You are indeed bold. Come. Cediela will not expect your immediate return."

"An'Avonelle will."

"Perhaps. But I myself am in need of refreshment, which is why I chose to join you." He led Severn toward the doors that opened on the interior of his stronghold.

Severn glanced once, with obvious longing, at An'Tellarus before he bowed to the inevitable and followed.

There were refreshments in the room to which the Lord of the West March walked. There were also chairs. There were no other Barrani, not even servants. The Lord of the West March gestured; he uttered three words very softly and at speed. Nothing in the room changed, but Severn was certain magic had just been used.

"I find the manner of your dress and your chosen behavior almost astonishing," the Lord of the West March said. "I wish my sister could have been here to witness it; it would amuse her for some time, and little does now. But it is not your...position...in Tellarus that is of concern to me."

"Why did you come?"

"Ah. I spoke truthfully. The Dreams of Alsanis requested my presence."

Not, Severn thought, in those words.

"Tell me, Severn Handred, did the Dreams surrender something into your keeping?"

"Yes."

"Is Cediela aware of this?"

"Yes."

"And Elluvian?"

"He knows. It was the reason he chose to enter Danarre in haste."

Blue-eyed, the Lord of the West March held out a hand. Severn hesitated, considering his options. Could he trust the Lord of the West March? Did he have any choice?

"I will not keep or destroy what you show me; I wish to examine it, that is all."

Without further comment, Severn withdrew the small
ivory branch, with its sharp emerald leaves. He placed it
gently across the Lord of the West March's palm, wondering if this was something that the Lord of the West March
desired for personal use.

If it was, his expression implied the opposite. He touched
the edge of a leaf; his finger bled. A wry smile moved the
corners of his lips as he returned the branch to Severn. "The
Warden of the green will grant you entrance to the green
if you show him this. It is genuine. Will Elluvian accept
Danarre, this time?"

"Not in my opinion, no. But I know far less of his history
than he does of mine."

"Do you wish to enter the green?"

Severn nodded.

"Why?"

"Because An'Tellarus desires it. Elluvian would leave
tomorrow—or earlier—if she were willing to allow me to
leave with him. He has no interest in the green, the Dreams,
or Danarre."

"Do not trust An'Tellarus."

"In this matter, I have little choice. There are layers of
trust; trust itself is complex. I trust our interests to coincide
here. I don't understand her position in this place, and I assumed Elluvian's position would be terrible because of his
chosen lord."

"Very well. When do you intend to approach Lord Barian?"

"Soon. Do you intend to be present?"

"I am not Warden; I am merely Lord of the West March.
But I believe my presence at your side will discourage those
who might prefer to see you dead and An'Tellarus thwarted.
I have returned entirely for that reason." He grimaced suddenly. "But, as always, no good deed—if indeed it could be
considered a good deed—goes unpunished."

Severn frowned.

"There seems to be an argument in the east courtyard, and it is growing contentious enough that my presence is required."

"And mine?"

"I would prefer to leave you here, but I am not certain that would prevent danger. Come, let us return. What I needed to know, you have offered me."

"I can't go back without a glass for An'Tellarus."

The Lord of the West March gestured; a servant appeared, carrying a tray. Severn chose a glass for An'Tellarus.

"You will not take one?"

"I don't drink while I'm working."

The Lord of the West March headed toward the door, lengthening his stride without losing any of the grace of Barrani motion.

As Severn reached the door on his heels, he heard raised voices, and the distinct sound of steel against steel.

CHAPTER EIGHTEEN

SEVERN COULDN'T DRAW DAGGERS WITHOUT setting down the glass, but even had his hands been empty, he would have left the daggers sheathed. This was the east courtyard and the stronghold of the ruler of the West March; unless and until that man drew weapon, any weapon Severn drew would be considered a subtle insult. It would strongly imply the defenses of the Lord of the West March were not to be trusted.

The fact that the Barrani famously proclaimed that trust was for children and lesser races while at the same time finding insult in obvious lack of trust was typical of the Barrani.

If he reached An'Tellarus, daggers might become an acceptable precaution—but she had guards.

He had no doubt that where blades clashed, he would find An'Tellarus; nor was he wrong. She was, of course, unarmed. So was An'Avonelle, who faced her. Severn made note of two unarmed men who had come, in his absence, to stand to either side of An'Avonelle. It was Avonelle guards and Tellarus guards who had drawn blades.

The Lord of the West March was in front of Severn; he

couldn't see the color of the Lord's eyes. He could guess by the texture of his voice.

"Perhaps someone would care to explain to me how swords have been drawn in my east courtyard?"

All eyes visible to Severn turned toward the Lord of the West March. The blades, however, weren't sheathed. Had Severn been one of those guards, he wouldn't have made that mistake.

No one offered an explanation.

Severn slid effortlessly between the Tellarus guards, glass in hand. He offered An'Tellarus what he assumed was Barrani wine, as if the congregation of naked blades were of far less relevance than An'Tellarus's needs.

"I see," he said in High Barrani, "I should not have left your side."

She glanced at him. "If the Lord of the West March wished to converse, the wise would accept his invitation. Not," she added, with a far more personal smile, "that I chose you for your obvious wisdom."

If the words were meant to be provocative, they succeeded, not that An'Avonelle's eyes could become any darker. One of the men took a step forward, toward An'Tellarus; Severn, now relieved of the burden of a delicate crystal glass, let his hands fall to dagger hilts and rest there.

"Do not," one man said, with obvious disgust, "interfere, mortal."

"I have no intention of interacting with you at all," Severn replied, his smile easy, relaxed. "Unless you force my hand. I had heard Barrani adhered to actual manners, and only in the lowest of taverns do drawn swords become part of standard etiquette. Perhaps I was misinformed?"

"You were not," the Lord of the West March said.

Severn could almost feel the air thicken around him, as if the chill of the Lord's voice contained literal ice. The man glaring at Severn apparently considered it safe to ignore the Lord of the West March.

"Lord Tanniase," the Lord of the West March said, his voice much softer. "Enough."

Severn made note of the name, and wondered, given the lack of intelligent reaction, whether it would remain relevant. He had moved to An'Tellarus's side and could now see the color of the Lord of the West March's eyes.

"Lord Tanniase." An'Avonelle's words had an effect.

"Lord Rowan," the Lord of the West March then said.

The man so named turned toward the Lord of the West March, and given the awkwardness of the interaction, offered a deep, perfect bow. "Accept my apologies, Lord of the West March. We are indeed a burden on the hospitality you so generously extend."

"No fault is found with you, or by extension Darrowelm."

An'Tellarus's guards sheathed their swords first. The guards of Avonelle followed. Lord Tanniase drew back, to stand in An'Avonelle's shadow. And above the gathering in the open courtyard, Severn could now see the dark, graceful figures of the Dreams of Alsanis.

"Perhaps you would care to tell your host how his hospitality has failed?" the Lord of the West March said, glancing first to An'Avonelle and second to An'Tellarus, as if neither Rowan nor Tanniase were relevant.

"We were not aware that you were the host," An'Avonelle replied. "Had we been, I am certain that there would have been no difficulty at all."

She was, of course, lying; she could see the flag of the West March just as easily as An'Tellarus had.

"I was unaware that others might raise my flag in my absence. But perhaps there were times in history when such subterfuge was used?"

An'Tellarus drank; her eyes were blue, but they weren't nearly as dark. Severn thought she was amused, but not entirely happy to be so. Any amusement he might have felt had drained from him the moment he became aware of the Dreams of Alsanis.

"Not that I can recall," An'Avonelle finally said, as if she had been silently examining what she knew of the history of the West March. "But I am certain that there has never been a time when the Lord of the West March entertained a human as a guest. We considered it a sign of extremely poor taste that he is present at all."

"I knew that he was en route to the West March, An'Avonelle. I am delighted to have him as a guest." The Lord of the West March lifted an arm. Severn recognized the posture. He had no desire to be anywhere near the Dreams of Alsanis—not when in the company of Barrani.

But the Lord of the West March could rule this place because he could hear the Dreams of Alsanis; if one of the great, black birds came to roost on his lifted arm, it would be assumed that the Dream had come for him—not Severn Handred.

If that was his intent, it succeeded; one of the Dreams began to spiral down toward the ground—toward the up-lifted arm—as if summoned. A hush fell on the gathering, although until the Dream began its descent, Severn had heard only the moving feet of servants, the armor of guards. Faces were raised, even An'Avonelle's, as if all present intended to bear witness to what was, by their reaction, an almost entirely unheard-of event.

Severn knew the Dreams were weightless unlike natural birds of prey, but that wasn't evident here. The Lord of the West March seemed braced for impact; the subtle signs of the bird's landing were clear to all who watched.

The Dream spoke.

Severn listened. He couldn't make sense of the words—they were an entirely foreign language, as they had been all but once. He couldn't be certain that the Lord of the West

March could hear the Dream until he saw the color of that Lord's eyes. They were gold and purple, although the gold faded quickly. The Dream bowed head to the Lord of the West March; when he lifted that head, a linked chain, from which dangled a teardrop pendant, was caught in its beak—as if it had been plucked from thin air.

The Dream then turned its head toward Severn—or perhaps An'Tellarus; they were standing close enough together it could have been either.

Elluvian was going to kill someone, Severn thought, refusing to flinch or cringe. He turned toward An'Tellarus. "Should I?" he asked softly. Her eyes were gold, purple, and blue. Beneath the curve of his arms, her shoulders were rigid. He wasn't even certain she'd heard his question.

He had some experience with the patience of the Dreams. Although An'Tellarus didn't answer, he nonetheless moved from her side to the watching Dream and the pendant that dangled from its beak. The Dream's gaze didn't waver, but it was clear that it was the Dream, this bird, that commanded here.

It wouldn't do Severn any good, but he understood there was no way to avoid this misfortune. Reaching out, he held his left palm cupped beneath the pendant. This time, the Dream squawked, dropping the pendant into Severn's outstretched hand. He accepted it; no one demanded to know what it was or why he now carried it. It was clear no one would until the Dreams of Alsanis were no longer so close to the ground.

Lord Tanniase was angry. Lord Rowan was pale. An'Avonelle, like An'Tellarus, made silence almost majestic. The guards had once again returned to their distant posts. Severn had no doubt they remained alert. But their absence emphasized the presence of a lone Barrani who had joined the Lord of the West March. He wasn't dressed as a servant, and he wore a slender tiara, which housed an emerald in its peak—one large enough to draw attention to the subtle crown.

He must be the Warden.

The Lord of the West March waited until the Dream of Alsanis once again took to the air. He then turned and offered his first bow. "Warden."

The Warden returned that bow. "Lord of the West March." He rose. "An'Tellarus."

She had not spoken. As Severn returned to her side, she glanced at his cupped palm and what it contained. He immediately offered it, as if it were meant for her.

She took it, lifting the pendant. She spoke a word, and then, after a pause, a second; he understood neither. But after the echoes of the second syllable died and silence reigned, she said, "It has been long since I have laid eyes on this pendant. I am grateful that it has returned, in the end, to Tellarus."

"It does not appear that it was to Tellarus that it was given." It was the Warden who spoke; possibly only the Warden would dare, if the Lord of the West March did not.

"He is mine," An'Tellarus replied, reaching out to place a hand on Severn's shoulder. "And as such, you are quibbling differences."

"Would An'Tellarus dare to say that if the Dream still rested on the Lord of the West March's arm?"

"Certainly." Her voice was sweet, amused, even affectionate—the exact opposite of her eye color. She smiled at the Warden. "I could say whatever I pleased—the Dreams of Alsanis do not hear me." She made no move to return the pendant to Severn. If he retrieved it at all, it would be in a much less public setting.

"They hear me," the Warden said. "But at the moment they do not seem to be offended." He then turned to Severn. "You are not known to the West March."

Severn bowed to the Warden but rose of his own accord. "I am Severn Handred. My home is the city of Elantra."

"A much different place—or so I am told—from the West March."

"The West March is not the High Halls, no." A murmur rose at the words. "And the Dreams of Alsanis have never flown so far to the east."

"I would speak with you in a less crowded environment, if An'Tellarus would indulge me."

"Why not speak with the mortal here?" An'Avonelle said.

"It would be mannerless to involve the Lord of the West March's guests in such a discussion," Lord Barian replied.

"It was to the Lord of the West March that the Dream flew," An'Avonelle countered, her eyes a martial blue.

"It was." Lord Barian's eyes were a similar color. "But it is seldom that the Dreams attempt to deliver physical gifts, and it is clear that the pendant is of Tellarus. Unless An'Tellarus wishes to discuss her private business in such a public gathering, I will refrain from occupying the center of this stage."

"She does not," An'Tellarus said. "But perhaps Avonelle is a bolder or less considerate house. Perhaps Avonelle wishes to discuss the business of Darrowelm and Kosmarre at such a gathering, for it seems to me it is because of their presence that her curiosity arises."

"We have nothing to hide," Lord Tanniase snapped, glaring at Severn.

"You are young, then, to have nothing you wish to hide," An'Tellarus said. "But certainly, if you desire to be so open, it would be far more entertaining to the audience we have gathered."

"Lord Tanniase." An'Avonelle's hands were now fists, and white with strain.

"I have nothing to hide, An'Avonelle. Certainly nothing to hide from Tellarus or her pet mortal. I have already spoken with the Warden. I have received the token of invitation to the green, and I intend to enter the green to take up the weapons that have long lain fallow at its heart." He spoke proudly, although his eyes were a martial, angry blue. "Your presence here, at this time, is suspicious but irrelevant. The green judges, not Tellarus."

An'Tellarus glanced at An'Avonelle; the look they exchanged was, briefly, the same. Severn would have joined them had anyone sought his reaction. He understood why An'Tellarus called Lord Tanniase young.

"The Warden, however, has been much occupied with the Dreams of Alsanis of late, and he has not yet granted the necessary permission. Given the token, it seems a lapse in fulfillment of his duties."

"It grieves me to hear the Warden so characterized," An'Tellarus said to Lord Tanniase. "But indeed, you are as bold as you have claimed. It is no wonder to me that Avonelle has chosen to support you." She then turned back to the Warden. "If you would care to adjourn to Tellarus, Severn will speak with you there." She frowned. "Lord Rowan, have you something to add?"

"An'Tellarus." Lord Rowan bowed. "It has been a long time since I last set eyes on that pendant or the woman for whom it was crafted with such care. It is the pendant your sister once wore, is it not?" It was a much better avenue of attack than anything that had yet fallen out of either An'Avonelle's or Lord Tanniase's mouth. Or so it seemed to Severn.

"It is. There must be some significance to the timing of its appearance, but the Warden, I am certain, will shed light on that when he comes to visit."

"I would hear what he has to say, if you permit it."

"She is not alive," An'Tellarus replied. "But that is ever our way: our workings oft survive us and leave a bitter echo of what we were in their wake."

"Not always bitter, but perhaps you are right. I feel the shadow of ancient losses in this. In my time in the West March, I have seldom seen the Dreams of Alsanis carry anything of value beyond the borders of the green." He bowed to her then.

She exhaled slowly. "Lord Barian, I fear the purpose of this meeting has been lost for the day; I believe it will soon rain."

"It will," the Lord of the West March said. "But I would offer, should it be acceptable, chambers within my domicile for this meeting, if the Warden's home, or Tellarus, should be problematic."

Severn was uncertain whether or not this was an offer or a command.

"It would be more than acceptable to me," the Warden said.

An'Tellarus considered the words for a beat longer before inclining her head. "It will rain," she said again. "Perhaps we should disperse before then."

Severn was surprised to see Lord Rowan follow in An'Tellarus's wake. Lord Tanniase attempted to do so as well, but An'Avonelle caught him and drew him back, her hand on his shoulder white-knuckled.

Lord Barian walked beside the Lord of the West March. The guards of the Warden remained with the guards of Tellarus and Darrowelm, but this time the servants of each lord also remained behind. They entered the building but didn't head to the room in which the Lord of the West March had briefly questioned Severn; the Lord walked past that door, and down a long hall.

He continued down that hall, and from there, through doors that opened into an interior courtyard. In the center of that courtyard was a fountain. The Lord of the West March approached that fountain, reaching out for falling water with cupped hands. Water hit his palms, and suddenly stopped falling. He bowed to the fountain, lowering both of his now empty hands.

"Lord Rowan, I assume your concern is more than idle curiosity."

"It is largely curiosity, Lord of the West March, but I

cannot consider it idle. Lord Leveanne was, in the distant past, a large part of my life. I am uncertain whether or not An'Tellarus is aware of this, but I have never stopped searching for her. Lord Barian knows, and may confirm the truth of that statement. That pendant is the first sign of Leveanne I have yet encountered in my many years of fruitless endeavor."

"An'Tellarus?"

She was silent for a long beat. The simple use of her name was a question; the Lord of the West March offered her the choice. In Severn's opinion, it was a genuine offer. Should she so choose, he would send Lord Rowan from the courtyard.

She glanced at Lord Barian for confirmation. The Warden nodded. "Very well. I was not aware of this. Perhaps, had I been, we might have joined forces. May I ask why she was of import to you? You were not in any fashion engaged or otherwise entangled in future marriage talks. She was to become An'Tellarus."

"Had she survived, had she remained within Tellarus, she would now and forever be two years younger than I. She was drawn to the green, or to its edges. I was not. But I was sent to the green often in my childhood and youth; it was hoped that my affinity for water would somehow catch the attention of the green. An'Darrowelm wished for a Warden that came from Darrowelm." He spoke without obvious bitterness or envy. "I met her then. Lord Barian was not Warden at that time.

"Our paths crossed often. I assumed that she, like I, was burdened with the responsibility of attempting to catch the green's approval. It was some time before I understood that she was meant to be An'Tellarus—and I envied her that. Imagine," he added, a bitter inflection seeping into his words, "having a role. Imagine having a place—and at that, a place atop the heights of her line. Imagine being considered—as a child—worthy of that. Or of anything."

"You knew this, but did not resent?" The lines of An'Tellarus's shoulders, rigid but nonetheless graceful, slowly relaxed.

"I envied, but no, I did not resent. What would resentment change? Her company would become a torture, not a privilege. And to my youthful eyes it seemed that, somehow, she deserved what she would be given."

"Even if she had no obvious power?"

Lord Rowan's smile deepened with chagrin. "Even so. As I said, I was young. I was a child when we first met, although I considered myself well beyond childhood at the time. But... as all children, youthful dreams, youthful longing, youthful dedication meant more to me than objective assessment. Ah, no—I believed I was entirely objective."

An'Tellarus's gaze did not move from the fountain, but she closed her eyes briefly. "She was loved."

"And we were not," Lord Rowan replied, all the words a longer way of saying yes. "She was loved by the green, in a fashion. She could almost hear its voice. Not always, and not enough to extract objective meaning, but that was not the way she listened."

The lord of Tellarus closed her eyes again.

"She could hear the Dreams of Alsanis."

An'Tellarus stiffened, but the quality of that stiffness was different; she was taut, as if she had become a drawn bowstring.

"I see you did not know. Did your parents?"

"If they did, they never spoke of it."

"Perhaps she never told them. She had no desire to become An'Tellarus, but our kin are long-lived; such a future was distant, not inevitable. She had even less desire to become Lord of the West March."

"She could not become...she could hear the water?"

Lord Rowan nodded. "And the water could hear her."

"How came you to know this?"

"In the green. I said that we came to the green; she was

drawn to it, and by that point, I was drawn to her. Where she went, I followed, whenever it was permitted. I remember the first day the Dreams came to her, circling in the air above where she walked. I couldn't hear them, of course—but it was the first time I had seen them so close they were more bird than shadow. In the green, their forms were more solid.

"She lifted an arm, just as the Lord of the West March did moments ago, and one Dream descended. I could not hear it then, or ever. But she could. Do you know what she did?"

An'Tellarus hesitated, and then said, "She sang."

Lord Rowan's eyes were almost green as he glanced at the ruler of Tellarus. "Yes. She sang. And the Dream heard her; they all heard her. I do not know if they joined her song or not—but the one on her arm did not take to the sky again. It…faded, vanishing as if it had truly been a dream and we had wakened from it.

"She said it eased their burden, this singing, this song. I could hear her voice, and it did not surprise me."

"You did not speak to An'Darrowelm of this."

"To what purpose? I was already insignificant, almost useless. I did not have great magical prowess, and I had not yet developed enough to be considered a warrior of note. Still, there was some hope that the green might eventually respond to me, that the Dreams might eventually become audible. To tell them that someone else existed who already filled those conditions? In the worst case, they might attempt to harm her. In the best, they would simply order me to withdraw, and I would lose what little chance I had to meet with her.

"I think she hoped the green might choose her as Warden. The Warden's position has never been considered political. To become An'Tellarus, to become Lord of the West March, required political power, political strength. To defend either title would require more of it. She was loved," he said softly. "But never truly seen. As children, we almost never are.

"We are seen for our potential, not our desire; for our

possible competencies, or our obvious weaknesses. When I knew who she was in the context of Tellarus, I knew there would never be anything permanent between us, but I still dreamed. If I could not be husband, I might be consort; if I could not even be that, I wished to be her friend.

"But that time, that amity, could not last. The West March was never far from war, and the war was the only thing that could unite our disparate factions. War came; the Dragon Flights came. The green closed its borders to all but a chosen few. She was chosen. I was not. I did not resent it; I hoped that the green would keep her safe. But if I could no longer enter the green—even with the permission of the Warden of the time—I had no use."

He exhaled. "I was offered to Danarre."

"It is a wonder to me that you remain of Darrowelm," An'Tellarus said.

"It was a time of war. Danarre was our strongest. Even you must admit that. And the Darrowelm council that chose to second warriors to Danarre is mostly dead, lost in the same war that destroyed Danarre."

"You did not die in that war."

"No."

"Why?"

"Many did not die in that war, An'Tellarus."

"That is true; I am here. But Danarre, in any true sense, died. Those who were of Danarre, those who served Danarre, those who fought in close quarters with Danarre—almost all perished."

"Your question is one I have never chosen to answer. Elluvian survived, after all."

She stiffened, as did the Lord of the West March. The Warden was almost disinterested, as if he had heard all of this before; he simply waited. It was to Severn, not any of the Barrani, that his gaze strayed, time and again.

"Have you spoken with the handful of survivors, An'Tellarus?"

"I have spoken—at length—with Elluvian."

"I have never been granted that opportunity, perhaps because he is wise. I wanted, and still want, his death, and I am no longer a weak and insignificant child."

"Nor is he," she replied softly. "Foolish. Stubborn. Willful. But not weak and not insignificant, except at his own desire."

"You know."

"I know far, far more about Danarre of old than it is safe to know—but it *is* safe, because I am An'Tellarus and Danarre was destroyed. You have spent far less time hunting Elluvian than searching for Leveanne."

He bowed head for a long moment. When he raised it, he said, "Leveanne was the reason I survived."

An'Tellarus frowned.

"She came from the green on the eve the Dragon Flights at last reached Danarre."

"Pardon?"

"She came where the troops of Danarre were gathered under the banner of An'Danarre. She walked through those soldiers, through the banner itself, as if she were a ghost. I did not see her until she called me. When I did turn toward her voice, the shadow of Dragons could be seen across the earth. An'Danarre had called the water, and the water had risen, shield against dragonbreath.

"The whole of my thought at that moment was that Leveanne would die." He shook his head, the upward curve of his lips too imbued with grief to be called a smile.

An'Tellarus was silent, her hands shaking. Severn was almost afraid to touch her, she was so brittle. But fear would not serve the role she had chosen for him.

"That is why I survived. In the end, it was not the Dragons I feared, not the death they would—and did—visit upon Danarre and my companions at arms, but...her. I ran to her.

I knew if she had passed through everything to come to me, she could not be present; I was afraid she was a ghost."

"We do not leave ghosts in our wake."

"I said I was young. She was young. I reached her side, but it took longer for me to travel; the war bands were being called into position, and the water shield was strong. I did not shout for fear she would be discovered and trapped as I was trapped. But I did reach out to grab her wrist, to drag her to some place safer.

"I was the person who was dragged somewhere safe. She was solid; she was real. She probably knew I would not let go until I was certain she was not in danger. I followed where she led, and she brought me to the green."

"To the green?" Lord Barian had become instantly more alert.

"To the green. To one of the small lakes at its heart."

The Warden's eyes widened, although no gold of surprise colored his eyes.

"We could see the battle playing out across the surface of the lake, as if it were an enormous mirror. She turned away from it."

"You did not?"

"I did, but she threw a stone into the water, and the ripples destroyed the images. They did not return."

"The green allowed you the entry that it had refused you."

"Yes."

"Because she asked?"

"I don't know. I could not ask. I was grateful that she was safe, that the fires and steel of war would pass over her."

"Was she alone?"

"She had her most favored servant with her."

"And you did not consider it strange that her servant was allowed passage to the heart of the green, where most of our own kin were refused?"

"Apologies, An'Tellarus, but no. She was a Barrani of

significance, and you must know that servants were seldom considered separate from their masters—and he was, further-more, a slave. The green might be just as likely to demand that she surrender her left arm. He was frequently present when we met, and I myself was still marveling over the mir-acle of my own survival. I have never understood why, of all people she could have chosen, she chose me; there were those from Darrowelm, present on that butcher's field, that were far more significant or worthy.

"I owed her a debt. I owe her one now. I have searched all these years in an attempt to find her to be free of that obligation."

Severn doubted that highly. He believed Lord Rowan had searched, but it was not out of a sense of debt or obliga-tion. No more was An'Tellarus's search for that same sister.

"I do not believe the pendant was delivered by accident. Nor do I believe the timing of its delivery was in any way random. If I cannot hear the Dreams, I can see them as well as any, and even here, in this courtyard, I can hear the voice of the water. There is a danger, An'Tellarus, a wrongness that has arrived in the West March."

CHAPTER NINETEEN

AN'TELLARUS TURNED TO THE LORD OF THE WEST March. "A wrongness?" Her question was quiet. It was also a command.

The Lord of the West March had no reason to heed it. His power was greater, both here and in the High Halls of his birth. His eyes were dark, but there was no hint of surprise in them; he believed what Lord Rowan said.

Lord Barian stepped forward. "A wrongness, An'Tellarus. This is the first time I have heard Lord Rowan's story, but I believe Lord Leveanne would have been accepted as Warden, had she survived. Only twice in our long history has one of our kind been so attuned to the green that they could walk its heart to reach areas in the West March to which the green has no connection.

"And I believe, as Lord Rowan believes, the timing is not irrelevant. The Dreams are restless, but there is a darkness in their voices, a coloring to their wings and eyes, that I have not seen before."

Silence fell. It was Severn who broke it. "Have such changes been noted historically?" He was uncertain that

Lord Barian would answer the question but asked it in a tone that implied confidence.

"You have been taught something about the green," Lord Barian replied, his eyes a shade darker at the interruption.

"He knows the green almost as well as I—who do you think taught him?" An'Tellarus's expression had taken on an almost languid possessiveness. In this fashion, she lent Severn her power.

"...Yes. Historically there have been similar changes in appearance. This is the second time since the final war."

The Lord of the West March then stepped in. "If I recall correctly, the disturbance occurred at a similar time."

"Similar?" An'Tellarus asked.

"You were not in residence at the time," he replied. "You had business in the High Halls."

"I am of the West March."

"Indeed. I make no attempt to imply otherwise. But at that time, a candidate came to the Warden with a token of invitation."

"Do you believe it was genuine?"

"That is not the business of the Lord of the West March, as you well know."

"I did not ask for irrefutable fact, but for your opinion—unless it is common for the ruler of the West March to have none when the Dreams are restless and the water, concerned. Ah, perhaps you have reasons you do not wish to offer an opinion. As you've pointed out, the green is not under the authority of the Lord of the West March. Lord Barian?"

"The business of the Warden is not the business of any other family of note in the West March." The Warden's words were stiff, but everyone expected that.

"But it is now my business, Lord Barian. The pendant, the Dreams, and Severn. This is not the first time he has met the Dreams of Alsanis; they flew all the way to Orbaranne like storm clouds to greet him."

This time, Barian's eyes were ringed gold for a moment; it passed, eclipsed by indigo.

Severn hadn't intended to share that information yet, if ever. But he accepted that the information wasn't his to control. An'Tellarus had been present, both at the foot of the Hallionne and within Tellarus itself.

"I will not insult you by asking your friend if this is true, and as I accept this as truth, I accept that in some small fashion, this does concern Tellarus." He exhaled. "Lord Rowan, I would greatly appreciate your withdrawal; this matter does not concern Darrowelm."

"Or you prefer that it not?" Lord Rowan asked, with a lopsided smile.

"Darrowelm has long been considered neutral by those who are not familiar with its structure and its subtle alliances," the Warden replied. "But it is not neutral."

"As you say. Very well, I will withdraw. But Warden, I do not support Lord Tanniase in his attempt."

"And An'Darrowelm?"

"Who can say? I am not privy to the councils of the powerful in my own family." He bowed. "Forgive my intrusion." When he rose, his glance lingered on An'Tellarus and her companion. He waited until the Lord of the West March spoke two words and stepped out of the courtyard.

"I would have allowed him to stay," An'Tellarus told the Warden. "Is there a reason you wished his departure? While it is true we are speaking of things that would best be limited to the smallest audience, it is also true that almost nothing we have spoken of came as a surprise to Lord Rowan."

"I do not wish to engage in political games. I am Warden of the green, not Warden of Avonelle, Darrowelm, or Tellarus; you may petition for information or entrance into the green, but you cannot command. Not even the Lord of the West March has that right."

"Be fair, Barian. I have never attempted to exercise any such power."

"No. But that pertains to your history, not to your future." He turned, not to An'Tellarus, but to Severn. "The invitation, such as it is, is false, in my opinion."

"You have not declared it to be invalid."

"No. As you suspect, that would have political implications, and it would require proof."

"How," Severn asked, voice soft and more deferential than it had been to this point, "would that be proven? I assume that, as Warden, you have ways of determining counterfeits."

"Indeed, although it is seldom that that expertise is required." He exhaled, his eyes a deep blue, his expression almost grim. "There is no proof that the invitation is fake. If I were to announce my suspicion, there would be very little to back it up. The power of the Warden is, in many ways, the power of consent; I am Warden because the green accepts me; I am Warden because I am acceptable to the West March, politically. It is the latter that would be in jeopardy if no proof is offered."

"You were chosen by the green."

"Yes." There was a hint of pride in the single word.

"How much of your suspicion is based on political knowledge, and how much on the intuition serving as keeper of the green has given you?"

Lord Barian tilted his head, and the hint of a smile touched his eyes, lightening the blue to a normal intensity. "It is, as you suspect, an amalgam of both. But the Dreams have been restless and the water disturbed. I have not touched the small branch that was offered me as proof of invitation; it passed from Lord Tanniase's hand to the water when I attempted to accept it. The water...moved it. I do not believe Tanniase will be allowed to carry it into the green, if he is allowed to enter at all."

"You've yet to grant permission?"

"I can grant permission, but in rare cases, the green decides; there is no way to override that decision."

"The last time this unrest in water and Dreams occurred was when another Barrani Lord received this branch?"

The Warden nodded.

"And that branch was considered false as well?"

"It was not considered false at the time, no. But...it could not enter the green."

"Its bearer could?"

"Yes—but the attempt was not successful. The bearer did not survive. We found his body outside of the Warden gates the morning after. The branch itself was withered with rot and worms; it was put to the fire." He exhaled. "The fire burned black and the branch screamed, enlarging itself before we were able to use the green's power to destroy it."

"Shadow."

"It is perhaps the one thing with which you might be more experienced, given your residence, than the denizens of the West March, but the dangers of Shadow are not unknown to us."

"You don't wish to burn Lord Tanniase's branch."

"I do—but if I am wrong, there will be political costs to be paid."

"I was told that anyone who had the Warden's permission could enter the green."

"Yes. But the shards are kept at its heart; you might walk the periphery of the green without reaching that heart. I am able to lead people to the heart of the green—but I lead very, very few, and of those, only the people I am certain mean no harm and intend to take no benefit that will not also benefit the green in some fashion. If you ask it, and I so choose, the invitation is not necessary.

"But if I do not so choose, the invitation implies that the green will. It is not a matter of concern. The green has ways of hiding and protecting those it favors."

"Then what is the purpose of the invitation if it is not genuine?"

"It is to convince me, of course, that by leading the supplicant to the heart of the green, I am following the will of the green."

Severn frowned. "You've just stated that the green has its own will."

Lord Barian smiled. "I did."

"Do they not understand this? It did not seem to be a secret."

His smile deepened. "An'Tellarus brought you here for a reason—you, a mortal, and at that, one barely out of childhood. Do you know what happens to a Warden who angers the green?"

"No. I was never taught that a Warden could."

"What, then, were you taught of the Wardens?"

"They serve the green. They protect the green. They respect the green. They can hear the voice of the water."

"We are Immortal, but I am not the first Warden; I will not be the last."

Severn frowned. "Were you Warden when the prior invitation was brought?"

"No."

An'Tellarus and the Lord of the West March were still, but their eyes were fixed to the Warden's face as the single word echoed into silence.

Severn broke it. "Was the previous Warden ever found?"

"No."

"But you knew he was...no longer Warden."

"The water carried the news, and the Dreams sang a dirge. It is a song I never wish to hear again while I live. I believe I never will; if it is sung for me, I will no doubt be dead or incapable of listening. Tanniase may make the attempt to reach the heart of the green, but I will not lead him."

Severn understood. Without proof, Lord Barian nonetheless accepted his instinct and the responsibility of his title. He had seen the price to be paid when those were rejected. "In your opinion, do the Dreams and the water imply a danger to the green?"

"I would have said yes had the Dream not come to this gathering. I would have been certain had the pendant not been carried by that Dream. If you want my suspicion, uttered in this safest of places, it is this: the Dreams and the green are waiting. They have invited someone to take the test."

"How did Lord Tanniase know?"

"Pardon?"

"If your suspicion is correct, it is not the timing of Tellarus that is suspect—it is the timing of Lord Tanniase and his sponsor."

An'Tellarus placed a gentle hand on Severn's shoulder. A warning.

"It is a question that I am now asking myself," Lord Barian replied. "I have no answer. The suspicions I have, I have kept to myself. In a different circumstance, Lord Tanniase's attempt, his invitation, would appear to be genuine, given the other signs. If you ask in an attempt to call my neutrality into question—and indeed, among my kin, it would be—I am willing to swear any oath you will accept that the information did not come from me. I have not spoken of it to anyone until now.

"But the water speaks. The Dreams fly. Those with experience can see portents—but not what those portents signify."

The Lord of the West March frowned.

"An'Tellarus," Lord Barian continued, "perhaps there is something you now wish to tell me, or something you wish to ask of me."

"I have never cared for the green," An'Tellarus replied. "I have nothing I wish to ask of you, and were I to be struck with that unfortunate impulse, I would immediately return to my abode in the High Halls."

Lord Barian surprised them all. He laughed, his eyes almost green. "I see there is a reason my mother considers you—in spite of your obvious power—frivolous."

She smiled. "And you do not?"

"Oh, I do. But I have seldom seen frivolity used in such a fashion; it is refreshing." He then turned to Severn. "You are not An'Tellarus. I believe she would abandon the West March should she feel an urgent need to act in a fashion not of her choosing. I do not believe that is true of you."

"I intended to visit you to petition you for permission to enter the green."

"Yes." Lord Barian was not surprised. "And I stand before you now without the clutter of servants and those who work by my side to study the green and protect it. It can get quite noisy, and the lack of privacy can be daunting. For you, however, I fear that daunting and deadly are now almost one and the same. What would you have of me?"

"I want your permission to enter the green."

"To enter the green?"

"To enter its heart."

"Do you want what Lord Tanniase desires?"

"I hope not." Severn's smile was easy; it wasn't genuine.

"Do you know that another rumor has reached me—from my own guards—about the events that occurred on the day of your arrival?"

"Lord Barian," An'Tellarus said. She was not a woman who was accustomed to being ignored unless she desired it.

The Warden ignored her anyway.

Severn exhaled. "And that rumor?"

"That the Dreams of Alsanis flew toward Elluvian. Is this true?"

Severn understood that this was a test, he'd been tested so often. He hadn't resented those early tests. While the humiliation of childhood failures still lingered, he understood that those failures traced a path to success, slowly but surely; that without failure, he wouldn't have learned what he needed to learn.

"No. No, as you clearly suspect, it is not true."

"Elluvian's flight was considered proof of that rumor—but one man noted that his flight included the Tellarus mortal."

Severn nodded.

"The Lord of the West March hears the water more clearly than I. He hears the Dreams of Alsanis more clearly. But he does not approach the green. None of my guards noted the way the water reacted to you when the gates opened. It is, of course, irrelevant to the water. I am curious to know why An'Tellarus thought to bring you, a mortal, to the West March—but I believe the timing of the various disturbances to be linked to that decision. And yours, of course, to attend her. What is it that you want from the West March?"

"I did not come here to seek the shards of Tyron; I did not know of their existence until I arrived."

An'Tellarus's expression had crumpled into familiar irritation. "Do not look at me," she told Severn, using a tone she had appeared to reserve for Elluvian. "You landed yourself in this mess; you may crawl your way out. Without," she added, "damaging the clothing or the jewelry you currently wear. Honestly, this is why I dislike the young."

"If you had no knowledge of them, why did you accompany An'Tellarus? The water does not believe you are hers."

Severn said nothing for a long beat, considering his options. He didn't intend to lie; a lie would serve no purpose here. He wanted to know what the water had said to the Warden, but conversely, could guess.

"The Dream of Alsanis dropped something when the gates opened." He reached into his interior pocket and pulled out the ivory branch. "I did not know its purpose; I was told only when I had reached Danarre."

Lord Barian held out a hand; Severn very carefully placed the branch into the extended palm, remembering that the leaves had cut An'Tellarus. As the branch touched Lord Barian's palm, it began to glow, the ivory becoming a pale light, the leaves a brilliant emerald.

"If you left this with me, it would be the proof I require," he said, voice soft.

"The other branch didn't do this."

"No."

"It's never glowed like that for me, either."

"Has it not?" Lord Barian shook his head. "I will return it to you, who were clearly meant to carry it."

"I do not understand the purpose it is intended to serve."

"You did not understand the purpose you were meant to serve when you set out, either."

Severn shook his head. "I did. But that purpose had nothing to do with ancient Barrani weapons. My Barrani master taught me to do nothing without a sense of my own purpose. He expected that I, a mortal child, would encounter those whose power was far greater than my own; he assumed that in those cases, I would be ensnared in the games others might play because the power differential might make separation difficult.

"But even given those constraints, I was taught to find a purpose of my own, a goal that might overlap the goals of the powerful I otherwise serve. He did not teach me to turn against those I had agreed—for whatever reason—to serve. But the powerful create paths by simple movement, and those paths, clearer and easier to walk, could be leveraged. Should be leveraged."

"Does An'Tellarus know of this goal?"

Severn nodded.

"Lirienne?"

The Lord of the West March did not reply.

"I believe you are meant to enter the heart of the green. I

believe you are meant to search for the shards of Tyron. But if that is not your intent, if that was not your goal, perhaps we might negotiate."

"You want me to enter the heart of the green?"

"It is not I that desire it, but the green itself." He smiled. "And I have served the green for most of my adult life. I do not see what the green sees or what it hopes to see in you. I do not know why Lord Tanniase chose this moment to make an attempt of his own. I think you will have little success—you are mortal—but the green is older than the Barrani, and its desires have often been opaque.

"Nonetheless, it is what the green wants. It is, I believe, what An'Tellarus wants. Lord of the West March?"

"I bow to your knowledge and your experience. If you accept Severn, I will, of course, accept it. But it does not seem to me that the mortal desires the shards."

"No. But all living beings desire something. We cannot force you to enter the green."

Severn kept a straight face. They could, and everyone here knew it.

"Therefore, tell us what your actual goal is, and we may aid you in the accomplishment of that, in return for the risk you will take at the heart of the green."

"You do not think I will survive."

"I think it highly likely that you will. I do not think you will find the shards of Tyron, and I do not think you can wield them, but I do not believe the green will make you pay for that attempt with your life. It is, however, a risk you take should you accept the invitation of the green."

"What benefit will that have for you?"

"The green will be content."

Severn studied the Warden's face; his eyes were blue, not indigo, his expression neutral. "I want," he finally said, "to inspect Darrowelm."

This elicited a frown.

"It is not on my behalf, Barian," An'Tellarus snapped.

"On whose, then?"

"I was not asked to do this. It is therefore on my own behalf."

It was the Lord of the West March who said a single word. "An'Sennarin."

Severn shook his head. "He did not ask it of me, but I owe An'Sennarin a great debt—and I am aware that the debt between a mortal and the ruler of a Barrani line is one that might never be repaid. There is only one thing I can do for him."

"You wish to find Yvonne of Darrowelm," the Warden said, voice soft.

"I wish to ascertain that she is alive—or dead, if she is dead."

"That is all?"

"That is all, for now."

"For now?"

"If she is alive, if she is captive, if she wishes her freedom, the answer to your question might change. If you intend to help me find the information I seek but expect me to make no further decisions based on what I find, you will be helping me under false pretenses. She may be alive and protected; she may be alive and content. That, too, is information that will alter the choices I might make."

"You cannot kidnap a member of Darrowelm," An'Tellarus snapped.

Severn nodded. "I have no intention of kidnapping her."

"That is your desire?"

Exhaling, Severn continued. "I had intended to petition you for permission to enter the green. I had no desire to find its heart. But the trees that house the great families are not rooted in the soil of the West March; they are rooted in the green. I hoped to find Darrowelm in the green, and to enter Darrowelm from it."

"And if you cannot?"

Severn shrugged, a fief shrug. "Then I will not."

"He is young," the Lord of the West March said. "He must experience such failure for himself before believing it is real." He turned to Lord Barian. "My advice, unasked for, is this: let the mortal try. Let him break himself against the shifting paths of the green, or let him succeed; in either case, it is in his hands." To An'Tellarus he said, "Can you keep him safe until such a time? The water is concerned."

"I will allow it," Lord Barian said. "But I will fulfill my duties first. I will lead the mortal to the heart of the green; where he goes from there is in his own hands—and in the hands of the green."

Severn was sick of High Barrani. Although he read and spoke it fluently, he'd never been in a situation where it was the only safe and acceptable language. Until now. High Barrani was very structured, and the language itself seemed to leech comfort or happiness out of every sentence to which it was applied. For the first time, he missed Elantra. Not home, not that—he had destroyed home with his own hands. But the Halls of Law, the streets of the city itself, noisy, crowded, far smellier.

The West March was pristine, almost perfect—as if even trees followed the unspoken rules of visible Barrani society— but it felt like art, not life; like a moment stretched out in eternity into which nothing else could be added. He didn't belong here. Every step taken was a reminder.

"I'm annoyed," An'Tellarus said, speaking the language of Elantra. "You've clearly spent far too much time with that boy—what were you thinking?" Her arm rested above Severn's; her words were pitched low, as if to reach only his ears.

"I was thinking Lord Barian meant to test me."

"You can't possibly think you passed."

His smile was genuine. "Barrani tests tended to follow, one after the other, until I finally failed. There was no end to them while I lived with my master. Yes, I think I passed. But passing just means I'll get to step into the next mess, the next test."

"And failure?"

"Failure means I have to go back to the beginning again."

She exhaled, leaning into his arm, his shoulder. From a distance, her public behavior was certain to cause embarrassment. "Yes, I think you passed. Barian has always been a strange child."

"It seems to me you've surrounded yourself with nothing but strange children."

Her smile was indulgent; it even reached her eyes, leeching some of the annoyance from their color. "It's both a strength and a failing. You understand that this could kill you?"

"Of course. But entering the West March was always going to pose that risk. I trust your intent, but you have many enemies."

"What are you thinking?"

"Lord Rowan," he replied. "Lord Rowan and the pendant that was returned to you."

"You can't honestly believe that the pendant was meant for me?"

He frowned.

"You gave it to me, yes. But the Dream of Alsanis gave it to you. It's not meant to remain in my hands." In a far softer voice, she added, "Nothing, apparently, is." A mortal life couldn't accrue so much bitterness. "Don't do what I've done."

He raised a brow.

"Don't realize the value and importance of something only once it has been destroyed or removed forever beyond your grasp."

He shook his head. "Too late." His smile was the equal of hers.

She reached up, caught his left cheek in her hand, and very gently brushed her fingers across his skin; they were cold. "Mortals are said to live far more intense lives within their finite span of years."

"You don't believe it."

"I do—but I also believe that emotions are emotions, and pain is pain. Sometimes I believe all of life is just an opportunity to grow the seeds of more pain in the future. Do you still have hope at your age?"

He had no answer to give; she lowered her hand and indicated that they should continue to walk. But as they approached the tree through which Tellarus could be entered, he said, "Yes. If not for myself, yes. In the absence of hope, I've set goals."

"Do they offer comfort?"

"Yours don't?"

"Ah, no. They offer hope—but hope is bitter to me now. It ends. It always ends." She reached into a pocket that was invisible to the eye and withdrew the pendant. "Stand still."

He stopped.

The pendant hung on a long gold chain; she didn't need to play with clasps in order to place it around his neck. "This is yours, for the time being. If you intend to go to the Warden, it will mark your import."

"Won't it make me seem like I might be one of your weaknesses?"

"Yes, of course—but you have drawn eyes. Elluvian has drawn eyes. We've split attention, but the moment you approach the Warden, that attention is likely to be seen as the screen it is. It's possible Elluvian will accompany you. It's almost certain that you will encounter Verranian." As Severn frowned she said, "You don't agree?"

"I agree, but...I think we might also see Lord Rowan."

"He will not be of aid to you."

"I think he might. If he's not, I don't think he'll be as much of a danger as Avonelle or Tanniase himself. Tanniase considers me irrelevant. Avonelle doesn't—because of your interest."

"You don't want An'Avonelle as an enemy."

"I don't want any Barrani as enemies."

She chuckled. "Sometimes that is safer than friendship, among my kin."

"If safety were my chief concern, I would never have agreed to this."

"Safety is chimerical, after all. Come, let us return. To-morrow—or perhaps the day after—we will visit the Warden in person."

"We?"

"I may not be allowed to accompany you into the green, but I will certainly see you off if I'm rejected." Her smile deepened, but it was a thing of edge and malice. "I imagine I will not be the only ruler of note to be present when you arrive. I almost wish to delay your arrival for a few days; I believe An'Avonelle and her people will remain rooted to the spot until you do."

CHAPTER TWENTY

LORD ROWAN'S PETITION FOR AN APPOINTMENT with An'Tellarus was waiting for her when they arrived in Tellarus. "This is not for me," she said, frowning. "Tellarus is a safer place to meet than any other, if you're determined to meet with him."

"I'm not against it. I don't believe anything he said to you was a lie."

"No. But truths among my kin are invariably half-truths; it's what is not said that can be dangerous. He has always been quiet."

"Meaning he's never drawn your attention."

"Meaning that, yes. Perhaps I will have to reconsider."

Severn's smile was broad. "I am considered quiet among my kin. Quiet, reserved, possibly boring."

"Boring?"

"It's a goal. An aspiration."

"Choose a better aspiration."

"If my goal were to entertain you, I certainly would."

"My entertainment preferences have never been predictable. Very well." Her smile became indulgent as her eyes shifted steadily toward green. "Surprise me. Lord Rowan is, as I just said, stiff and boring. If you wish to meet with him—"

"The appointment he petitioned for was with you."

"Neither of us believe that. Do not waste my time." She walked into the interior, toward the stairs that led up, and up again, to the multiple platforms that comprised her home. "I will have him brought to you—along with suitably staid refreshments—when he is granted entrance."

Severn's usual encounters with "staid" refreshments didn't involve daggers. The servants, however, appeared to consider the oversize dagger set to one side of the various plated snacks completely ordinary. The dagger itself was impressive; he could see the folds of steel in its blade and had no doubt the edge was sharp. The handle was ivory and ebony, but not ornate; it seemed both plain and solid: a statement.

A statement that didn't blend well with hospitality, such as it was, in Severn's normal life. He wasn't certain if this was meant for his use but doubted it. He had daggers of his own. So, no doubt, did Lord Rowan.

An'Tellarus didn't lead Lord Rowan to the platform. Another servant did, as she'd promised. He wondered if she could see or hear what occurred in her absence; it was safest to assume that she could.

He rose from his chair as Lord Rowan entered and offered Lord Rowan a Barrani bow. Lord Rowan hesitated for one breath, and then extended the same courtesy to Severn, which probably surprised them both. Perhaps it shouldn't have. Severn wore the pendant that Lord Rowan had instantly recognized.

"An'Tellarus felt that your petition involved me and wished to give you privacy should that suspicion prove correct," Severn said.

"It is, of course, correct." He glanced at the food laid out, his gaze pausing on the same dagger that had struck Severn as inhospitable. To his surprise, Lord Rowan exhaled on a sigh. "She is canny and dangerous."

"But not boring."

At that, Lord Rowan's brows rose into his hairline. He laughed. "You have clearly spent much time with the Barrani if you can say that and survive it."

"Over half of my life," Severn replied, returning a quieter version of the smile that lingered on Lord Rowan's face. "You don't seem surprised to see a weapon there."

"And you were?"

"I was. It is not the custom of my people, but I have attended Barrani functions, and have never seen a similar knife before."

"It is ceremonial, and I am uncertain that it will have any meaning for you."

"Its purpose?"

"Do contracts exist among mortals?"

Severn nodded.

"How are they composed?"

"In pages and pages of High Barrani with multiple lines, clauses, and subclauses."

"Only on paper, then?"

"Not only, no. But the paper is considered the relevant part—it is proof of the existence of the agreement. Do the Barrani not have similar?"

"They do—treaties and such. They are, however, worth only a little more than the paper on which they are written."

"We sign our contracts."

"More writing," Lord Rowan replied. "More ink. The writing itself is of a piece with the document. Barrani might avoid breaking those written agreements, but not because of the writing, or the public nature of such contracts."

"The consequences?"

He nodded. "There are ways, however, to sign—if you

will—that are far more permanent, the consequences more personal and more immediate."

"And they involve daggers?"

"No; a dagger is not necessary. I could break the glass from which I am currently drinking and draw blood with one of the remaining shards. We swear blood oaths when we make agreements we wish to signal are serious."

"So...this is the equivalent of a pen."

This also amused Lord Rowan. "Perhaps."

Severn understood then. "An'Tellarus clearly believes you have come here to negotiate."

"She does."

"And she wishes to discourage you if you are not serious?"

"Indeed. And you are now exposing ignorance to a person with whom you have not yet entered negotiations. I am not certain she would be pleased."

"I'm certain she would be intrigued. One of the few things she values about me is my ability to surprise her."

"Intrigued?"

"She might wonder why I was willing to expose such ignorance to you."

"And if she asked, what would your answer be? I confess I am curious."

"I would consider it a small repayment for the risk you took in the presence of the Lord of the West March and the Warden of the green."

"You will not drink?"

Severn shook his head. "Barrani wine is too potent. If my thoughts are not always clear to the Barrani, I wish them to remain clear to me."

"Very well. I welcome a little less clarity of thought, myself; the edges of the past are too sharp."

"What have you come to ask of me?"

"I wish to accompany you into the green. The Warden will lead you there; he will not lead Lord Tanniase. At one point

in time, he would have, but Tanniase is not who he once
was. He has spent too long in the company of An'Avonelle.
Avonelle desires that the shards of Tyron come to the hand
of a reliable ally. Kosmarre is willing to be that ally."

"And Darrowelm is not?"

"Darrowelm will side with Avonelle, in this. It was once
an ally of Sennarin, before Sennarin moved almost entirely
to the east, where the High Halls wait."

"And now?"

"Now?"

"An'Sennarin is, as you've said, in the High Halls, but you
do not refer to the current lord, do you?"

"The current lord? No. He is, by all accounts, barely out of
childhood. Sennarin was not friend to Avonelle. But Darrowelm was not considered an enemy, and An'Sennarin is not
An'Avonelle. He will not interfere in the West March; he is
unlikely to survive. Darrowelm has never been an enemy of
Tellarus, but it has never been a friend, either. If An'Tellarus
has played her hand—and after the events of today, she has—
they will not step forward."

"But you are here."

"I am Lord Rowan, not An'Darrowelm. My visit is purely
social, and as such, cannot be easily forbidden. But yes, I am
certain it would ruffle feathers were it known."

"It will be known if I grant the favor you ask."

"It is not a concern." He leaned forward in his chair. "You
wear the pendant now."

"An'Tellarus gave it to me."

"Or returned it to you?"

"It was not, and is not, mine. You recognized it. The
woman who once wore it did so centuries ago. How could
it have relevance to me? Whole mortal lines rise and vanish
in far less time."

"The Dreams meant for you to have it. I wish to know
why."

"You feel that accompanying me into the green will answer that question?"

"Given the green? Probably not. But it is the only hope I have." He leaned back. "You are here for your own reasons, of course. I cannot offer you any aid when it comes to the shards; you must seek them, you must find them, and you must pass their test—a test only those who have wielded the weapons understand. But if you did not come to the green to seek them, you must have your own reasons for being here."

"You do not believe that I came for An'Tellarus's sake."

"Oddly enough, no. Almost everyone who witnessed your arrival in the east courtyard, however, would disagree."

"I would not be welcome in Darrowelm."

"No, largely because An'Tellarus would not be welcome; she is not trusted, and her anger has destroyed whole families, root and branch, when it is invoked. You must know her well enough to know she is not entirely predictable; the lack of predictability with the historical consequences of her anger lead to extreme caution."

"Would I be welcome were I to visit without An'Tellarus?"

"No, as you must guess, because you are hers."

Severn reached for a glass of water, ignoring the plated food. "What do you hope to accomplish in the green?"

Lord Rowan's gaze fell to the pendant.

"She is dead, according to An'Tellarus. Do you believe An'Tellarus lied?"

"Frequently. But not about this."

"Then what do you seek?"

Lord Rowan shook his head. "I cannot answer that question; I have asked it, often, of myself. I have searched for her and searched for her traces; I have found nothing. But the pendant was hers. I am certain of it." Lord Rowan lifted his chin. "You do not seek the weapons. What, then, do you seek?"

"I will enter the heart of the green at the behest of An'Tellarus. She desires it."

"That is not an answer."

Their eyes met. Severn's narrowed as he studied Lord Rowan's expression. He took the first risk; he had something Lord Rowan wanted. "I owe a great debt to An'Sennarin."

Lord Rowan blinked. "An'Sennarin? Not An'Tellarus?"

"I owe a debt to An'Tellarus, and my payment is to enter the heart of the green. It's a lesser debt, one easily discharged."

"Not so easily; it may kill you."

Severn shrugged, a fief shrug. "Nothing has, so far."

These weren't the answers Lord Rowan had expected. He was silent, no doubt considering the history of relations between Tellarus and Sennarin. Severn waited, knowing he would find no answers there. "What is your business with An'Sennarin?"

Severn raised a brow. He was young, not foolish.

Lord Rowan smiled. "Very well. Let me retract that question."

"And the insult that spawned it?"

"That as well. I told you: Darrowelm was entwined with Sennarin, but Sennarin—before the death of the previous lord—was the greater power. The ties that bound the two families have been severely loosened; Darrowelm remains and Sennarin is no longer ascendant. What would An'Sennarin have of you?"

Severn shook his head again. "He has, of course, asked for nothing. The debt I feel is personal; I doubt he sees it as a debt at all. Did Lord Leveanne save you from death during the war as a bargaining position?"

Lord Rowan's eyes darkened instantly. After a long, angry pause, he swallowed. "Your point is made. Accept my apologies."

"Apology implies there will be no recurrence. May I trust that?"

"Inasmuch as you seem to trust anything, yes." He smiled.

If Darrowelm had been a strong ally of the previous lord of Sennarin, it would explain Yvonne. If it were attempting to leverage a shift in the alliance—to become the dominant power—that would also explain Yvonne. Severn considered both outcomes likely. But it was also true that if Yvonne of Darrowelm were dead, not confined, it would be in Darrowelm's best interest to hide that fact for as long as possible. If she were alive, her presence could otherwise be an olive branch offered the new An'Sennarin; a gesture of good faith, in the hopes of continuing a previous, fruitful relationship.

He wasn't Barrani, but his training made clear that he had to look for the power and its shifting landscape if he wished to know the truth. What Darrowelm might do to appease An'Sennarin now would depend much on their belief in An'Sennarin's weakness.

"I wish information," Severn finally said.

"In return for allowing me to accompany you?"

Severn shook his head. "It will help me to make that decision, but what I want in trade will depend on your answer."

"That is not generally the way these things work."

"It's the way negotiations with Severn Handred work."

Lord Rowan frowned; his eyes were blue, but the color seemed to shift and swirl, as if the man behind those eyes was struggling to sever himself from his emotional reaction. "What did you just say?"

"I said it's the way Severn Handred negotiates."

"Handred."

Severn nodded.

Lord Rowan rose and walked to the platform's edge; he faced the portions of forest beyond the platform, beyond Tellarus. "Ask your questions."

"Is Yvonne of Darrowelm a captive in Darrowelm?"

Silence.

"Is Yvonne of Darrowelm alive?"

"This is another family's business. It is not yours."

"I will personally ask the Warden to exclude you from the green, or the heart of the green, until I, or my corpse, emerges if you continue in this fashion."

"And you think you have the power to demand that? That is a very sloppy threat."

"It was not a threat, Lord Rowan. It was a promise. I understand that bluffing is common in games of chance and fortune, neither of which we are playing. It will be my request, not An'Tellarus's, but I will not step into the green until he agrees."

"You must ask another favor."

"No. You may offer a different favor, but you will waste both your time and mine, and you will forgive me if I consider my time to be more precious."

"You have so little of it."

Severn said nothing. He waited.

"She is not a captive in Darrowelm." Lord Rowan's hands clenched by his sides, but he made no move to arm himself.

"Is she dead?"

"You may or may not choose to believe this, but I do not know. She was insignificant as a child and was likely to remain so. Darrowelm had no interest in her; it had little interest in most of its children, and she was not of the direct family descent. Her parents are dead. She was granted the opportunity to live within Darrowelm itself far earlier than most."

"When did her parents die?"

Lord Rowan exhaled. "At almost the same time Ollarin's died. That is why you are asking."

Severn nodded.

"Then you understand that the offer to take in a worthless orphan was not the kindness it seemed. Please tell me that your negotiations will not or do not involve Yvonne."

"I could lie. You wouldn't believe it."

"We are aware," Severn noted the use of *we*, "that

An'Sennarin must have more power than he did when he was a child in the West March. We knew of his potential, and we knew the previous lord wished to utilize it. He paid; he is dead. Ollarin is alive, and he is now An'Sennarin."

"An'Tellarus attempted to visit her."

"Before Ollarin took the title, yes. And once after it came into his hands."

"She was refused entry."

"Yes." Lord Rowan turned to face Severn, an odd smile changing the contours of his face. "You were not tasked with this. It was not An'Sennarin's request. I ask, now, that it remain this way. What I tell you, you must not repeat."

Severn shook his head. "If she is dead, I will inform him."

"I have told you she is not. But now, Severn Handred, all paths lead to the green. She is not—and I will swear a blood oath upon this information if you insist—within the confines of Darrowelm. Very well. If you discover evidence of her death, you will do as your conscience dictates. In that way, you are very like our young. The information must not be traced to me; if you stumble across it without the aid of any of Darrowelm, I will make no attempt to bury either you or that information."

This turned his goals, briefly, on their head. "You believe Yvonne is...in the green?"

"Perhaps An'Tellarus has not informed you, or perhaps An'Sennarin himself has not, but An'Sennarin hears the water more clearly—and speaks to it more easily—than any other lord in the West March."

Severn didn't ask the next question, the obvious question; it wasn't necessary. Danarre had the fountain at its heart—it was highly likely Darrowelm did as well.

"Very well. I am to meet with the Warden in three days. Meet us there or return to Tellarus before we set out."

"I will meet you there." He glanced at the knife.

"I can swear a blood oath if you desire it—but I am not Barrani. I doubt it would bind me."

"It would bind me," Lord Rowan replied.

"I believe what you've said. A binding oath would change nothing. It won't change what I have to do. It won't change my goals." He grimaced and repeated the words in High Barrani.

"I understood you the first time," Lord Rowan replied, although he didn't shift languages. "If I were not afraid An'Tellarus would kill me, I would demand to speak with her next. Were I your age, I would take the risk of death regardless." He offered Severn a very formal bow. "In three days. I should warn you that the Warden takes his appointments—unless an emergency arises—before the sun reaches its height."

Lord Rowan wasn't the only person waiting for Severn when An'Tellarus finally decided it was time to depart. Elluvian was waiting within Tellarus, his foot beating a staccato rhythm of impatience. His eyes were very blue, his arms folded. An'Tellarus ignored him; had she been able to magically walk through him, she would have. The Barrani Wolf had no choice but to pull up the rear, given Severn's prominent position by An'Tellarus's side.

Lord Rowan waited beneath the shade of the tree that served as a half portal to Tellarus itself. He offered An'Tellarus a perfect bow—one he hadn't offered in the east courtyard. As if to emphasize this, he also offered Severn a similar bow.

Tellarus guards were present; she had chosen four. Two servants also followed. Had it not been for the color of her watchful eyes, they might have been returning to tea in the east courtyard of the Lord of the West March's abode. Severn wasn't surprised to see the guards of the Warden out in greater number. If Avonelle and Kosmarre had littered their own guards, under false colors, throughout the Warden's forces, that would become clear soon. He wanted to drag his arm from An'Tellarus's to bring his hand closer to his daggers.

"There is no one invisible in the streets." She spoke Elantran. "You'll have time to react unless archers are put to use. Some of the guards, however, are definitely in the Warden's service; I recognize them. They might choose to ally themselves with Avonelle or Kosmarre if the incentives are good enough, but I haven't generally considered them fools."

Severn grinned.

"You won't relax until we reach the Warden, will you?"

"Sorry. If hostility had a stench, I'd never be able to clear it out of my nose."

"They would have to be brave or desperate to attack you; you are obviously mine."

"And Elluvian?"

"He's a big boy. He can look after himself."

"He's joined our party."

"Yes. I told him not to, but he insisted. It's almost as if he expects trouble." Her smile almost sparkled in the sunlight, as if she were hard as diamond. She lifted her chin, exposing the length of a pale, perfect throat. "The Dreams are coming." She felt his arm tense beneath hers and shook her head. "Unless they demand your attention, ignore them. I pointed them out on the off chance their presence would provide some comfort. It will certainly make any of the guards along this road think twice if their intent is to harm or kill you."

"Why?"

"Lord Barian's movements are never precisely secret. It is possible—perhaps likely—that he sent his guards out in greater numbers to avoid a lackadaisical assassination attempt. Regardless, those who serve will understand that he's waiting for a guest who has been invited.

"The news will filter out, and it will not filter out slowly. You have upset a precarious balance in the West March. I admit I find it enormously entertaining."

Of course she did.

"I will also admit," she added, as the Dreams began their descent, "I find it exhilarating. I've never seen the Dreams so close or so present as they have been since we arrived in the West March."

Severn lifted an arm, bent at an angle, just as the Lord of the West March had a few days past. One of the Dreams condescended to land on his arm, but the others—five in total—remained airborne, at a far lower altitude than he had seen such birds fly before.

Lord Rowan, who walked on the other side of An'Tellarus, stumbled and righted himself; Severn wondered what Elluvian was doing but couldn't shift his gaze to look; the bird was on his arm, staring at him, eyes unblinking.

"Speak if you wish to speak; ride if you wish to ride," Severn told the Dream. "I'll listen. I have nothing else to offer you, or I would." His tone was soft, the words low; he spoke almost as if the bird were a natural creature. The Dream remained silent, but the weight of that silence was underscored by the presence of the low-flying escort. Severn wondered if these Dreams could die. It wasn't a question he felt comfortable asking. The claws of the Dreams were real, and he was certain they could be deadly.

But these birds didn't smell like birds. They bore the scent of forest, of branches, of leaves; he caught the faint sweetness of something floral as well. He wasn't surprised when the Dreams began to sing, their voices in no way matching their forms. Flocks of squawking birds never sounded musical, but these weren't squawking. He wondered if anyone else walking the streets—or guarding them—could hear the dreamsong.

It didn't sound like a dirge to Severn, but he'd heard so few, and always at a distance; he wasn't certain if, in Barrani context, this was a chorus of mourning.

"I almost feel I owe you an apology," An'Tellarus said, her voice pitched low.

"Please don't. As long as you uphold your end of our deal, you owe me nothing."

"I didn't imagine that you would become so...obvious."

Severn grimaced. "It's not my favorite position, no."

"There are many who would kill for the attention you are so clearly receiving."

He nodded. "Perhaps because of my childhood, it's not attention or envy I seek. Both have always been a danger."

"Not attention, not envy, and not affection, either, if I'm any judge." She was. They both knew it.

"That wasn't always true," he confessed, watching not An'Tellarus but the Dream.

"Oh?"

"It's painful, to have and lose."

"You are too young to say that. And I confess that the seed of affection has been planted in me. You are not what I expected—and I knew you wouldn't be, but...this is not what I envisioned."

"Can you hear them?" he asked.

"Yes. Yes, Severn. The dreamsong is audible. If I am able to hear it, I imagine the whole of the West March can. I had hoped that you would meet the Warden in relative privacy. That will not happen, now." She smiled, her eyes an odd shade—almost green, almost purple. "Still, I'm not at all bored, and in this moment, I feel the fleeting hint of an awe I thought had long deserted me. I don't know if this is what your first master intended, but I almost hope he's watching."

Severn glanced at Lord Rowan; his eyes were raised, his lips compressed as if he feared to utter words that would embarrass him. Severn hesitated and then said, in Elantran, "Please protect Elluvian."

He heard the annoyed intake of breath that came from

his right and ignored it. The birds didn't stop their chorus of song; they made no reply at all.

The Warden's gates were open by the time An'Tellarus and her party reached them. Standing on the outside of those gates were men and women who wore long robes—green robes—with the insignia of the Warden. Standing apart from them stood Lord Barian; he wore similar robes and the slender tiara. Black hair framed his face and fell away, disappearing down his back. His eyes were almost green, his face raised as Lord Rowan's face had been raised.

He nodded to An'Tellarus but didn't acknowledge Severn until An'Tellarus released his arm and nudged him in the Warden's direction. Severn took a step, his raised arm still a perch for one of the great, black birds, and then glanced back at Lord Rowan. For the first time, Lord Rowan hesitated, as if he were no longer certain his request could, or should, be granted.

"You know why he wants to be here," he said to the bird, who now cocked head to one side as if half believing Severn couldn't actually speak. "Unless there's a reason the green would reject him, he'll be my second." As if this were a pointless duel.

The song didn't change, but the bird seemed to nod, and Severn, lifting voice and switching into the more cumbersome language, said, "Lord Rowan, you have permission to accompany me."

Lord Rowan stepped forward instantly. An'Tellarus remained as she was, as did her guards. Only Elluvian moved, but he came to a stop at her side, probably because she'd grabbed his wrist.

The Warden offered Severn a deep bow and held it an uncomfortably long time. Or it would have been, had the bow been meant for Severn; it wasn't. It was meant in its entirety for the Dream that perched on the mortal's arm. For the song the chorus of birds, all hovering a man's height above the ground, continued to sing.

Only when the song finally tailed off into an almost unnatural silence did the Warden rise. "I welcome you, Severn Handred."

Severn glanced at the bird on his arm; the others rose, taking once again to the height of the skies, where they glided in a circular pattern. This one, however, appeared to have no intention of joining them, and Severn's arm was becoming stiff. It was very difficult to observe normal Barrani courtesies when one of his arms was useless. The Warden accepted this with more than good grace. He turned to those who clearly obeyed him and spoke so softly Severn's ears didn't catch the words.

No one, however, could fail to catch the words that came from behind and to the left.

"Wait!"

People were running toward the Warden—or toward Severn, it was hard to determine without looking. Lord Rowan, unencumbered by the honorary sentry, did turn; his hand fell to a sword Severn hadn't seen until that moment. He shifted away from Lord Barian to see banners in the street; he recognized Avonelle from his earlier studies but didn't recognize the second banner.

He did, however, recognize Lord Tanniase, and assumed the banner to be Kosmarre's.

An'Tellarus abandoned the pretext of perfect etiquette then. It was clear that Tanniase at least intended to join Severn. An'Tellarus was closer and stepped in, once again, to his exposed side, keeping distance between herself and the reach of the Dream's beak.

It was An'Tellarus who turned toward Lord Tanniase. "The Warden," she said, voice cold and loud, "is occupied, Lord Tanniase. I am certain he will greet you with all due respect when he is finished."

She could have cursed—in Elantran—to no greater effect. Her words, or perhaps her tone, rippled outward, changing the speed at which the guards behind Lord Tanniase moved.

"That is not your decision." The familiar voice came from behind the line of Avonelle guards. It was, of course, An'Avonelle's. "You are not Warden, An'Tellarus; Lord Barian is."

At the sound of her voice, the Tellarus guards moved up; the Avonelle guards spread out. Hands fell to weapons, but the weapons remained in their sheaths. Severn thought it unlikely they'd remain there.

Lord Barian turned and snapped audible orders to his own guards, and even if the guards under his colors spied at the behest of other lords, they moved at his command here.

It is not the time to shed blood, the Dream said.

Severn turned toward its moving beak; so did Lord Barian.

It is not the place, not yet.

As if those words, that voice, could carry, a third banner joined the two on the street. It was larger, its fall weightier; it was carried on a large pole, undisturbed by the movement of wind or breeze, an image of a white bird of prey on a black background.

"No," the Lord of the West March said. "It is not the time, nor the place."

CHAPTER TWENTY-ONE

THE LORD OF THE WEST MARCH HADN'T CHOSEN to depend on the power of his title; he had come with his own guards, and they outnumbered Avonelle's. Avonelle's guards weren't the four considered polite in rarefied West March society; Tellarus, should it decide to stand and fight, was clearly outnumbered.

Elluvian, however, was with An'Tellarus. Severn was certain he counted for more than a half dozen of these Barrani guards, in the worst case. The worst case was unlikely to emerge. In these circumstances, the Warden's guards and the guards of the West March, who stood beneath the banner of a large bird of prey, would join forces. Tellarus might choose, with only four guards, to remain neutral, but given the color of her eyes, Severn doubted that.

"An'Avonelle," the Lord of the West March said. "Lord Tanniase." The words were both acknowledgment and command. "Do not anger the green." He glanced at Lord Barian; Lord Barian, eyes the color of An'Avonelle's and An'Tellarus's, nonetheless offered the Lord of the West March a deep bow.

"We do not seek to anger the green," Lord Tanniase said,

his tone clearly making an objection of the words. "And indeed, it might be seen as protection and defense of the green that we travel in such haste. The Dreams—"

"Can you not see where the Dreams of Alsanis have chosen to land?" The Lord of the West March looked, pointedly, at Severn's arm. "It is to honor the passage of this party that the Dreams flew. It is to honor the will of the green that they chose to sing. Or perhaps you did not hear their song."

Severn thought it impossible; all of the Warden's people had, as had An'Tellarus and Lord Rowan. Given Lord Tanniase's instant flush, he revised his opinion.

"My apologies for the interruption, Lord Barian," the Lord of the West March then said. He bowed to the Warden. "I was asked to come, to bear witness."

Lord Barian didn't doubt him; Lord Tanniase did. An'Avonelle was glaring at the bird that rested on Severn's arm. If he had caught her attention in the east courtyard, it was nothing in comparison to this; she was livid. Severn was certain that, had it not been for his escort, he'd be dead in the streets.

"We wished to ascertain that the Warden was safe," An'Avonelle finally said.

"From a *mortal*?"

"A mother's concern can on occasion produce haste where it is not required, and he is my only surviving child." Severn wondered idly if she'd killed and eaten the rest. Certainly she'd sent at least one to their death in the High Halls.

"I am safe," Lord Barian said, when no one chose to speak in response. "I serve the green. I have never once failed in that service. And today the green is awake." His eyes were green, but it was not entirely the green of very rare Barrani happiness; it was other. Brighter and darker, both.

"You have not done your duties with regards to Kosmarre," Lord Tanniase snapped; he was visibly angry, his self-control almost nonexistent. "A week ago, you received my proof of invitation, and you have not yet led me into the green. It is almost an insult."

"Lord Tanniase," An'Avonelle said, her voice cold.

"But—"

"The Warden's decision must be respected. And clearly, the Warden has been very busy. It has been many years since I have seen such a gathering of his liegemen. It takes time to accumulate those disparate servants. Perhaps the wait was necessary."

Lord Tanniase withdrew a small ivory branch, with larger leaves of emerald attached to it. The bird on Severn's arms tightened its claws; Severn, without thought, reached out to grab the bird's leg. It felt far smoother than the legs of the Imperial messenger birds, as if he was touching ebony. He didn't want the Dreams to touch the branch Lord Tanniase held.

He didn't really want the Warden to touch it, either, but the Warden had previously held it for long enough to be suspicious of its origin, its nature.

"I offer my most sincere apologies to the Warden," Tanniase said. "But this is a matter of such import to me, I fear I have been unable to fully contain my worry." He bowed, the branch now cradled in both of his upturned palms.

Severn frowned. It came to him then that Tanniase had accepted this invitation in good faith, or in as much good faith as he could muster. In that, his circumstance would be no different than Severn's. Tanniase wanted the weapons. Or perhaps Tanniase wanted what the weapons would signify: that Tanniase was special, that he was to be respected, admired, perhaps exalted.

Severn hadn't known about the shards, but regardless, the benefits to Tanniase would never be Severn's. The most he could hope for, were he to somehow succeed in finding them and passing their test, would be envy, anger, and the echoes of both: resentment and fear. He was not, and would never be, Barrani. He was foreign, an outsider. He had no place here.

He was accustomed to that feeling, even when he was surrounded by his own kind. There was no place for Severn in any of the spaces mortals occupied. No place, except perhaps the Wolves. But if he had no place, he had a purpose, and that would have to suffice.

Lord Barian's eyes had turned to Severn, and Severn understood the wordless command. The ivory branch was in an awkward place to reach with the hand he had free; he therefore withdrew it with far less grace than Tanniase had his own.

Word spread out in a widening circle, followed by silence. The texture of that silence was a mix of reactions: awe, suspicion, dread, anger. The gathered Barrani were very like a human crowd, but smaller in number.

Lord Tanniase's eyes were gold with shock, but the gold was swallowed by a darkening blue. He turned toward An'Avonelle, but her eyes were as dark as they could get and still be within a Barrani range. An'Tellarus's were lighter, of course; she was enjoying herself.

Lord Barian lifted a hand. "Lord Tanniase."

The Barrani Lord stepped forward and placed his invitation into Lord Barian's hand.

The Dreams of Alsanis began to screech. No, that was the wrong word; they began to *roar*, their voices overlapping like the rumble of thunder at the heart of a storm. Severn tightened his grip on the Dream. "It's all right," he said, in very soft Elantran. "The Warden knows. He won't allow the branch to enter the green."

He should not touch it at all!

"He knows that as well—but this is the realm of the West March, not the lands of the green, and the rules here are different."

The bird's claws tightened, piercing cloth, a reminder of just how little primal ancient forces observed the distinction. "He will do nothing to threaten the green. Nothing."

It is not the green that will be harmed, but the guardian of the green, the watcher, the Warden.

The Lord of the West March stepped past Severn, toward Lord Barian; Lord Barian lifted his free hand, palm out, a warning of its own. It was the Warden the Lord of the West March chose to obey.

One of the robed people stepped toward Barian, hands cupped around the flat but rounded bottom of what appeared to be a large basin—a basin of stone or marble. Runes were engraved around the outer lip. Severn had no doubt similar runes girded the interior. Lord Barian transferred the branch received from Tanniase to the bowl; it fell with a splash, as if the bowl contained a greater depth of water on the inside than it looked to hold from its visible dimensions.

The water rose in a twisting pillar; the bowl tilted and Lord Barian immediately placed his hands beneath it to steady it. Steam rose from the pillar. Severn was surprised to see that the pillar appeared to contain, at its heart, white fire, a flame that burned what it touched.

It touched only the branch, but Severn understood Barian's concern, for as the branch burned in the white flame, it screamed. The scream sounded similar to the anger of the Dreams. The leaves wilted first, but they didn't burn to ash; as the outer edges of emerald blackened, the entirety of the shape and seeming of a leaf twisted, becoming distorted when seen through the moving wall of water. The smoke that emerged was clearly not natural; it was far larger than the leaves or the branch, and its darkness, murky, solidified instead of dissipating, as most smoke would.

But most smoke, most fire, didn't occur in the heart of water, either.

Tanniase was almost frozen in place, his eyes wide, his brows high. He turned toward An'Avonelle. Her eyes were indigo, her arms rigid, her hands curved but stiff. She didn't return Tanniase's glance; her eyes were fixed on the pillar of water, its unnatural fire, and the thing that twisted and burned there. Severn reached the limitation of inferences drawn from Barrani eye color. There were far too many things of which she might be frightened, and far too many that might enrage her.

He knew he was one. An'Tellarus was one. And he was certain she found Lord Tanniase's outburst almost humiliating because here he was associated with Avonelle, and his behavior would reflect poorly on her.

"Severn," Lord Rowan said, gently nudging his shoulder. "The Warden is waiting for you."

Severn nodded, but waited, watching until nothing remained at the heart of the water but the flame itself. He then approached Lord Barian, the branch in his free hand.

"This is not how you intended to arrive, is it?" Lord Barian asked, the question so soft Severn barely heard it.

Severn shook his head, a hint of rueful grin offered to the Warden. He held out the branch. Claws tightened again; this time he was certain they left small wounds.

Lord Barian bowed to the great bird of prey and spoke to it in a language Severn didn't recognize. The Warden clearly understood that the permission he sought, he sought from the wrong person. The Warden served the green, but he lived in the West March; unless the power with which he was now imbued could be used at his whim, he must make concessions to the politics that governed him.

Whatever Lord Barian said caused the claws to loosen. Severn then approached the Warden and carefully placed the ivory branch in his hand. He expected that it would also undergo trial by water, as the first branch had.

He was wrong.

As soon as the branch touched Lord Barian's hand, it began to glow, just as it had done in the Lord of the West March's home. But the glow was brighter; the leaves glittering as if they were the emerald their color resembled. The light they shed was green, and it cast shadows, rippling toward the ground beneath the Warden's hands, a vine of a paler green.

The Barrani holding the basin set it down and rose, as if to emphasize that it wouldn't be necessary.

Barian, holding Severn's branch, turned to the silent Lord Tanniase. "I do not believe you deliberately came to me with a fake. I believe your intent was to enter the green and attempt to prove your worth to things that sleep. Your impatience, if you acted in good faith, is understandable. But I, too, had reasons for denying your request. There is nothing left of the invitation you received, but I invite you to examine the circumstances surrounding your discovery with more care.

"This, however, is genuine. You can see the difference now. Perhaps it will better explain what appeared to you an unnecessary delay." His eyes remained green, his tone respectful.

Lord Tanniase swallowed. "Will you not test this branch the way you tested the first one?"

"I see no necessity for such a test. Do you?" Before Tanniase could answer, Lord Barian lifted head and voice. "Does anyone present see such a need?"

Silence. Lord Tanniase trembled but bowed again. He then rose and stepped backward, toward the Avonelle banner under which he'd arrived. If An'Avonelle had raised voice, he might have insisted, but she didn't. Wouldn't, Severn thought. She might be ambitious. She clearly wasn't stupid.

With obvious respect, Lord Barian returned the branch to Severn. "If you are ready, please join us. We will partake of refreshments before we enter the green."

Severn glanced at Lord Rowan, who nodded. He then turned to look back at Elluvian but could no longer see him in the crowd.

An'Tellarus didn't accompany Severn, although she did make a very public show of kissing the cheek farthest from the perched Dream of Alsanis. "This isn't what I intended," she said, speaking Elantran as if it were the only language of love. "But I admit you've surpassed my hopes. Elluvian is enraged, but he has far better control of his temper than he once did.

"Of course, he is known for his rage and fury. Perhaps in time you will find out why. In the meantime, I ask that you not get yourself killed in the green. Preferably at all. Elluvian will blame me."

"He won't."

"Oh?"

"I'm fully capable of making my own choices—and there's no true choice if there's no risk of, no acceptance of, the consequences of that choice."

"Spoken like the young man you very much are."

"What would you expect of an older man?"

"Experience tempers resolve. Tell me, do you believe children should be killed for their mistakes?"

"It depends on the consequences of those mistakes to others. Children take dares and tests of courage in the streets of the fiefs at night. Sometimes they survive the Ferals, sometimes they don't. It's not about whether or not they deserve to die by Ferals. It's not about how good or bad they are. Some mistakes are more costly than others." He exhaled. "No. I don't believe children should be killed for their mistakes. But my beliefs don't change facts.

"And An'Tellarus, I'm not a child." He turned once again to Lord Rowan; Lord Barian stood silent, waiting for An'Tellarus to finish. "Elluvian has already acknowledged that fact. If I die here, it's on me."

"Very well. I do hope you come back to me." She lowered the hand she had lifted and stepped back.

Only Lord Rowan accompanied Severn, but Lord Barian seemed to accept his presence.

★ ★ ★

"Normally," Lord Barian said, when they were far enough down the small cobbled path behind the Warden's gate, "you would be required to bathe in the waters, and you would be clothed in robes of entreaty. Lord Rowan?"

Lord Rowan bowed. One of the robed men led him away. When he had disappeared from view, Lord Barian said, "You are not what we are. The waters have already cleansed you, and it is not to entreat the green that you have come." He smiled and added, "I believe you would find the robes cumbersome should you be required to fight. The green will take no offense at their absence."

"But the green will be offended by Lord Rowan?"

"He is Barrani, and he is of the West March."

"And as such, expected to know better?"

"Indeed."

Severn had no desire to wear robes, the hems of which might entangle his legs, but he felt a visceral desire to show the green the respect it demanded. "Do you have a cloak that is similar in design to the robes?"

"We do."

"Let me borrow that, then."

Lord Barian nodded, and robed people fluttered at his silent command. "If the Dream chooses to accompany you for the entirety of your journey, I ask that you accept it."

Severn nodded. He hoped the Dream would do so from the air; his arm was now stiff with the effort of maintaining the elevation and bend its perch required. A cape could be put on while the Dream remained where it was; robes couldn't—no doubt the real reason Lord Barian didn't insist.

"You have chosen to allow Lord Rowan to accompany you."

Severn nodded.

"You are certain that is wise?"

And grinned. "No. Very few seem to expect wisdom of me. You disapprove?"

Lord Barian shook his head. "I know Lord Rowan's long and fruitless quest, and I was not surprised to hear that he desired to accompany you."

"But surprised I allowed it?"

"You are of Tellarus. If any house would, it is Tellarus." A woman in robes approached Lord Barian. She bowed, rose, and handed him a satchel that seemed, given the way it reflected and trapped light, to be made of silk. Silk wouldn't have been the material Severn would have used for a satchel or pack of any kind. "It is difficult to offer you a meal, given what you must carry on your arm. I do not believe you would be allowed to sit in peace. If you later have the opportunity to eat," Lord Barian said, as a servant presented Severn with a satchel, "this will be of help."

"Do you have any advice to offer me?"

"Do not offend the green."

"What will offend the green?"

A brief smile touched Barian's lips. "Do not harm the trees. Do not set a fire. Do not defile the waters of any lake or stream you might find. If you are attacked by predators, you may kill them to defend yourself—but do not attack them first. The green is not unreasonable, if it chooses to harbor you. And if it perceives that you have done it a service, it may choose to aid or guide you."

Severn glanced at the Dream. The Dream bowed its head.

Lord Rowan returned in robes of forest green. He bowed to the Warden and rose. His eyes were almost green. "Will you lead us yourself?"

"I will lead you into the green, but I have assigned the difficult tracking to Lord Onuri." He turned to the man who stood at his left; of all the gathered servants, Onuri was the only one who carried a visible staff. His hood was down around his shoulders, and his hair flowed past it; his eyes were blue, but the blue had flecks of green in it.

Lord Rowan nodded, as if he'd expected as much. "He has never been lost in the green," he told Severn.

Lord Onuri, robed, shook his head. "Lord Rowan is kind, but wrong. The green, however, has never allowed me to remain lost. Once," he added, "I slept. It caused inconvenience and worry."

"Barrani don't need to sleep."

"No. I will apologize in advance; I am not as fleet-footed or graceful as most of my companions, but on occasion the green creates a path to make my passage less cumbersome."

Severn smiled. "I am not fleet-footed or graceful compared to most of your kin, either."

"Come. We follow the sun," Lord Barian said. He walked ahead between trees and the shadows their leaves cast; to Severn's eye, his feet barely touched the ground. When Severn looked back over his shoulder, he could no longer see the Warden's gates, or any of the people who served him.

When the Dream of Alsanis chose to finally vacate its chosen perch, Severn breathed an audible sigh of relief. He lowered his arm and began to exercise it as they walked.

"Some of my kin would be highly gratified to have drawn so much attention," Lord Rowan said, a half smile touching his lips and the color of his eyes. He lifted a hand to forestall a response. "You are not of my kin, and even were you, I realize it would never be your ambition."

Severn shrugged, an easy, natural shrug—favoring the shoulder of the arm that still felt stiff. "I couldn't avoid attention at An'Tellarus's side. And yes, I know it's not the same." He glanced at Lord Barian's back, and then to the side at Onuri.

To his surprise, Lord Rowan said, "Onuri was once of

Danarre, before it fell. He was never a warrior; that was not his strength."

"It was the only reason I survived," Onuri said. "But I was injured; I walked close to death. I cannot run, if in the end running is required. I bear no sword. I am here as guide, not guard."

Lord Rowan nodded; none of this information came as a surprise to him.

"Where do you intend to guide me?" Severn asked.

Onuri smiled for the first time. "You are certain you have never entered the green?"

"I am certain I have no memory of ever doing so."

"As you clearly suspect, it is not my guidance that is of value here. It is the guidance of the green itself. I intend to follow the signs that might lead us to your destination; they are oft subtle."

"And Lord Barian?"

"Lord Barian can, if it is necessary, stand and fight."

Lord Barian stopped walking and turned toward Severn. "The green does not give commands in words even those who can hear its voice understand. The only living being who could is Alsanis, and he speaks to no one now, except through his dreams. There are shifts in geography, changes in paths that have been well-worn. We look for those changes. Onuri is our most gifted guide. His sensitivity is greater than even mine.

"He is also the most gentle of us. The green rewards many things, but perhaps because Onuri is, and has always been, who he is, Onuri is valued."

To Severn's surprise, Onuri reddened. He was clearly unaccustomed to praise. He made no reply, but bowed his head and continued to follow the Warden while staring at the ground.

Only when Onuri suddenly said, "Stop!" did Severn understand that it wasn't humility that caused this; it was a necessary part of his assigned duties. Everyone came to a halt. Onuri bent, stiffly, at the knees. He reached out as if to touch something, but to Severn's eye, there was nothing there.

Only when Onuri's hand came into contact with a plant no one else could see did it become visible; it was a large white flower, the weight of the bloom bending the stem. Severn glanced at Lord Barian and instantly met his gaze; the Warden seemed intent on watching Severn. Whatever Onuri was doing, he'd clearly expected.

"This is where it becomes more difficult," the Warden said, as if offering an explanation. "Onuri?"

Onuri failed to reply. Severn thought it was because Onuri hadn't actually heard the Warden. He seemed to be almost hunting through foliage—all of which remained invisible. After ten minutes, Onuri exhaled and shook his head.

The white blossom clearly indicated the correct path, or perhaps a waypoint. "Were you looking for a second flower?" Severn asked.

Onuri nodded.

"What do you do if Onuri is not the guide?"

"We follow the path," the Warden replied. "If the path we take doesn't lead us to the heart of the green, that is the will of the green."

Severn frowned. To his eye, there was no path. They had begun walking on one, a narrow path of cobbled stone; he couldn't remember the moment when that path had ended. "Do you see a path here?" he asked the Warden.

The Warden frowned. "We are standing on it."

"I'm not. Onuri?"

Onuri shook his head.

"Lord Rowan?"

"I see no path, either."

The Warden exhaled. "Very well. It is your invitation. It is therefore your pilgrimage. How do you wish to proceed?

We may follow the path I see; we may step off that path and follow you. The choice is yours."

Severn reached into his internal pocket and withdrew the ivory branch. In the light of this particular forest, it looked natural; the leaves seemed slightly wilted, although they retained their brilliant hue. If he'd hoped for guidance, the leaves failed him. He stood in a patch of knee-high weeds, surrounded by trees. The task every other Barrani seemed to anticipate or dread was, in the end, secondary to Severn. If there was no easy way to accomplish it, he would accept that failure; it wasn't why he'd come.

Pocketing the branch, he turned to Lord Rowan. "Tell me, now, about Yvonne."

Lord Rowan glanced at the Warden; he clearly had no fear of Onuri. The Warden frowned at Severn but nodded. "The green is not meant to be a place for ordinary conversation."

"No," Severn agreed. Just that. He didn't turn to the Warden. The Warden had clearly left things in his hands.

"Might we at least find someplace to sit?"

"We don't usually find chairs in a forest, but yes, unless the Warden has objections."

"The green will not be offended," the Warden replied.

Severn offered Onuri a hand up. The Barrani guide accepted that hand without obvious hesitation or suspicion; his bad leg was stiff and his gait more encumbered than it had been before he'd spent so long on his knees.

The forest felt familiar to Severn, in a way that the normal forests on the road to the West March had not. He couldn't say why; there were insects here, and birds—some of whom were loudly unhappy about their company. He passed between trees, looking for signs of a footpath. He didn't expect to find something more suitable to carriage or wagon traffic; he couldn't imagine that either had ever been allowed to pass the Warden's gates.

Clearly the green allowed few people to come this way. He watched Onuri as they trudged past trees and over particularly gnarly roots. If the green were content to flatten land when Onuri required it, no hint of that showed in his movements. Severn was aware that Onuri saw more than anyone else present.

He was almost ready to give up the search for a resting place when a glint of light in the distance caught the corner of his right eye. "That way," he told the guide. Onuri nodded.

"I've never seen this part of the green before," he said, and his eyes, as he turned them briefly in Severn's direction, were green. His steps weren't any lighter, and the walk had clearly been long enough his gait was a disadvantage, but he didn't appear to notice this. He moved ahead, picking up what speed he could, until they found themselves free of the trees. Before them lay a still, placid lake—a lake which reflected sunlight as if sunlight were gold.

The beach was a beach of small pebbles, not sand. There were large boulders that towered above the smaller rocks, and it was to those that Severn led; they were flat enough that everyone could take a seat and rest—or discuss. Only Onuri failed to take that seat. He was exploring the water's edge, his hands, hair, and robes wet.

Lord Rowan picked up the conversation he had gently refused to begin. "Yvonne, as I said, was not considered a relative of import. She was not magically gifted, and while she was not considered lacking in terms of physical coordination, her aptitude for traditional combat arts was not significant.

"She was, however, much favored by her parents; she was their only child. Her father was a warrior of some minor renown in the third war; he had students, although none were from ranking families. Barrani understand their respective place. Yvonne's friends, and the friends of her family, were people who weren't expected to amount to much. In times of need, they might join war bands, but they were content with the smallness of their lives. They had no desire to aspire to power beyond their station.

"Yvonne's friends were therefore similar in stature, and similar in expectation. But one of those friends showed a surprising, early aptitude for the water. His parents were proud, and they encouraged him, perhaps in the hope that he could rise above the station to which he'd been born. He was young, this friend; young, hopeful, determined to better his own family and his own standing.

"But his clan was not Darrowelm, it was Sennarin. Perhaps, had he been a child in Darrowelm, his eventual fate would have differed, for Darrowelm prizes the West March above all, and aptitude with water is of significant concern to the West March."

Severn nodded, frowning. "If that was true, why did Darrowelm support Sennarin?"

"Do you believe that all mortals support and desire the same things?"

"No."

"Indeed. Do you believe that all of Tellarus desires what An'Tellarus desires?"

Severn shook his head.

"Gold is not always our currency. Power is, but power is subtle, a web that connects many things. Sennarin offered that child's parents that power: an increase in their rank, a better place to live. But An'Sennarin wished the child to be sent out of the West March; he demanded the child be sent to the High Halls in return for his largesse."

Lord Rowan hadn't mentioned a name, yet, but it was obvious who that friend had been. "Ollarin's parents refused."

"As you say. They refused. His parents paid for the refusal of a direct command with their lives. Ollarin was bewildered, but he had no desire to leave the West March. An'Sennarin was therefore left to find other levers. The lever he found—given Ollarin's age and general naiveté—was Yvonne."

"An'Darrowelm agreed, then."

"No. But An'Sennarin's power and support had long been a pillar of Darrowelm, and he could not simply refuse. Yvonne's parents met the fate of Ollarin's. Yvonne, however, was injured in that attempt. She was, in her fashion, fearless, and she took up the sword she had been learning. Effort and care had to be taken not to injure her, but no such care was taken. Sennarin wanted her alive, but perhaps felt obvious injury would serve their purpose just as well.

"Understanding this, Darrowelm chose to bring Yvonne into the clan home, to allow her to recuperate. She was injured enough that excursions would have been awkward. Sennarin's forces therefore dragged Ollarin to Darrowelm. They could not meet Yvonne without An'Darrowelm's presence, but that signified little; An'Darrowelm was willing to entertain them.

"Ollarin left for the High Halls the next morning."

"And Yvonne?"

"Yvonne had lost her parents. She had almost lost her life. The last thing she wanted was to lose Ollarin as well. She was willful, angry, determined. What do you think she did?"

"How injured was she?"

"She did not lose her arms, but she lost the use of one; her right hand would no longer obey her commands. Darrowelm would not allow her to be taken to the Sennarin West March stronghold, but he otherwise cooperated with An'Sennarin. Given the deaths caused by Sennarin forces, it was considered wise.

"Yvonne, injured, did not agree. She understood what was at risk, but to her there were other risks that were far greater; she was desperate."

"How do you know this?" It was the Warden who asked, his voice much softer.

Lord Rowan had not forgotten the existence of the Warden. He bowed his head for a long moment, and when he
lifted it, his eyes were tinged purple.

"How do you think? She made an attempt to escape what
was, by then, captivity. Understand that An'Darrowelm,
whatever you think of him, intended to preserve her life;
to keep her safe from the political storm until it had passed.
He fully expected—we all fully expected—that Ollarin had
walked to his death in the east. The Test of Name in the
High Halls would consume him utterly. There was no way
Yvonne could prevent it.

"Nonetheless, she intended to march to the Empire and
find Ollarin. She intended to rescue him. She was desperate
to rescue him, to prevent him from committing what we privately believed was suicide. Ollarin had never been strong."

The Warden waited.

"I was one of the people assigned to protect her." His
smile was bitter. "We are not a race equipped to protect even
our young from themselves. But given her determination, I
thought she had a far greater chance of escaping the Tower
of Test. I made clear that her parents had died because the
power arrayed against them was too significant—what could a
child do that their parents could not? As I said, she was young.
Death was better than the failure to try at all."

"You said she was alive."

"I said she was not dead," he countered. "But there was
only one place to which she could run with any guarantee
she would not immediately be found by either Sennarin or
Darrowelm." He then turned to Lord Barian. "Only one
place, and to enter it at all, she required permission. Your
permission, Warden."

CHAPTER TWENTY-TWO

SEVERN TURNED TO LORD BARIAN. ONURI WAS THE only person who continued to forage, unaware of, or perhaps unconcerned with, the conversation.

"Yvonne," Lord Barian finally said. "I did not expect that Yvonne would be of relevance today—not even when you came to me as Severn's chosen companion."

"She was not my goal," Lord Rowan replied. "But it was to receive information about Yvonne and her whereabouts that Lord Severn requested my presence. I have my own reasons for coming, and those reasons are well-known to you. To most of the West March, with the exception of Sennarin and Darrowelm, Yvonne is of no significance, no interest.

"The motives of either line are now substantially different than they were when Yvonne left home: Sennarin wishes to find her and ascertain her safety; Darrowelm, to find her because Sennarin's demands have grown increasingly...fraught. If it were possible, Darrowelm would surrender Yvonne to An'Sennarin.

"That has not been possible. An'Darrowelm does not care if I search—pointlessly—for signs of Lord Leveanne; he has been willing to allow me to do so with the understanding that if I should somehow encounter Yvonne, I bring her home. Her absence works to my benefit.

"Severn, however, wishes to find Yvonne, not the traces of Leveanne—although he bears the most solid proof of her existence around his neck."

"And how did you come to learn of Yvonne?" the Warden asked Severn, far more demand in his tone than there had been when he addressed Lord Rowan.

"The water," Onuri said.

All three turned to look at Onuri, whose robes were now thoroughly wet. In his left hand he carried smooth pebbles, in his right something that looked like water weeds. His eyes couldn't be seen, as he hadn't finished his odd foraging.

"The water?" the Warden asked.

Onuri nodded. "Its voice is strange today, but it is speaking Yvonne's name. If you come to the lake, you can hear it."

Severn immediately rose, leaping lightly off the rock on which this conversation had unfolded.

"The water told Yvonne to come to the green," Onuri continued, as if Severn hadn't moved.

"Yvonne couldn't hear the water," Lord Barian said.

Onuri shrugged. "Ollarin could. The water loved Ollarin. Here, or there. Always. Maybe the water made itself heard because Ollarin wanted it."

Severn turned toward the man who could hear the water's voice: the Warden. "Where is she?" His voice was soft, almost quiet.

Both of the Barrani Lords stiffened at the sound. Or perhaps at the sound coming from a mortal with no status at all in West March society. Severn wished he had ditched the expensive clothing and ridiculous jewelry before he'd come here.

"I do not know where she is." Lord Rowan was the first to reply. "But as she was safe in the green, and her continued residence here suited my purpose, I admit I did not search with any urgency. Lord Barian?"

"Do not," the Warden said, his eyes a darkening blue, "offend the green."

"Is asking, is searching, an offense to the green?"

"No. Demanding, however, is. I cannot tell you where Yvonne is. I can tell you that she is alive."

"Have you seen her?"

Lord Rowan tensed.

"Lord Barian is Warden," Severn said, his gaze on the Warden. "He is not the green."

Lord Barian lifted a hand in Lord Rowan's direction. "He bore the branch and carries it still. He wears the pendant that was given him by the Dreams of Alsanis. If I give advice, I must also accept it: I, too, wish to avoid offending the green. He has been given the right to question; he would not be here otherwise.

"But I admit I was not prepared to answer the questions he does ask."

"What questions were you prepared to answer?" Severn asked, in a far softer tone.

"I was prepared to offer answers about the shards of Tyron and the heart of the green—although the answers would not, and cannot, be definitive. I was prepared to lead you, the green willing, to its heart, where you might receive answers that are far more complete than those I might hesitantly offer.

"Yet it appears you have not come for the shards, and your interest rests with Yvonne of Darrowelm, a young woman recently out of childhood who has no bearing on the fate of the green or the shards the green shelters. I did not expect to hear her name. Yes, Severn. I have spoken with Yvonne. I had to speak to her the first time to allow her entry into the green—but Onuri speaks truth: the water was restless that day, and it spoke with the most urgent of its many, many voices.

"I knew Yvonne of Darrowelm would come. And I knew the green intended to house and protect her—but against what, and for what future, was not revealed. She was... injured by those who killed her parents. Her eyes were dark when she arrived; she had no hope for herself, no hope for the future. She did not come to the green as a supplicant. She did not come to beg its favor or seek some glimpse of the future. Even had the green offered her that glimpse, were it hopeful, she would not have believed in it.

"We are not like mortals. Our memories are long, harsh, sharp; we do not forget the things that have caused us pain. Perhaps we forget the things that have caused us joy—or perhaps, in our pain, joy cannot reach us. Her only wish at the time was vengeance. Vengeance or death. It is not easy to be...less than perfect in Barrani society."

Onuri rose, the sleeves of his robes dripping water across the pebbled beach. "It is not easy." He repeated the words. "But I value my life and the time I've been given—time I would not have had had I not retained the injury that marks me as useless in the eyes of so many. I have never come across Yvonne, but I have come across some of the traces of her life in the green. If I could speak with her, I would tell her: I am happier now than I was when I was fully capable of being sent to war. Perhaps I am happier because of the green. Perhaps she is happier now than she was the last time she met the Warden."

"Could you find her?" Severn asked. "You are our guide."

"If the green wills it." He looked at his sleeves in some dismay. Severn almost laughed as he realized the Barrani man hadn't fully realized just how wet he'd become.

Onuri then tilted his head, looking at Severn, his eyes narrowed. "Come into the water," he said.

Severn nodded, but paused to look down at his boots; they were very fine, but weren't meant for overland journey. Although they'd been given to him, they weren't his. He bent, unlaced them, and removed them, setting them aside on what passed for beach. He then made his way to the water's edge. Onuri simply waited, his sleeves dripping water, his feet no doubt just as wet, although he wore shoes.

"Why do you want to find her?"

"She is a close friend to a man I respect and admire."

"Does she?"

"Respect and admire him?" At Onuri's nod, Severn said, "You would have to ask her. She isn't hiding just to be found—but she must have known her intended use. Perhaps she meant to free him from the burden of concern, but if she did, no word was sent to him. He does not know what happened to her." Severn found it odd; An'Sennarin was beloved of the water, and if the water knew, An'Sennarin should have known.

"Lord Barian, what were you prepared to tell me? I know of the existence of the shards. I know they remain unclaimed, and have for centuries. I know there is a test devised by either the shards or the green—or some combination of both. I know nothing about the test itself, and nothing about the shards or their capabilities."

"There is a test. I can tell you nothing of it. I have never been invited to take that test myself, and even were I, I would decline unless I felt it would offend the green. I can tell you that the people who have been chosen by the shards are all people of honor; they were respected—ah, no, perhaps that is the wrong word. They were *revered*. When they passed on, the shards returned to the green; any attempt made to hold on to the shards failed. In one case, it failed spectacularly.

"You know of The Three."

Severn nodded as he stepped toward the water. "The Three choose their wielders; those who are not chosen but who dare to make the attempt to wield them perish."

"Not all perish. But yes. The shards are similar, but in the worst case, more extreme. Those who do not catch the attention of the heart of the green are prevented from making the attempt—for their own sake. If the green is unknowable, it is not malicious. Its desire is not the death of individual Barrani. But the shards take a form that is meant for the wielder, and the abilities of the shards are drawn from the wielder. More than that, I do not know."

Severn took a step into the lake; he was surprised. The water was cool, but not cold; it was almost refreshing. Onuri came to stand by his side.

"It is easier to swim than to run," the Barrani guide said.

Severn couldn't see him. All he could see was the rising of the water. Without thought, the mortal Wolf reached out to grab Onuri's right arm, as if to steady him or save him from the unnatural movement of the lake.

But it wasn't the water that rose; it was something that now appeared to be growing out of the lake bed, a plant of some kind. A slender trunk appeared first, thickening as Severn watched, its bark...ivory. "Can you see that?" he asked his companion.

"Yes."

A tree grew from the lake: an ivory tree, branches shooting out from the central trunk as the trunk gained altitude and size. Across the pale, yellow-white branches were small nubs, but even as the branches continued to stretch, he recognized them as buds. The buds opened, as if caught in the whirlwind of a sudden change of season. The leaves were emerald; they glittered in the light.

From such a tree the small branch Severn held in his right hand had grown.

Severn began to walk, but slowly; Onuri kept pace beside him. "Have you seen this tree before?"

"No. But I think it is only to be found when the green wills it. I am not certain I will be allowed to touch it or to take samples from it." It was clear he intended to try. To

Onuri, the tree was the miracle; the shards were almost irrelevant.

Lord Barian and Lord Rowan didn't join them as they made their way across the water; the lake bed sloped down toward both tree and the lake's center. Onuri was accustomed to being wet; Severn, less so. But when the water reached waist level, Severn's feet hit the roots of the tree.

"Will you climb?" he asked Onuri.

Onuri hesitated.

"There are roots beneath our feet."

"There are roots beneath your feet," Onuri replied, his eyes downcast briefly, as if by doing so he might hide his obvious disappointment. "You might be meant to climb." Lifting his face, he added, "I will not drown if you let me go. Swimming is easier for me than walking, and the water in the green pays attention." He gave Severn a nudge.

Severn then released him. Beneath his feet, the roots felt like ivory, not bark; he began to walk carefully, sliding rather than stepping as he made his way to the trunk. He shouldn't have been surprised when the heart of the tree cracked and split, as if it had been struck by invisible lightning. What remained in place of ivory bark was a gap the size of a person, as if this were an oddly placed door to a Hallionne.

He turned back; Lord Rowan was now in the water. The Warden was not. He remained alone on the shore, and the shore, in Severn's eyes, appeared to be receding. If Onuri was somehow forbidden this door, Severn very much doubted Lord Rowan would be permitted to enter. Nonetheless, he waited. Even at this distance he could see the unguarded expression that transformed Lord Rowan's features: desperation.

What was Leveanne to you? He didn't ask the question aloud.

Does it matter? It was a question he could ask of himself, but he hadn't asked it. He turned toward the gap in the tree and saw the darkness; nothing emerged except the voice.

"Clearly it does," he replied. "To me, it does."

*If he is not granted entry, will you take the risk that you will
both be rejected?*

"I gave him my word."

It was not an oath sworn in blood.

"Mortals don't swear blood oaths."

A tinkle of sound, like wind chimes striking each other,
was followed by words. *They do. They do, child. But yes, their
oaths, sworn in blood or sworn on it, do not have the weight of their
Barrani counterparts. Very well.*

Severn caught the edge of the gap; felt it beneath his
palm as if it were newly broken stone. He then reached out
to Lord Rowan, holding his arm steady as the Barrani man
approached. Lord Rowan reached out in his turn to grip the
hand that Severn had offered; their hands were slick with
water, knuckles white, as Severn pulled him up.

"Don't let go," Severn said.

Lord Rowan nodded, lips compressed and white around
the edges, his eyes blue. Hands anchored to each other, Severn
took his first step into the darkened gap, dragging the Barrani with him.

Severn thought he had entered a tunnel. He adjusted that
belief; the moment he stepped into the darkness, the darkness dissolved. He tightened his grip on Lord Rowan's hand,
as if to drag him the last few steps; Lord Rowan responded
in kind.

The lake was gone, the water with it; Severn's feet and
clothing were completely dry. He could see trees in the distance, but none of them were the tree of invitation; they
were the trees of the overland trek to the West March. Shadows cast by sun fell across the forest floor in sharply defined
spokes. Above, he could hear birds. Clearly his sudden appearance had caused either alarm or annoyance.

But there was a footpath between the trees. He glanced
at Lord Rowan.

"We're in a forest," the Barrani Lord said, understanding the unspoken question.

"You can see the footpath?"

Lord Rowan nodded, his breath unsteady. He didn't tell Severn to release his hand, and he allowed Severn to lead. It was awkward to walk hand in hand with a grown man, but he'd had practice doing exactly that with a child or two, and the muscle memory allowed him to follow the path. No roots crossed it, and no weeds grew anywhere but along its edges; only the shadow of moving birds passing overhead made clear that the path was a part of the forest they called home.

"What do you know of Handred?"

"Lord Leveanne's slave?"

Severn nodded.

"He was good with his hands; he carved and he created things that were of use to him. They were inferior to Barrani works, but Lord Leveanne found them amusing or endearing." He hesitated, and then said, "He could fight. Had slaves been considered for purposes of combat in war, rather than timid support, he would have served well. Lord Leveanne was unwilling to risk him; of all the things she owned, he was the most valued."

"Was he Lord Leveanne's? I thought him a Tellarus slave."

"If An'Tellarus has told you as much, I will confirm. But he was allowed to attend Leveanne—at her very specific request." A hint of a smile touched the tone of the words, almost transforming them. "No one who knew her considered it a request; it was a command uttered as the heir of Tellarus."

"Did her lord disapprove?"

"No. Many, many people did. Handred was not as you are now; he was not built for display. He was scarred, and almost ungainly in build and size; his hands were callused and sun dark with labor. She could not change that, and after a single attempt, did not try."

"Was he young?"

"By our standards? Even the most ancient of your kin are young. But he was older than you when she was last seen by any of her kin in the West March. No one thought much of it, for the first few days; it was not the first time she had chosen to enter the green, nor was it the first time she had taken her mortal with her. He was her most constant companion.

"But that made sense. If he was owned by Tellarus, he was not of Tellarus; he was not of any of the other families that owed service to Tellarus. Not even Verranian was as close to her, in the end, as Handred." He hesitated. Severn marked it and glanced at him. "This will not make sense to you, perhaps, but…it was only in Handred's presence that I heard her laugh. Her laughter was like light in a very dark place. Perhaps that was why she valued him.

"Understand that we hide our weaknesses, and we eventually learn to hide our attachments—as Yvonne demonstrates, those attachments become almost fatal weaknesses if we do not. But it is the joy that we must cloud or obscure; Barrani joy is delicate and so easily broken. Handred would not live long enough to become a truly deep threat.

"She learned his tongue; they would speak it in the presence of less friendly Barrani Lords—which annoyed those lords. I often wondered if that was her intent…but I could not make myself believe it."

Severn nodded, as if this made sense. It would have made sense to Verranian, had Verranian ever thought to talk of joy.

The path he followed widened as the last of the trees fell away. The ground beneath his feet became harder as they both emerged from tree line into a clearing that was bound, on the far side, by what appeared to be the edge of a cliff. To the right and the left, Severn could see footpaths, but they weren't the focus of his attention.

He heard Lord Rowan's sharp intake of breath and was almost certain his breath had caught in the same way, if for different reasons.

Standing yards away were two Barrani. One was a woman, and one a very familiar man. The woman was wearing the robes worn by the servants of the green. Her brow was unbroken by the tiara that the Warden had chosen to wear, but her eyes were as green as the emerald at the peak of that tiara; her hair was long, and in the light, almost brown. She looked young, to Severn, but maybe that was because she seemed almost incandescent with joy.

The man wasn't likewise attired, as if his lack of robes were meant to make a subtle point about his allegiance here. He wasn't standing; he was kneeling, one foot to ground, head bowed. His face was partially hidden by his posture, but that made no difference; Severn knew him instantly.

He was Severn's guardian and teacher.

Lord Rowan released Severn's hand before he, too, adopted the posture that Verranian had adopted. That left two people on their feet: the woman and the mortal Wolf. She stood as if anchored to the ground; it was Severn who moved, leaving Lord Rowan behind. He meant to greet his master, but found he lacked the words as his gaze was drawn to the woman, and held fast there, as if by magical compulsion.

He knew who she was, who she must be, by Lord Rowan's behavior. Thinking this, he stopped, and gently removed the pendant that hung loosely around his neck.

"I believe this belongs to you," he said, holding it in the cupped palm of his left hand.

"It did, once. But I surrendered it to the green, as I surrendered all else." Her smile was gentle and tinged with regret. "Have you come to find me?"

He wanted to lie but couldn't. "No, lady."

Her smile deepened, which wasn't what he'd expected. "Why have you come?"

He held out the branch that had been the start of his tangled interaction with the West March and the green.

"I recognize it. You have come to seek the shards?"

"No."

"That is what that branch signifies."

He shook his head. "The branch signifies the green's acceptance. Perhaps it is what the green wants—even those who have devoted the whole of their lives to the green cannot say with certainty. But it is not, in the end, why I am here."

"What, then, do you seek?"

"I seek a person—a different person. Have you met Yvonne of Darrowelm?"

"I have not met her, but I have heard her voice. You have come for Yvonne?"

He hesitated. "I hope to find her and to deliver word to her."

She smiled and held out both of her hands, palms up; they were empty. Severn shook his head; he didn't understand the gesture—but it reminded him, oddly, of Elianne's mother. It was not something he expected of a Barrani stranger. When he failed to move, she said, "Come here. Let me look at you."

He obeyed without intent, his feet moving, his hands rising. The green of her eyes seemed too brilliant to be contained by something so small and natural. He placed both of his hands across hers, only realizing that he still carried the branch in one of them when he felt its texture instead of her palm. The leaves could cut; he'd seen it before. Her hands tightened before he could lift either of his.

He thought the leaves would be crushed.

"You are young. You are too young to be here."

"I am not considered too young by my own kin."

"Your kin?" She smiled. "Verranian?"

By her side, kneeling, Severn's master looked up at the sound of his name. "He is considered adult by his own kind."

"Kind. Kin." She shook her head. "Why are you here?"

"I was invited to the green by the green." He looked at the

branch almost crushed between their hands. Perhaps because the leaves had started to wilt, their edges drew no blood.

"And you accepted the invitation?"

He nodded.

"Have you become a child who accepts random invitations from strangers?"

It was an odd question, but he accepted it, accepted the condescension implied by it. He was here, after all.

"Have you not come to find the shards of Tyron? They have been waiting for a wielder."

He shook his head. "Others have that desire."

Her lips turned up at the corners. "You are not drawn to the power you might wield if they come to your hands?"

"I am not Barrani."

"Yet you speak our language so well."

"He taught me." He looked down at his master, who had not yet risen.

"Yes. I admit some surprise. I thought he might find you a mortal family, in a sea of mortal families, in a place where no slavery exists."

"How...do you know him?"

"We were once—long ago—distant kin; we dwelled within the same house. Now I live here—but not for much longer. He remains by my side as he can; sometimes the green does not allow it." She looked over his shoulder, to where Lord Rowan knelt. "Tell me, why have you come, if you have not come to retrieve the shards? It was Verranian's wish that you become a man who could."

"They are Barrani weapons."

She laughed, but the laughter was gentle, shorn of the edge that would make it a weapon of humiliation. "Is that what you were taught? Verranian, I am surprised."

"I taught him nothing of the shards," Severn's master replied. "I could not know whether or not he would move and speak among our kind; I taught him the language, the manners, the appropriate customs of the West March. But he has spent near half his life among mortals now; he has made no attempt to join a Barrani household of any note."

"He did not come here on his own."

"No, Lord."

Severn understood very little of this conversation, but not none. "I came with your sister." He paused, and then added, "An'Tellarus."

Her eyes darkened a fraction—blue intertwining with green until her eyes seemed like a very dark turquoise. "I did tell her," she said softly, "to let me go. I had no intention of becoming An'Tellarus when I left. She was angry," she added, her smile tinged with regret and nostalgia. "She was furious. So many years of rage and envy and wanting. I had taken all the advantage of the heir. I had received all of the respect, all of the devotion, all of the lessons offered the heir. I had been given my pick of the best of our guards, the best of our servants—and even, in the end, the best of our slaves.

"Everything." She bowed head. "She was not wrong. I had not deliberately kept those things for myself, but I had not considered the differences in our stations. I had been given things without demanding them, and I accepted those gifts as if they were natural. As if, indeed, they were meant solely for me."

"They were gifts," Verranian said; he still had not risen.

"Yes. And so they were; they were given freely. And accepted in just such a fashion. I did not, and would not, demand. I understood my position. Tell me, Severn, what do you think of An'Tellarus?"

"She's...older than you are. She has aged, in the world beyond the green. She rules Tellarus, and people fear Tellarus. In many ways, she is what the Barrani want of a lord. But... she's unpredictable. She's chaotic. She privileges whim and indulgence—but never so much that it costs her the power she needs to rule."

"Is she beautiful, to you?" It was such an odd question. She must have known he found it confusing; she chuckled. "Is it a difficult question to answer?"

"Are mountains beautiful? Are oceans? Are forests? She's Barrani; by existing, she is beautiful. Ageless, fearless, powerful. She is…what she is. My opinion is irrelevant. Why did you ask?"

"You see all Barrani as beautiful? You cannot distinguish?"

"Compared to us, yes. But…beauty seems irrelevant. It's a judgment."

"You do not judge."

"I try to see what is actually in front of me. Beauty is sentiment. It is too personal."

"I found her beautiful. She was…open in her anguish, her anger, her envy; open in the very little joy she had. She was jealous and possessive by nature, and she compared herself to me endlessly. I hated that, but I could not make her stop. She could not see herself, except as a mirror, a lesser reflection of me. But what she wanted of me, I could not give her; she wanted me to be worthy of what she thought others saw in me, of me. I think, if I had, she might have made peace with herself. If I could live up to her ideals of perfection, the painful comparisons others made would at least be justified.

"I have surprised you."

"She misses you," he said, almost without thought. "I think, with time and distance, she no longer sees you the way she once did."

"Yes. But it is entirely because of that absence, that distance, that she can. She wanted to prove herself. She wanted to be An'Tellarus. I…no longer did. I thought she would be happy when I told her I was leaving; I had been called to the green. That was not a lie; I had. I do not think I have ever seen her angrier than she was on that day."

Severn nodded.

"You understand her anger?"

"You had everything she thought she wanted—everything. And to you, in the end, it was nothing. Yes, I understand her anger. You did not leave for her sake."

"No. I told you: I had been called to the green. The Warden of the time—not the current Warden—demanded my presence. I had refused; I was heir to Tellarus, after all. He did not have the power to force me. I thought his demand political. He was, in some fashion, an ally of my sister's. But in this, he moved against her will. I *had* been called. In the end, it was not the Warden's voice I heard—it was the water's. And I came because the Dreams of Alsanis were desperate.

"I came late," she continued, voice softer. "Perhaps, had I come earlier, things would have been different. Perhaps I could have entered the green and retreated at my own will. But the green..." She shook her head. "The green was injured. I could not leave. And when my sister at last came to seek me out, I could not greet her. I was not allowed." Her smile deepened. "I will not repeat what she said, although I could hear every word of it clearly.

"It was only in defense of me that she could express her love—and it was incendiary. If you feel it will not upset her, tell her that I, too, miss her. That I regret our childhoods, and the years we could have had together, all wasted. She did not send you here."

"Not directly, no. She asked me to be her companion in her journey to the West March, and she promised me information that I wanted in return. I accepted. But upon entry into the West March proper, the Dreams of Alsanis dropped the branch on my head. I did not tell her immediately, but when she did learn of it, she accepted that I, too, would come to the green.

"I think it would amuse her if I found the shards of legend;

it would gratify her if I could pass whatever test they set and wield them."

"And so you seek them on her behalf?"

"No."

"They are reputed to be weapons of great power."

"For the Barrani. But it is not among the Barrani that I intend to live. An'Tellarus does not require the weapons, and I am sworn to another's service. I will not bring the weapons to Tellarus, even if I could wield them. She knows this. I think she intends to annoy Avonelle and Kosmarre."

"Does she do that in order to protect you?" Verranian asked, from waist height.

"No, of course not."

"Does she do it to protect Elluvian?" At the mention of the name, Lord Leveanne's eyes darkened to indigo.

CHAPTER TWENTY-THREE

VERRANIAN ROSE THEN, AS IF HE HAD REMAINED kneeling because he didn't wish to disturb her happiness. Her anger—if it was anger—was less intimidating.

"Why did you mention his name?" she demanded, turning from Severn for the first time, although she didn't loosen her grip.

"Because the boy traveled with An'Tellarus *and* Elluvian. He has seen Danarre; Elluvian attempted to protect him from the interest of the Warden's guards by dragging him to Danarre—and entering it."

"Severn, how come you to know Elluvian? Why was he traveling with my sister?"

"He is her relative. I believe she is fond enough to be indulgent, although he is clearly a constant disappointment."

"He cannot be trusted. He *must not* be trusted."

"He serves the Eternal Emperor."

"Pardon?"

"He serves—truly serves—the Dragon Emperor in the east."

"And the Dragon Emperor sent him to the West March?"

It was Severn who tightened the grip on her hands, this time. "The Dragon Emperor allowed him to accompany An'Tellarus; he did not send him. He has no interest in ruling the West March."

"It was the Emperor's flight which destroyed Elluvian's home. His flight destroyed Danarre."

"His flight didn't destroy their ancestral home."

"His flight was responsible for the death of almost all who served or were related to Danarre! I watched it. I saved the very few I could. Lord Rowan."

Lord Rowan rose for the first time since they had entered the clearing.

"Tell him."

"He knows."

"He knows that Elluvian was *riding* the leader of the Dragon Flight when the Dragon flight attacked?"

Verranian said nothing. Lord Rowan came to join Severn. "He does now. But he is not Barrani. It will not mean, to a mortal, what it might mean to us. I would kill Elluvian if I could, but to do so I would risk the wrath of An'Tellarus. For reasons that are not clear to most of us, she has always favored him; she desires him to become An'Danarre."

"He *is* An'Danarre," Lord Leveanne replied, her voice very like her sister's when coldly, profoundly angry.

"He will not take the name. He almost never comes to the West March. The choice he made, he adheres to now; he serves the Dragon."

"He betrayed his people. He betrayed his line. In time of war he chose the Dragons over his own people."

Severn felt the conversation moving beyond him. He didn't believe Lord Leveanne was lying. Lord Rowan accepted her words as truth. Verranian did as well. What did he know of Elluvian, in the end?

And if Elluvian was that treacherous, how did it affect private Severn Handred?

In any practical sense, it didn't. He wondered what had passed between the Emperor and Elluvian at the end of the war. He was certain Elluvian wasn't bound to the Emperor by anything other than his oath. But he was also certain Elluvian genuinely served the Emperor. Given the Empire, given the Emperor's intent, given Imperial law with all its clumsiness and subtlety, Severn was certain that Elluvian would far rather serve the Emperor than a Barrani Lord. Any Barrani Lord.

He didn't say this. But he felt moved to speak, regardless. "His betrayal of Danarre is a Barrani crime. I am not Barrani. But I will say this: if he chose that solution, the problem behind it was real."

"You trust him?"

Verranian's frown was instant. "What have I taught you?"

"My trust changes nothing. Trust him, fail to trust him, he remains Elluvian, and he remains the Emperor's." Severn answered with a confidence his onetime master had not expected. "In the end, he has nothing to do with my reason for being here. Danarre has meaning to the West March. It has meaning to me in only one way: I am not willing to die for it. I am not willing to die for Tellarus. I, too, have sworn oaths—oaths my death will undermine." Very carefully, he disentangled their joined hands.

He had been wrong about wilted leaves. Lord Leveanne's hand was bleeding, although the cuts were shallow. His own, however, were not.

He offered her a perfect Barrani bow; his master was watching. "I have things I must do while I am in the green, if the green allows it."

"Do not offend the green," Lord Leveanne said, her voice far more neutral.

"If it offends the green that I must fulfill my responsibilities, I cannot avoid it."

"What responsibilities?"

"I must find Yvonne of Darrowelm. If she wishes to leave, I will help her leave; if she wishes to stay, I will pass a message to her and retreat."

"But you have been chosen—"

"Perhaps." He bowed again, this time to his former master. "But even the chosen must choose. This is my choice. There are two paths that lead from this clearing: one to the left, and one to the right."

Lord Leveanne swallowed and nodded. "You can only take one. When you leave, you will not return to this place again; it has been held here for far too long, and the green does not like stasis." She exhaled. "I wanted to see you at least once. You are Handred, and Severn. I cannot help you beyond this point, but I would give you a gift.

"To the left, if you are cunning enough to follow the path, you will find Yvonne. To the right, you will find the shards of Tyron." She lifted her head, turned her face toward Lord Rowan. "What would you do if offered the choice?"

"I would take the path to the right, for I have finally found what I seek in the green." His eyes remained fixed upon Lord Leveanne. "Or perhaps I would choose no path, if I could remain here until this space is once again lost to the green."

"Verranian?"

To Severn's surprise, his master smiled. "I, too, would take the path to the right, had I been called to the green. But that is not the answer, in the end, for young Severn. Can you not see? He has made the choice he feels he must make. Even were he to desire weapons of legend, he will honor his choice while he lives." To Severn's surprise, his master bowed. "You are no longer my student. I am no longer your guardian. You made your choice then, and you make it now.

"But I am not disappointed in what you have become."

Severn was surprised. He could keep expression from his face, but his master had always seen what lurked beneath it; he therefore didn't try.

"If I must make all your choices for you, you are, and will remain, a child. Children without parents seldom survive long. I could not direct the course of your learning for the entirety of your life. And it was your life. You are mortal; your life is meant to be spent among mortals. Barrani purpose is not your purpose."

"And my purpose?"

"It is hard for any of us to define our purpose—but it is, in the end, an intimate, internal goal. You left, and I allowed it. You were a child, but you understood choice and consequence. I was told," he added, "that I had been irresponsible in allowing you to make that choice at that time—and perhaps that was true. Had you been Barrani, I would not have allowed it."

"But I'm not."

"No. I am content to be alone; loneliness is not the result of isolation. I might spend your lifetime, even should you die of old age, without speaking to another Barrani and not feel the discomfort of their absence. But mortals, in my observed experience, are not Barrani. Perhaps, if you were Immortal, you would become as we are; perhaps the Ancients had their reasons for gifting you age and death. What you needed, I could not give you."

"What you needed brought you here."

Severn frowned. He didn't correct his master—that had seldom worked out well. If his master had been unusual for a Barrani, he was still Barrani at heart.

"You were lonely. You had become aware of all of the interactions your upbringing to that point could not provide. You did not resent me, but I feel that would have followed, although perhaps not. For a mortal, you were unusual in a way that circumstance alone could not explain." He frowned at Severn's expression. "I have a greater power than you had—or have now. While that would be true of mortal parents with regards to young children, it would not remain that way. It would always be true of me. Measure yourself against me, and you would always come up short.

"Or so I believed, at the time. If you chose to take the test of the shards of Tyron, if you could wield those weapons, that would be less certain."

"You intended that I try."

His master smiled. "We wish to give our young whatever advantages we can. Even Barrani."

"I'm not Barrani."

"No. And if it was my intent that you try, it was never guaranteed that you would succeed; there is risk in even making the attempt. Understand that while we want what is best for you, your life is not our life, and our determination of *best* can be found wanting. I, like any other Barrani in the West March, do not know what the shards desire of their wielder, and you suffer under the disadvantage of mortality." His eyes were almost green. "But I, like perhaps a foolish parent, understand your decision. It is a burden, a debt of honor, and you will shoulder it until the end.

"It is neither a choice I would have made in my youth, nor one I could make now, and perhaps I would argue that by arming myself I might be capable of carrying a greater burden in the unforeseeable future. But I am uncertain that it would be a genuine argument, rather than a justification.

"This is not the last time we will meet, if both you and I survive. Ten years from now, perhaps fifteen, I wish to see where your choices have led you." He reached out then, and laid his hand briefly on Severn's shoulder. "Loneliness is a vacuum that we struggle to fill, in one way or another.

"Tell me, Severn Handred, are you lonely?"

He couldn't answer the question. There was either too much to say or too little. Either *yes* or *no* was layered. He had no desire to speak of the choice that had destroyed what remained of the home he had found, although he was certain none of the Barrani present would judge him for the choice he did make.

But to speak of it was to speak of Elianne, and he wouldn't expose her to strangers.

He exhaled and offered Verranian a very solid fief shrug. Verranian had never been fond of them.

Lord Leveanne watched him, her eyes shading to purple, which Severn hadn't expected. "You don't look like him."

He stiffened, meeting that gaze.

"But you remind me of Handred."

"Did you name me?" he asked, voice as soft as he could make it.

She smiled. "Mortal names are not like our names. Yes, I named you. I wanted some hint of what Handred was to continue; his people are long gone. I would have liked to watch you grow. I would not have made the same choice as Verranian. But…I cannot leave the green. Once, perhaps, when I first entered it, but that time is long past. I offered the green something of myself in exchange for something I desired."

"An'Tellarus offered you information about your parentage." The last few words tailed up, as if in question.

Severn nodded.

"I do not know how she came to believe she could. Nor do I think it relevant to you as you are now. Go. Go; let the green make of you what it will. If I can, I will watch. But if it is possible, I ask you to keep the family name you were given while you live."

"Can you tell me the information you believe she can't?"

"Not yet. Go and do what you must, and perhaps—if we are lucky or if the green is merciful—I will."

Lord Rowan didn't choose to accompany Severn, nor did Verranian.

"This is not a path that any others can walk. You choose. See that choice to its end," his master said, although Severn hadn't asked. He didn't move from Lord Leveanne's side. Nor did Lord Rowan.

The boots that Severn had abandoned on the shore of the lake stood before him; he put them on. He then walked to the left. When he reached the mouth of the left path, he turned to look back. No one was watching. Leveanne said she'd wanted a child who could carry Handred's name forward. What Severn wanted to know, now, was where that child had come from. Had Verranian simply gone in search of a mortal baby?

In the Empire, such a search would have been illegal; one couldn't sell or buy children, and one certainly couldn't just grab an infant and abscond with them. Not according to the law—but if laws were all that was required to end certain activities, the Halls of Law would be irrelevant. It wasn't.

The ground beneath his feet was less flat, less smooth, than it had been when he stood in front of Leveanne and his master. For one, tree roots cut across the path, and where there were no roots, there were fallen branches. Stones that were taller than he was obstructed the footpath, almost as if they'd been part of a riverbed that had long since dried out; he moved around, not over.

The light dimmed as he walked, as if the sun was sinking. Here and there, insects scuttled, birds screeched, either anger or warning behind the sounds they made. He wondered what night looked like in the green; given the change in light, he was going to find out if he didn't reach a destination soon. He didn't expect the passage of time to conform to any normal internal clock—this was the green.

It was like, and unlike, the Hallionne.

What do you have when you are removed from every context you understand? How do you communicate when you cannot speak the same language as those who surround you? What, in the end, is language?

Perhaps because he had seen his master, the questions returned to him as they so often did. Or perhaps the questions returned because they were relevant. He was, in theory, in the heart of the green. He knew, on a visceral level, that *heart* was not a location; the green was not simple geography. Only the Warden's gates conformed to expected reality: they stood in one place, and that place didn't change.

Didn't have to change, given that the green always did.

Where was Yvonne? Was she in a tree, much like the trees which the oldest and most significant of the Barrani families claimed? Was she in a hovel? Was she in whatever the poor or independent Barrani chose to call home? Even in the West March, he hadn't seen the type of slums that comprised the warrens in Elantra. Nor had he seen the derelict buildings that characterized at least half of the fief of Nightshade. He knew the Barrani prized power. He had just assumed that power, to the Barrani, meant wealth.

No, he thought, that wasn't entirely true. Magical talent was important, just as physical strength might be to mortals. But it was a way of standing out, of leveraging skill in exchange for...for what?

An'Tellarus clearly had wealth. Even Elluvian did, given how much he was willing to spend to appropriately clothe a recruit of the Wolves. But it seemed to Severn, upon consideration, that the craftsmen, the farmers, the tanners, fishers—people who could be seen easily in Elantra—had become invisible. He had seen no Barrani farmland on the overland journey, and while he was certain farms must exist, perhaps he had missed them by taking portal paths.

If Yvonne, if Ollarin, had been insignificant members of branch families, what had they done to live? What could Yvonne do now, if she were to leave the green? A darker thought followed. What if she wanted to leave, but couldn't?

What was the green? What secrets did it hold? Why had he—taught to examine and observe for all of his remembered childhood—accepted the green as a fact of nature, like a mountain ridge, a waterfall?

Do not offend the green.

How did one offend a mountain or a waterfall or an ocean? How could one make a deal with any of those things? He shook his head. One couldn't. If the green was sentient enough to somehow make bargains with those it allowed entry, what did the green want?

What did the green want of Severn? If the branch he still held was an invitation to take the test the unknown weapons set, was ignoring that test to find Yvonne of Darrowelm somehow offensive to the green?

But no. No. There had been two paths. He had chosen one of them. The green might not be the reality in which Severn had lived almost all of his life, but Severn was still Severn. If he couldn't scan a familiar city street at varying levels, if he couldn't watch the people in the streets themselves, he knew the importance of silence, of stealth, of awareness of his environment. He could focus on those; he could empty his thoughts of questions that wouldn't help him here.

The path grew far narrower by the time he hit rock face and cliff—or two cliffs; the stone through which the path appeared to end was cracked. There was enough space above ground level that Severn could fit through the wedge. That crack was what remained of the path's forward direction, but it seemed to go on for long enough he couldn't clearly see an end. It wasn't as simple as using two tightly packed walls to climb to reach roof, but it was similar; if it wasn't flat, it was rough enough to easily find foot- or handholds. It was difficult only when the gap narrowed so much it was difficult to move without turning sideways, but even then it was possible.

He'd been straddling the divided stone for what felt like hours when he heard moving water and froze for a moment.

Beneath his feet, water appeared, its heights capped with foam, as if this long crack had been created to form the V-shaped bed of a river. The water began a body length below his feet, and he began to climb, pushing himself up, and up again, to avoid the water's rise. If water itself wasn't deadly, people still drowned, and the current was moving fast enough he was certain he'd join them if he couldn't avoid it.

He had a bad feeling about his progress. He looked up; he could only barely see the rock's height. Adjusting his footing, he chose to continue to move forward, in the direction the water was rushing. His arms and legs were tiring, but that was to be expected; this wasn't the type of physical exertion for which he'd been trained by anything other than necessity. In the narrow gaps between old fief buildings, the nighttime Ferals couldn't leap high enough to catch him; sometimes they had trouble fitting themselves into the space.

Still, even in those circumstances, he'd sought height—rooftops were safer than the sides of walls. Here, that didn't seem to be an option, and even if it was, he wanted to be certain that the forward path didn't depend on contact with the ground. He didn't want to lose it, because it was the only clue he had to Yvonne's location.

The gap continued, and as it did, night fell, as if poured out of a large pitcher. Where there had been clear blue skies some hours past, there was now a similarly clear nightscape: he could see stars, and a moon that was low and bright. It seemed to cover the bottom third of the sky, and its lowest point was in line with the river that now flowed beneath his feet.

Beyond that, however, he could see where the water went: a lake. He grimaced; there was no hope of finding a footpath on the lake bed—but he had a decent chance of surviving what was clearly a drop from this cliff to the water below. His master had insisted that he learn to swim; it had been one of his most dreaded activities as a young child, but he was grateful for it now.

What had Lord Rowan said? The water had delivered a message to Yvonne; the water had spoken to the Warden. Severn knew An'Sennarin had touched the water in the bay of Elantra, homesick and worried. The water had clearly responded in the West March. He wondered if the water was separate from the green, or if they coexisted; he knew elemental water was summoned, in theory. Had An'Sennarin summoned water from the bay? Had that water returned to… wherever it was elemental water returned when the summoning ceased?

The water in the green, the water in the West March, was elemental water. It was aware, sentient, capable of movement to a limited extent—he'd seen that before he'd stepped foot in the West March proper.

If the water beneath his feet—water that rushed forward and seemed to fall into the lake below—was normal water, he ran the risk of drowning if he hit rock on the way down. If the water was somehow connected to, or allied to, the will of the green, it might be safe. Safe or no, it didn't look like he had a lot of options. As he approached the end of the crevice, as moonlight became more prominent than the darkness of rocky wall, he saw that the water that passed beneath his feet did, as suspected, drop. Had he been standing on the shore of the lake, it would look like a waterfall.

Severn chose to shuffle to the left to get a better idea of how far down the water fell; mist rose where rushing water struck stone, over and over again. The rock was slick with water. He could see, but color was muted, and the shape of objects softened by moonlight.

He couldn't see a way down. The rock through which he'd traveled jutted out at an angle; without the proper tools it was impossible to climb.

He transferred to the right side of the crevice, but the view was the same. The only obvious path forward was down. If the rocks jutted out at an angle, down might be navigable. What he couldn't clearly measure was the height of the drop.

It wasn't Severn's way to trust what he couldn't see. It wasn't his habit to believe in things he only barely understood. Nothing about this water looked magical, for want of a better word. To drop into it, to follow its fall, seemed the only option. He couldn't sleep here, and waiting for dawn and better visibility was risky. He could, and did, rest, back against the left wall, feet against the right.

Life will test you. It is both impersonal and deadly if you cannot pass.

"Yes, thank you, I know that," he snapped, as he would never have snapped at his master in childhood. "Tell me something that I haven't learned on my own in the past eight years!" His voice bounced off rock, echoing.

The water in the bottom of the crevice began to rise.

Severn considered his options, inching up, and up again, until the gap between walls of rock was too wide. He was in the green. The water had called to Yvonne; the water had called to Severn. An'Sennarin, an elemental adept, hadn't known that Yvonne was here. The water hadn't bothered to tell him.

Or maybe he hadn't asked the right question.

Finding Yvonne was the one thing he could do for An'Sennarin that An'Sennarin couldn't do for himself. And An'Sennarin had, decades past, done the one thing Severn would have asked for—pleaded for, even killed for—had he been alive and aware at that time. He'd come to the green because of An'Tellarus, but his goal in the West March had been An'Sennarin's goal.

It was his goal now. Could he trust the water? Could he trust the green?

He knew better. He'd been taught against trust almost before he'd been taught to read and write. He'd absorbed all of his master's many lessons, had learned how to put them into practice, choosing those he could accomplish with the strength of a child, a youth, a young man. He'd grown into as much of it as he thought possible.

Don't trust.

But he had chosen to trust, before. He'd chosen to take the risk, knowing that for the unwary, trust led eventually to death. He had chosen to trust Elluvian, if imperfectly; he'd chosen to trust the Emperor in the same way. Trust in either case was almost irrelevant; it affected Severn Handred, but it didn't affect Elluvian or the Eternal Emperor.

It was the same situation he faced with the water and the green: his trust could damage or kill him, but it couldn't damage or kill them. Two paths had been created for his use. He'd chosen one—but he'd had no hand in the creation, no hand in the intent.

Was that true? The two choices offered him had been offered with some knowledge: Yvonne. The shards. The green had offered choices that were relevant to Severn—a test, perhaps, of his determination. And that path had led here. It was impossible to trust something so alien, because it was impossible to understand all of the motivations involved. Wealth, power, status—they meant nothing to the green.

He should have meant nothing to the green. But...he did. Even if only for this moment, this one visit, this entry into a wilderness that couldn't be reached without permission or invitation, Severn had meaning here. The landscape had formed a path his feet could—until this moment—follow. He hadn't reached a dead end.

He'd reached the end of a path he could navigate entirely under his own strength.

Yes.

Gritting teeth, Severn forced himself to loosen both hands and legs, and dropped into the raging currents beneath him.

CHAPTER TWENTY-FOUR

THE WATER WAS COOL, NOT COLD, AND THE current was almost like muscle, sinew, as if the water had figuratively stretched out its arms to catch him. Under the low moon, he couldn't feel the drop his eyes had definitely seen. The water lowered him to the lake and left him there.

He began to swim toward the shore but paused, treading water as he looked at the lake itself, remembering the tree that had sprouted from the first one.

The water remained unbroken, ripples from the waterfall interrupting the moon's reflection. There was no sandbar, no hint of the small islands that sometimes appeared in lakes. He swam to the nearest shore in sight, dragged himself out of the water, and attempted to wring that water out of his clothing.

To his surprise, this wasn't necessary. As he considered the state of his shirt, his tunic, the collarless but ostentatious Tellarus-provided clothing, the water drew itself out of the fabric and into the sand beneath his boots. The water from the fountain in Danarre had done the same.

He had spent what felt like over half a day following the

path; it was night and he was tired. But if he fell asleep here, he had no certainty that he'd wake up in the same place. Or at all. He was hungry, but he'd long since learned to ignore hunger when there was no easy way to eat; he had some food in his pack but decided against eating it for the moment. The air was cool, not cold, the breeze gentle, the light bright enough to see by. He could walk back to the waterfall or away from it, and chose away, looking for any sign that another person had passed this way.

He drew daggers three times. There were no trees near the beach, but there were boulders behind which he could shelter should the need arise. While he had no desire to attack or kill any wildlife he might encounter, he had even less desire to become an animal's next meal; when he heard growling, he armed himself, but didn't stop moving.

None of the growls produced animals; all produced an instant tension, a wariness that he recognized. Only a fool went into the streets of Nightshade at night, but the desperate could be forced to them, and he'd known his share of desperation. He didn't expect Ferals to suddenly emerge in the green, but he knew so little about the green he considered it a possibility.

It is.

He turned to his right at the sound of the voice and smiled. The water had gathered in the shape of a woman who was a foot taller than he, the movement so silent or instant, Severn hadn't had time to notice.

"How? The Ferals are Shadow."

The creatures you call Ferals are not entirely of Shadow; they are animals that have been transformed by what they have touched.

"But if they're here, that implies Shadow exists in the green."

Yes. At its edges. The green is…tired. There has been little opportunity for rest or renewal. Do you know how forests die?

He frowned. "No."

They age, and as they do, the many branches of their trees block sunlight; the forest floor becomes less wild because weeds cannot easily grow without sunlight. Trees wither, they die, and a single spark can cause a fire that rages across the whole of ancient woods.

But in the passage of those trees, sunlight once again touches forest floor, and things begin to grow anew.

"And the animals and birds that lived there?"

Many die. Some do not. The forest neither knows nor cares.

"The green isn't a natural forest."

No, as you've surmised. And the green does care. But what it requires now you cannot give it. It is time. You search for someone.

"Yvonne of Darrowelm," he replied, not knowing if the name had any meaning for the water. When the water failed to reply, he attempted to describe her, without ever having seen her. He knew she'd been injured; knew her arm had never recovered; knew the color of her hair and her height. He had never seen her and knew very little else.

The water failed to respond, and in the silence, Severn could once again hear the growls of distant animals. The water's words had done nothing to still the growing tension.

"She is precious to An'Sennarin," he finally said.

You do not serve An'Sennarin.

"No. But I owe him a debt, and this is the only way I can repay it. Nothing else I offer will be of value to him in the long fight to come."

There was a child, the water said. *She was injured in two ways. We called her to the green when we understood An'Sennarin's fear.*

"Why didn't you tell him?"

We were not certain—we are not certain—that she can be saved. Severn didn't like the sound of that at all. "Is she dead?"

No, not yet. But...it is complicated. You spoke of Shadow. You do not carry its taint.

"...She did?"

Yes. But...it had not devoured her, and An'Sennarin was

desperately unhappy so far from home. He could not return, because she was in the hands of his enemies. We thought we might contain the damage if we could separate her from those that caused it.

"She survived."

She did. But…she is not whole. We cannot wake her, here. The green will not allow it; if she wakes, the damage she will do while the green is weakened is far too great of a danger.

"Can I take her out of the green?"

Perhaps. But not safely. She cannot harm us, but the green is not what we are. There is a reason you were offered two choices. It is possible that you can do what the green cannot safely do.

"…If you mean that she's somehow infected by Shadow, there's nothing I can do to cure that. But…I can escort her out of the green if that's allowed."

If she is tainted, if she cannot be cured, she must be left with Alsanis.

"The Hallionne destroy Shadow."

Yes.

Severn exhaled. "Can you take me to where she is?"

Perhaps. She is not awake in any sense of the word you would use.

"Is she aware?"

We think so, but we are uncertain; she cannot hear us clearly, and even our speech now takes great concentration on our part.

He wondered what it would be like to be trapped in the green for decades, unable to move or interact with the environment, but aware of each passing hour. He thought it would drive him insane. "Do you sleep?"

I am water, but water is many things. To you, to your kind, I sleep often, I sleep constantly; I wake only when I am called.

"And to you?"

There are waves and currents. I am not always aware of every part of me. Do you understand how your heart beats? Sometimes the undercurrent is strong enough that I am anger and destruction; I am storm in your mortal harbor. You are not all of one thing; no more am I.

"Even in the green?"

Clever child. Come. We've arrived.

In Severn's eyes, they stood on a sandy beach. He could see the odd pebble, glinting under moonlight. There was no path, no building, and no people other than himself, unless one wanted to count the water.

"I...don't see her."

No. We could not be certain that she would survive unchanged, but the green was willing to accept her at my request. I offered the green what promises I could. I told you—Shadow will not change or corrupt the heart of the water. She is here. The water turned as it spoke, until it faced the lake to which it was still attached. When Severn stilled, the water rippled, small waves extending outward from the form the water had adopted. *I will not let you drown,* the water said, understanding Severn's concern.

"She's...beneath the lake?"

She is. You will have to find a way to bring her to the surface.

"You can't?"

I made promises to the green. They cannot be broken.

"You want me to break them."

You have made no promises to the green; the green will not be offended.

Severn chose not to remove his boots; he was certain the extended exposure to water would ruin them, but he wasn't certain what his feet would encounter on the lake bed. He accepted the water's direction and began to walk into the lake. The water's Avatar made no move to follow or to lead.

He was surprised when the lake bed fell away beneath his feet; between one step and the next the gradual slope down became an underwater precipice. But he could breathe here, and the fall, cushioned on all sides by water, wouldn't kill him. Without the steadiness of the water's voice, the water—lit by moon above—seemed far darker, the threat of Shadow more real.

Ferals were some blend of physical dog and Shadow; their forms didn't change or alter to suit the convenience of their daily hunts through the fief streets. He wondered if subtle Shadow might contaminate fish in the same way; would small swarms suddenly begin to attack? His movements, agile in air, were slowed by water. If something attacked him here, he was unlikely to survive it.

He accepted the risk. He'd accepted that risk from the moment he'd accepted An'Tellarus's invitation. Once again his master's voice returned as he floated slowly down, in water that seemed to have no end.

Risk is risk, Severn. Whether you choose to take the risk for "good" reasons or "bad" reasons does not change this fact. You may choose to take risks for reasons you personally consider good, as we all do. But risk is a moral vacuum. The universe is not concerned with morality. The choice, as always, is yours. The consequences, as always, are also yours to bear.

The moon's light alleviated darkness, but also accentuated it. Severn shifted position and began to swim down, into the depths. If the green and the water felt it necessary to contain a danger they had nonetheless chosen to risk, it would be here, where the water surrounded everything. He wished, briefly, that he had asked An'Sennarin what Yvonne looked like; when they were joined in the Tha'alaan, he could have seen her image clearly. He let the regret go. She was likely to be the only Barrani woman he'd see in the heart of the lake. It wouldn't be hard to recognize her, if he could find her.

He was wrong.

Visibility was poor, and lake bed was nonexistent when he encountered the first Barrani woman. He felt a flush of relief, which didn't last, because to the right of this first woman, he could see the dim, pale outline of a second. He couldn't, at this distance, differentiate between the two, but couldn't tell if they were somehow identical, either, which would have made some kind of warped sense if the water had been intent on hiding Yvonne.

But...the water had guided him here. He changed the direction of his arms, tilting up to slow his forward progress. If these weren't illusions designed by the water, had they somehow been put in place by the green?

Do not offend the green.

Severn had been taught to be polite, politic, careful. He knew how to navigate his way out of a brewing fight with the clever use of both words and body language. He'd learned Barrani culture and customs first, because if he offended a Barrani, he'd die. Mortal customs, however, had followed, although his master had had a very odd view of humanity. His lessons had had very little to do with the streets in which Severn lived. But as a child he'd observed, and he understood that lessons were only one part of the equation. The other was context. In all situations, power ruled—but the elements that defined power were different. In order to give no offense, he had to assess, and the initial assessment involved silence, observation, the ability to deflect attention.

All of his interactions naturally devolved into these learned behaviors. All, except for his interactions with Elianne and her mother.

He understood from observation that people of all ages wanted attention. He had never, considering all of the possible consequences, understood why. Not even with Elianne, in the beginning. She became some small and less predictable part of the space he occupied, but he occupied it in the same way: he observed, he watched for signs of anger, fear, desire. With Elianne in tow, he'd had to shift his responses. In some cases, this meant engaging in physical fights he would have easily avoided otherwise.

He had wondered in frustration if she were so careless because she was ignorant. Or if she was ignorant because she was so young. He'd obviously been her age before, but none of his memories of himself resembled Elianne. It took him time to understand that her fearlessness, her openness, the way she shared both tears and joy, was entirely her own, and by the time he understood this, he was far too entangled with her not to understand how precious it was. No child could be a child forever. No one walked through life unscarred.

But he had wanted to allow her the space to be that child for as long as he possibly could, because something about her immediacy and openness moved him, where so little else did.

That was gone now. He'd destroyed it with his own hands, in order to save Elianne's life. It was a choice she would never have made, would never have allowed him to make, if she'd known.

Ah. No. Why was he thinking about that now? It was irrelevant. It couldn't be changed. What he had was the present and the future.

And on some days, the present and the future looked very much like the water in which he now swam: cold, dark, bottomless, cut off from most of the light. He would never have known the difference if he hadn't left his master. Was it better, then, to have the knowledge and live with the pain that never quite left him?

Again, he shook himself. The answer didn't matter. He couldn't change the past, could never revisit his choice and make a different one. He had the future, or as much of it as remained if he made the wrong choice here. It was this choice, this path, he could affect.

Arrayed before him at different heights were at least a dozen Barrani women. They seemed tethered in place by shackles he couldn't see. Their eyes were closed, and dark hair moved in the currents like fronds of seaweed. They weren't evenly spaced, but they didn't appear to be bound to each other; he swam around their formation, circling closer and closer.

"Yvonne." His voice sounded oddly strangled as it left his lips and traveled through water.

As one, all of the women he could see pivoted to face him; as one, their eyes opened. In the darkness he couldn't see the color of those eyes; he could see pale, almost liminal skin, the sweep of moving hair, but their eyes seemed black to him—even the whites. They lifted their left arms in concert, and then their right, and from that position, they linked hands, interlacing fingers until they appeared to be forming concentric circles at different heights.

"Yvonne." He spoke again, his voice unfamiliar in his ears.

She—they—must have heard him; he was certain they wouldn't have opened their eyes, otherwise. Wouldn't have linked hands, as if to form a barrier through which no one could easily pass unnoticed. He was certain he would have to go through them but thought he could swim in the spaces between feet and hands.

He was wrong about that, too.

Even as the thought emerged, he could see the forms of Barrani women begin to elongate, feet bending and... spreading, to join up with heads that had also become stretched and warped, until the women no longer resembled Barrani; the faces, stretched so fine in places he could almost see through them, now seemed trapped there, neutrality becoming rictus as he attempted to find an opening before the whole of the sphere was entirely sealed.

His movement was slowed by water. The growing encasement seemed to struggle in the medium as well, but perhaps that was the water itself. He could no longer hear the water's voice. He swam up to the height of the formation; he could see the darkness where hair overlapped, could see the pale length of stretched faces. He could fit between them if he swam straight down. He didn't want to be caught halfway between.

"If you can hear me," he said to the water, "help me now."
He began to swim.

The water didn't answer, but the gap where hair and flesh
extended held steady for just long enough that he could approach it and propel his body through the space. Hair attempted to cling to his legs, but currents swept the strands
aside. Above his head, the space he'd entered as those strands
writhed together snapped shut, pulled by something that
couldn't be seen.

The interior of the sphere wasn't dark, which was what
Severn had expected. He could see light, pale and almost
green, emanating from what he assumed was its center. That
light caused the elongated flesh to glow faintly, the color better suited to corpses than living Barrani.

He wondered, briefly, how he would escape this sphere;
wondered if it would collapse if he reached its center, simu-
lacrums breaking and flowing inward, toward the intruder.
He had daggers, but not in hand, as they made swimming
more cumbersome.

The sphere, however, held while he swam toward its heart,
and toward the light.

The light itself had no shape. It was like a sphere within
a sphere. He squinted—he had to squint as he approached,
the light was so bright. He called Yvonne's name three times
but stopped before a fourth; he could hear something like
a sibilant whisper ride water currents to his ears. If Yvonne
couldn't hear or answer, he wanted no more attention from
what did.

But Yvonne wasn't the source of the light in the water; the
heart of the light was the wrong size, the wrong shape, for a
person of any race. He stopped swimming as he reached the
source: two long daggers, attached to nothing he could see.

He failed to understand the why of it; how was consigned
to water, to the green, to things he'd been clearly taught

were like acts of nature, not acts of man. He'd been offered a choice. He'd chosen.

Had Lord Leveanne lied to him? Had she decided, for reasons of her own, that the weapons were, in the end, what she wanted him to have? Had the water somehow lied? The water knew what he'd chosen. She'd led him to the edge of the shore, pointed him in the direction he must swim, and left him. Had the water known that this was what waited?

Bewilderment and confusion gave way to a very rare anger.

He knew what lack of choice was; as a child he had accepted it. But he'd been offered a choice and he'd *made his choice*, and yet, here he was, in the center of a lake, before two glowing daggers, no sign of Yvonne of Darrowelm in sight. He wanted to ignore them, to swim up and break through the sphere that encased these daggers as if protecting them somehow. He wanted to simply walk away.

Do not offend the green.

He couldn't be certain that the voice was the water's voice; it might have been simple memory.

"I don't understand what you want," he said, the words precise and over annunciated. They weren't followed by invective, but that took effort. "Yvonne, if you're there somehow, I came on behalf of Ollarin. I came to find you. Your safety is the only thing he wants of the West March."

The sphere of light shed by the two daggers cracked, as if it were glass, the outer containment of a lantern's heart. The daggers remained, but their light was now housed entirely in their blades, and as Severn watched the light dim and shift focus, those blades began to move.

They moved toward him, blade first.

Anger fled. He lifted both hands, pushing himself up as if by that minor motion he could avoid them. Had they floated, handle first, he would have understood that he was meant to take them. As it was, they gleamed in dark water, like two fangs that were part of some invisible maw.

He drew his own knives in time to parry the slow attack of the two daggers; it should have been simple. It wasn't. There was a weight behind the slow thrust, an intention. That he could readjust his grip and compensate for the unexpected strength of his unseen adversary was the result of training.

Weapons training was also the only training that Mellianne didn't complain about; the only thing she thought was relevant and worthy. She joined Severn in some of his other lessons, but she was sullen. She had long since learned not to disturb such lessons with outright hostility.

She would have been smug, had she been by his side, the proof of the importance of these lessons, this training, so obvious. He'd never argued otherwise, but she found his interest in language and history, his interest in magic, his interest in society's various structures, annoying—as if, by having those interests, he was criticizing hers in a passive-aggressive way.

The daggers retreated and attacked again, this time at different heights, different speeds; the water didn't seem as viscous for them as it was for Severn. None of his training sessions had involved water as anything other than rain and the conditions in which rain could leave the ground. He would have to do something about that, if he managed to return to the city whole enough that he could.

Now, however, he shifted the positions of his own daggers. He kicked the one blade that had chosen a lower trajectory, parried the other; both knives once again withdrew.

The third attack was faster. Severn couldn't parry both blades in time; the blade on his right struck a glancing blow, sliding off Severn's dagger with a grinding sensation and cutting his hand. Severn never wanted to shed his own blood, but he dreaded it here. Blood in water was never good, and this wasn't a known body of water. He didn't know what might sense and seek blood—but he imagined the shell of non-Barrani might react to it badly. Badly for Severn, that was.

Badly, it seemed, for the blade: it dimmed, as if drawing blood toward itself and tarnishing the newness of its light. Blood slowed it. Severn looked, briefly, at the cut hand. To his surprise, the cut was far shallower than the blood shed into the water implied. He glanced at the brilliant glowing knife, and then at his own daggers. He sheathed one and waited for the fourth attempt. This time, he chose where and how these foreign weapons would cut him. He meant to take the blow on his right hand; it was already injured.

But the dagger had other ideas, and he received a wound to the left hand, positioning the edge of his palm in a way that wouldn't allow the knife to cut important tendons in his fingers. Flesh wounds could be survived more easily. He'd only barely started life as a Wolf. He doubted that he'd be given the same opportunities Rosie had been given when she'd lost the use of her leg.

The job that he'd chosen out of a bitter necessity had become something far more important than he could have anticipated. He could make a place for himself in the Halls of Law, but he had to survive. Blood once again billowed in the water; the cut was deep. This time, Severn watched the wound he'd received. The edges of the cut began to close.

He sheathed the dagger he'd brought as he watched the light dim. Blood flowered in water again. This time he could see that the cloud of blood and water elongated to a point—the blade itself. Both knives slowed motion, as if they were snakes that had just been fed.

Severn reached out with both hands and caught these new weapons, one hilt in each hand. He didn't understand the green. He barely understood the water, and of that, only the tiny part of it that had also been touched by An'Sennarin. They had said that the shards of Tyron tested their bearers, and if the bearers were found wanting, they could die.

As tests went, this wasn't much of one. Severn had taken far worse damage fighting for his life in the not-distant past. Here, the blades had cut him, once on each hand, and then… surrendered. He took them, wondering briefly if they had sheaths in the lake that he couldn't see. No one willingly carried unsheathed blades in anything other than their hands.

"I chose to find Yvonne," he told the blades, as if they were somehow sentient or alive. "I didn't intend to find you. If I was offered a choice, I hope that the choice I made will be respected—by the green, by the water, and by those who accompanied me." A brief thought came: perhaps these weren't the coveted weapons hidden by the heart of the green. Perhaps they were meant to allow him to leave the sphere he'd entered—it showed no signs of dissolving on its own.

But he knew, on a visceral level, that the thought was wrong. He held two legendary weapons in his hands, as if they were garden-variety daggers.

"Yvonne," he said, lifting his voice.

There was still no answer.

"All right," he said to the enchanted blades. "We have some work to do." The blades, like the missing Barrani woman, failed to reply.

Severn wasn't generally squeamish. He understood that the distended, warped bodies that formed this sphere weren't actual bodies; they weren't actually Barrani women, drowned and chained in place. He'd seen bodies in the morgue before. He knew what to expect from corpses. But there had been no Barrani bodies in the morgue, and even if there had been, he'd been given very little practice in cutting into those corpses. He'd watched. It had been late, because the Wolves didn't enter the general areas otherwise occupied by the Hawks or the Swords during their normal hours.

But the morgue had information Elluvian considered important. The reports generated by the morgue had to be understood by the Wolves, even if investigation of murders was the province of the Hawks. The sight of treating what had once been a living, breathing person as dead flesh to be investigated had been arresting—but corpses didn't scream when they gave that information up to the men and women who could then translate what they found into language other officers in the Halls of Law could understand.

He could make cuts into dead flesh, but he wasn't entirely certain that what surrounded him was, in fact, dead. Yvonne wasn't here, or wasn't visible, which meant that he had to leave or look elsewhere. To leave, he had to exit this terrible sphere. He had to cut through flesh or hair. Hair was preferable.

Shadow infested Ferals. Ferals came out at night and began their hunt. But at dawn, they retreated, over and over again, crossing the border between Nightshade and the darkness around which all of the fiefs were built. Ferals could be killed. He'd seen it before. Their bodies didn't melt or disappear when the sun rose.

He hesitated, and then looked straight up, where the dome itself was sealed with joined black hair, the color matching the situation almost perfectly. If Yvonne had somehow been affected by Shadow, was she lost? No, he thought. The water thought she existed, entwined somehow with the Shadow that any thinking person feared.

It was Shadow that the green somehow accepted, but Severn didn't understand the green. The Towers in the fiefs would have destroyed Yvonne utterly. Of that he was certain. He was less certain of the disposition of the Hallionne. And Severn himself?

He could kill her, if she could be killed. But he couldn't bring himself to tell An'Sennarin that this one faint hope was gone, and at Severn's hands. But she wasn't here. What was here was a mockery of Yvonne, made physical and real, but not alive in the sense that Severn understood life.

He was willing to accept that there were lives he could not, or at least did not, understand. Not all of that strange life was inimical; not all of it could be like the Ferals. He wasn't certain if he felt this way because he'd chosen his goal, his purpose, and it better suited that choice. That was too much like lying to himself, and if he couldn't trust his own thoughts to be truthful, to be objective, how different was that from madness? He had to be able to see what was in front of him. He had to separate that cleanly from what he wanted or what he feared. There was no other way to move forward, not for Severn Handred, raised by a Barrani Lord in the fiefs.

He couldn't sheathe the daggers he'd picked up; he didn't try. Instead, he swam up to the height of the dome and studied the twined hair. The daggers no longer glowed so brightly their light hurt his eyes, but they shed light regardless. It wasn't a bright light, but that wasn't required now—his eyes had acclimatized to darkness.

He nudged the mass of combined hair with the left knife. It immediately separated, as if it were alive and the blade burned it. Perhaps it did; he could almost taste the change in the water that passed through his lungs as if it were air. Strands of hair untangled and retreated. A space very similar to the one he'd entered began to open up.

He began to swim up through the gap, and stopped, treading water as he watched the movement of hair. Instinct told him to leave, but instinct also told him that he wasn't done here yet. Severn had learned, at a very early age, to trust his instincts, but warring instincts made that difficult.

He preferred to have objective fact back instinctive reaction, because sometimes instincts were composed of the minor details that he'd observed and internalized without simple words. He knew he'd have none of that backing here. He was breathing in water, surrounded by a sphere made of the warped flesh of multiple Barrani women.

He could assume these were the artifacts of the Shadow the water had mentioned; that somehow, this was Shadow's expression. But the heart of the sphere wasn't a person. It was these weapons. Maybe the sphere itself was meant to keep the weapons at bay; maybe it couldn't collapse further without somehow destroying itself because the weapons lay in its center.

Or maybe there was more to it.

The water said Yvonne bore the taint of Shadow. But if the Shadow could do this, it wasn't simple taint or contamination. If this was Yvonne's burden, shouldn't Yvonne be here somewhere?

Severn understood the instinct then. He swam up to the body of the nearest Barrani, lifted his left knife, and very gently drew it across the line between her exposed shoulder blades.

The water shook with her screams.

CHAPTER TWENTY-FIVE

ALL OF THE BODIES SHUDDERED; ALL OF THE bodies screamed. None bled, but Severn hadn't intended to cut. He pulled his arm back as the body he was closest to began to buck wildly. It wasn't the only one; all of the bodies, stretched and attached, began to squirm and struggle in the same way.

He moved to the next one to test his theory. He drew the back of the blade across the thighs of this segment of the Barrani chain. The screaming continued. He then drew the back of the other blade across the untouched thigh in the same fashion. This time, every part of the wall undulated and the water itself grew cloudy, as if with blood, although he hadn't pierced flesh.

Hair detached first, and formed braided tendrils; their target was Severn. The hands of the multiple Barrani women continued to be almost melded together, but the legs and feet separated from the foreheads to which they'd been attached. Hair streamed together, and Severn pulled back, his movements slowed by water.

Severn bled when struck. If he'd needed any further confirmation that this wasn't normal hair, he had it. His blood was, unlike the odd opacity shed when these twin blades touched the formation, red. He wasn't certain how deep the puncture wound was and couldn't pause to check. He shifted the blades in his hands and began to use them to cut.

The hair itself seemed longer than normal Barrani hair, but not by much. If he remained in the center of the formation, it was safer—but safer wasn't *safe*, and the tendrils struck his back, his shoulders, his arm. He cut those that seemed to be reaching for his face, his eyes.

Cutting the ends of the tendrils released the bound hair, and it spread in the water in loose strands, as if released from the bondage of ties and clips that might otherwise preserve its shape. He moved through those strands slowly, waiting to see if they regrouped. They didn't. Shoulder blades—theirs—tightened and spread in an almost rhythmic way, as if the bodies, still attached to arms and by hands to each other, were attempting to tear themselves free.

Throughout, the air vibrated with screams of pain, and sound became an almost physical assailant.

He made no attempt to cut wrists or fingers, but once again, drew the backs of the knives across them. This time he was knocked back. A foot had hit his rib cage, kicking backward. But the wrists and hands he touched with the blades separated. Fingers pulled out of the single lump of bumpy flesh that had been conjoined hands, and arms were free.

For the first time, one of the women could turn in place, turn her face toward Severn. She did, and brought her hands up, almost across her chest, as if to defend herself from a deadly attack.

Her eyes were black; he could see no Barrani color in them. She made no move toward him, and he moved to the side, cutting tendrils of hair into their disparate strands. He brought knife to skull, to roots of hair, and from there, to the front of a face he couldn't see, his arm bent around the side of a face.

Only when he had done this did he once again move to touch melded fingers, and to watch this woman pull her hands free of the joint lump. She turned, just as the first woman had done, to face him, to look inward, her arms crossed against her chest, her teeth bared. No words emerged, but the screams of pain were eclipsed, momentarily, by snarls of anger. She made no move to attack him, or no immediate move; just like the first woman, she seemed intent on defense.

Her eyes were dark as well, but he thought he could see the glimmer of whites around that distended, black iris.

He then moved slowly, bleeding as he made his way to each and every one of the Barrani women who had been stretched to form a living sphere, cutting tendrils of hair before he ceased to cut anything.

It grew silent as he worked, or more silent; not every Barrani who turned to face him snarled. Some sobbed instead, curling in on themselves more tightly, knees drawn up to their chests, arms wrapped around them, their postures differing, their reactions becoming individual.

At last, when the last two joined hands were free, all of the Barrani women were now facing the interior of what was no longer a sphere. Every single one of them seemed almost identical, although Barrani often seemed that way to the untrained eye. But the shape of their faces, their jaws, their arms, the length of their legs, their feet—they seemed to be the same, as if all of these were Yvonne of Darrowelm.

Or parts of Yvonne.

Severn didn't understand the why or the how. Instead, wincing as he moved, he swam down to the bottom of the sphere, where his feet touched sand as current whipped around his ankles. Lifting his face in water that was now almost muddy, he shouted, "Yvonne!"

All of the Yvonnes, as he thought of them, paused; some

stiffened, some loosened their posture. They looked down at him as he stood beneath their many gazes.

And then, as one, they looked away—toward an Yvonne who was curled in an almost fetal posture, her knees beneath her chin, her arms bent at the elbows, her hands covering her face as if she meant to hide her tears. As if they weren't part of Yvonne, but recognized who Severn sought. Or as if they were waiting for this one last Yvonne to unfold, to join them.

"Yvonne," he said, his voice loud enough to carry, but soft enough that it implied speaking, not shouting.

She didn't react; he wondered if she couldn't hear him or didn't want to acknowledge him. He wanted to sheathe the long daggers, but had no way to do it without just letting them go. Given the color of Barrani eyes here, that seemed like the worst possible idea.

All heads remained turned or lifted to this one Yvonne. He swam toward her, but they no longer seemed to be looking at him. At least not for now.

"Yvonne." She didn't lift her head, but her arms tightened. "Ollarin asked me to find you."

A murmur came from the other Yvonnes. "Ollarin?" It passed between them like an echo, or perhaps a ball bouncing between players of a game without pause. Where there had been screams, snarls, sobs, there was now a single name. The name grew louder, the texture of the spoken word shifting between voices: curiosity, fear, anger, and something more tremulous.

All of them were her voice, and none of them were her voice.

"Ollarin is An'Sennarin now."

This time, the lone silent figure lifted her hands from her face. Her eyes were blue—but they were Barrani blue. Her hair moved in water currents but didn't seem to move on its own.

"Lies."

Severn shook his head. "He sent me to find you, if you could be found. I have a letter—" He hesitated. He wasn't certain the letter, in an interior pocket, had actually survived his first fall into the lake water. "I *had* a letter. I don't know if it can be read anymore."

Eyes narrowed, she said, "Why not?"

"Most letters don't survive being soaked in water. Which is where we are."

"You're human." Her words were slurred.

"Yes."

"Why would he send you?"

"I came with An'Tellarus."

This time, her eyes widened. They narrowed immediately, but not before it was clear that An'Tellarus wasn't the name she'd expected to hear, and also wasn't a name that she feared.

"You belong to An'Tellarus?"

"No. I serve the Emperor. The Dragon Emperor."

"Has he come to burn down Darrowelm?" It wasn't the question he'd expected, and it was asked with far less fear than the words themselves implied. There was something that hinted at either hope or anticipation in the question.

"He hasn't come to the West March. He doesn't rule it. But I serve the Emperor, not An'Tellarus. An'Tellarus lives in the Imperial City some of the time, and it's illegal to own people in the Empire."

"How did you meet her?" As she spoke, she lowered her knees, letting her hands rest on her lap. She appeared to be seated on a shelf of water.

"I met her when I was asked to visit the High Halls."

The grimace she offered in response to the last two words was very...human. "But you survived?"

Severn shrugged. "She did try to kill me before we'd been formally introduced, if that helps."

To his surprise, Yvonne laughed. "That sounds *just* like her."

"She tried to visit you."

"Here?"

"No. In Darrowelm. She wasn't given permission to enter."

Yvonne nodded. "Is Ollarin really An'Sennarin?"

"He is. He's been An'Sennarin for all of my life, which according to An'Tellarus is practically yesterday. He had no way to reach you—everyone thinks you remain in Darrowelm."

"But not you."

"I was told by Lord Rowan that you were no longer in Darrowelm. Which is good because I intended to try to sneak in there."

"That isn't a very good idea."

"No. But it was the only idea I had. Darrowelm, like Tellarus or Danarre, has roots somewhere in the green. Where we are, now."

"You can't walk in from the green."

Severn shrugged. "I no longer have reason to do so." He turned toward the sphere of women. They had fallen utterly silent when she first began to talk. It was eerie. He hoped they'd vanish somehow, if they weren't necessary.

The long knives began to glow.

"I won't force you to leave. I won't harm you. If you're safe and happy here—"

"Do I *look* happy to you?"

Severn grimaced. "That was a stupid comment on my part."

"It *really* was."

"How did you end up here? I mean, here specifically. In the water surrounded by..."

"Surrounded by what?" Her eyes narrowed.

Severn stared at her. "What do you see?"

"You. The fancy magical long knives. The holes in your clothing. Is that blood?"

"Not enough of it to kill me."

"What do you think you see?"

"A very large number of Yvonnes."

"Pardon?"

"I see a very large number of Yvonnes. There are Yvonnes to either side of you, and above and below you as well. The one to the right of you is glaring. The one to the left is hugging herself with her arms. Below you, one is now crouching in the water, and above one is standing, arms crossed. There are other Yvonnes besides these; there are enough to form a Barrani sphere." He chose to skip the part about how that sphere was formed.

"Are you hallucinating?"

"My wounds are from those other Yvonnes. I don't consider them hallucinations."

"And the knives?"

"I don't have sheaths that fit them. But they were here—they were at the heart of the sphere. You're at the side, at the widest part. Can you move?"

"I've obviously been moving. Do you mean swim?"

Severn nodded.

"To where?"

"Up."

Her throat stretched as she lifted her face. "To where?" she asked again.

"Can you follow me?" he asked, swimming up toward the moonlight, with the expectation he'd hit the lake's surface by the time he arrived.

The blades became brighter again as he waited. He almost offered one to her for the light but hesitated. If these were the blades hidden in the green, she might not be able to carry one—but she'd certainly want to try if a mere mortal like Severn had managed it.

Yvonne unfolded fully, rising from her invisible bench. "I can try."

Severn swam up. Yvonne followed, but came to a halt at the upper reach of what had once been a sphere. Her arms and legs were moving; she was clearly a good swimmer. But her arms and legs couldn't propel her past the ring of Barrani look-alikes. None of them tried to touch her. None of them tried to impede her progress. Clearly they knew she couldn't leave.

Severn seldom cursed. He rarely saw the point in it. He therefore said nothing. But he looked for any physical impediment, any sign that the Barrani women were holding her back or down. They weren't. She was swimming in place.

"Have you ever tried to leave the lake?"

She shook her head.

"Why not?"

"This is the only safe place for me." When he failed to continue, she said, "I was injured, when I got here. And I was exhausted. I wanted to be safe, and this was safe."

"Why did you come here?"

"Why do you think? If you know Ollarin, truly, you know what Darrowelm wanted. You know what Sennarin wanted." Her eyes narrowed, her lips thinning. "My parents died. I almost died with them." There was a moment of wild glee in the final words. "I should have, but I couldn't. They didn't want me dead. If my parents hadn't been so stupid, they wouldn't have died, either."

"You would have gone with them?"

"Yes—what was the alternative? My family dies and they take me anyway? But my family *did* die, and after that, there was no reason at all to preserve my own life."

"How did you almost die?"

She stopped attempting to move upward, since up wasn't allowed, and turned herself around to face Severn. "I jumped in front of one of Darrowelm's blades. Here. You can see the scar for yourself."

He could see a good deal more than that, but focused on the puckered, dark scar beneath her right collarbone, just above the swell of breast. None of the Barrani that otherwise resembled Yvonne had a similar scar, or any other imperfections Severn could see.

"Have you ever been injured before then?"

"Not like that, no. I broke an ankle once," she added, with a grimace. "But that day was different. I knew it was different." She hesitated. "I took the first blow meant for my mother. It pierced us both; it killed neither of us. They froze because…they weren't supposed to kill me. I would have been happy to die. It was the only way to…resist."

To spit in their faces, Severn thought. It wasn't something he'd be willing to die for, but he understood the desire. "Was there anything unusual about the sword that you were stabbed with?"

She gave him a look that was very familiar—but it reminded Severn of Mellianne, not anyone Barrani.

"I ask for a reason." He exhaled, which was an odd sensation in the water. "The water said you had been tainted by Shadow. The green accepted whatever that taint was, possibly because the water wanted you to flee to the green; the water wanted you to be safe."

"I know that," she said, her voice just shy of snappish. "But I don't feel any different. I don't feel like I've been transformed into something dangerous or monstrous."

Severn glanced at the physically solid echoes of Yvonne. "No, you probably don't. Do you want to stay here?"

She shook her head, and then added, "It doesn't look like I'm being given the choice. I can't swim up—I can't even *see* up."

Severn turned to the Yvonnes, or the nearest one. Lifting both knives, he approached, but the Yvonne now had eyes for what Severn considered the real one. He had apparently become as invisible to the Yvonnes as they were to her. He brought the knives around, aiming for a shallow cut across the Barrani's thigh.

Yvonne shrieked. "What are you *doing*?"

He looked at her; her leg was bleeding. "Testing something."

"How did you even do that? You weren't anywhere near me!"

"Magic knives?"

Her expression was angry, not fearful, but she frowned. "Were you trying to damage one of the invisible Barrani—the ones you can see and I can't?"

Severn nodded. "I don't think you'll be able to leave the lake if they're still here. But they're clearly part of you in some way I can't see, and I can't cut you free without killing you." As the currents around his legs grew stronger, he added, "I have no intention of killing her." The water stilled. "So...about the sword."

"It was a sword," she replied, with more gravity. "It wasn't glowing, but it wasn't radiating black Shadow, either. No, I haven't been stabbed before, so I can't compare the wound with other injuries. It hurt, but it only hurt after the fact—more on the way out than on the way in."

"But these were Darrowelm forces?"

She frowned. "It was An'Darrowelm who demanded my surrender." Her frown deepened. "I don't know everyone who served or lived in Darrowelm. I wasn't part of the main family, and my parents weren't, either. But the forces of Darrowelm—the guards, the warriors—wear the symbols of Darrowelm." Barrani memory should have come in useful here; it didn't. She couldn't remember.

Had she been mortal, had she been human, this would have been entirely natural. Human witnesses had incredibly unreliable memories for things they had witnessed, even firsthand. But Barrani? They forgot nothing. They could remember everything with a bit of time and effort. Yvonne couldn't.

He rode the undercurrents of his own frustration. If cutting one of the Yvonnes caused the wound to appear on Yvonne herself, he was at a momentary loss. Were they somehow part of Yvonne? And if they were, why could he see them so distinctly? Was it his own vision he was meant to distrust?

Were these Yvonnes part of Yvonne, extruded somehow by Shadow? Or by something else? Was that even possible?

The blades he held were now once again too bright to look at without squinting. Yvonne saw them the same way, given her own squint and the way she raised a hand to shade her eyes.

"I want to try something," he said, swimming once again toward the Yvonne he considered the real one.

"You want to cut me."

"I want to cut you. Or I want you to cut yourself."

She grimaced and held out her hand. "Give me one of the knives."

The water moved around his arms as he attempted to lift the blade.

"...Or not."

"I don't know if you've ever heard of the shards of Tyron."

Her eyes rounded, her expression one of outrage. "Of course I've heard of them!" Then, as his words and her answer sank in, she looked at the blades. "You think that's what these are?"

"They shouldn't be. They're in the wrong place. But...yes. I think that's what they might be. I don't know a lot about them, but people who know more have implied that picking them up can be death for some people."

"And not for you?"

Severn shrugged. "Not yet."

She'd clearly heard the stories, but she left her hand, palm up, where it was. "They haven't killed you yet. Is my hand okay?"

He nodded. "It's just an experiment." This time, the water released him. He wanted to reach out to steady her hand, but he had no hands free. "I'll hold the blade still; you run your palm across it. You'll have more control that way."

"You can't put them down, can you?"

He grimaced. "I'm afraid to try. I think...I think the blades kept the multiples at bay. They were attached to you in some way, but—"

"They couldn't devour me?"

"Something like that. To me, when I first arrived, you were just one part of them."

She shuddered, but lifted her hand, grasping the edge of the right blade and pushing her palm against it. When she pulled her hand back, it was bleeding. But so were the palms of all of the other Yvonnes.

"They're all bleeding," he told her. "Not just you."

"So you could kill all of them at once if you killed me, or you could kill me by just killing one of them."

"That's what it looks like to me."

"You should have brought Ollarin with you. He could talk to the water anywhere, and I'm sure the water would have told him what to do."

"If he could have come here, I wouldn't be here. The water wanted you saved. If you want to wait until he can come here, I think the water and the green can preserve you."

"And the Shadow?"

Severn shook his head. "I don't know." But he had his suspicions now and didn't necessarily like any of them. "I grew up hearing very few stories about either the green or the shards—but it almost seems to me that the green might have moved the shards here to preserve you. I don't understand how the green views Shadow, I just know the green is ancient, and somehow sentient, but not in a way we can easily understand.

"The shards—or their light—seem to absorb or destroy bits of Shadow."

"But those Yvonnes aren't bits of Shadow, as you call them. Not if stabbing them hurts me."

"It's Shadow."

"What does that mean?"

"If anyone understood Shadow fully, *Ravellon* probably wouldn't exist. Shadow is chaotic, it defies expectations. Anything we know of it is, by the mutating nature of Shadow, incomplete. The water implied that you'd been altered by Shadow the way animals can be." He realized this was the wrong phrase almost before it left his mouth, and mentally kicked himself. He wasn't usually this careless.

Yvonne bristled, as he'd expected. To his surprise, she kept angry words to herself. Her eyes were a dark blue, but they didn't dip into the indigo of rage. "You are going to explain that."

"Yes. My wording was poor, I apologize. Where I grew up, there were creatures we called Ferals. They were like giant dogs, and they came to the streets after sundown, and hunted whoever was unlucky enough to be in those streets. At dawn, they left. They were never anything other than giant dogs with giant teeth, and the Towers obviously considered them not quite Shadow, or they could never leave *Ravellon*.

"I think somehow you're like the Ferals. But…I don't know how. And if we can't figure it out, even if you do get out of here, you're likely to end up in Hallionne Alsanis."

She fell silent. "I want to try something. Hold out the blade again."

He did as she asked. She lifted the hand she hadn't cut, and cut her palm, this time more quickly. "Is it the same?"

He nodded. All of the Yvonnes now had two bleeding hands, not one.

"I'm glad Ollarin isn't here."

"Why?"

She smiled a fey smile, a hint of wildness, a hint of darkness, transforming it. "Because he was always far too squeamish. Always."

Severn knew all the ways in which the Ollarin she'd known had overcome that squeamishness. "He's An'Sennarin, now," he replied, implying everything else he didn't put into words.

"He's Barrani," she said. "Keep your left hand exactly where it is. He isn't incapable of violence. But he's incapable of it when he actually cares. I thought he would be better off if I were dead, did you know that?"

"He wouldn't agree."

"Of course not. That's why I said he's squeamish." She caught his left wrist with both of her hands; young or not, her grip was strong. Had his life been in danger, he could have stabbed her with the right hand. It was no longer his life he was worried about. It was hers.

"Don't move," she said, and this close he could see the light of the one blade reflected in her eyes. "I don't remember who stabbed me. But I remember where, and how."

He could feel the water entangle his legs, his thighs, his chest. Yvonne herself didn't seem to be similarly impeded. If the water had spoken to him with words, in a voice he recognized, he would have been far calmer because he understood what Yvonne intended.

But she had no momentum, as she drew closer to the blade. She used Severn as an anchor point so she could pull herself up to the blade's point, the blade's edge, and slowly impale herself on it. She grimaced, clenching her jaws together as she traveled slowly up the stationary knife. But he saw what she intended: the blade entered her body along the same lines as the reddened scar.

She bled, the incision was so slow; he wanted to help, to put his own muscles into it, to shorten the time it took for the knife to sink into her flesh; he couldn't. Her grip was too tight.

"I remember," she said, her voice shaky. "How the sword entered. Where it entered. Where it exited. It didn't kill me then."

"These aren't swords. They're long knives."

Her eyes widened. "Is that how they appear to you? To me, they're swords. Long swords. Barrani swords." As she spoke, blood trickled out of the corner of her mouth. "This does hurt."

"Ollarin wouldn't have allowed it."

"He would have let me do what I wanted until it actually hurt me. You don't think this is the wrong thing to do."

"I think it's risky."

"But not wrong."

"I think it's risky and smart, unless you die from a wound I have no way to heal. If I'm wrong about what these weapons are—"

"I'm certain you're not."

"Weapons aren't known as healing devices." He didn't flinch as she pulled herself up the knife, but her arms began to tremble as her hands lost strength. There was a lot of blood.

"Let me finish," he said.

She shook her head; drops of blood slid off her face and the sheen of sweat she'd built up. "I remember what it felt like."

"What do you think reinjuring yourself is going to do?" But even asking he turned; the many faces of all the other Yvonnes were now twisted in grimaces of pain. Although some bore it silently, some screamed, some mirrored the grimace on the actual Yvonne's face. All bled.

So did Yvonne. He could see the widening gap in her flesh; she bled as if there was only wound, no blade, although he could clearly see it.

But the nature of the wounds seemed to change as Yvonne continued. Red blood—the Yvonnes shed red blood—became darker and thicker, until what fell was black and oily. The light of the blade Severn held dulled once again, as it had dulled without breaking skin when he'd run it across the multiple Yvonnes, breaking their formation, but the process was different.

Yvonne's pain didn't seem to come from contact with the blade; it came from the wound she was inflicting, slowly, on herself, in an attempt to match present pain to the remembered pain of the first injury. If, as they both suspected, Shadow had entered through that wound, she hoped the light of the blade would kill it. This wouldn't have been Severn's first choice, it was so risky—but the light of the blade wasn't dimming the way it had earlier. To his eye, it seemed that Yvonne was absorbing that light; her chest and the shoulder nearest the wound were glowing faintly, as was her arm.

He was grateful when her hands fell away from his wrist; his arm was numb, her grip had been so strong and so consistent. He wanted to pull the blade out, but her eyes widened and she shook her head. He understood why. Her body continued to absorb all of the light the sword shed. Only when that light resided entirely within Yvonne did she lower her head and exhale.

"Now," she told him, her body tensing.

He pulled the knife out in a single, straight motion, and then reached out with both arms—his hands were still full of hilt—to catch her as she pitched forward.

CHAPTER TWENTY-SIX

ATTEMPTING TO HOLD A PERSON WITH ONLY THE crook of one's arms was more awkward than Severn had anticipated, never having tried anything like this before. Yvonne helped, in a way; she pitched forward, and he took most of her weight against his chest.

"Yvonne."

She stirred.

"Stay awake. It's important to stay awake."

She nodded, but it was feeble. Severn looked up. The rest of the Yvonnes, wounds bleeding black, were...unraveling. There was no other word to describe what he could now see.

He tightened his arms; he couldn't cross them properly while knives remained in his hands. He wouldn't let go of them until the water cleared; at the moment it was murkier than it had ever been, as the other Yvonnes continued to crumble.

The current was strong, but it seemed to be moving in a very tight circle, collecting and condensing the particles suspended in it, rather than dispersing them. This detritus was gathered and compressed into one dark, shivering ball. Severn looked at it, then looked at Yvonne. If he was forced to let go, she would sink to the lake bed, where she would likely die. She wasn't conscious enough to hold on to him while he attempted to navigate water with weapons in either hand.

These weapons were magical. They had the ability to counter, to destroy Shadow. He was certain he wouldn't find their like again.

Lord Leveanne had offered him a choice. He'd chosen. *Do not offend the green.*

The weapons weren't where they should have been, but they'd been where they were needed; the light they'd shed at the center of the sphere probably kept the Shadow anchored, if not jailed. He was certain the positioning of the blades had allowed Yvonne to survive *as* Yvonne.

It was Yvonne's choice that had freed her from Shadow. It had never been a safe choice, but it was the only choice she had if she wanted to leave the lake, the green; the only choice that might allow her to finally be free. But now, struggle as she might, she couldn't remain conscious. If he couldn't carry her, she was almost certain to die.

"Help her," Severn said, to the water, to the currents that were in no way natural. "Help her rise. Carry her to the shore."

The water failed to respond. Or perhaps it answered, wordless: it didn't touch Yvonne at all. The choice was Severn's to make. Weapons or Yvonne. He wondered if this was supposed to be an agonizing or difficult choice; if he was supposed to hesitate while she bled out or let her die while he returned with the shards.

He'd hesitated for long enough. The sword Yvonne had pulled her way up fell first; he caught her, hand around her upper arm, arm behind her back, and began to kick his way toward the dense, roiling ball.

He then drove the second blade, still shining with brilliant light, into the center of the ball. It stuck there as if the ball itself were flesh. He let the hilt go.

Before he left, he offered the black mass the equivalent of a Barrani nod. "I don't know if you were keeping her safe, somehow," he said. "If you were, I'm sorry for what I've just done. But we can't coexist with Shadow the same way the Ferals can, and she needs to be free of you to be safe."

He wrapped his second arm around her because he now could, and began to swim up toward the lake's surface, carrying her.

This time, nothing impeded their progress.

The water aided their rise. He hadn't expected that; he might have held on to the weapons, otherwise. But he couldn't turn back yet, couldn't try to retrieve what he'd dropped. He had a feeling he wouldn't be able to find them. A choice had been offered, a choice made.

He accepted both the choice and its consequences.

Yes, the water said, as if she could hear the thought. *I am not certain it will be enough to save Yvonne. She was brave. Brave and foolish.*

Severn agreed, but silently. He didn't ask the water why she hadn't spoken until now. He made no accusations. Instead he said, "I tried my best not to offend the green."

The green is not offended. You would know, if it were. Come, bring her to my shore.

Severn nodded; the water lifted him. He held Yvonne tightly until the water stopped.

The shore was not the shore he'd left when the water had pointed him in a general direction. It was a beach of sand, but the sand was so pale it was almost white; from a distance, it resembled snow. The water itself was warm enough snow seemed unlikely, but Severn understood that nature in the green didn't abide by the usual rules.

The sand, when he stepped onto it, was warm. Water didn't drip from his clothing as he stepped out of the lake; it withdrew. Yvonne wasn't wearing any clothing to speak of, but the water left her hair and skin. Severn's shirt was a bloody mess, which was expected; the water didn't, or couldn't, clean that.

He considered asking the water if clothing could somehow be created but resisted. Even if it could, it wasn't likely to survive their exit from the green. He turned to look back, but the lake was still, almost serene; there was no person-shaped pillar behind him.

He set Yvonne down on the sand; she was cold, but the sand would keep her body warm. He then began to sort through the small pack he kept with him, hoping water—or the damage water could do—would disappear as easily as the water itself. He examined Yvonne's wound. It was deep, as expected. He then removed both shirt and jacket; the jacket was for the moment useless; the shirt could be cut into longer strips. He took out a needle, thread, and grimaced, grateful now that Yvonne was not awake.

He then began to stitch the wound on two levels. He turned her over when he was done, turning her face carefully so she could still breathe, and stitched the exit point. Only after he finished did he cut the shirt into strips he could use to bind the whole of her chest. More than that, he couldn't do. There were no doctors in the green.

He would have to look for the way out, but later. He was tired. He was certain that this close to the lake, the water could offer protection if protection were required. He joined Yvonne on this bed of sand, closed his eyes, and slept.

He dreamed.

He seldom dreamed, but knew he was dreaming regardless. The beach on which he lay had become a bed—a straw bed, covered with heavy cloth. Yvonne was sleeping beside him, but the bandages his expensive shirt had become were missing; instead, she wore a long robe, through which no blood leaked. This wasn't reality, but the fog of dream that allowed most dreamers to misplace reality, or reassign it, was missing.

He brought his hands to his chest. He wore a shirt more in keeping with his regular clothing, and loose-fitting pants.

"Are you awake yet, you sleepy wastrel?" A man's voice. Low but laced with frustrated affection. He didn't recognize it, but it was similar in texture to Helmat's voice.

Oh. Not Barrani. He considered closing his eyes, but decided against it, sitting up and shifting his legs to the floor. The floor was wooden plank beneath his bare feet; there was no sign of boots or shoes anywhere. Yvonne didn't stir. He reached out to touch her forehead; she didn't seem feverish. Perhaps because he was certain this was a dream, he felt it was safe to leave her here.

He turned from the bed toward the room's single door; it was a small room.

Standing in the doorway was a man he'd never seen before. His face had one distinct scar, wider than the one Severn carried on his own. He was a bit shorter than Severn, but wider across shoulders, chest, and thigh. His hair was long, and it hung to either side of his face in dark braids.

His eyes were blue, and open, and unblinking.

"I'm coming. If you want to speak with Yvonne, you're going to have to wait."

The man shook his head. "She's safe enough here, and I've little to say to Barrani."

"You realize you're in the green, right?"

"Ah. Yes. Yes, I do. But I've spent a long time seeing nothing but Barrani faces. They all look suspiciously alike. It's been a while since I've seen a face like yours."

"Or short hair?"

"I've never seen hair as short as yours." This was said with obvious, but mild, disapproval.

"Where I work, it's your hair that would be unusual."

"Work, eh? Never mind. Come eat. I don't think we'll have much time."

"Much time for what?"

The man laughed, the sound deep and resonant. "Food first."

Severn was surprised to see Lord Leveanne at the table when they emerged into what appeared to be a small dining room. He froze as the man kept walking, and then offered her a perfect bow. A Barrani bow.

She rose and offered him a similar bow in return, which surprised him. Lord Rowan and Severn's former master were not in the room.

"Was it difficult?" She returned to her seat only when Severn started to move again.

"Was what difficult?"

"Finding Yvonne."

He shrugged and took one of the three chairs at the table. The man had disappeared, but returned with two large platters, which he set on the table. "I cooked," he said.

"This is his way of warning you that criticism will be taken personally," Lord Leveanne added, smiling. There was affection in the smile, but the purple of sadness permeated her eyes.

"I'm a good cook," the man said, dragging his chair across the floor, sitting in it, and dragging it back to the table. "She hates it when I do that."

"I can see why," Severn replied. He was speaking Elantran. So were they. Another indicator that this was somehow a dream.

"You came with Cediela?"

"With An'Tellarus, yes."

"Still the same?"

"I have nothing to compare her against, but she hasn't changed since I first met her."

"At your age, that's not much time for someone like Cediela. Eat. The food will get cold."

Severn nodded, but failed to immediately eat. Instead he looked at Leveanne and at the man on the opposite side of the table. "Are you Handred?" he finally asked.

"Did he forget to introduce himself?" Leveanne asked in turn.

"Guilty as charged. I'm not used to visitors. Yes, I'm Handred."

"I'm Severn. Severn Handred."

"I'd heard. Honestly, Severn?" He asked this of Lord Leveanne. "What kind of name is that?"

"Would you have preferred I call him Handred?"

"It's a better name."

"It's your name."

"Yes, that's why it's better." The man grinned as he spoke. "Eat. You're too scrawny. You're never going to get places like that."

"Which places?" Severn asked, assessing.

"Places that lead to survival." The man's smile dimmed as he answered. "What have you been doing?"

Was this, then, An'Tellarus's answer? Was he somehow related to this man? To a man who had, in theory, died four centuries ago?

"He doesn't know," Lord Leveanne said quietly. "He's not testing you, Severn. I don't know, either. Verranian gave reports from time to time, but mortals grow so quickly, those reports were irrelevant. The child they described was not the Severn Handred you are now. And even the Severn Handred who has come to visit will not be the Severn Handred who might have arrived in another ten years, or twenty."

"Aye, but we won't see that Severn," Handred said. "Will we?"

Leveanne shook her head.

"So I want to hear about the Severn Handred who's managed to survive until now." He turned in his chair; the food, like dream food, forgotten. "You don't seem to have a sword. Or an axe."

"They're hard to conceal."

"And you work in a profession that requires concealed weapons?"

"I live in a city that is far, far more crowded than the West March has ever been. People who carry weapons openly are often looking for trouble. Even if they're not, trouble can find them when the taverns begin to empty out. I was only taught very rudimentary sword work."

"Verranian failed to teach you better?"

"I was too young to handle a real sword when we lived together."

This was clearly the wrong answer. Handred had more to say, but Leveanne reached out to touch the back of his hand, and he fumed silently.

"I never thought it was right," Handred finally said. "Having Verranian raise the boy when he doesn't understand mortals."

"He was a good guardian," Severn said quietly. "A good teacher. I didn't starve. I didn't have problems with Ferals. I didn't have problems with Nightshade's Barrani guards. I was as safe as I could be, given where I lived." He hesitated, and then said, "I was young. Where I lived seemed like the entire world, to me. I didn't think to ask my master why he'd chosen to live in the poorest and least safe sections of the city.

"When I was old enough to wonder, I was no longer living with him." His smile shifted but remained. "I did have to worry about starvation, Barrani, Ferals then. I wasn't certain to keep a roof over our heads."

"Our?"

"I—" He fell silent then. There was too much to explain, and it led to things he didn't want to share.

"Who did you lose?" Handred asked, voice much softer, as if he could see past the words Severn couldn't speak.

Severn swallowed. "My family. I left Verranian and became part of a mortal family. Mother and child. The child was five years younger than I was. We didn't have much money, and we were living in the fiefs. There aren't a lot of doctors in the fiefs."

"They died of illness?"

"The mother did. The daughter didn't. But when the mother was dying she asked me—she begged me—to take care of her daughter."

"Did you?"

Severn nodded. "For as long as she allowed me."

"She's still a child if she's five years younger."

"She ran away from home. She survived, but I can't protect her anymore. I did something to save her life that she'll never forgive."

There was more to the story, but Handred nodded, as if Severn had said enough. "Do you regret it?"

Severn shook his head. "I regret the necessity. She was the only family I had. I had to keep her safe. I had to protect her."

"She didn't understand that?"

Severn shook his head. "I couldn't explain. If I had, she would have died. I would do it again if offered the same choice in the same circumstances."

"Even if she hates you?"

Severn nodded.

"You preserve her in order to lose her?"

"I didn't want to lose her. Maybe in the future—" He shook his head. "I didn't think about the future. I promised her mother I'd protect her."

"Protection can mean many things," Leveanne said softly.

"So can promises." Severn shook his head. "I made the

promise to her mother. We both knew what she wanted. Her daughter was five at the time."

"And when you parted?"

"Twelve. Almost thirteen."

"How could you be certain that you understood what her mother asked of you?"

The question made almost no sense; the insistence on asking about it, even less. Severn reminded himself that he was dreaming, and dreams had their own rules, their own odd window into a slanted reality. "She wanted her child to *survive*. I wanted her child to survive. I was considered a child myself at the time—but I was five years older. I told her I would protect her daughter, with my life if necessary; she told me that if I died, her daughter had no chance. I had to survive for the child to survive. Do you think she was wrong?"

Handred and Leveanne exchanged a single glance. It was Handred who spoke. "Survival isn't everything."

"But without survival there's no hope of change," Severn countered.

"That's Verranian speaking." Handred's voice and expression were sour.

"It is—but the words seemed fair to me. They made sense. My master was both rational and pragmatic. He seldom gave advice. He simply tormented me with enough questions that advice rose from the answers I gave him." Severn grimaced.

Handred chuckled. "You didn't enjoy it."

"You didn't enjoy it, either," Lord Leveanne said. She was smiling. "You almost took your own life just before we met."

"It's better to die on your feet than to live on your knees," Handred replied. But he, too, smiled.

"Give the boy some credit. He has not lived on his knees."

"You trust Verranian too much."

"And you trust him too little. There is a compromise

between our two views—and that compromise is Severn himself."

Handred nodded. "I didn't grow up a slave. I wasn't raised as one. But our village unintentionally offended a Barrani war band. Half of the villagers died; the rest were sold into slavery. I was one of the rest." He paused, as if expecting questions. Severn had none.

"I was considered dangerous, for a human, but that was seen as a positive. I was an angry dog, not a rabid one. An'Tellarus chose to have me as part of his household. That would be the former ruler, not the current one."

"Why?"

"Because his beloved heir wanted me."

Lord Leveanne's expression didn't change. "I saw something in him, in his anger and his despair, that called to me. My father considered it pity, but pity for the lesser creatures was, in moderation, an acceptable trait. My sister demanded that he be given to her. I refused. It was an unpleasant argument. I am certain my father regretted his indulgence of me, ere the end. Handred taught me many things—odd things, unusual things, things that a Barrani of my status should find beneath her.

"I can weave baskets," she added, with a soft smile. "I can dye cloth. I can make clothing suitable, at the least, for Handred and his kin. I found the work oddly relaxing. He assured me that was because I was spoiled; people in his village were required to work. To *work*," she added, changing intonation in obvious mimicry of the larger man. "When he had been with me for five of your years, he would sometimes speak of his family. Did you know he had children?"

Severn shook his head.

"Had I known, had he spoken of them when I first laid eyes on him, I would have tried to buy them as well. And when he did speak, I made the attempt to find them, but I wasn't successful; my father was unwilling to put the resources necessary at my disposal. He wasn't happy with the request, and we argued.

"I was foolish," she said.

"I should have stopped her," Handred added. "It was also my greed. Living in Tellarus was not what I expected of life among Barrani, and I felt certain that if my children were here, they would at least be safe. And yes, Severn, I understand the words of the mother who died. I understand the desperation behind them. When Leveanne offered," he continued, without the use of a title, "I accepted. I should have refused."

Lord Leveanne shook her head. "You said it so many times: I was master. You were slave. You had not come to me of your own volition, and no matter how the relationship between us changed, it would always be shadowed by the fact of that slavery. I didn't want that; I couldn't change it. I could try to give you volition and choice while you lived; it wouldn't be long enough to cause difficulty, because you were mortal. I intended to free you.

"In the end," she said, "I intended to free all of the slaves. But for me it was simple: they weren't Barrani; they couldn't influence the fate of Tellarus in any significant way. I could, with great condescension, look down upon people who argued against it. But one can argue—and Handred did—that many of the Barrani were as much slaves as he, without the obvious markings.

"And in one case, it was true—but worse." She shook her head. "I will not waste the time we have on such topics. They are buried in history, now. Handred's friendship allowed me to view the world in a way I had not."

"You named me," Severn said, the statement tailing up at the end.

"I did."

"Why?"

She glanced at Handred. Handred ran his hand across the

back of his neck, looking faintly embarrassed. She shook her head, smiling.

"Because you are a child of the green. You are the child given to me—to us—by the green."

CHAPTER TWENTY-SEVEN

"DID AN'TELLARUS KNOW THIS?"

"No."

"Verranian knew."

"Yes. He was the only one who did."

"Why did he separate us?"

Her eyes were blue, but tinged with purple. "Because I asked it. The green is many things to many people, and it is special to all of them, but it is not a place for children. There is a power in the green, and the unwary can lose themselves entirely to that power. In the best case, the green absorbs the person in their entirety; they become part of the green.

"In the worst case the power transforms the young, and the young cannot control it; they do not have a will that matches the will of the green, and they cannot fight to separate themselves, to *be* themselves, when confronted with the ancient power contained here.

"You could be born here. You could not safely be raised here."

Severn frowned. "But if I'm a child of the green…"

"Ah, I have not been clear. What grieved Handred the

most was the loss of his children. What he desired most was not me—it was the children he had been unable to protect. If he had died, he might have had an excuse he could accept, but dead, he wouldn't need one. They are gone; they are long dead, and if they had children, those children, too, will have perished of old age if they were fortunate enough.

"We couldn't have children; he is human. I am Barrani. The very nature of children, of procreation, handed us by the Ancients was entirely separate. You couldn't be half Barrani and half human. Perhaps, in another era, when the Ancients walked the world and created us all, an Ancient might have somehow allowed it. But not now."

"The green is ancient."

Here, she smiled. "The green is ancient. We have stories of the Ancients—of law and of chaos—that are myth or legend now, but in those stories, the Ancients could bespeak us, and we them. The green has never been that force. We call it sentient because it responds to our ceremonies and our rituals, but not so consistently that we are ever truly in control.

"We could make love; we could not have children."

"I didn't want children," Handred said, voice gruff. "I didn't want a child I would have to fail again, and lose again. I found a life I didn't expect—and didn't want—when our village was destroyed. I didn't—" He shook his head, face redder. "Not then. Not when she first said it. Not when she said she wanted my child.

"But she was heir to Tellarus. She could bespeak the water. She could enter the green at any time of day; if the Warden was too busy, the green wasn't. It was, in the end, to the green we fled when she made her first choice. Me," he added, in case Severn was dense. "But when Levē focuses, she's hard to move.

"She asked the green for time because she knew it would take time, and it was time I didn't have. I told her I didn't need it—but I'm greedy. I told you. Here, without all of

Tellarus and its many responsibilities, we could be together. I wanted it. I'm ashamed to admit it, now."

"Why?"

"Because she would never have left Tellarus otherwise. She was a power in her own right; she could have been—she *was*—a mage of significance. She worked for years to try to somehow prolong my life, but she couldn't rid me of mortality, and she knew by that point why children are important to so many of us: they're the only form of immortality we have. They're a part of ourselves that we can leave for the future. If we can't become people of renown, if our name itself doesn't become significant in history, it's our sons and daughters that remain.

"We couldn't have those. I didn't expect we could. I understood that I ended here, as a slave, in Tellarus. But I expected *nothing* when I arrived, and...she wasn't nothing. She expected far, far more than nothing. She seemed a little peeved that she couldn't have it." He grinned across the table.

"Clearly you're mistaken," she replied. "I couldn't have it *then*. But I realized I needed more time, and it was time you didn't have. I came to the green."

"You can't leave the green, can you?"

"No. I will never leave the green again. I will never be able to speak like this, to you, again. I am deeply curious about my sister's offer of information, but even if she tells you—somehow—I cannot be guaranteed to hear what you would be willing to share. Once, I could have left, even after I abandoned all responsibility to my sister. But Handred could never leave the green." She hesitated. "We didn't leave Tellarus before I asked the green for shelter. I wished to hide Handred from time, from the passage of time. I wished Handred to remain as he was until I could somehow create a solution to our problem.

"I was the difficulty. In the end, it was a fault built into my very nature. What I was, what I had been born to be, could not be significantly altered without grave consequences. I was willing to risk consequences. Handred was not. I think he felt it was safe to care for me because I would never meet the fate of his former family; I existed before he was born; I would exist long after he was dead. I would be untouched, unchanged."

Handred said nothing.

"But my people had taken everything that he valued, almost everything that defined what he was, and what he was given instead was not what he wanted. I wanted to somehow return something that..." She shook her head. "I was the problem. The child that another mortal might have given him I could not. Even if pregnancy were possible, our children don't wake unless the Lady chooses a name from the Lake of Life.

"I asked the green to change me. I asked the green to alter me in such a way; to give me what mortals were given. The green is sentient, but to bespeak it requires great effort. It is not simply asking as one would ask another person."

"She didn't ask for my permission, and even if she had and I had refused her, she would have done what she wanted anyway. She didn't understand—she had no children of her own—that having a child and abandoning him to the outside world without being able to teach him and watch him grow was not what having a child meant to me.

"If I'd understood, I would have made that clear: having a child that we couldn't raise or hold or teach would have been just another loss. But while we struggled for many years to understand each other, our understanding was always going to be imperfect. It was thus with my first wife as well.

"I didn't know. I didn't understand until she was pregnant. She'd told me clearly why pregnancy would be impossible. I thought... I don't know what I thought. I thought it was a miracle. I thought the green had somehow allowed it."

Leveanne's expression was complicated. "I had to surrender two things to the green to achieve my goals. The first was my freedom. If the green could grant what I desired, I—like Handred—would never again be able to step foot outside of the green. The second was the source of my own life: my name. My True Name. I was afraid to lose that; our children, our infants, don't wake without a True Name. I had no idea what I might become if I voluntarily gave up what can't be separated from my people except by death.

"I didn't make the decision quickly. I didn't make it recklessly. I left the green once or twice, in secret, because my sister's ascension to An'Tellarus was neither bloodless nor safe. But I didn't speak to her; I didn't attempt to meet with her. She might have suspected my hand in some of the incidents, but as they were directly beneficial to her, I doubt she spent too much time questioning them. And perhaps I had lost some of my edge by that point.

"When she was secure enough, I accepted the green's offer."

"Lord Rowan?"

She shook her head. "I will not speak of the war. It is over. But yes, there were advantages; I was closer to the green; the green could hear me. But now? Now the only voice I hear for most of the day is the green's, and soon, I will hear no other.

"I was changed, slowly and irreversibly. I bore the child, Handred's child. You." Her smile was gentle, but it was, as most Barrani smiles of its kind, tinged with sadness. "But you cannot truthfully be said to be mine, because I am not what I was. I am part of the green in all ways. Handred wanted to leave with you, when he understood the damage the green might do to you. But he also understood that if he left, he would die. He would wither and perish—and his child, his son, would have no one to watch over or protect him.

"Verranian said he would take you. He would make certain you were safe. He would see you settled with a human family. But he hoped to find a village that resembled Handred's village."

"He wouldn't know a human village if it bit him on the—" Handred cut off the final word as Leveanne raised a hand.

"The green offered one gift when our child was born. This moment. This time. But we didn't expect it would come so soon, and that we would be so unprepared."

"Could I stay in the green?"

She shook her head. "You can visit. But the heart of the green is not yet for you. In the near future, perhaps, but we will not be here to greet you or to speak with you if you return."

"You didn't expect that I could wield the shards, then."

Another glance passed between them.

"Were you tested?" she asked softly.

"You tested me. You offered me a choice."

"The green offered you a choice. You chose. But the green didn't promise that the path would be easy to follow; it didn't promise that there would be no danger. You made the choice. Why did you choose a woman you have never met—a woman moreover who carried the taint of Shadow within her body—instead of weapons of legend?"

"Because I owe An'Sennarin a great debt. I wished to discharge that debt in my time in the West March, and there was one certain way to do it—find Yvonne and confirm either her safety or her death. An'Tellarus gave me no orders. I was to be her adornment."

"Do you believe that?"

Severn exhaled. These two would never meet An'Tellarus again; what he said wouldn't affect the weathered ruler of Tellarus at all. "No. I believe she intended to tell me of her suspicions about my parentage. I would have scoffed at them in disappointment, which would be embarrassing because she would have been right, and I, wrong. I believe that what I wanted to do for An'Sennarin's sake, she wanted done for his sake as well—but she'd probably die before admitting it.

"I think she made an offer she felt I wouldn't refuse. She had reason to suspect that I could find Yvonne, or the truth about her, where others might find it more difficult." He frowned. "I think she knew that if I followed her to the west, Elluvian would follow me. I don't think she meant to remain idle, either. I think she meant to irritate the power structure here as a way to unsettle it.

"She didn't intend for me to receive an invitation to the green. She didn't intend for me to take whatever test the shards of Tyron offer. That would probably be a step too far for An'Tellarus."

"Do you think so?"

"I'm demonstrably not Barrani. Those weapons are for the Barrani. She might like to tweak noses—or worse—but she's still Barrani. She likes me because there's no cost to it; there's no risk involved. I'll never be able to kill her, even if I want to."

"That does sound like my sister."

Handred had been listening. "Why do you think mortals can't wield the shards?"

"They're Barrani weapons."

The larger man shook his head. "They're the *green's* weapons. Do you think they'll kill you if you touch them?"

"No." He hesitated. It had never been his way to share information unless at need. He'd woken in a dream and had accepted the unusual story of what was purported to be his own birth, but normally he would take some time to examine all of the known elements before reaching a decision. Here, he hadn't done so.

But if they spoke truth, he had so little time.

Exhaling, he said, "I've already touched them."

Neither Lord Leveanne nor Handred seemed surprised.

Lord Leveanne, however, seemed concerned. "What do you mean?"

"You said the green offered two choices: Yvonne or the shards."

She nodded.

"But the shards were where Yvonne was."

Handred glanced at Leveanne. Leveanne, however, was staring at Severn, almost unblinking. Her hands had curved into gentle fists. "Tell us."

He did. He told her where he'd found Yvonne, and further explained the state in which he'd found her. He then gave up on doubt and assessment. "I think the shards somehow anchored her in place—because they could anchor Shadow in place. I don't think the Shadow could affect them. I'm not sure what I would have found had I made a different choice."

Handred said, "Nothing."

"Nothing?"

"Nothing except the disappointment of the green. Do not offend—"

"—the green. I know." Severn frowned. "There was no test," he finally said. "I could grab the blades. If it weren't for the blades, I think Yvonne would be dead, lost or trapped where I found her forever. An'Sennarin…cares for Yvonne. He was worried. The water cares for An'Sennarin in a way it doesn't for most of the Barrani who can hear its voice.

"The water understood his greatest fear, and I think the water dragged her into the green—but Yvonne was tainted. The green allowed her entry in spite of the taint. The Shadow can't warp the water, and the water thought the green was less concerned about Shadow.

"But…I think the green was less concerned about Yvonne's Shadow because the shards of Tyron were here. Something about the shards could…hold the Shadow? Bind it in place? It didn't destroy the Shadow, but it might have contained or constrained the damage it could do to Yvonne." He hesitated again. "That's not quite accurate. The shards did destroy the Shadow."

"When you equipped them?" Handred asked.

"When I equipped them. But they clearly had some power before that. Yvonne was anchored to their location somehow. She was…asleep, but she couldn't have reached the weapons regardless."

"Why didn't you bring them with you?"

"I couldn't carry the blades and carry Yvonne as well. Yvonne was bleeding. I had to get her out of the water, and I couldn't rely on her to swim. I needed my hands."

"So you just *dropped* them?"

"I thanked the green. I was grateful. But I'd already chosen the path that led to Yvonne. I didn't think dropping them would cause them to be lost forever. I didn't," he said, more thoughtfully, "wish to offend the green.

"Taking the weapons instead of Yvonne wouldn't have discharged any debt, and it would have made a lie of my choice. I don't know how to offend the green—there's a chance I could do so unintentionally—but it seemed clear to me that choosing the weapons instead of Yvonne would be offensive. It would make the earlier choice and determination a lie."

"I wanted you to have the shards, if they would accept you," Leveanne said, her voice soft. "One Barrani child in the West March is unlikely to make your future any safer."

Severn nodded. If this woman was almost his mother, she was Barrani.

But Handred shook his head. "Leve, he made the right choice."

"She's a stranger to him. They share nothing."

"It's not what she is or what he owes her. It isn't, in the end, what he owes the other child, An'Sennarin, either. It's what he owes himself when he makes a decision, when he accepts a responsibility."

"Unless An'Sennarin saved his life, I cannot see the sense

of that." She once again turned to Severn. "Will An'Sennarin attempt to kill you if you fail in this mission? Was saving Yvonne saving your own life?"

Severn shook his head.

"The weapons you might have taken from the green would be of far more use to you—and to any of those you choose as allies—than Yvonne, a child who will be of no help to you, even should you remain in the West March."

"Leve."

"There is no pragmatism in him. I thought, if Verranian was his master, he would have taught our son at least that much."

"I'm not going to defend Verranian. I've never liked him."

To Severn's surprise, Leveanne rolled her eyes in obvious annoyance.

"But in this one instance, I think Verranian may have made the right choice."

"He *abandoned* our child when he wasn't old enough to be considered adult even by human standards."

Handred shook his head. "He taught him what he could of Barrani lore and customs, and when he thought it wouldn't be enough, he allowed Severn to find a family of his own people."

"Who almost immediately died."

"Leve—Severn could never be of aid to Verranian. He could never grow into his strength if he remained in Verranian's care. Verranian would never need or rely on him to do...anything. Children are fine with that because children *are* dependent. But to grow out of that, to grow into adulthood, that would never be enough.

"Look at him. Look at him now. The boy might not have my work, but he has work, and the work is meaningful to him." He walked around the table, and gently took both of her hands; she wasn't as large as Handred. To Severn's surprise, Handred knelt, still holding both of her hands as if they were precious and fragile.

Severn smiled, thinking that there was something familiar about this discussion: it reminded him of Helmat and Elluvian, two men he trusted, all childhood lessons aside, but who could not see eye to eye on many things.

"It is not meaningful—" She stopped as Handred's hands tightened briefly. "We cannot be with him. We cannot protect him. We cannot give him the currency of his realm. But the weapons at least…"

"Weapons are tools, love. Their use, their significance, is defined by those who wield them. It's more important that he be the right wielder, not that he have the right weapon. I don't know—we don't know—what his life has been like. We can see our fear and our own guilt in his circumstance, or we can try to see as much as we can of things that give us more hope."

"I do not see hopeful in this."

"No. You don't."

"You do."

"I do. The boy has developed the desire to protect, to guard, to help. He's not a fool; Verranian saw to that. But until we mortals can see ourselves as people who *can* help, we can't see beyond our need *to be* helped. I don't know what Verranian intended—but maybe he listened to me more than I believed. What *we* need is not what Barrani need. What Severn needs isn't what I need. What he chooses to protect isn't what I chose to protect—we haven't lived the same life.

"But he promised a mother that he would protect her daughter; he gave that mother what little peace she might have had before she died. The daughter is alive because he did everything he could to keep that promise. He's become an adult." He turned to Severn, although he didn't let go of Leveanne's hands. "I have no right to feel proud, but I do. I'm proud of you. I'm proud of you for keeping that child alive. I'm proud of you for choosing Yvonne's life over some magical tools.

"If you had taken the weapons—if you'd tried to take the weapons—instead, you'd know it as a failure. You'd have chosen greed over duty. You'll meet people who make that choice, time and again. They don't understand duty. There's nothing you can do to teach them. That family took you in. They didn't have to. They didn't have much. You accepted it; you became part of their family. And you protected your family."

"Yvonne is *not* his family. An'Sennarin is *not* his family. If they were, we wouldn't be having this argument!"

"We would," Handred said, although he smiled. "Perhaps because Barrani are Immortal, they can live more easily in isolation. They do, now—they trust no one, not even family. They consider accumulation of power the only safety, and that power is individual. They help when it is beneficial."

"So do humans."

"Yes, of course—but the fact that you can't understand how Severn's choice is beneficial *to him* implies a narrow scope of what *beneficial* means. When the boy goes to wherever it is he calls home, he can stand tall, he can stand straight, he can face himself and know that he is all he should be."

"And who defines that should?"

"Severn," Handred replied. "Severn Handred."

Severn nodded. "We don't know what the shards require as proof of worthiness, for want of a better word."

"But you know what you require of yourself."

Severn nodded again. And smiled at Handred. "Verranian isn't trapped in the green, is he?"

Leveanne shook her head.

"He was my guardian, my master, my teacher. I hope to be able to thank him properly some day in the future."

"Do so by surviving."

Severn's smile deepened. Neither of these people were

anything like Tara, Elianne's mother. Neither of them were like Verranian. But he understood that they expressed concern, hope, and worry in ways that suited who they were, and he accepted it. After today it wouldn't matter.

"You can't stay with us forever," Handred said. "But you can stay with us for a bit longer. Come, boy. I've a mind to see what you've learned in weapon handling."

Leveanne exhaled. "That's what you want to do in the time we have left us?"

"There won't be another time."

"There won't be another time for anything."

"What would you have us do? Talk? I think the boy has talked more today than he usually does in a week. I know I have."

They left the kitchen through a door that Severn was almost certain hadn't existed until Handred spoke. It led out to a yard that looked familiar to Severn: it was a drill yard, but a small one. Two men would have no difficulties sparring here.

Along the wall farthest from the door was a weapon rack; the weapons, from this distance, seemed made of wood. Handred walked to that rack and retrieved a wooden sword—a sword that was longer than the practice swords in the Halls of Law. Or at least in the rooms the Wolves used.

Severn hadn't lied; he hadn't been well trained in sword use. He had, however, been working on it under Elluvian's bruising guidance. He, too, retrieved a wooden sword, although his was shorter than Handred's. The weight of it, on the other hand, was not what would be expected of wood; it was heavy. He considered the practice here, and after a pause, took a second sword—a shorter one—in his left hand.

"Let's see what you've got," Handred said, stepping into the center of the yard.

Severn bent slightly into his knees, lifting the practice

blades. He waited for Handred's attack. Severn had nothing to prove here. He'd been honest about his skills. He was very curious about Handred's. To his mild embarrassment, he would have assumed Handred's skills were nonexistent, given his status as a slave.

Handred wasn't fast on his feet; he wasn't light. But he wasn't a man who would lose his footing easily, if at all. He tended to hold his blade in both hands, not one. Severn had practiced with a one-handed sword, and sometimes a shield, but he disliked the shield. It was useful, and perhaps on a battlefield its usefulness would outweigh other disadvantages, but a shield had no reach unless he extended his arm; he couldn't finish anything with a shield.

He therefore began to learn with a practice sword in either hand; he'd some practical experience wielding two daggers at a time. He couldn't hide behind either of them; he had to be far more aware of the actual arc of incoming swings in order to parry them. But he could use his left hand to end a fight, because even a shorter sword had more reach.

He quickly found that Handred attacked with the momentum of greater weight, greater size; parrying required the blades in both hands. He learned two things as he moved: that his father knew how to leverage greater reach, and that his size didn't make him slow. He kept his feet planted, and when he moved he didn't overextend. Had he, Severn could have knocked his legs out from under him at least four times. As it was, Severn almost lost his footing twice because Handred didn't just stand still while Severn was attacking.

Handred's skill was by far the better of the two.

A twinge of regret caused his expression to tighten. He could imagine meeting this man in the drill yard for a couple of hours a day, could imagine attempting to absorb the skills on display here. He could also imagine how useful those skills might be in his duties as a Wolf.

It was in the drill yard that Severn discovered Handred

cast no shadow. Severn did. The movements of shadows beneath the feet of his opponents were one of the subtle things he watched for. It took no deliberation; he realized it only when he identified the source of his discomfort.

But if Handred wasn't solid enough to cast shadow in sunlight, he was certainly solid enough to cause Severn to stagger back at the weight of his blows. He was fast enough that dodging wasn't guaranteed to succeed, or Severn would have spent the lesson dodging. Perhaps because he wasn't corporeal in the same way Severn was, Handred could speak—with daunting ease—while he attacked.

"What will you do with Yvonne?"

Severn, learning Handred's patterns of attack the hard way, grunted. Clearly, given the shift in attack pattern, that wasn't an acceptable answer.

"She's not mine—it's her decision."

"Good. An'Sennarin?"

"Childhood friend. She was hostage for his behavior until he became head of his line."

"Would she be safer in the High Halls?"

Severn shook his head; drops of sweat flew off his hair. "What happens to you?"

Handred's turn to grunt, but Severn's attempt to press him—by physical force—fell flat. "The child? The one who ran away from home?"

"She has Barrani friends. I keep what watch I can. But—" Handred's blade hit the side of his left thigh, with the flat. It would bruise. "She's safe. As safe as I was with Verranian."

"And that's enough for you?"

"It's all she'll allow."

"So she knows?"

"No. She'd probably try to kill me if she knew."

"What are the Wolves to you?"

Severn stiffened; it was subtle. He continued to parry, to move, and to strike—not that his blows landed. He'd never mentioned the Wolves.

CHAPTER TWENTY-EIGHT

HANDRED WAS PART OF THE GREEN; HE COULDN'T leave it. That's what Leveanne had said. Severn had taken care not to mention the Wolves since his arrival in the West March. An'Tellarus knew, of course—but even if she'd mentioned it, she couldn't speak to Handred.

He was in the green, now. He had no idea what the green could hear, no idea how much of Severn's life it now knew. But Handred knew, and he shouldn't have.

The sword in his left hand flew.

"You're not concentrating," Handred snapped, as sure in his criticism as any teacher Severn had weathered in the past. The larger man stepped in, and instead of using his sword, attempted to knock Severn off his feet with a well-aimed kick.

Severn remained on his feet, but barely, as Handred withdrew. "Get your sword."

He did as ordered. As he turned his back to retrieve the fallen blade, he said, "How do you know about the Wolves?"

"Does it matter?"

"To me, yes." He crouched, lifted the practice blade, and rose, pivoting in place and ready for attack.

Handred, however, didn't charge in. "Why?"

"I don't talk about it outside of the office. The Wolves are...Imperial executioners."

"Assassins?"

Severn shook his head. "Some people can't, or won't, acknowledge a difference between the two. If the Emperor sends us to kill, we kill. But it's not done often. What we do, for the most part, is retrieve, or attempt to retrieve. If the target dies in the line of that attempt, the Emperor accepts it, but his goal isn't their death."

"And if he sends you to kill?"

"We either kill or die in the attempt."

"And that's not assassination to you?"

Severn exhaled. "He's the Emperor. The laws we follow—Imperial laws—were conceived of and written by him. He's the final court of law. He can condemn a criminal, and when he does, we execute at his command. No one else has that authority. We can't randomly kill. We don't take orders from anyone except the Emperor."

"You kill at his command for money."

Severn faced Handred fully, blades in hand. "Is that how you see it?"

"Are you paid to do your work?"

"I am."

"And that work involves killing."

"It does."

"I fail to see how it's different."

"That," Severn said, as he bent into his knees, "isn't my problem. It's yours. I'm the one doing the work and to me there *is* a difference."

"Convenient."

He offered Handred a fief shrug. "The only person I have to justify my actions to is the Emperor. And myself." He exhaled. "Myself, first. I know that I can kill when killing is necessary. I know that I don't when it isn't. I've sworn an oath of loyalty to the Emperor; the Emperor is my master. I wouldn't have sworn that oath if I couldn't believe in the value of it, the rightness of it.

"The oaths you swear, or swore, are your own. You made them—I assume you made them—for your own reasons, and I want to believe that you were true to them."

Handred's eyes were unblinking. "Why?"

"Because some part of you is my father."

"You believe that?"

He hadn't had the opportunity to really think it through; he answered instinctively. "I do." Instinct had deep roots, but as the words left his mouth, he felt that they were so firmly entrenched he wouldn't be able to easily dislodge them. "Yes. I do."

"So I'm to live up to your expectations and not the other way around?"

"You should live up to your own expectations," Severn replied. "And I'll try to live up to mine. I...don't know you. I didn't grow up here. I don't know what you want or expect—if you want or expect anything. But if you're somehow a story that the green is letting me tell myself, if you're a dream, if you're not real at all, then the story I choose to tell is this one."

Handred lifted his blade. "And that's all you want?"

The question made little sense.

"You don't want to make a family of your own? You don't want to find a place to call home?"

Ah. "No."

"Why?"

He supposed that having this conversation with a father he had never met was somehow inevitable. "I had a home. I destroyed it with my own hands. I won't—I *will not*—ever do that again."

"You're too young to say that. You're too young to give up."

Severn shook his head. "Are you going to fight or talk?"

The older man stared at him for one long breath, and then he roared with laughter. If a bear laughed, Severn thought it would sound like this.

Severn was disarmed only the one time. Although his hands were sweaty with effort and the heat of the midday sun, he managed to retain his grip on the wooden blades. His father was *good*. His style of fighting was practical, not polished; if he was armed, he intended to take his opponent down. That suited Severn; it was, in the end, similar to his own. Severn was lighter on his feet, more agile, but his blows lacked the strength, the solidity, of Handred's. He could dodge and balance better than his father, but his father had clearly built his own attack and defense on his strengths, not his weaknesses.

Blunt weapons—which were what practice blades were, in the end—didn't favor Severn. But they were what he held, and as was his wont, he worked with what he had at hand. That had been his master's earliest lesson: see what's in front of you, use what's in front of you. If you want better, find it later. What you have to survive is now.

He intended to remain in this sparring contest until the older man called an end to it. But the green, the power of the green, seemed to be endless; Handred's endurance was astonishing.

"Why aren't you angry?"

Severn's answer was broken by the heaviness of exhausted breath. "At what?"

"At anything, boy. At the world. At the gods. At the unfairness of your life compared to the lives of so many others. You're mortal. You'll age. You'll die. The Barrani—curse most of them—will live forever, and the blood on their hands will be washed clean by time."

"Would anger change that?"

"What?"

"Would anger change anything? Can anger obliterate all differences between us? Can it right wrongs? Can it bring justice?"

"Justice?" Handred roared. Severn expected the full-force attack that followed the second syllable. He didn't brace for it; he moved, leaping to the side as the earth took the force of the two-handed sword. He clipped Handred's leg with his own and kicked it a second later.

Handred actually stumbled.

Justice was a human word. The Barrani didn't use it. It was, according to Severn's first master, quaint, naive, a word that children might dream of when they were too idle.

"Justice," he said. He came to a stop near a wall, waiting for Handred to right himself. Handred did.

"Is that what you think you're doing? Is that what your killing will achieve?"

"Imperial justice," Severn replied. "It's never going to be perfect, because we're not perfect. But if I have to work to eat, if I have to work to live, it's a better goal to have. I won't rule. I won't be Emperor. I won't have thousands at my command.

"But I don't want that."

"You'll never be seen as a power."

"No. But how would that help me?"

"Being seen?"

"As a power," Severn replied, nodding. "I won't live to meet the expectations—or hopes, or dreams—of others. But I won't do nothing, either. This is how Severn Handred has chosen to live."

"What does Yvonne have to do with that?"

Severn lowered the blades but didn't set them aside. "If you can't understand that, I can't explain it." He turned to meet Handred's gaze; it was dark.

"I want you to try."

"I told you—I'm indebted to An'Sennarin."

"Because of the Tha'alani?"

Severn barely reacted. "You really do know things I've never told you."

"I didn't have much time, and it's slipping away even as we speak."

"If you already know the answer, ask a different question."

Handred chuckled. "If I knew the answer, I wouldn't ask."

"Yes, because of the Tha'alani. Because of the crimes his actions stopped. Because his concern decades ago, his horror—even his sense of guilt—would have been what I felt had I been born then and not when I was.

"They were strangers to him. In the end, he saved everything he could. He understood that the damage done to the Tha'alani, with each death, was done to the entirety of their race. Did he kill? Yes. Did he do it to protect people who couldn't otherwise defend themselves? Yes. Would I have done what he did if I'd had the opportunity and the power? Yes.

"Yvonne was the reason he headed to the High Halls. Her life was important to him. Even now, it haunts him. If he'd just gone when called by his family's lord, if he and his parents hadn't rejected the 'invitation,' nothing would have happened to Yvonne. His parents would still be alive."

"His parents made their choice."

"Yes—but it was the only choice they felt they could make. And had he argued with them, had he demanded the right to go to the east, they would have allowed it. They died to prevent that, and in the end, he went east regardless. If he'd known that he would head east, and take the Tower's test, he should have just left. His parents would be alive. Yvonne would be unharmed. You can call it a choice—"

"I meant that the boy shouldn't be burdened by that particular guilt. Or the guilt of Yvonne. He wasn't responsible for their deaths or their injuries; that rests on the shoulders of the former An'Sennarin. And you, boy—you shouldn't take on burdens that aren't yours to carry. Your parents made their own choices. Selfish choices, perhaps. But those aren't *your* choice, and they aren't your weight to carry. Understand?"

Severn nodded. "The only thing I might offer An'Sennarin that will give him some peace is Yvonne. She was a civilian, if that word means anything to the Barrani. If I can protect her here, I will."

"And that's what you think your weapons are for? To protect strangers?"

"To protect strangers—where I can—who can't protect themselves. I can't and won't be everywhere. But if I can't even make the effort when something is right in front of me..." He shrugged. "I'm not a hero. I have no desire to be a hero.

"You asked about the Wolves. They're the smallest branch of the Halls of Law. Had I been offered work with the Hawks, I would have taken it; had I been offered work with the Swords, I would have taken it. All three, Hawk, Sword, and Wolf, attempt to uphold and enforce the Emperor's laws. Hundreds of people work in the Halls of Law, supporting different aspects of Imperial laws. Most of them probably come to work, do their job, go home to their families. They might not see why the work is important—but I do.

"We're not perfect. But the work we do makes the world a little more just. That's it. That's my goal, now. That's my purpose. To make the world a little bit fairer. It's a way of protecting those who can't protect themselves."

"What about those you fail to protect?"

Severn shook his head. "I told you, we're not perfect. But we save what we can, when we can. I think about those people, instead. People like Yvonne."

"Who isn't a citizen of the Dragon's Empire."

Severn unbent his knees. "Are we done here?"

"I don't know." Handred lifted his face. "Are we done here?"

The very skies seemed to answer, in a clap of cloudless thunder.

Yes.

Severn would have dropped the practice blades if he could. He'd opened his hands, or had intended to open his hands, as the single word shook his body. His hands didn't open. Ah, no, the blades didn't fall.

He looked up from his hands to Handred, who was watching him, his own hands empty, his arms crossed. His expression was almost grim.

"You had one choice," he told Severn. "There was only one choice."

"You mean at the start?"

Handred nodded. "You were told you could search for Yvonne or you could search for the shards."

"Which is two choices, in the normal world."

Handred chuckled then. "There was, as you discovered, only one choice."

"Two."

"Don't argue with your father."

"A right choice and a wrong choice, by the standards of the green."

"Ah. No. There was a right choice and a wrong choice by the standards of Severn Handred. You didn't even hesitate."

"I didn't want the shards."

"If you'd found them, you'd leave them behind, is that it?"

"I did." He met and held his father's gaze. "But you're right in one way. There was only one choice I could live with. Had I been any of the Barrani, there would also only be one choice—the one I didn't make. I don't know what choice Lord Tanniase would have been offered if he'd been allowed to enter the heart of the green. It wouldn't have been the same."

"No. But he was never invited into the heart of the green. The heart has been restless of late; restless and worried."

"Why are you telling me this?"

"Because you made the right choice. The green, like the water, is many things. And the shards, like the green, are not singular in intent or desire. They are heavy, heavy weapons," he added, voice softer.

"How do you know?"

Handred shrugged, looking slightly pained. "I embarrassed my wife by trying to wield them—I didn't realize what they were."

"I'd heard the shards could be deadly in their rejection of a possible wielder."

"They didn't kill me. Maybe because I wasn't Barrani. Or at least that's what I told myself. That's what Leveanne told me."

"I'm not Barrani."

"No. And clearly the shards are willing to have you wield them. Look down."

Severn obeyed. The practice blades he'd wielded against Handred were no longer practice blades; they were no longer wooden, and they were no longer the length of a long sword. But he wasn't holding them. He'd opened his hands to let them fall.

They hadn't fallen. Instead, they'd transformed; they floated above the ground, as if gravity was inconsequential. Between them he could see links of chain form, from hilt to hilt. "These…are the blades I saw in the water, where Yvonne was."

Handred nodded. "I hope I don't have to tell you never to do that in a real lake. You'd drown."

Severn stared at the floating blades.

"You don't understand."

"I don't."

"Well, someone smarter than me will have to explain it, then. But it seems clear to me."

Severn raised brows at Handred.

"What the weapons want, you want. It's probably why it's been so long since Barrani have been able to wield them. What Barrani are taught to want, for the sake of survival, isn't what you were taught. I wouldn't have thought Verranian had it in him."

"He probably didn't. I spent almost half of my life with a human family, and a lot of that meant I had to ignore some of what he'd taught me."

"He thought you might be the wielder he's been looking for."

Severn frowned. "Verranian's been looking for someone to wield the weapons?"

"For some time."

"Verranian isn't aligned with a family."

"No. He was aligned, once, with Tellarus—but that was for Leveanne's sake. He will not serve An'Tellarus."

"He doesn't trust her?"

"He doesn't like her." Handred grinned. "Makes her sound appealing, doesn't it?"

"You don't like her, either."

"I didn't, no. She was a walking ball of envy and jealousy when she was younger. There's no context in which that's appealing. You don't mind her."

"She said it's been four hundred years since she last saw her sister. She regrets the envy, the jealousy. She regrets the loss. I guess even Barrani can change when they've had four centuries to reconsider."

"She wanted to be An'Tellarus."

"She is. I'd say she's good at it, but maybe a bit irreverent. She doesn't really care what others think of her now.

She might have thought being An'Tellarus would give her what she lacked."

"You think it has."

"I didn't know her when you knew her. I've got nothing but other Barrani as a comparison. But yes. I think becoming what she wanted to become made clear that it wasn't a solution. I've never asked. I'm not about to ask, either."

"I never said you were stupid. You're talking to avoid the blades, aren't you?"

"Maybe a little. But…if I pick them up now, you'll vanish, won't you?"

Handred said nothing.

"All of this will vanish. It's a dream. Maybe it's a dream you asked for, maybe it's a dream that the green can give me for now. I want to spend a little longer with you. Without the bruising," he added, with a wry grin. "I couldn't take the blades with me when we left the lake; I had nowhere to put them, and I couldn't carry Yvonne with two hands full of knife. They're going to need sheaths of some kind if I'm meant to take them out of the green."

"Yes, they will." Lord Leveanne's voice came from the house; he turned toward her. She was wearing a robe of startling green, as if the concept of green had been defined by the folds of its fall and the way its sheen reflected sunlight. "But I can offer you sheaths. What neither of us can offer you is training. These weapons can't be used the way normal weapons can; they are, as you are aware, special."

She came into the drill yard carrying two sheaths; they were simple, and at this distance seemed unadorned. "The sheaths are not decorative; like the blades, they conform to the needs of the bearer." She held them out. Severn glanced at the floating blades, and then turned his back on them and walked toward Leveanne.

It was hard to think of this person as a mother. Harder to think of her as *his* mother. She was too intimidating, too distant; she was a Barrani Lord. But he approached her with as little caution as he could, holding out his hands. She placed the sheaths across his palms. They were warm. He'd thought them brown and unadorned, but he could see a pattern of leaves and vines engraved in their surface, as if they were wood.

She walked to where Handred stood. Her eyes were green, but the green was ringed with purple. "You were right," she told Handred. "How do you feel about him now?"

"Good. Full of regret, but you expected that. The boy lives in a better world than either of us lived in, and he sees clearly. He doesn't see far enough yet, but I think he will in time. And yes, he'll leave a bit of my name in a world that would never have heard it." He slid an arm around her shoulders. "Go on, boy. We've outstayed our time."

Severn closed his eyes. Inhaled. Exhaled. Opened them. "Thank you," he told them both. "I'm alive. I'm still grateful to be alive. I'll do what I can while I am. If it weren't for you, I wouldn't have the chance."

Handred's smile deepened. "Go on," he repeated.

Severn turned toward the weapons that were waiting. Stopped. If he were Elianne, he would run across the drill yard to where his parents were waiting. He'd hug them or offer them the silent opportunity to hug him. He might even cry.

But he was Severn. He examined the sheaths he'd been given; they were long, and it would take time to become accustomed to their weight. But he attached them to his left and right hip for the moment because he needed to free his hands.

He grabbed the hilt of one weapon in his left hand. Nothing happened. Exhaling, he grabbed the second in his right.

The world exploded.

Shards of dream, as if dream were reflective glass, passed by his eyes. He could see the two people who had claimed to be his parents, watching; could see part of the dining room table; could see the blue of clear sky, the green of leaves and branches, hints of smaller colors that implied flowers.

He could also see blood; it was his. If the dream were glass, he'd been standing too close to the shatter radius. One of the shards was embedded in the fleshy part of his left thumb, another in his right wrist. The shards were small. If his hands were empty, it would have been trivial to remove them.

His hands, sadly, weren't empty. But glass shards didn't magically continue to appear. They were gone. In their wake he stood on a shore of pale white sand; at his feet was Yvonne of Darrowelm. She was pale, but seemed to be sleeping, and the blood across the dressing Severn had made of his expensive, peacock clothing was dark brown and dry.

In his hands were two long knives; between them a chain that seemed far too long.

He'd never been certain whether or not magical weapons were sentient weapons; in some of his master's stories, they were. In some they weren't. These blades seemed to follow the second branch of stories. They made no attempt to speak, no attempt to guide. But they were glowing faintly.

He could move his arms freely, but the blades seemed glued to them. Yvonne, unconscious, was more cumbersome here than she had been in the water; he still couldn't carry her while wielding two weapons. Given her height and weight, he was unlikely to get far wielding even one.

But the sheaths he'd been given remained empty; he couldn't sheathe either blade.

He was tired. No, he was exhausted. The moment the dream shattered he felt the weight of sleepless hours—or longer—spent in the green. And he felt the weight of these blades; they hadn't been heavier than he would have expected given their length and size. Until now.

He wondered if he could even consider this reality. He was still in the green. He was still beside Yvonne. She hadn't been magically healed in the time he'd spent listening to Lord Leveanne and Handred. And he was attached to weapons he couldn't sheathe.

He tried. His arms strained against the growing weight of the blades; the weight subsided when he stopped making the attempt to put the weapons aside. He had very little ego, a gift from his first master, but he hesitated to speak to the weapons where anyone else could hear him. Yvonne was sleeping; she might wake. If he were to deliver her safely from the green, appearing to be unhinged wouldn't help at all.

Still, after what felt like hours of pointless struggle, he took the risk of appearing unhinged. He tried to talk to the weapons. He tried to make them move. He asked. He begged. He pleaded. He explained the situation, the *why* of the necessity of the sheaths. Nothing made a difference.

"What do you want me to do?" he finally asked. Blood trickled from the cuts on his hand and wrist. It colored the beach's white sand. Only when he looked at that beach—really looked—did he realize his blood wasn't landing in the normal way. The sand absorbed it, yes—but only parts of the sand. As his blood spread, the discoloration racing ahead of where he stood, he realized that the blood itself was like ink. Where it fell, it began to form words.

He could read the words although he didn't immediately recognize the language. They weren't Elantran, and they weren't High Barrani.

"No," a familiar voice said, over his left shoulder. He didn't even tense at the sound of Verranian's voice. "They are the language of the green."

"Can you read it?"

"It is not written for my eyes; it is written for yours."

"Can you carry Yvonne?"

"She, too, is your burden to bear. Am I capable of it? Certainly. But not here, not now."

"Can you tell me what the shards expect? What they want?"

"They attempt to tell you that now, but you are fighting them."

Fighting them? Severn turned toward his master then. Verranian's eyes were blue, with strong flecks of green. He seemed almost at peace. "I would not have brought you here now," he said, voice soft. "But Lord Leveanne has desired to see you in person since the day I removed you—for your own safety and theirs—from the green. Had I known you had encountered An'Tellarus, I might have approached her to ask that you be kept from the West March, but as I have often told you, regret is pointless."

"You didn't want me to meet my parents."

Verranian was silent.

"Because you knew what the end must be. You won't be able to meet with her again."

"No. But that is the will of the green. What it gave her was time, but the time was brief. You cannot remain in the green."

"And you?"

"There is very little in the green for me, now."

"What happened to Lord Rowan?"

Verranian's brows rose before falling into an expression Severn knew well. "Why do you ask?"

"He came with me. He wanted to see Lord Leveanne again."

"He is no longer within the green. And he is not your concern. Let the shards speak." He frowned. "You remember our early lessons?"

"As much as any mortal can remember, yes."

"When I taught you to write, when I taught you to play with the spinning top, there was a reason for both lessons. You don't have the quill; you don't have the toy. But those lessons are the ones which will serve you best here. Had you failed those lessons, the shards would be irrelevant now."

Severn understood. "You were testing me for magical ability."

"I was. The shards are magical in nature, although the magic is complex. It is not something any of our kin, even the most renowned of scholars, understand perfectly. Had they, the shards would not have been waiting for you in the heart of the green."

Severn could write with either hand but favored the right. He closed his eyes and began to write as if his hand was attached to a very large, very stiff brush.

He couldn't remember what he'd written, imperfectly to his master's annoyance, as a child. But he was certain there were no clues in the sentences that his master had had him transcribe. It was the act of writing itself, the act of extending will and forming words that someone else might be able to read. Silent communication.

The blood that had fallen fell in the shape of words— words Severn couldn't read. What would weapons want, if weapons wanted something? As if he were once again four years old—the age at which the quill seemed impossible, it was so awkward and shaky—he struggled with the shape of written words, understanding that they must be his own.

But what would satisfy silent weapons?

What had caused them to become actual weapons, not the practice swords he'd used when sparring with Handred? What was it he'd said? What was it that proved that he was somehow worthy?

Worthy, unworthy—these words had had little meaning in Severn's life. He accepted that he would be judged by people, because judgment was a necessity when survival was one's goal. But Handred was right: survival wasn't just about Severn Handred's life. Survival was about making choices that Severn himself considered the right choices, and surviving the consequences of those choices.

Saving Yvonne.

Saving Elianne.

Protecting the Tha'alani.

He began to write; he wrote in Elantran. *Help me protect the things that need protection. Lend me your power. I will walk the path of guardian, of protector, of executioner, of...service.*

Verranian's silence was loud. He could read what Severn struggled to write, and he wasn't impressed. But he made no attempt to stop his former ward.

Only when Severn signed his name did the blades flash almost white.

CHAPTER TWENTY-NINE

"I BEGIN TO UNDERSTAND WHY THESE WEAPONS have lain fallow for so long," his former guardian said, in as pinched a voice as he ever allowed himself. "*Service?* Why would you promise servility?"

Severn wasn't surprised. "I thought you said you couldn't read what was written."

"What was written? No. What you wrote, however, yes. For half your life, I raised you. I am certain I did not raise you to write *this*." His eyes were blue, but flecked with green; he was, inasmuch as he had ever been, happy, something his spoken words didn't convey at all.

"What does service mean to you?" Severn asked.

"I served Lord Leveanne."

"Why?"

"You ask that as if you do not know."

Severn exhaled. "I know you taught by asking questions to which you already knew the answers. You taught me how to do that as well. But you were my teacher, my guardian. I asked you questions when I didn't understand or didn't have the answers."

"It is a personal question. But I admired the lord, and I wished her to survive and conquer. I was willing to dedicate my life to her and her goals."

"You don't consider that service?"

"Speak Barrani. And no, it is not service as you have promised service. Understand that the blades are not merchants, not wily politicians. They accept your words as oaths."

"Because they *are* oaths. I didn't promise the shards anything I couldn't deliver. I didn't promise them anything I'm not going to do anyway. Can't you accept that service, for me, is what you offered Lord Leveanne?"

"I would accept it if it were true. You believe they are the same. They are not."

"Why are you so certain?"

Verranian was silent for a long moment. "Tell me of your service, then."

"I don't want to rule. I don't want to be Emperor. I don't want a family—I've proven that I can't protect it without destroying it. I don't want to kill, though I have and will; I don't want to hurt others. But I'll do that, as well, sometimes unintentionally. I don't trust myself enough to try to be An'Tellarus. I might, in desperation, become An'Sennarin, if that's what it took."

"You can't."

"I meant I might be analogous to what he's become—I'd do what he did. I'd have done it sooner than he did it. But becoming a ruler wasn't his goal. It isn't mine. That doesn't mean I don't care about how I'm ruled. Or how others are ruled. Dragons are Immortal. They have memories like Barrani memories. They know what they've tried, they know what's failed and what's succeeded. They can perfect things over time."

"If you die of old age before that perfection is achieved, how does it affect you?"

"I trust his intent. Barrani could never have created the

Halls of Law. The Halls of Law, the Imperial laws, are meant for people like me, not people like you. They're meant for those who won't live forever, who haven't amassed power, who haven't spent their lives learning how to kill."

"Why do you think the Emperor privileges the weak?"

Severn shook his head. "I don't think he sees us as weak. We're mortal, yes. But we are what we are. I can't see everything he sees. I'll never see everything he's already seen. But in ruling, he also serves."

"That is not the way rulership works."

"Not for you, no. Not for An'Tellarus. Not, perhaps, for the Lord of the West March. But it's the way it works for the Emperor. I'm willing to be part of that vision. I'm willing to serve it because it's so much larger than I am, in the end. His reach is far greater than mine will ever be—but what he's trying to grasp, I want him to grasp. If standing on me—if standing on the service of people like me—extends his reach enough, he will.

"You don't understand it. You don't understand the Emperor. You don't understand why I admire him because you can't see what I see. You should sit down with Elluvian—the two of you would see eye to eye."

"He serves the Emperor," was the distinctly chilly rejoinder.

"Yes. He serves the Emperor the way you would serve the Emperor if you offered service. He doesn't serve the way I do because he can't see what the Emperor means to people like me—and he can't see what we mean to the Emperor."

"Your view is not the normal mortal view."

Severn shrugged. "I'm not responsible for anyone else's view. I know what I serve. I know why. If something changes, I'll reconsider my commitment then. It's not mindless loyalty that I offer. I don't offer mindless loyalty to anyone."

Severn could feel heat in the hilts; heat and ice. The light dimmed. The blades remained. The chain between them had lengthened.

"You will need to wrap the chain around your waist," Verranian said.

"Who attaches swords to a *chain*?"

Verranian laughed. It had been a long time since he'd heard that laughter. "Remember, Severn: do not offend the green."

"I won't. I owe the green a great debt."

"As great as the debt you owe An'Sennarin?"

"No," he replied. "This debt is personal."

"And you have no method of repaying it."

"None that I know of. The most I can do is use these weapons as promised." He sheathed the weapon in his left hand and then, as his master had commanded, began to wind the chain around his hips. He left enough slack to sheathe the right weapon.

"When you leave, I will accompany you."

Severn nodded. Bending, he carefully slid his right arm beneath Yvonne's knees and his left beneath her back, lifting her as he rose. He understood that carrying Yvonne from this place to the West March proper was symbolic, and symbolism mattered to the silent green.

Severn followed the shoreline. He had no sense of the compass direction but was almost certain it wouldn't be necessary. He'd accomplished what the green desired be accomplished. He assumed the green would reveal a path that would lead to the West March when it was ready. He wasn't worried.

This was unusual when he was in an unfamiliar environment, especially when he carried the wounded, which would make both fight and flight far more difficult.

He realized why as he walked: his master was by his side. Verranian, his first and earliest guardian, his first teacher. He was Barrani. He'd made clear from the start that he was—obviously—not Severn's father. Not his parent.

But the safest Severn had ever been in the life he could remember was under Verranian's care. Verranian had never considered himself Severn's parent, but for Severn, *parent* had been a word that had no meaning. Only when he began to mingle with other children, other mortals, did the concept grow teeth: all the other children had parents, or knew who those parents had been.

Even so, if Severn asked—and he had—he didn't demand to know. Verranian, Barrani, was better than any mortal parent, safer than any mortal parent. Illness didn't bother Verranian; mortal gangs traced a wide circle around Verranian's lodging. Ferals might be stupid enough to attack the Barrani guardian, but it was the Ferals who died—and swiftly.

Verranian had left him with Tara and Elianne. He'd left as if Severn had made a choice, one he couldn't claw back or revoke. Verranian was willing to protect one mortal boy, but not a mortal mother and her younger daughter.

Are you lonely? His master's last question, a question to which Severn had had no answer. He'd understood that the answer would define whether or not he was to be abandoned, but he'd had no answer to give. Not then. Loneliness was not a much-discussed concept in a Barrani childhood.

He gazed at Yvonne, who stirred but didn't waken. Loneliness wasn't much discussed, but clearly even Barrani children sought peers, friends, even family. When he'd spoken to An'Sennarin, through the retired castelord of the Tha'alani, an echo of that same question remained in An'Sennarin's memory.

Are you lonely?

Yes, Severn thought. Not at age four, from which he pulled the dimmest of his memories, but at age ten? Yes. There was a warmth, an affection, a silliness in that mortal

home that had never existed within Verranian's, and Severn
had leaned into it, like a flower seeking sunlight.

But even so, Verranian had been Severn's first parent.

A footpath appeared between two trees. He followed that
footpath to its natural end, and that end was a familiar gate,
one that seemed to be freestanding. Severn couldn't bow
while carrying Yvonne, but he turned his back to the gate
and offered the green a silent, but long, gratitude in mixed
Elantran and Barrani.

An'Tellarus was waiting beyond the Warden's gate. Elluvian was not. She watched Severn as Lord Barian opened the
gates, looking first at the Barrani carried in Severn's arms, and
then at the more visible sheaths and chain that girded his hips.

It was evening. Evening of which day, Severn couldn't
be certain. He might have asked, but An'Tellarus's eyes had
gone from the usual blue to a more martial one as she looked
at Severn's companion.

Verranian offered An'Tellarus a deep, and perfectly correct, bow. It wasn't designed to annoy her, but she was unusual; she could take offense at anything if she so chose.
Given the presence of the Warden and his servants, she chose
not to, but her expression made clear it was close.

"Come," she said to Severn. "You must be both hungry
and tired. Let us repair to Tellarus for the time being. Someone is waiting for you there."

At a guess, it was Elluvian, but it didn't matter. If Severn
could be certain of nothing else, he was almost certain
Yvonne would be safe in Tellarus—if she survived. She was
pale, her brow beaded with sweat. He nodded. He wasn't the
peacock he had been when he'd first entered the green; his
jacket was wrapped around Yvonne, and his shirt had been
reduced to cloth strips. But he knew it didn't matter: as the
Warden's eyes took in what An'Tellarus's had seen, the Warden offered Severn a low bow.

He added no words. An'Tellarus's invitation was a command, a demand, as anyone Barrani hearing it already knew. Severn was, if not her servant in the traditional sense, hers in the eyes of the West March; where she commanded he follow, he must follow.

But he paused, Yvonne in arms that were growing numb. "Did Onuri return?"

Lord Barian frowned, but nodded.

"I have something to give him, as thanks for his guidance." He turned to Verranian, who nodded; he took Yvonne's weight from Severn's arms as if she weighed nothing. Severn then fished around in the pocket of the jacket that was Yvonne's only covering. From it, he withdrew a small ivory branch, adorned with emerald leaves. "You said it could be planted if I returned from the green.

"I would like Onuri to plant it, if that is acceptable."

Lord Barian's eyes were almost green. "Will you hand it to him yourself?"

Severn glanced at Yvonne. "I would, just to see his joy, but Yvonne requires aid."

The Warden bowed and rose. Severn placed the branch across the Warden's palm, and then turned toward Verranian, and held out his arms. Verranian nodded and once again transferred what was almost deadweight into Severn's keeping.

The pace An'Tellarus set would have been punishing even if he hadn't been carrying Yvonne; he was. The crowds in the street were staring, some with open hostility. Word had clearly traveled. Verranian's eyes became the same martial blue that An'Tellarus maintained, and Severn understood why Verranian hadn't offered to carry Yvonne for the last leg of her journey. Of the two, Severn and his master, it was the master who was far more skilled at combat, should combat become necessary.

It shouldn't. The blades Severn now wore weren't the type that could simply be stolen and equipped. Any denizen of the West March must understand that. Most denizens of the West March, however, would consider the bearer an insult, a disgrace, a stain upon the myth of the shards of Tyron.

But to attack Severn here was to attack Tellarus. Legends and myths would be poor protection against the lived history of those who had seen the conflicts won by An'Tellarus; hands were stayed, silence maintained. It was the silence of a crowd on the edge of a mob's rage, but it remained on the right side of that edge.

Elluvian was waiting by the stairs when Severn, An'Tellarus, and Verranian cleared the vestibule that granted entrance into the tree-home of Tellarus. His eyes became the same blue that the other two had maintained since Severn's exit from the green. He clearly wanted to ask what business Verranian had in Tellarus, a question he had no right to ask. An'Tellarus might be fond of Elluvian, but she was a Barrani ruler who appeared to be in a less than indulgent mood.

Elluvian, however, didn't appear to care about Yvonne or Severn's new weapons; his gaze was focused entirely on Private Handred. Only when he seemed satisfied that Severn—down layers of clothing—was materially unharmed did he lose the rigidity of his standing position.

"I have asked that a room be prepared for her," An'Tellarus told Severn, as if Elluvian didn't exist. "Follow me. I have healers here, although none of them are particularly powerful. How was she injured?"

Severn shook his head. "It's a long story. Let me put her down before my arms fall off." He spoke entirely in Elantran.

"Very well. I will have food prepared—will you eat at her bedside, or will you join us?"

"If I can be spared for long enough to dress myself, I'll join you."

She nodded.

"In my own clothing," he added.

Yvonne woke when Severn set her down. She startled, attempted to sit up, and fell over instead. Severn caught her. "Where are we?"

"Tellarus."

"Why?"

"An'Tellarus met us when we left the green. I came here as An'Tellarus's companion. Would you rather convalesce in Darrowelm?"

She lay back against the bedding, her eyes blue. "Does An'Darrowelm know where I am?"

"If someone from Darrowelm recognized you, yes. There were far more people waiting outside of the Warden's gate than I'd expected."

"No one interfered?"

"An'Tellarus was in a hurry. No. No one spoke. I think they were probably more concerned with the weapons—and the person who now wields them—than they were with an unconscious Barrani woman. I'm sorry."

She shook her head slowly. "I'll convalesce in Tellarus, then."

Severn hesitated. "You might be safer in Danarre."

Her brows rose. "Danarre?"

"Danarre is open, for the moment."

"That's impossible."

"Elluvian of Danarre opened it."

"Why?"

"You'll have to ask him."

"You don't have the right to offer me shelter in Danarre."

Severn nodded. He didn't.

"You don't know what Danarre was. You don't know what it means," Yvonne said. She closed her eyes. "If An'Tellarus is willing to allow me to recover here, it's safest for me here."

"I had a letter for you, from An'Sennarin."

"Had?"

"I think it might be waterlogged and illegible." Regardless, Severn handed her the sealed scroll, edges worse for wear. "I am soon returning to Elantra, if you wish me to carry a message to An'Sennarin."

"Could I deliver the message myself?"

"You will have to make the request of An'Tellarus; I will be returning in her company. If I survive dinner."

She smiled, her eyes shading toward green. He bowed and left the room, racing to his own to change.

By Halls of Law standard, Severn made himself presentable. But he added the weapon chain. It was awkward to unwind it, awkward to rewind it. He really didn't consider a chain to be a useful addition to a weapon. Even a thrown weapon would be made far more awkward with the weight of a chain attached.

He headed out of his room, and then paused there, realizing he had no idea where he was supposed to go to eat. Elluvian, however, was waiting on the stairs just outside of the platform assigned to Severn; he was leaning against the trunk of the tree, his arms folded.

"Try not to cut off your arms while you're wielding those," he said, straightening out.

Severn grimaced. "I don't understand why there has to be a chain, but I don't think it's a good idea to attempt to remove it."

"You can't control its form?"

"Should I be able to?"

"In theory, perhaps. There are stories about the shards, but none of us can claim any personal experience observing former wielders. You found what you were seeking."

Severn nodded.

"And you offered her the shelter of Danarre."

He'd heard that. Severn wasn't even surprised. "She decided it was too risky."

"Clearly she's not completely foolish. How was she injured?"

"I have to answer An'Tellarus's questions—at dinner—if you can wait until then."

Elluvian nodded.

An'Tellarus's dinner guests weren't just Verranian, who was clearly there on sufferance, and Elluvian, who appeared to be invisible. The Lord of the West March was also seated, and he smiled as Severn entered the room—or whatever it was one called a platform without actual walls or doors. An'Tellarus made clear where Severn should sit by a simple motion of hand.

"We are waiting on one more person," An'Tellarus said. Severn took the chair by her side, opposite the Lord of the West March.

Severn wanted to ask who that person was, but the Lord of the West March was present, and An'Tellarus was in her more rigid mood. She didn't offer the information. But the information came regardless. Lord Barian stepped onto the platform and made his way to the seat beside the Lord of the West March.

"It has been an eventful day," An'Tellarus said, after Lord Barian was seated. Servants appeared, moving through the room as if they were a gentle breeze—a breeze laden with food and drink.

"Yes," Lord Barian replied, lifting a glass of dark wine. "Eventful and chaotic."

"Have you heard from your mother?"

He smiled, his eyes blue. "As you suspect, she is not entirely pleased with the outcome, but I am her son—she will not offend the green. Offending the Warden, however, is well within her jurisdiction." His smile deepened. "She made some attempt not to blame me for her lack of fortune, this time. I admit I was torn. Your invitation allowed me to escape an unpleasant interrogation, but it certainly added wood to the fire."

An'Tellarus laughed. "You must point out that Severn is mortal; the shards of Tyron will not remain an impossible goal for long."

"I am sure you will remind her of that fact. Often."

The Lord of the West March smiled. "Cediela, you are impossible."

"Demonstrably not. Do you have words of wisdom you wish to pass on to Severn? We will be leaving in two days."

"I fear my lack of experience with the weapons he now bears will not allow me to offer words of wisdom." His smile dimmed. "Avoid the High Halls. I am certain you've been taught to avoid Barrani in general; hone those lessons."

"That is harsh advice, given his current company," An'Tellarus said. She was amused.

"He will not be keeping his current company when he returns to his home. I am curious. Many of our kin have attempted to take the test set by the shards; fewer have survived. The dead leave very little in the way of records, and the living declined to add to our history. How, then, did you approach the shards, and what was the test you faced?"

Severn's smile was something he'd learned from An'Tellarus. "I am not permitted to speak of the test. I don't wish to offend the green."

Verranian raised a brow, but also nodded.

"Speak, then, of Yvonne of Darrowelm. And speak, if you will, of her injury. Did you cause it?"

"No. She chose to injure herself." His expression became more serious. "She was taken into the green by the water— or at least that was how she perceived it. An'Sennarin was and is beloved by the water itself, and the water understood both his fear and his desire to protect his childhood friend.

She was injured when those who wished to control the young Ollarin attempted to take her into their custody. The injury was contaminated, somehow, by the Shadows we face more closely in Elantra."

Everyone's eyes darkened instantly to indigo. Had Severn's eyes been subject to the same color changes, he would have joined them.

"The shards of Tyron appear to damage Shadow. Yvonne tested that; she wanted to cut away the Shadow that had infected her. She impaled herself on one of the two blades I was wielding. It seems to have worked—but she injured herself in exactly the same way she'd been injured when she'd been kidnapped."

"I see." The Lord of the West March frowned. "You live in Elantra, which surrounds the fiefs—and *Ravellon*. Perhaps the weapons will see their best use in your hands. I would like to see them."

"Not at the dinner table," An'Tellarus said, before Severn could comply.

The Lord of the West March glanced at An'Tellarus. She was smiling, but her smile was steel—all edge. This was Tellarus. The Lord of the West March was a guest. He nodded with obvious reluctance.

"They are not toys," Verranian said quietly. "They are not simple badges or adornments. To mortals, to those with whom Severn will work, they are not significant weapons. I believe it best they remain hidden."

"They cannot be used—"

"Apologies. I meant that their significance be hidden. They chose, and they chose Severn Handred. But as An'Tellarus says, his reign will be brief. He is mortal. Even if he lives out the full span of his peaceful years, he will not be able to wield the weapons at the end of his life. He has perhaps, generously, half a century, no more. The weapons will return to the green."

"If we understood why they arrived at their choice, they might be in use before another half millennium has passed."

Verranian glanced at Severn. "I highly doubt it," he replied. "But perhaps, when it might be relevant again, we can discuss it further. It is possible that other Barrani will attempt to hasten their return to the green. In vain. The blades will not be wielded by those who engage in such activities—or those who hire others to do that work."

"Very well." The Lord of the West March raised a glass. "To Severn Handred, wielder of the shards."

He was joined in this toast by everyone but Severn, after which discussion moved on, guided firmly by An'Tellarus.

Severn spent a day with Verranian, in the Tellarus version of a drill yard. He found, to his surprise, that the chains that bound the blades were extensible; if he couldn't remove them—which would have been his first choice—they shrank to a manageable length when he chose to wield them as weapons. Winding—and unwinding—the chain would be the practice of days or weeks, given the clumsiness with which he did so on his first day.

But he discovered a use for those chains in the late afternoon. He held both weapons; Verranian requested that he spin one by the chain, using the hilt of the other as its pivot point. Verranian seldom made pointless requests, but Severn wasn't confident. A spinning length of chain was one thing, a spinning length with long blade attached, quite another. If he tried this in the city streets, he'd injure someone. Probably himself.

He did manage when Verranian's eyes were almost black with annoyance.

"You think you—with *any* weapon you choose—could possibly injure me? By *accident*? Spin the chain, boy. Spin it and support that motion until I tell you to stop."

Severn began to swing the chain in a wide, circular motion. When he got up to speed, it was simple, but getting up to speed wasn't as easy as it should have been. Only when Severn had succeeded to Verranian's satisfaction did Verranian attack.

The attack wasn't physical. It was magical. Fire shot forward from the tips of his master's fingers, heading toward Severn's head. Severn stayed his ground because on some level he trusted his master. Still.

The fire broke against the moving chain. None of it passed through the links. Severn exhaled and continued because Verranian hadn't finished. Water came next, and after it, a much larger burst of green fire. Nothing Verranian attempted broke the barrier the chain had become. Some of it did damage the floors and blacken the walls to either side of where Severn stood. He flinched. An'Tellarus wasn't likely to be happy.

It was another twenty minutes before Verranian called a halt to his tests; Severn discovered that slowing the chain safely was more difficult than starting it up. More than that, Verranian was willing to consign to future training, where by *future* he meant in Elantra.

Yvonne surprised Severn; she was waiting for him when he emerged from the training room. The training room was an actual room, unlike the guest rooms and dining hall hosted in the higher branches of the tree. She wrinkled her nose, and with reason; he had sweat profusely.

"I could read An'Sennarin's letter," she told him. "The water didn't destroy the words."

"What does he want you to do?"

She snorted. "Ollarin doesn't want other people to do anything. Not because of him. He wants us to make our own choices, choices we can enjoy." Given her pinched expression, this had caused frustration—at least to Yvonne—in their childhood.

"Did he have any suggestions?"

"If you call groveling apologies suggestions, yes, plenty. Have you been to the High Halls?"

"Can I bathe before we talk?"

"Sure."

Severn headed toward the baths. Yvonne followed him. Of course she did. She was unlike any Barrani Severn had ever met. Unlike An'Sennarin, certainly. "Why don't you wait in your room?"

"I'm bored. The healer was excellent. His lecture was less excellent but listening to him tell me I'm an ignorant child was the price for recovery."

Severn reached the room in which a heated, built-in bath waited. He then removed his clothing and settled into the water.

"I'd join you but I'm not supposed to get the incision wet. So, have you been to the High Halls?"

"Yes."

"Often?"

"No. The first time I went, An'Tellarus tried to kill me. I think she would have been disappointed had she succeeded."

Yvonne laughed. "That sounds like An'Tellarus. Did anyone else try to kill you?"

Severn shook his head.

"Would it be safe for me? Before you answer, remember where I was when I got injured the first time."

It was the question he'd been half dreading since she'd surprised him outside of the training room. "If you go to the High Halls as An'Tellarus's attendant or servant *and* her servants don't resent you for it, it should be safe. It would be far safer if you remained in Tellarus; I'm sure she'd allow that."

"What if I don't care? I've nothing to lose, now."

"An'Sennarin would care. People in the West March knew that you were his weakness."

"I wasn't the only one."

"You were the only one who survived. Given that you lost

your parents, I can't see how you're less of a weakness now. It would be far safer if you stayed in Tellarus."

"You really *have* talked to Ollarin."

"When we don't have much we often fear loss more, not less. He's lost almost all of his family and friends. He can't be what he was to you, because you'll be targeted again and again by those who want to kill him or control him. He can't do anything until he has a solid base of power he can trust."

"So, never. But if that were true, why are you even here?"

"Most Barrani couldn't conceive of a friendship between a lord and a mortal. There's no way I could be of import to An'Sennarin in the eyes of anyone who would want to use me that way. You don't have that advantage."

"If I stay here, Darrowelm and Tellarus will come into conflict."

"If you go with An'Tellarus, that's even more true."

"Yes—but she's accustomed to people trying to kill her. They all die. My presence wouldn't make her life any worse. She'd be in the High Halls, not here. It's not An'Tellarus who would face the hostility; it's her servants. It's people like me, who don't bear her name but serve her house."

"You would *be* one of those servants." Severn, frustrated, drowned out words by rinsing his hair beneath the surface of the water. When he came up for air, she hadn't stopped.

"I want to see him," she said quietly. "You know how power changes people. You know that he's a power now, and he's fighting to remain a power. I want him to survive—but I want some part of him, even if it's small, to remain Ollarin."

"You want him to remain a child." Severn rose, dripping, from the water; Yvonne held out a towel. He took it without comment and began to dry himself off.

"Is that how you see it?"

"It's how it will be seen."

"That's not what I asked."

"If you go and you're killed—or kidnapped and used as a lever against him—it will almost destroy him."

She was silent. He thought she'd finished talking and was grateful for the quiet. But perhaps because she was young in Barrani years and experience, she failed to retreat.

"I don't want to destroy him. But if he loses everything that made him even a tiny bit happy, how is that not destruction?"

He opened his mouth. Shut it. Maybe he, considered adult by his own people, wasn't much more of an adult than Yvonne. "I won't talk about this until you've at least asked An'Tellarus's permission."

"Do I seem that stupid to you? Of course I asked her first. She said it's up to you."

Why me? Severn wrapped a towel around himself, ignoring the hanging robes, and headed up the stairs to find different clothing to wear. Yvonne followed. "Then no. Stay here."

"It's my risk to take!" Her steps grew far heavier against the slender stairs.

"Not if it's up to me." He exhaled. Turning on the stairs, he said, "Convince me. Convince me that it's worth the risk." He then turned and hurried to his room to get dressed.

She continued after him. "Threats won't work."

He dressed quickly. "Not really. You won't attempt to hurt or kill me in Tellarus."

"I want some part of the Ollarin I knew to remain—and that's not going to happen if I'm here. Here, I can protect nothing."

"Protect?"

"There is more to life than existence. He can't be what he was. But if nothing he once was or believed survives, what does survival *mean*? It's a name. It's a rank. It's a crown—all things he never wanted in the first place. It's not that I want him to be a child. It's that I want him to somehow be allowed to be himself some of the time. Would you hide here forever, if you were me?"

Severn wanted to say yes. It would be a lie but lies weren't difficult if they served a purpose. He opened his mouth and failed to verbalize the single syllable. Everything he had said to her was true.

But what she had said to him was also true. If Elianne were somehow to become like Ollarin, and if he had not destroyed their family so completely, would he remain in Tellarus, as he wanted Yvonne to do?

"...No. I wouldn't." He turned to her then. "We leave tomorrow."

Her eyes were green, but he could see, across her cheeks, the faint trail of tears that he hadn't seen fall.

EPILOGUE

AN'TELLARUS WAITED IN THE GREEN. SEVERN HAD spent the day with Lord Verranian, a man practically name-bound to Lord Leveanne, he was so much her servant. Dinner had been pleasant, and after the initial seating, frictionless. But her guests had been circumspect. Severn maintained his quiet, neutral expression throughout most of the meal. It was only after the guests had departed—quite late—that he had approached her far more awkwardly.

She disliked the bow he offered as the opening gambit of a conversation, although conversely, she approved of its crisp, graceful lines. All irritation, all appreciation, vanished when he spoke.

I met your sister. She is in the green, part of the green somehow; she cannot leave it. She told me that we—she and I—could not meet again if I returned; her time had passed.

An'Tellarus understood the boy's words, or the motivation behind them: she would not be found in the green should An'Tellarus visit, either. Nonetheless, she asked the when, and perhaps the why—but the boy didn't have answers. Later, she would ask for every detail of the conversation the boy had had with Leveanne. They would have weeks together on the road as they returned to Elantra; they had no need of speed now, and therefore no need to risk the portal paths the Hallionne offered.

But they were Leveanne's words to Severn. Leveanne had left few words with the boy for An'Tellarus. Not none, but Cediela had never been fond of secondhand words. She had, for years, resented her sister. Envied her. Even, perhaps, hated her. But centuries had worn those feelings down, smoothing out their edges, and when they had become smooth enough, distant enough, other thoughts had begun to intrude.

Had she ever really understood her sister?

No, of course not. She had assumed—as all children assume—that what she personally wanted was a universal desire. Leveanne had had, from the moment of Cediela's awakening, everything Cediela could want. Had wanted. She was respected as heir; she was respected as a leader; she was loved. Both their father and mother had looked only to Leveanne. While they cared for their second child, they treated her as if she were helpless, as if she were lesser, as if she would always remain a child in the shadow of her elder sister.

And that had been true. She had lived in Leveanne's shadow. But the sun, in the absence of shadow, could be merciless and unrelenting. All of the bitter advice her elder sister had tried to impart over the years, Cediela had slowly begun to use. And it came to her, in the early years of her reign, that it was work. She believed, to start, that Leveanne wanted the adulation and power she received by simply existing, that Leveanne had been better prepared for the politics and the wars that erupted in their lee; that for Leveanne it would have been *easy*.

But even that bitterness, that certainty, faded over the centuries, until she could no longer believe what she had told herself. Barrani memory was a blessing and a curse. Memory had its own thorns, its own traps, with which to bind the unwary. Free of those, she could examine the sister in her memory, without envy or resentment or the desire to find flaws. Without those things, she could see her sister more clearly—if one could ever see someone who had engendered such pain clearly.

And she could see, as well, her own tangled responses, removing the harshest, layer by layer, until only a lonely desire remained: she, too, wanted to be loved. She wanted Leveanne to love her. But Leveanne was long gone.

She did not believe Leveanne was dead; she could not believe she was alive. But she knew that the window in which she might meet that sister of nightmare and dream was almost closed. Might be closed now, given what Severn had said.

Regardless, she had come, dressed simply, as she might once have dressed in the youth she'd spent angry and envious and forsaken. Her hair was long and unbound, her dress unadorned with lace or pearls or gems. Her boots were practical, her jewelry as simple, as ancient, as the style of dress. She was anxious, her hands curled almost to fists, her voice mute, even when she tried to lift it, because the only word she could think of to say was her sister's name.

"I told you I would take everything from you," she said to the breeze that rippled through bent wild grass. "I was so angry. Do you remember? Can you remember, now? And I did. I have everything you were to be given."

"Does it make you happy, Cediela?" That voice. That familiar voice. An'Tellarus turned instantly toward it. No one was there.

Closing her eyes, she said, "Not always. Sometimes not at all. I never thought I would say this, but I miss you. I miss you, sister. I think you would have been better at this than I am."

"Different, not better. I always thought you better suited."

"You never said that."

"Not to you, no. I did try, but you were not receptive.

You thought I was attempting to mollify you—or worse, pity you."

Cediela nodded. "Where are you?"

"I am with the green. I am part of it, and soon, I will not be myself. But I thought you might come, and I have been struggling to hold on to my sense of self." As she spoke, the air in front of Cediela began to waver, to shift in place. Leveanne, dressed much as her sister was, stood before her. The grass beneath her feet didn't bend. "I'm sorry for the pain I caused you. I didn't know how to stop. Nothing I did seemed to work. If I tried to step back, you were angry. If I offered help or advice, you were angrier. It is hard for those who love you—parents, servants, siblings—to approach when you are so constantly angry, so bitter."

Cediela nodded. It was true. "I am not what I was then. I...grew up."

Leveanne smiled. "You did. And look at you: you are far more responsible than I was, in the end. You have been An'Tellarus for centuries, and the line has never wavered. I have no right to be proud of you, but I am."

"Why did you not come back?"

Leveanne shook her head. "I cannot. Do not ask me; it will cause us both nothing but pain and regret. I made a choice, and even if it wasn't a wise choice, the consequences are mine to face."

"And mine. I never meant—"

"You did. You meant it then. I was never certain you would grow to regret it. It would have been better if you hadn't."

"For you?"

"For us. I can't come back. I could only barely wait, in case you did come to the green before I could no longer speak with you." Leveanne's eyes were green. They were an odd green; not quite Barrani, but close.

Cediela's eyes were, she was certain, purple; she would

have changed the color if she could, because she understood that this was her last chance to see her sister off, to truly say goodbye, without anger, envy, resentment. But in the absence of those things? Regret remained, regret grew.

She hadn't understood Leveanne, and soon, there would be no Leveanne to learn from, to grow with, to make amends to. Of love, she did not speak or think. She was An'Tellarus.

But when Leveanne opened her arms, Cediela moved to close the distance between them, opening her own, as if the weight of all the years had momentarily fled. Her steps were light, quick, and her arms, her hug, fierce—as if she could, by dint of will, keep her sister here for even a moment longer.

She knew she couldn't. Whatever it was the green sought from those who served it, she had never had; she had nothing to bargain with, nothing to offer. Even this moment had been bought by Leveanne.

She took it. She took it gratefully. Arms around her sister, words left her mouth in a rush to be said, a rush to be heard.

All the while, Leveanne held her, until even that was no longer possible.

Yvonne shouldn't have chosen to travel. If the Barrani healers were exceptionally competent, the reach of their magic wasn't overly impressive; she was told to lie abed for at least a full week, and to take time returning to what passed for normal.

Predictably, she refused to be left behind, refused to follow later—she knew, by bitter experience, that that later might never come. She slept, uncomfortably, for most of the journey back, but the first few days required overland treks through forest, between the Hallionne. This time, An'Tellarus didn't suggest that they take the portal paths.

Severn was tasked with watching and guiding Yvonne. An'Tellarus, perhaps disappointed with Severn's decision, kept her distance, but did not deny Yvonne permission to join them upon their return. The journey home therefore took longer than the journey to the West March had; if Yvonne was stubborn, she nonetheless tired quickly.

She asked questions only when they reached the carriage outside of the last of the Hallionne. Those questions were practical: they involved the High Halls, the rules of the High Halls, and the possible dangers inherent in them for a simple servant who had no desire to join the court of lords. She knew that Ollarin had taken the Test of Name; she could easily deduce that he had passed it. She didn't want to take the same risk, as she saw no practical use for it; being a Lord of the High Court wasn't relevant for someone who had no lineage, no family, no wealth. All it would do is garner attention, and Yvonne didn't want the attention of the powerful.

An'Tellarus warmed slowly to the girl, but she did warm; it was hard not to like Yvonne. Her odd mix of sentiment and pragmatism made her seem both fearless and cautious. It was clear that she'd chosen to trust An'Tellarus. An'Tellarus did call this foolish perhaps a dozen times. Yvonne agreed that it was. As the carriage approached the city, An'Tellarus grew more forthcoming, and some of what she imparted to Yvonne about the High Halls was new to Severn. It was, clearly, annoying to Elluvian.

Annoying enough that he chose to disembark two weeks from Elantra, to make his own way back to the Halls of Law or the Emperor. He didn't trust Verranian, of course, but he trusted Verranian to protect Severn. He didn't appear to care about the fate of Yvonne at all, and no one was fool enough to worry about An'Tellarus.

Severn was grateful to return to work. He was grateful to be able to spend most of his time speaking Elantran in an environment in which the wrong words or the wrong phrases wouldn't start a small war. He was grateful to be in an environment in which he was rarely expected to speak at all. Also: grateful for the lack of An'Tellarus's gaudy, expensive clothing.

He was less grateful for the presence of Verranian, his former—and current—master. Helmat had almost thrown both Verranian and Elluvian out of the office, which would be tricky in Elluvian's case, when they had come together to ask permission to use the drill room on a set schedule. Helmat wasn't impressed by the weapons that Severn had brought from the green. This had caused friction between the Wolflord and Verranian, although Elluvian seemed to find it amusing.

Verranian, however, had demonstrated the utility of the weapon's chain, after which Helmat gave his grudging permission. Helmat, like Severn, had been appalled by the chain. Like Severn, he had withdrawn his complaint when he saw the chain in action.

Over the next two weeks, they worked together, becoming more comfortable with the weapons and their capabilities.

Severn, no longer the child he had been, nonetheless fell into the old patterns of master and student. It annoyed Elluvian. Verranian, however, seemed impervious to annoyance, irritation, or even anger. He had always been like that, and Severn knew that much of his own steadiness had been derived from living with a man who could not be shaken.

He was grateful for that.

At the start of week three, Severn was busy with Records work and the continuation of special training. The one thing he was certain would irk his teacher was interruption of those exploratory lessons—and interruption was demanded. An'Tellarus had sent Severn an invitation to attend her in the High Halls. Helmat was far more openly annoyed than Verranian, but Verranian wasn't happy.

"Why is she calling you to the High Halls?" His voice was

measured and calm, but he seldom asked questions to which he did not expect answers.

"I don't know," Severn replied, although he had some suspicion.

"You can tell her to—" Helmat bit back the words. "You're not her servant. You're an Imperial Wolf. You work for *us*."

"It's an invitation, not a command."

Elluvian snorted.

"You go with him," Helmat told the only Barrani Wolf.

Elluvian glared at Severn. "This is the last time. And you can't go dressed like that."

"No, of course not," Severn replied.

The High Halls were still not a place safe for Elluvian to enter. Severn better understood why. Had it been up to him, he would have left Elluvian behind, but the Wolflord's orders were quite clear. Verranian hadn't been invited, and had no desire to attend. Severn had no idea where Verranian chose to stay; he half suspected that he had returned to the cramped apartment that had been their childhood home, but didn't ask.

He dressed as he'd dressed for his first visit to the High Halls, and followed Elluvian's lead, as he had done the first time. He wore the weapons, but not openly. This time, there were no tests within the cavernous halls themselves; no attempt to bisect the new Wolf to test his reflexes.

Instead, there were guards—Tellarus guards—who met them as they reached the height of the impressive and intimidating front stairs. Those guards formed a wall between Severn, Elluvian, and anyone foolish enough to approach them. They walked at Severn's speed, led him to the hall that opened to the Tellarus apartments, and left him there.

There were no odd adornments in this hall; it was almost featureless, now. Only the two statues which had annoyed Elluvian so much remained at the end of the hall: a human male and a Barrani female. But now, Severn had names for both: Handred and Leveanne. An'Tellarus had not removed them; he doubted she would while he lived.

The High Halls were never going to be a safe place for Severn to visit. Not as a Wolf. He stared first at Handred and then Leveanne, as if to burn these graven images into memory, where he might safely look at them when he couldn't visit.

Elluvian said nothing, content to wait—but he probably would have preferred to be left in the hall if the alternative was An'Tellarus's command performance.

The doors rolled open. An'Tellarus wasn't there to greet them; instead, a servant waited between the two doors. He recognized her instantly: Yvonne. She bowed, as if Severn were the most honored of guests, which apparently annoyed Elluvian.

"This way," she said. "An'Tellarus has invited a guest; there will be a small party." Although her expression was neutral, her eyes were a bright, deep green.

Severn nodded. "Has she invited this guest before?"

"No. And he hasn't invited her, either." She hesitated, and then added, "I really like her."

"I do as well. And oddly, I trust her."

"Don't tell her that—it really irritates her."

"Your Elantran is excellent," he said, with some surprise.

"Barrani memory. We learn languages pretty easily."

"Elantran isn't spoken in the High Halls."

"No. That's why I'm learning it." She grinned. "I have permission. Thanks for coming."

"It's An'Tellarus," Severn replied. "She doesn't send out invitations expecting to be declined."

"I was told she almost never invites anyone to visit. Elluvian, maybe. The High Halls aren't like the West March."

"No. You don't mind?"

"I don't like them—too much stone. But I think it's safer for me here. Not for too many others, though." She turned a corner, and Severn followed her through a delicate arch and into a larger room; it opened onto a balcony, and the breeze was gentle. Wine had been poured, and food lay across a table, but the table was unoccupied. An'Tellarus was on the balcony, glass in hand. She turned at the sound of Yvonne's chatter, and smiled at Severn, although her eyes were blue. She even offered Elluvian a curt nod, which he accepted with obvious resignation.

Severn joined her on the balcony, as did Elluvian, although Elluvian kept a greater distance.

"Yvonne has been, to my surprise, a delight. I am happy to have her company."

"You forgive me for allowing her to join us?"

"I do. She is not feckless or unwary, but she manages to be happy. I think she would manage that almost anywhere. She is understandably somewhat nervous today, or I wouldn't have invited you at all."

Elluvian snorted.

A chime sounded from the heart of the unoccupied dining table. An'Tellarus looked over her shoulder and nodded to Yvonne, who left the room, no doubt to greet arriving guests.

"I advise you to avoid the High Halls in future," An'Tellarus continued. "You will not be well received once word travels from the West March, as it no doubt will. You are an odd child, and not at all what I expected, but I am glad to have met you."

Severn turned toward the room, although one hand remained on the balcony rail.

Yvonne came into sight first, but directly behind her was An'Sennarin, his eyes—at this distance—an astonishing green, a green that matched hers.

He couldn't hear what they said to each other. He was certain An'Tellarus and Elluvian could. But neither made a move to enter the dining room; they seemed content to let the two childhood friends become acquainted again.

Only when Yvonne came, all perfect posture and servant invisibility totally discarded, to grab Severn by the hand and drag him back into the room did the two Barrani detach themselves from the balcony and the illusion of privacy they offered Yvonne and Ollarin.

Severn, at least, had a story to tell, and it was clear that An'Sennarin wished to hear it, or at least Severn's part of it. He was certain that An'Sennarin's fear for Yvonne would return, but there was no sign of it in his eyes now. He was certain there would be no sign of it in Yvonne's for much, much longer.

Helmat Marlin sat at his desk, staring at his reflection in a silent mirror. He expected the knock at the door, and gestured in the door's general direction, adding a curt "Enter" when the door failed to open.

Severn Handred stood in its frame. The boy was calm, collected, and utterly without worry. Helmat couldn't decide if this pricked his pride or not.

"Don't just stand there. Come in. Close the door behind you."

Severn nodded and did as commanded; he came to stand in front of Helmat's desk. Helmat, however, rose, abandoning it; he walked to the window and looked out, hands folded behind his back. When it had been silent for a beat too long, he said, "Come here."

Severn crossed the room, passed the desk, and came to stand beside the Wolflord.

"I spoke with En," Helmat said, without further preamble. "I've heard his version of events in the West March. Do you have anything you'd care to add?"

Severn shrugged. "I'm sure Elluvian told you anything of relevance when it comes to the events that might have future repercussions."

"For the Wolves, yes—in a crude and obvious way. He doesn't understand you."

"I won't claim to understand myself well, either."

Helmat grinned, the expression clearly reflected in the glass they were both theoretically looking through. "I did point that out. En wasn't amused. You came back with a weapon that's better known to the Barrani than I'll ever be."

"Yes."

"And that'll make you better known to Barrani than you ever wanted to be."

Severn nodded.

"En said you were offered a choice. Weapon or girl. You chose the weapon?"

"No. I chose to rescue the Barrani *woman*."

"Yes. En said that you said that was your choice." Helmat's grin deepened; he was genuinely amused. "For what it's worth, he believes you believe what you told him. He's having trouble believing it himself. If it's true, he's found and trained a fool; if it's a lie, the girl you rescued should still be trapped. He was quite annoyed by the entire situation."

"And you?"

"You were offered a choice. You chose rescue and protection over a shiny, powerful weapon. In the end you got both—but you'd've been happy if you'd just rescued the girl."

"She's not a girl—"

"To the Barrani she is." Helmat glared at Severn before continuing. "I think it's a stupid weapon," he added. "I would have forbidden its use, but En said, properly wielded, it's a spell breaker. Which needs a different trainer. I don't like that there's yet another Barrani interfering with my people—En's bad enough."

Helmat could complain, amiably, until the sun set, the moon rose, and the sun rose again. He wasn't angry at the moment. He was, Severn thought, happy—happier than he'd ever been in Severn's admittedly short experience. "Has Elluvian offended you?"

"Constantly," was the cheerful reply. "But nothing annoys him more than ignorance—specifically his own. He doesn't understand what I saw in you. He doesn't understand what the Emperor saw in you. He knows what he saw: competence, and a surprising amount of it given your utter lack of proper training. He saw potential. He thinks you could be one of the best Wolves he's ever raised. Better than me.

"But while I see what he saw—as does the Emperor—we see what he can't see. He's in a foul mood—I'd suggest you avoid him for the remainder of the day."

Severn almost told Helmat that less visible smugness would probably better Elluvian's mood but decided against it. It was clearly a part of the history of these two men who between them defined this current generation of Imperial Wolves.

"You don't see things the way I do." Before Severn could answer, Helmat continued. "I look at you. I admit—grudgingly—that you're better than I was at your age, in all the ways Elluvian would have cared about when I was young. But you're better in ways he wouldn't have noticed as well.

"You need something to protect. You need a purpose. But you're not waiting for any of us to give it to you—you choose. You continually choose. I don't even think it was hard for you to choose the Barrani over the weapon. Doesn't matter if it was hard. Doesn't matter if it was easy. What matters is the choice you did make, the responsibility you did choose.

"You are the Wolf I've been waiting for."

Severn glanced at Helmat's profile.

"You don't have my abiding rage; you do have some anger, but it's never in control of you. I barely survived my temper, in my distant youth. I have no children," he added, something in his voice shifting unexpectedly, as if he'd just stepped onto what he believed was solid floor and found it rotting beneath his feet. "Probably for the best—I'd've been a terrible father."

"I don't believe that."

"Do you know how many Wolves have died on my watch?" It was a rhetorical question, but Severn nodded, which surprised a bark of laughter out of the older man.

"That's probably the kind of father I'd be as well. It's never a wise idea to become attached to your people when the likely outcome for them in the field is injury or death. Hells, you don't have to be in the field—you can just be at a desk in this damn office.

"But...if I'd ever had a son, and he were remotely like you, I'd've felt like I'd done the right job. This isn't a safe life. I'd like you to survive it. But I don't want that enough to tell you to quit."

"Even if you did, I wouldn't quit." Severn exhaled. "I spent much of the last year being unmoored, uncertain about the future and my part in it. I want this as much as you want it, and maybe even for the same reasons. I won't die."

"I'm sure Darrell thought that as well."

"I'm not Darrell."

"Then let me be maudlin. Let me be old and foolish. I'll believe you. Stay here while you can. Serve the Emperor. Be my Wolf. Survive it."

"I won't die on your watch. I won't leave the Wolves unless the first oath I ever made is invoked. I'll be your Wolf, the Emperor's Wolf, until then." He paused, looking through the pane of glass. "I think you judge yourself too harshly."

"I've heard that before."

"And I think my father, had he ever met you, would have approved of you."

★ ★ ★ ★ ★

ACKNOWLEDGMENTS

THIS HAS BEEN YET ANOTHER YEAR OF CHAOS, where norms are upended, gently put on their teetering legs, and then upended again. None of our work routines have been the same since our first lockdown in early 2020.

This is true of almost everyone I know. We're still all working from home—and that would include editors and publishing professionals like art directors, marketing people, etc.

For those who are essential workers, it's been chaos in an entirely different way. John, our UPS driver, said, the last time I asked, that it was like Christmas Rush *all the time*. In general, we gear up for, and then settle down from, that kind of rush. Not in 2020. Not now. Health care workers have barely been given a chance to breathe between Covid waves. Many of the doctors still aren't seeing people in person—they call on Zoom first.

So, in our second year of Covid: thank you to all of you who have worked in stressful circumstances to keep the rest of us going. We're standing on your shoulders, no matter how bowed those shoulders have become with the weight you've been carrying for so long.

We are eating because you've kept working, kept delivering food, kept delivering necessary packages. We're medicated, where necessary, because pharmacies have remained open. We're vaccinated because Vaccine Hunters Canada existed and used social media to not good, but *great*, effect. Some of us are alive because of you and the work you've done, even when obnoxious idiots are trying to protest outside hospitals the necessary work you do—and not outside Parliament, where laws are actually made.

We're all in this together, yes—but some of you have been carrying far more weight than we have.

I'm grateful that you haven't shrugged.